Dark Sisters

Also by Kristi DeMeester

Such a Pretty Smile

Beneath

Everything That's Underneath

Dark Sisters

Kristi DeMeester

ST. MARTIN'S PRESS
NEW YORK

This is a work of fiction. All of the characters, organizations, and events portrayed in this novel are either products of the author's imagination or are used fictitiously.

First published in the United States by St. Martin's Press, an imprint of St. Martin's Publishing Group

EU Representative: Macmillan Publishers Ireland Ltd, 1st Floor, The Liffey Trust Centre, 117–126 Sheriff Street Upper, Dublin 1, DO1 YC43

DARK SISTERS. Copyright © 2025 by Kristi DeMeester. All rights reserved. Printed in the United States of America. For information, address St. Martin's Publishing Group, 120 Broadway, New York, NY 10271.

www.stmartins.com

The Library of Congress Cataloging-in-Publication Data is available upon request.

ISBN 978-1-250-28681-9 (hardcover)
ISBN 978-1-250-28682-6 (ebook)

The publisher of this book does not authorize the use or reproduction of any part of this book in any manner for the purpose of training artificial intelligence technologies or systems. The publisher of this book expressly reserves this book from the Text and Data Mining exception in accordance with Article 4(3) of the European Union Digital Single Market Directive 2019/790.

Our books may be purchased in bulk for specialty retail/wholesale, literacy, corporate/premium, educational, and subscription box use. Please contact MacmillanSpecialMarkets@macmillan.com.

First Edition: 2025

10 9 8 7 6 5 4 3 2 1

For the impure girls. And for Annie Bolton,
who graciously lent me her very Puritan name.
I love you all.

Dark Sisters

PROLOGUE: 1750

I died once before.

At thirteen, the river water rushed into my lungs. Hungry. Insistent. My older brother had been there to pump it from me and command my heart back into life.

"You stupid girl," he said, but there were tears in his eyes. "Your place is at home."

But I was tired of caring for the little ones Mama left behind after her death. She had taught me the hidden magic of the natural world. How a root might be ground into fine powder and used to heal a cough. How the wind and water bent to no power but what they held themselves, and how if you were still enough, you could let that same power enter you. I had no use for the confinement of a house. For the tug of a babe at my skirts with its always hungry, screaming mouth.

So when the accusations began in my thirty-fifth year, in whispers that warned of violence, I marveled at how one could cheat death twice in her life. Once, I'd faced it without fear, but now, it coiled through me, hot and slick as oil. I saw its poison everywhere. I felt it in every muscle as I hurried home, my cap pulled down to cover my face as much as possible.

I was not the first accused. There were two others before the rope's shadow fell over me. Women who courted more suspicion than I by virtue of their lack of a husband. Unmarried with a little coin outweighed my small ministrations to the sick. A poultice for a wound that would not heal or a tonic for a cough were small compared to what could be gained from a woman with property who'd refused marriage.

We'd all been there to see them tried. Every woman turned her face toward heaven as she watched her neighbor or friend garble a final prayer before the rope did its work. Mercy dying on our lips as we made ourselves small so that terrible, holy eye might not swing toward us.

But my mother had taught me how quickly a whisper can turn to a scream, and I knew there was little time to do what was necessary. A few days. A week at best. I could draw no suspicion that I understood the shadow fallen over my doorstep. To do so would only hasten the end. And there was no promise Reverend Brenton and his men would not come for me in sunlight. Such things were typically done in darkness, but when those who deem themselves favored by the Lord discover a witch, a delay in punishment is akin to the profane.

The morning sun clung to the leaves and grass, already verdant and lush with the start of summer heat. The birdsong that typically cheered me sounded to my ear as nothing more than a dulled sort of noise. The natural world with its heart beating above and below held no joy, and the houses with their thatched roofs carried only threats rather than comfort. I went quickly past them, hoping anyone who happened a glance outside would not see the panic blazing from my every movement.

I was only a woman carrying water for the washing. They could not have known how I'd planned my path. How it carried me directly to Benjamin Gillett as he drove his cows to pasture the way he did every morning. How it afforded me but a moment of greeting. And then a request of the man who was soon to become my son-in-law.

"Mrs. Bolton. A blessing to see you this morning," he said as he removed his cap to reveal a tangle of dark curls.

"Indeed. I must beg forgiveness to be so brief. The red cow has escaped her pen again. It seems my attempts at securing the lock are a series of failures. Florence hunts her even now."

There were ways of drawing a man in. A lowered voice. A demure gaze. The suggested need of a savior. I had no want of any of it, but I had to do it all the same. It was the only way to ensure our safety.

"I'll see to it this afternoon." He offered a lopsided smile. The one I knew had drawn my daughter to him and then kept her there with its warmth. Its gentle kindness. Florence had chosen well. Knowing she had done so pained me all the more.

"We would be most grateful. And I know Florence would be happy to see you," I said. He had the piety to blush. It would have been better if he reached through the thin cage of my chest and tore out my traitorous heart.

"I trust she knows I feel much the same."

I kept my gaze trained on the earth. "We'll look for you then, Benjamin."

I did not look back lest I, like Lot's wife, turn to a pillar of salt, but hurried on, ignoring the sharp ache of every rock against my thin leather shoes. I passed no one else on the road, save for Edward Harrison's sow, who spared me a single glance before resuming her rooting. A small blessing.

I slowed only when the path bent toward our cottage. The farmland stretched away with its darkened soil and sprouting barley, and the end of the path marked the boundary of Edward Harrison's land. There was no proper path to our cottage, but there was a worn line that led to and from our door. There were no other houses beyond, only the vast wildness of the forest. The dark and the devil so close I could sense him if I believed in such nonsense.

Perhaps this lack of belief was what Reverend Brenton could see within me. That while I was in attendance every Sabbath, Florence beside me with her devout prayers and service, I had no use for his god. Or his devil.

Above me, three vultures circled, and death's heavy sweetness flooded my nose. The handkerchief I kept tucked in my pocket did little to dampen it, and I breathed through my mouth. Tried not to think of that scent on my tongue.

Hidden in the deep grass, a rabbit lay still, its scarlet viscera shimmering in the light. A light meal for such carrion. Shivering despite the warmth, I could not help but interpret the rabbit and those creatures of death for what they were. An ill omen.

"I'D NOT THOUGHT it was already so warm out. Your face is flushed." Florence held a cool hand to my cheek, and I leaned into her touch. My daughter. The only love I carried in this life since her father went into the earth when she was still barely walking. I've often considered it a blessing she did not know him well. That she did not have to live each day of her seventeen years with that unhealed wound inside her as I did. She'd grown into his likeness with her wild ebony hair and dark eyes. The only part of myself I'd ever read in her face was her mouth—the curving upper lip that gave the appearance of mischief or a secret that desperately wanted told.

She'd stood beside me during the hangings. Averted her eyes and winced when their necks mercifully snapped. Gripped my hand with a strength I didn't know she possessed when they had not. I knew it didn't matter how devout Florence appeared. Reverend Brenton and his men would not suffer her to live. She was my daughter and tainted by my blood. My teachings. The fear that threatened to consume me was not for my own life. It was for hers. Her flesh was tender. They would see her as a morsel worthy of their teeth. An image of their fingers pressed against her shuddered through me, and I stumbled.

Florence took me by the arm and settled me on the stool beside the hearth. "Here, Mother. Rest for a moment."

I kept my eyes closed as she fluttered about me, smoothing my hair and pressing a damp rag to my cheeks and neck. "There was no sign of the red cow as far as Mr. Pulferd's fields. I'll go out again after I've started supper. Perhaps she'll have stumbled into someone else's pasture. It would be a blessing if it were that simple."

It was as I planned. Every moment falling precisely as I'd hoped. And yet I could not keep myself from hesitating. From wondering if my daughter would listen to reason and see the truth in my fear. We would be accused of witchery and there would be no mercy or allowance for her constancy.

Despite all I'd taught her of the magic flowing through the natural world, she was the town's daughter. Born to its teachings and the beliefs Reverend Brenton poured in her ear every Sabbath. Florence would not begrudge me my tinctures, but I knew she worried after my soul. Saw the deception of it. How it wore one face to cover another. But I was also her mother. She would not publicly condemn me for such duplicity, for she saw how I cared for those who came to me with their illness and pain and how I helped in the ways I could. She saw the depths of my heart. How it held multitudes.

Perhaps there was a chance yet.

"Florence." I reached for her hand and held it still. How small—the delicate bones beneath her skin something so easily crushed. "You have seen the swiftness with which a single word leads to a hanging."

"I have," she said.

"They will find us next."

She snatched her hand away. The warmth of it still spread through my palm, and I watched as heat tinted her cheeks and neck. "They won't, Mother. We are covenanted. In the meetinghouse every week. They've no reason to bring such things to our door."

"Reason has little to do with what's happening. You must see that, Florence. We've no more time to hope for it. There could be merely hours separating us from being named, and there will be no stopping that blade once it is in motion. We must go. With haste."

I watched as her body went rigid. The silence between us growing like some immutable beast. My own heart was leaden, laboring through its beats. Often, I wondered if it would be easier if it stopped of its own accord. My body taken back into the dirt. But it carried on. I would not leave this world without knowing my daughter was yet safe within it.

"I would not flee like someone carrying guilt on her soul. Not when I have nothing to fear." Tears threatened, but she blinked them furiously away. "I would not abandon the only life I have ever known—to be Benjamin's wife, to have a family—for an imagined threat." She squared her shoulders, and even as dread pulled at me like the river water that had tried to claim me as a girl, I was proud of the fire in her. Proud of the woman she'd become.

I nodded even as I wished I could sob. Or scream. Anything to lessen the pain of knowing what I must do to guarantee our safety.

"All will be well," she said. "God will see to it." She smoothed her skirts and cap. "I'll be starting supper then. And then the cow."

I watched her go, and only when I was certain she would not return did I rise and hunt out the carving knife. I'd taken care to sharpen it the night before, and I folded it carefully into my apron.

Outside, the air smelled of grass and wild onion and the woodsmoke from the cooking fire Florence had built. There would be stew that night, but I knew I would have little appetite.

As I approached the hen house, the hens went quiet. It was strange that I would come at this time of day. I'd already collected eggs that morning, so there was no reason for my presence. They watched with bright eyes as I undid the latch and reached inside.

"Hush now," I said as I lifted the largest black hen into the air. She squawked and set her wings flapping, but I only gripped her tighter as I knelt and withdrew the knife.

"Let all that will hear and all that will see attend me now. For blessed are those who know the earth and her wants. Blessed are those who would provide offering." I drew the blade across the hen's neck, the blood warm against my hands as I let it flow into the dirt. "A blood exchange that I might know strength. For a heart that would not bend or break."

The knife slid easily through the meat, cutting along the breast until the heart lay exposed, slick and pinkish among the blood. It was a sacrifice even Reverend Brenton would understand, for hadn't his god bled for the good of his people? I was no less than he. In the end, we all wear our brutality like beautiful cloth in the name of love.

I pressed the organ to my mouth. "So it is spoken, and so let it be."

I bit down.

CHAPTER I

2007

Sundays were for Chanel.

For Jesus, too, but mostly Chanel.

Camilla Burson sat in the front pew of The Path's sanctuary, her gaze trained on her father's place in the pulpit as she tried not to fidget with her hair or skirt. Even though she'd spent over an hour on her hair that morning, making certain that the curls were a blond, shining miracle, she could feel every individual strand that had fallen out of place. Heat rose along her throat, and she willed it away. The pastor's daughter wasn't meant to look distressed during the sermon. She was meant to look perfect.

Jesus tap-dancing Christ, she was so sick of perfect. The weight of it. How it tugged at her and kept her locked in place when all she wanted to do was have a little fun. Before she turned into her mother and the other Bible study ladies with their prim smiles and Botoxed foreheads and broods of children. Another wife, dutiful to her husband. Obedient and God-fearing and, above all else, dull as dishwater.

"And so, as the seasons change, so do we change. Husbands to fathers. Women to wives and mothers. It seems only fitting to discuss such things in this season. As we prepare to guide our young ladies toward the correct path. As you prepare to commit yourselves to your future. I know it's easy to get caught up in the excitement of the dress, the hair, the jewelry. I can't tell you the number of hours such conversations have taken up in my own house. If I had a dollar for every time I heard my daughter utter the phrase 'who designed her dress?' I'd be ... well, able to afford a *second* beach house."

He flashed a smile, and Camilla laughed along with the congregation even as embarrassment threatened a return of the heat she'd tried to banish. She hated when he used her as a point in his sermons. As if she was nothing more than a series of failures held up as an example of how not to serve the Lord. As if she wasn't trying to be all the things he expected of her.

"But you see, young ladies, beyond the fancy dresses and the glitter and the high heels, there's the heart of this very special night. The night of your Purity Ball. The night you pledge yourself to your father and your Father God to remain pure until your marriage."

Beside her in the pew, Camilla's mother shifted, her mouth turned down in the hidden frown she always wore whenever her father mentioned anything about the Purity Ball. The sunlight filtering through the windows settled about her face in a dazzling corona. Even with the frown, she was beautiful. Camilla often found it hard to look at her. To see her beauty as anything other than devastating. As a sum of everything Camilla was decidedly not.

Throughout her childhood, she spent hours staring into the mirror, wondering when she would finally find her mother's features in her face. When she would look in the mirror and not see her father's blond hair and pale eyes, but instead the lush dark of her mother's hair. The deep golden green of her eyes. When she would be able to carry that darkness with her rather than the light.

"As we approach that day, I want you to listen to what Jesus said. 'Put on the Lord Jesus Christ and make no provision for the flesh, to gratify its lusts.' Romans chapter thirteen, verse fourteen. Just like those pretty dresses, you should wrap the Lord Christ about you. A reminder against the temptation of the world. That you make no provision for the flesh."

Inwardly, Camilla squirmed. It didn't matter how many years she'd heard a variation on this sermon—the one her father always gave in the months leading to the Purity Ball—hearing her father talk about lust made her die a little inside. And now, knowing she was finally going to participate in the Purity Ball after years of begging her mother every spring only to be met with a number of excuses, the feeling was somehow worse.

Even more awful that Grant Pemberton was sitting somewhere in the sea of pews behind her. Grant Pemberton, who'd left Hawthorne Springs behind for law school three years ago. She'd been invisible to him then, but she wasn't fifteen anymore, and her body had made good use of the three years. She couldn't help but hope he wouldn't find her so invisible now.

She glimpsed him that morning as they filed inside the sanctuary, her Sunday smile plastered to her face so no one would ever think she was anything but thrilled to be there. The sight of him instantly transported her into the awkward, unformed body of her fifteen-year-old self. Somehow, she'd managed not to trip.

Even now, she found herself dazzled by his easy smile. How it transformed his face from sharp cheekbones and jawline into something softer. Something kinder. He'd been handsome back then, in an urgent, aggressive sort of way, but he'd grown out his hair and let it fall over his eyes. A further tempering that lessened the brutality of his beauty. The raw edges filed away in favor of approachability. But she saw him. *Knew* him. Despite the groomed five o'clock shadow he wore now, she could still make out his jawline. There'd been nights she fell asleep to the vision of herself running her tongue along it, the salt taste of him filling her mouth.

Camilla felt it then. The flush she'd tried to hold at bay creeping up her neck and cheeks. If Noah and Brianna knew she was thinking about Grant Pemberton in the most lustful way possible in the middle of her father's sermon on feminine purity, they would piss their pants laughing at the irony. She pressed a hand to her throat, hoping no one would see.

"That you make *no provision* for the flesh," her father repeated. "Young ladies, when you make allowances for sin, expose yourselves to temptation, wrap yourselves in immodesty rather than purity, you cannot exist in God's light. There is simply no room for it. Those who do so find themselves cast away from the warmth He provides. It's in that dark where the abominable dwell. Satan. Demons. Disembodied spirits. The Dark Sisters."

He paused, letting the hush of the sanctuary fill the space he'd created. Camilla felt it in her chest. All that space. How she waited with the rest of them, her breath aching in her tightened lungs, for him to fill it. She hated him for it. That he held this power over not just the congregation, but her as well. Because she knew what was coming. The appearance of the Dark Sisters in her father's sermon meant someone was sick.

She scanned the congregation, but there was an unending sea of faces. Even if she knew all the members of her father's massive following, she wouldn't be able to know who was absent from their pew and why.

And even though she knew the Dark Sisters were a load of shit, a scary story her father trotted out as a reminder to keep on the straight and narrow, there was a dim part of her that still feared them. That felt a faint lick of hellfire at her feet. She couldn't help but lean forward and wait for her father to begin.

"But we all know this story, don't we? Every few years, we hear it. Whispers about what somebody's daughter or sister saw in the woods. It passes from house to house." Her father swept a hand through the air, and she kept herself from rolling her eyes at his theatrics. "Like an illness. An infection.

"Sin is a lot like that, isn't it? It starts as something so small. A whisper about something you saw in the woods. A pale hand reaching from a tree with ropes of hair instead of leaves. Two sets of eyes, pale as milk, looking out from the dark. Two women creeping along the ground, their hair intertwined in a single braid. Forever bound to whatever hell they created for themselves. Forced to wander the earth as ghosts or demons or the smeared remainders of a sinful heart. Because make no mistake, these creatures, the ones our girls call the Dark Sisters, are exactly that."

She'd heard her father talk about them in his sermons when she was younger, but she hadn't paid any more attention than she did to his stories of David or Moses or Job. But then Tricia Allman threw a slumber party for her ninth birthday. Fifteen tiny girls crowded into their family pool house as the sun set over the discarded toys and suits still dripping on their designated hooks.

Outside, Darren and Catherine Allman chatted over bourbon cocktails, comfortable in the knowledge the girls were tucked safely away inside. Proud they'd given their daughter the theater of privacy and freedom without truly granting it. They were good parents. Careful and strict when it was needed, but still young and carefree and cool. They poured more bourbon. Smiled. They were *good* parents.

Inside the pool house, full dark fell over those tiny, girlish bodies. The walls seemed to drop away, and shadows opened great, heaving mouths on all sides. They were no longer girls. They were bits of meat meant for a saliva-slick tongue.

They huddled together, shivering against the chill of their still-wet hair. Tricia Allman held court among them, her cherry popsicle–stained mouth the only color in that bled-out room as she leaned in, her voice dropped to a whisper.

"My cousin saw them once. She was mad at her mom and said she was leaving and never coming back. She'd been crying and stopped under a tree. Said she felt something touch her shoulder, and when she looked up, they were up there. In the tree. Reaching for her," Tricia said.

"That's not true," Brittany Johnson said.

Tricia frowned. "Is so. She said their hair was braided together. One of them looking forward and the other backward. And that they didn't have eyes really. It was just all white. And then they made this sound." She closed her eyes and opened her mouth as the girls went silent. Waiting. Listening. Until a small whine crept from Tricia's lips, her eyes fluttering slightly open as it pitched lower into a throaty rattle. "I can't do it as good as she can. Makes my throat hurt. Anyway, she ran before they could grab her and eat her. Because that's what they do if they catch you. Pull their mouths apart with their hands until their jaws break and then slurp you up whole."

Camilla had been the first to fall asleep. It was her first sleepover. She was an only child. No one had ever told her not to be the first one to fall asleep.

She woke to a pressure on her abdomen. A faint tickle over her face that smelled of synthetic strawberries. The dark bloomed around her, stretched out and out until she wondered if she'd tumbled into the sky, but there was no air in it. She gasped and pushed against the thing on her abdomen. It did not move, and beneath its weight, her body went cold with panic.

And that sound. A slow rattle. So much like the impossible beginning of a death. Air as it fled the failing lungs for some other, unknowable vessel. Across her face, she felt that same delicate tickle as the sleep-hidden world around her came into sharper focus. A pale form crouched on top of her, its face bending to study hers, its hair falling over Camilla's face as it opened its mouth wider, the hands creeping up its face so it could break its teeth and jaw before swallowing her.

She screamed. Clawed at the shape that still pressed against her until she felt the soft tear of flesh. The quick warmth of blood under her fingernails. Again and again, she lashed out, until the shape squealed and tumbled away. Her chest freed of its weight, Camilla pulled breath into her in great heaves. The air that rushed back into her lungs was sharp, and she panted as light flooded the room.

Tricia Allman lay curled beside Camilla, her hands covering her face. But they could all see. All the girls. The blood weeping from Tricia's right eye like some misplaced stigmata. As if the nail that pierced Christ's palms had somehow found its way into Tricia Allman's right eye. That was how they would all describe it after. Like a horror show. Even if it was only a scratch. In their girlish minds, it was a bloodbath.

"She scratched me! She scratched my eye out!" Tricia howled as the other girls crowded around her in confusion. They ignored Camilla, who sat in the quickly cooling urine-damp of her sleeping bag trying to understand what was happening.

At some point, amid the chaos of Tricia screaming and Camilla sobbing, someone hit the intercom button, and Tricia's parents came rushing in. And that was the end of Tricia Allman's ninth birthday party.

Camilla's mother came to pick her up, her mouth pressed in a thin line as Tricia's mother explained what had happened.

"A silly prank. You know how girls are. Telling scary stories and whatnot. We're just thankful Tricia wasn't more hurt. I can't imagine what could have possibly possessed Camilla to react that way."

"Maybe your daughter sitting on her chest and scaring her half to death had something to do with it."

"Ada, please—"

"It's a shame, really. That Henry and I trusted you with our daughter. He'll be so disappointed when he hears about this." She took a step forward and then another, forcing Tricia's mother to stumble backward. "More of a shame that I wasn't here when it happened. Because if I had been here when your daughter decided to play her blasphemous little prank, you'd be dealing with much more than a scratch."

Whirling on her heel, she grasped Camilla's hand and marched her to the car. The drive home was quiet, but her mother held her hand the entire time. She carried Camilla inside as if she were four years old again and then ran a bath and helped her inside the warm water. Passed a washcloth over her face again and again until her tears finally slowed.

"Hush, now." Her mother hugged Camilla to her, not caring that her daughter was going to ruin her Derek Lam blouse. "It's just a story. And little girls exaggerate. The Dark Sisters have never eaten anyone. At least not as far as I know." Her mother winked at her. It didn't make Camilla feel any better.

Later, Camilla would be embarrassed by what had happened at the sleepover. How she'd reacted. No one held it against her. No one made fun of her or reminded her how she'd sliced Tricia's face open with her fingergerate. But in that moment, as her mother wrapped her in a towel and rubbed at her arms, she felt only fear. Fear that the Sisters would find her. Wrap their hair around her like a cocoon. Squeeze her body until it burst like ripe fruit, their mouths stained with the juice of her as they ate her body and drank her blood like some profane Communion.

Back then, the story of the Dark Sisters felt so much bigger. There'd been nothing allegorical in it. It had been visceral. Real. She carried her fear like a second skin, slipping it on and off from year to year until she was old enough to understand.

The Dark Sisters were not a story. They were a *lesson*. One Camilla had been learning her entire life. Be good. Be pure and modest and chaste. Because the temptations of the world wore many faces. Some of them lovely. Even Satan was beautiful when he fell, after all. She imagined the Sisters had been the same.

Still, down in the sleeping parts of her she tried to ignore, there was a fear. The Dark Sisters might not have been real, but the illness was. And it had come among them again.

Again, she scanned the crowd and darted a glance at the Whitten pew. Noah sat beside his father, his gaze on the pulpit but soft with boredom. She craned her neck further, a pretense at stretching, and found Brianna in her family pew at the back of the church. Brianna rarely talked about it, but even this simple push to the outer circles of visibility within the church spoke of an otherness Camilla knew she resented. A bitterness born of her darker skin. Even after four years of membership in The Path, Brianna's family was often left off invites. Dinner parties and galas and prayer circles came and went without their names included on the guest list. Their money didn't matter in the face of such dimly veiled prejudice.

Camilla had brought it up with her father only once, and he'd frowned and told her she was mistaken. He didn't want to hear about such ridiculousness again. That moment counted among the first cracks in her girlish belief her father could do no wrong.

Brianna caught Camilla's eye. *Who's sick?* she mouthed.

Camilla shrugged. *Outside. Later.*

Brianna gave a brief nod, her dark eyes going even darker with concern.

Camilla ground her teeth together and caught at a loose bit of skin at her cuticle and tugged, the release a delicious sting. She both hoped and did not hope for blood.

She wanted the blood for what it meant. Cleansing. Penance. A release of all the sinful thoughts and feelings contained within her treacherous skin. But to bleed so publicly would invite questions she did not want to answer. There were no ways to mold the complexity of those thoughts and feelings into anything resembling cogent speech. She thrust her hand beneath her thigh and looked back at the altar.

The last bit of her father's sermon washed over her, and soon enough, every head in the congregation bowed in prayer for the benediction. The band took their places—some quiet approximation of Christian pop—and the service was over. Her mother stood, her willowy body lovely in its divine, silken armor, and drifted to her husband's side. From this spot, they would greet the congregation and exchange blessings for the stolen minutes Camilla needed with Brianna and Noah away from prying eyes.

Camilla moved through the throngs of women comparing dresses and jewelry, all chattering about the upcoming Purity Ball or the sermon. The Dark Sisters and the possibility of more sickness had taken root despite any distractions the Purity Ball offered. Her father had warned them, and they all felt the edge of it. Finally, she burst through the vestibule doors and drew the first clean breath she felt she'd taken all morning.

She hurried through the parking lot with its gleaming collection of Maseratis and Mercedes, hoping no one—particularly Grant Pemberton—was watching as the pastor's only daughter darted past the immaculate landscaping.

Noah and Brianna were already there, a wall of unmanageable kudzu at their backs. Brianna's face was screwed into a frown, the burgundy lipstick she wore immaculate somehow despite the contortion, as she whispered furiously at a rather amused-looking Noah.

In her black Tom Ford crepe, Brianna was a fierce vision of elegance. A warrior goddess disguised in her Sunday best. The twist outs she wore fell to her collarbone and emphasized the grace of her neck and shoulders. That same grace inhabited every breath. Every movement. So much so that Camilla often wondered if Brianna had been set on this ugly, wasted earth by mistake. If every day God cursed Himself for not keeping her among the angels where she belonged.

"Ask Camilla. She'll tell you," Brianna said.

"Ask me what?"

Noah loosened his tie as he turned to face her. It made him, as always, look younger than his eighteen years and more like the boy she'd known all her life. The freckled, dark-haired kid with darker eyes who'd been the only other one to laugh when, in the first grade, Mrs. Stewart had seriously intoned "Dear Lloyd" instead of "Dear Lord" at the start of morning prayer. Camilla's best friend until Brianna moved to Hawthorne Springs in the ninth grade, and their trio was made complete.

"The Sisters," he began.

Camilla rolled her eyes. "What a crock of shit. A made-up story to scare little girls and keep the rest of us on the straight and narrow. *Be good or you'll end up like the Dark Sisters.*"

"Exactly," Noah said. "We used to dare each other to go out in the woods at night and find the tree they're supposed to haunt. See how long we could sit there before pissing our pants. No one ever saw anything."

Brianna stiffened. "What about all those girls who say they saw them? Every year, there's at least a few."

"Kids' stuff. They're little girls. They think they see something one night, and that story's already in their head, and so they fill in the blanks with whatever's easy. Everybody gets excited for a few days and that's it," Noah said.

Brianna turned to face Camilla. "And what about the ones who get sick?"

"Correlation doesn't imply causation. Come on, Brianna. You took Statistics with the both of us." Noah rolled his eyes at Brianna, but she kept her gaze solely on Camilla.

Because Camilla knew. Knew that for every story someone's daughter brought home, her fear a terrible, heaving thing that closed her throat and numbed her tongue as she tried to find a way to retell what she'd seen in the woods, there was a woman in Hawthorne Springs who fell ill.

Fundamentally, Noah was right. Logic implied that something nonexistent could not impact the living world. But it happened regardless.

Camilla shook her head. Silly to get caught up in a fear she'd put aside the moment she turned fourteen. "It's environmental. Like the flu or something."

"Except some of them fucking *die*, Camilla," Brianna snapped.

Noah stepped away. This wasn't his fight. Never had been. Because it was never the men who got sick. Only the girls. The women. The unbaptized coven of the Dark Sisters brought like lambs to the slaughter. The illness always began in the same way. A sore throat. A cough that wouldn't go away. Until, eventually, their teeth and gums went gray. Boils in the inner cheeks and mouth that would not heal. In the end, their teeth and tongue and gums rotted and fell away in small, painful bits.

"We all die, hon. That's part of it. And the ones who died were already old," Camilla said.

"That's not— Forget it." Brianna lifted a hand to her face, but remembered her makeup and lowered it. "It doesn't matter."

Camilla pulled her hair off her neck. The late spring heat had only just begun to bloom. Soon enough, the air would carry a damp weight, and every breath would feel like drowning. Even still, a shiver ran through her belly, and she swayed for a moment, willing the sudden nauseating, oily sensation in her mouth away.

People got sick. It was just how it was. Countless doctors came to Hawthorne Springs to draw blood and run tests. No one could explain why the women got sick. What caused it or how to stop it. They threw the weight of their collective wealth behind it, and still, they were no closer to an answer.

Every year, her father preached on the will of God. How there was no point in worrying over what was in His control. It felt better to give it all over. To close her eyes and pretend that because it was in God's hands, she had no need to worry. Because she was her father's daughter, that particular cup would pass from her lips. That poison averted because of her last name. Her blood.

She needed a distraction. They all did. Something that didn't carry any of the responsibility of the Purity Ball or the vague uneasiness of disease meant for people older than them.

"You know what?" Camilla clapped her hands together. "We need something fun. Something that's not doom and gloom and modesty and virginity until your wedding night."

"Thank you. Exactly," Noah said.

"Let's throw a party."

"It's like you're asking to be sent on Retreat," Brianna said.

"Not this little baby angel birthed from the loins of our divine leader. Not the preacher's own daughter. He wouldn't dare!" Noah reached to ruffle Camilla's hair.

"Mess up the hair and die, Whitten."

He chuckled and dropped his hand.

"We'll call it a vigil then. For whoever's sick." She clasped her hands together and fluttered her eyelashes.

"Shameless," Noah muttered.

"Not shameless. *Bored.*" Camilla took a step toward Brianna. Who cared if her father threatened her with Retreat. It wouldn't be the first time, and it surely wouldn't be the last either. "Come on, Brianna. Whoever's sick will be fine. And we'll pray for them. That's what Communion is anyway, right? A little prayer. A little wine. I'll ask my dad if we can use the pavilion." She bumped her hip against Brianna's and waited for the smirk she knew was coming.

"You two are going to hell," Brianna said, but her mouth quirked upward.

"Only if you're there to keep me company." Pursing her lips, Camilla blew a kiss toward Brianna. "I should get back before they start looking for me. I'll call you later. We'll plan." She let out a diabolical laugh.

Brianna swatted at her ass, and Camilla danced away, waving over her shoulder as she went. She skirted the edge of the parking lot, ducking behind cars until she was close enough for it to look as if she'd been there all along. By the time she straightened, her heart felt as if it was lodged in her throat, and she forced herself to breathe slowly, glad to be able to blame the heat for the flush in her cheeks.

Her mouth stretched into a smile as she nodded at a group of women clustered near the door.

"A lovely sermon today," one of them said as she passed.

"Thank you," Camilla said, and angled herself to maneuver past them, but the woman shot out a hand, Cartier bracelets glinting in the sun, and gripped Camilla's forearm with ballet-slipper-pink fingernails.

"Your father," she began as the other women averted their eyes, their chatter gone quiet. "Would you tell him I said so? About the sermon?"

"Of course," she replied as she tried to place the woman's face. To remember her name.

"You'll tell him?" she repeated, those pastel fingernails pressing indentations into Camilla's flesh as she drew closer, her tone a confidential hum.

Camilla pulled her arm out of the woman's grip, keeping her smile fixed in place as she realized how she knew her. Tania Fullerton. Back in Hawthorne Springs after two months at Retreat for sleeping with the contractor who installed her new kitchen cabinets. Her husband had caught them. Closed his practice early that day to get a head start on packing for the fishing trip he'd planned for the weekend only to find his wife spread-eagled on the marble countertops she'd had shipped from Italy.

Camilla studied her. How she stood just outside the circle of women. Desperate to be seen. Included. Allowed entrance back into the life she had before her indiscretion. The one before the two months of immersive workshops and prayer sessions and counseling all mandated as part of Retreat. No phones. No outside contact. A Biblical boot camp for those who dared give in to their base desires.

And now, all those judgmental eyes were locked on Camilla. Waiting to see how she would respond. If, after her father's sermon, she would *make provision* and give even the slightest allowance. The smallest bit of grace.

She let her smile drop. "I should find my father. If you'll excuse me."

She heard the approval in the women's voices as she walked away, but it was a small comfort. Answering according to expectations didn't negate that Tania Fullerton's husband was a supercilious prick. One who made a habit of publicly teasing his wife about her weight problem, pinching and squeezing her sides as he chuckle-yucked his way through yet another tired joke.

Camilla's heels echoed through the emptied vestibule as she wound her way through the central hallway that led to the offices. Her father's was the last, the large double oak doors standing open to reveal him seated behind his desk, his suit jacket thrown over the back of the leather chair, and his Bible open before him. Trent Glover, the youth pastor, stood off to the side, his hands in his pockets as he let his gaze travel the length of Camilla's body only to pause at the hemline of her skirt before cocking a disapproving eyebrow.

"Well, well. Look what the cat dragged in."

She forced into her voice a brightness she didn't feel. "Hi, Pastor Trent." She leaned against the edge of the desk, slid off her heels, and let her feet sink into the plush rug her father had imported from Iran. A shiver of pleasure ran up her back.

Her father glanced up, and then resumed his reading. "Isaiah. We were discussing the next Youth Meeting."

"Judgment and restoration of the virtuous. Seems fitting with the Purity Ball happening so soon," Pastor Trent said.

Camilla ignored him and focused on her father. "Daddy, I was thinking—"

"Mmm . . . that can't be good. Usually means it's going to cost me money." Her father flipped a page, his finger tracing the thin paper.

"I was thinking we could have a prayer vigil. For whoever's sick."

Pastor Trent frowned. "And where would this vigil be?" he asked, but she kept her gaze trained on her father, who still had not looked up from his Bible.

"At the pavilion?" She knew her father would be more likely to say yes if the vigil was at the church, but the pavilion was outdoors, removed enough from the main campus so there would be fewer prying eyes. Fewer opportunities for anyone to say the vigil goers weren't praying at all but instead getting shit tanked on a nice red.

"I don't think that's the best idea," Pastor Trent said. Her father snapped his head up, his face momentarily warring against indignation before settling again into placid lines. "I seem to remember the last event you had at the pavilion. A Bible study, wasn't it? Must have been a good one. Chelsea Puckett was so full of the Holy Spirit, she had to have her stomach pumped."

Camilla's face burned. It wasn't her fault Chelsea Puckett couldn't control herself. And they *had* talked about the Bible. They played Fuck, Marry, Kill with the twelve disciples and then the Old Testament prophets because why not? And then Brianna did a dramatic reading of the sexy parts of Song of Solomon. By the time Chelsea started puking, they'd all participated in a thorough Biblical discussion.

Her father closed his Bible and leaned forward. "Trent, if I could have a word with my daughter. Privately."

"Of course."

Pastor Trent pushed past her, she and her father locked in stasis until the door closed quietly behind him. Camilla knew what would come next—she would apologize, and her father would cave, but she wished she didn't have to go through the motions.

"Daddy, you know what happened with Chelsea wasn't my fault. I just thought the vigil could be a help," she said.

His shoulders immediately relaxed, the tension draining out of his body as he picked up his Bible. "I know, princess. I know. You have to understand that Trent means well, but he doesn't know your heart like I do. And after the last time, I don't think it's the best idea."

She let her lower lip jut out the tiniest bit.

"Sorry, baby. I know you're trying to do something good, but there's just no way I can do it. Not so soon after the Chelsea Bible study incident. You understand?"

She nodded her head even as she internally rolled her eyes. But just because he'd said no didn't mean the vigil wouldn't happen. There was, as her father was so fond of telling her, more than one way to skin a cat.

"That's a good girl." He picked up his suit jacket and draped it over his arm. "Now, let's get out of here. Your mother is probably wondering where we've gotten off to. After you," he said, and she slid her feet back into her shoes and went silently past him, his hand at the small of her back to guide her.

Some enterprising church leader had already gone through the back offices and turned off the lights. She hated the church when it was dark, emptied of the people who were supposed to fill it with praise and light. It felt haunted in those hours—a bleached memory of the joint fervor it was supposed to contain.

Her mother was already in the Mercedes, sunglasses in place, the visor flipped down so she could touch up her lipstick. "Where have the two of you been?"

Her father buckled himself in, his eyes trained on Camilla in the rearview mirror. "Just a little father–daughter chat," he said before the engine roared to life.

Camilla leaned her head against the window and watched as the houses grew farther and farther apart, mansions changing into estates with rolling fields set back from the road, the trees an emerald smear as she focused on her breath instead of the silence fallen between them. Despite the estates, Hawthorne Spring was a small, insular community. Practically everything was within walking distance for anyone who might prefer physical exercise to riding in leather-seated, air-conditioned comfort.

Ahead, the road veered right, her father punched in the gate code, and their drive with its arch of oak trees swallowed them. Finally, the trees gave way to hydrangeas, their branches drooping with heavy white petals, and the house appeared before them. A European-style imitation of a more ancient house, its pale brick façade stretched upward toward a gabled roof, the arched, full-glass doorway winking in the soft afternoon light. Ivy snaked along the front, expertly trained around the entry's cedar beams, the wood adding a warmth to the cooler tones of the house's exterior. The driveway looped past the main house and led to a separate four-car garage that housed her father's everyday vehicles. His specialty collection lived in a larger garage elsewhere on the sprawling property, next to the stables, pool, guesthouse, and the family's private tennis court.

"Lunch?" her father said as he cut the engine.

"Not hungry. Besides, Vera's coming over for Pilates." Her mother opened the door and stood, not bothering to look back as she drifted toward the covered stone breezeway that led to the main house.

"Ada," her father called.

Her mother paused, her back still facing them. "Henry?" she asked before turning.

"The Bransons are coming for dinner tonight. Six o'clock. We'll dress for dinner."

Camilla bit down on her groan. Dress for dinner meant something that wouldn't allow her more than a nibble of whatever Chef had decided as the evening meal.

Her father continued. "The gray Kiton would be best, I think. Hair up for that neckline. Don't want to look like you have a double chin," he said.

"Of course," Ada said, and turned back to the house.

They followed behind. Camilla focused on her steps so she wouldn't scream in frustration. A feral thing set loose in the lovely house her father had built with his faith and money. Because she knew what that final comment meant for her mother. That she would hear it and starve herself a little bit.

She would think it was her own idea. She wanted to fit into the clothes. No lumps. No bumps. All smooth angles and curves only when it came to her breasts. Cheekbones sharp and a hollowing in the space behind her collarbone. A hollowing in her stomach. Beautiful in all the ways men told her to be. All the ways she came to believe as her own truth.

All those small suggestions. No one had ever told them to starve themselves. To sweat through hundreds of Pilates classes from private instructors in the name of a tight ass and flat stomach. To pay for liposuction. A breast augmentation. A brow lift. But they were quiet daggers offered up at an altar they imagined they'd built. This was how you found a husband. This was how you kept him. And didn't they want that? To be found desirable? Worthy of attention? Didn't they want to look good so their husbands would not stray? Would not sin?

It was impossible not to internalize it all. Those comments. The jokes that wore a veneer of truth. *Whoa! Guess someone was hungry. You can tell this one likes her bread! Just because they make it in your size, doesn't mean you should wear it, you know what I mean? Never hurt to help the natural beauty along, now did it?*

They added up to a belief in not good enough. Not thin enough. Not attractive enough. And the fury within Camilla existed because she believed it, too. Had adopted those beliefs as her own, and now she felt their fingerprints all over her body. Marking her as theirs rather than her own. The ache of that knowledge rooted ever deeper because she knew she allowed it. Had been the one who let it eat her alive and imagined she liked the way the teeth felt at her throat.

It felt like being haunted by an unattainable version of herself. A ghost she could not exorcise.

Angela, the live-in housekeeper, had already opened the heavy cedar doors for them and vanished into the bowels of the house to finish setting out lunch. The entryway opened on twin white marble staircases twisting away from each other before meeting once more on the second level; the Baccarat chandelier—a twentieth wedding anniversary gift from the church—hung in the center of the foyer, allowing pale golden light to shimmer through the crystals. Beyond, the entryway opened into a formal living room done up in various shades of cream, every surface free of dust and clutter. A rotating team of church members descended on the house twice a week to clean, not because they needed the money—no one in Hawthorne Springs suffered financially—but because it was God's will to support and aid the head of His church.

"I'll take lunch in my office. Keep working on next week's sermon. You should join your mother. Some movement would be good for you," her father said.

"Yes, sir," Camilla said, and her stomach cramped around everything she'd not eaten that day and the anger she'd swallowed instead. He gave a little wave once he got to the top of the stairs, and then she was alone. The silence of the house bore down on her. It seemed as if the lunch Angela had prepared would go uneaten by the women in the Burson house. She waited a beat and then followed her father.

Upstairs, the hallways branched left and right. Left to her father's office, the library, her parents' bedroom. Right to her own bedroom and the other fully furnished, but unused rooms. When she was younger, she sometimes swapped rooms, experimenting with sleeping in a different bed for the night, imagining she'd wake up someone else only to rush to the bathroom mirror the next morning and see the disappointment of her own face with its pale, nondescript features, the sloped nose she still felt was too large. Her father had offered to make her an appointment with a renowned plastic surgeon in Buckhead, but she couldn't bring herself to do it. Not yet. She feared the pain. The recovery. The blood.

She closed her bedroom door behind her and tugged off her dress, her pantyhose, and kicked her shoes across the room before wrapping herself in her ivory silk robe and collapsing on the canopied bed her father had custom-ordered from France. He'd been the one who decorated his daughter's bedroom in the subtle complexity of French provincial elegance as a gift for her sixteenth birthday. In spite of her irritation that Daddy had been the one to decorate her bedroom, she loved the gilded antique mirrors and calming tones of gray and blue her father chose.

The bed enveloped her, the duvet velvet soft, and she wished, as she had when she was young, that she would wake to find she'd transformed overnight into someone who wasn't constantly watched and evaluated for any possible misstep. She ran her fingers over the duvet, watching the blur of her lavender fingernails. She was surprised her father hadn't noticed that morning, how the color clashed against the dark skirt she wore. The color had been her own pathetic rebellion against the years of pale pinks and creams he suggested.

What she wanted was to sleep. Wrap herself in the duvet and follow whatever darkness would come down into a deep blank erasure.

But no. There was Pilates with her mother and Vera Stephens, her mother's oldest friend. Aunt Vera to Camilla despite the lack of a blood connection and the age gap that could have made her Camilla's grandmother. Vera had been there her entire life, woven into the fabric of her family.

Sighing, she sat up and pushed herself off the bed. Pulled something made of Lycra from her closet and tugged it over her hips and chest. Felt how it molded to her skin and contained all the ugly parts of her. Smooth. Tight.

Even as she pulled her hair back, she felt the fatigued protest in her muscles. A ghost memory of the thousands of other movements made in the name of someone else's standards of beauty.

She could skip it. But that would mean seeing her father's pursed lips over the dinner table. His admonishments that if she wasn't going to take the classes along with her mother, he may as well stop paying for the private instructor. He thought she'd be a little more appreciative of how he provided for them. He only wanted them to be healthy.

Before she could find all the reasons not to go, down the stairs she went and then down again into the subterranean hallway that led to the workout studio where her mother waited. With any luck, her mother and Vera would have already started on the Reformer, and Camilla would only have forty-five minutes of agony rather than the full hour and a half.

But when she rounded the final corner, she didn't hear the thumping bass line of whatever classical music the instructor typically blasted through the speakers, and the studio door stood open. Normally, they kept it closed with the lights off. Warm and humid and dark as a womb as they transformed themselves into something sharper. Harder.

"Even now, I've told him I don't want her at the Ball. But Henry insists. Says it's strange that his daughter is the oldest of all the girls. That he's indulged me. *Indulged.*" Her mother's voice went hard. "That was the word he used. Like I'm a child who wants extra dessert."

Camilla stopped and pressed herself to the wall, hoping they'd not seen her and that the instructor wouldn't happen along at that exact moment and reveal her hiding place. Her mother had spent years keeping Camilla from participating in the Purity Ball, and the excuses were flimsy at best. The Ball was going to overlap too closely with a planned trip to Rome. There wasn't time to plan the dress the way she wanted to. She wasn't ready for Camilla to grow up quite yet. She still saw Camilla as her little girl and wanted to hold on to that for a bit longer. If there was an actual reason, Camilla wanted to hear it.

"My dad said it was a dream."

"A dream so many of the other girls have had?" Vera snorted. "That's not how dreams work. How many times have we had this conversation, Ada?"

Camilla inched forward. Her blood pushed through her with such force it made her head light. Another step and she could see into the studio. Her mother on the floor, one leg extended outward as she stretched. Vera, seated on her left, mimicked her movements. Both fluid. Both graceful. Both wearing frowns.

"I still dream about it. My Purity Ball. Everything's so heavy, and I can't move. Like I'm being swallowed. Someone's laughing, but I can't see. I can't see, and it *hurts*. And I wake up with this dread. Like this cold running through me that won't stop, and I think about Camilla, and what if that feeling is right? What if something bad happened that night? What if it's still happening? How would we ever know? It's not for us anymore. The moms. Just the fathers and church leaders and the girls while we sit at home with whatever these memories or dreams are." Her voice broke as she folded into herself. So small. Like a child.

Her hands scrabbled at her thighs and the bodysuit she wore, but the material was strong. Expensive. Tearing it would require a strength not even Pilates could grant.

"These fucking scars," she said. "My father said I was dizzy. Hadn't eaten all day to make sure the dress fit. That I fainted that night, but I would remember that, wouldn't I? Something like that?"

"Of course you would." Vera scooted closer to Ada and put her arms around her. "Of course."

The fear her mother described seemed to bloat outward like an infection. It wrapped sharp fingers around Camilla's heart and squeezed.

She shrank backward into the hallway, not wanting to see her lovely, perfect mother broken in such a way. She didn't want to wonder if her mother's memory of her own Purity Ball was accurate or a childish misinterpretation. The Purity Ball was just another sermon. A ritual wrapped in silk and gold, sure, but there was nothing insidious about it. Nothing that would inspire this fear.

Her mother's voice dropped to a whisper, but Camilla could hear her all the same.

"And that sound. Running under the laughter. Horrible. Wet. Like someone eating."

CHAPTER II

1953

Mary Shephard stared at her kitchen counter, where her third loaf of bread of the morning was currently resting. It was barely nine, and she'd already cleaned up the breakfast dishes and dusted the living room and mopped the floors. And the damned bread. She'd done that, too.

Her daughter was sleeping peacefully in her crib, the house a sparkling, domestic quiet any new mother would envy. She washed and dried her hands, the diamonds in her wedding band catching the sunlight, and stared out the back window into the wooded expanse that stretched over the ten acres of her husband's land. He told her when they got married he would clear out a section of it and plant her a rose garden, but she got pregnant and then the baby came, and he hadn't quite gotten to it yet. But she wasn't upset with him. Robert was so busy—exhausted when he came home from work and practically falling asleep over his dinner. Besides, she could always ask around, see if any of the other Hawthorne Springs ladies could recommend a gardener.

She wiped down the kitchen counters again, and wondered how many times she could clean the same rooms before she crawled out of her own skin with boredom. Leaning against the counter, she looked at the loaves of bread, how prettily lined up they were, and before she could think, seized the loaf still in its pan and marched outside. The grass was cool against her legs, the morning call of birds raining over her as she walked to the tree line and, with a scream, hurled the bread as far as she could into the woods.

Shoulders heaving, she turned back to the house. The bread had not been enough to fill whatever it was that was hollowing her out. Her hands itched with the need for destruction. For broken glass and shattered porcelain and the delicate give of something breaking. Robert's golf clubs were still in the entryway closet, and for a moment, she let her eyes drift closed against the sun and imagined what it would be like to take his nine iron and smash the oven he'd given her on their wedding day. She wondered if it would feel something like freedom. She wished she had a cigarette. But Robert had not liked women who smoked, and she gave it up after their second date.

Maybe she'd throw out all the bread, and Robert would ask where his toast was in the morning, and she'd tell him—what, exactly? She'd never been intelligent enough to come up with a lie that was remotely believable, and even if she did somehow manage it, she knew he'd sense it the moment it crossed her lips. Her own body was little more than a series of betrayals. She went flush across her neck and chest when confronted for even the tiniest thing, and on their wedding night, he'd kissed the lines of scarlet embarrassment that appeared on her chest and laughed as he called her his "nervous little bird."

From the house rose a wail that Mary knew would soon turn to screaming, and she turned and hurried back inside to the pink-and-ivory nursery where her daughter had wriggled free of her blanket.

Mary lifted the baby from the crib and hushed her as she buried her nose in the top of her daughter's sleep-scented hair. She wished she could bottle that smell so even as her daughter grew, she'd always remember her as she was now: tiny and beautiful and perfect.

"You were supposed to sleep for another half hour, my beauty," she said as she carried the baby into the kitchen to start a bottle. Mary settled her in the playpen, where she stared around her with bright, tear-damp eyes.

Mary started the water boiling and pulled a can of evaporated milk formula from the pantry. She'd tried to breastfeed, but her milk was slow, and Dr. Benson told her it would be better in the long run to make the switch rather than trying to force something that simply wasn't working. She'd been secretly relieved when he told her. They could afford the formula, and the vitamins were better for the baby.

The baby cooed as the water heated, and Mary flipped through the April issue of *Vogue*, bypassing the advertisements and then pausing at a full-page photo of Mrs. Leopold Stokowski, née Gloria Vanderbilt. Mary stroked glossy red fingernails along the graceful curve of her jaw, accented by a daringly short, scalloped haircut, the slim contours of her waist, the subtle swell of her mouth.

The knot Mary carried in her chest tightened, and she told herself it was envy. That it was a desire to possess the same striking figure and delicate features rather than wondering what it would be like to press her lips against that bowed mouth and then let them part, her tongue tasting the sweetness there. The very thing she knew was an abomination in the eyes of the Lord and in the eyes of The Path.

She was happy. Her husband was handsome. Kind. Wealthy. Not that the last part mattered because everyone in Hawthorne Springs had more money than they knew what to do with, but she'd been raised for a good marriage and a cherubic daughter and a beautiful home. All the things, as women, they were supposed to seek out because it was as God intended. She traced the page once more before guilt and shame burned like acid at the back of her throat, and she seized the magazine and buried it at the bottom of the trash, making sure she covered it in coffee grounds so she would not be tempted to dig it back out.

She was happy. She *was*. She offered the words up like a prayer as she fed her daughter, marveling at the tiny fingers that curled around her own. She would raise her daughter and keep the house and sit beside Robert every Sunday in his family pew. These were simple, straightforward things, and she was a simple, straightforward woman. There was no need for more.

The rest of the day passed in a series of repeated motions—cleaning, feeding, burping, diaper changing. Golden light softened the edges of the house as the afternoon wore on, and Mary made dinner and changed out of her housedress and into the red silk dinner dress Robert ordered for her as an early Mother's Day gift. She sent up a silent prayer of gratitude when it zipped, the darts at the bust straining against the extra baby weight she still carried. Keeping trim was next to holiness according to her mother, and the last time she'd seen Mary, she pursed disapproving lips and reminded her that her own waist had gone back to a svelte twenty-six inches only two months after she gave birth to Mary.

Glancing in the mirror, she smoothed her hands over the decorative cummerbund loop at the waist before touching up her lipstick and dabbing a bit of Givenchy perfume on her wrists and neck. Robert had never placed any sort of expectation on her about her appearance, but she was her mother's daughter. Her most devoted student in the art of snaring a good husband and then keeping him. These survival tactics would ensure she outdid any potential rivals. At the top, resources were slim, and if she wanted to marry well, there were rules to follow. Rules Mary eventually swallowed as truths. Robert might claim to love her with no makeup and undone hair, but he knew nothing of feminine competition.

Mary was changing the baby when she heard her husband's truck pull up the drive. He honked the horn twice, and she lifted the baby and went to peek through the window.

"What is Daddy doing?" she asked. Robert was standing in the front yard, his tie dangling from his neck as he reached through the truck's window and gave another series of honks. When he spied her in the window, he waved and then bounded for the front door.

"Daddy is silly," she said. "Let's go see what he's doing."

Robert was framed in the doorway, his dark hair falling against his temples as he grinned at her.

"Give me the baby and close your eyes," he said.

"What in the world?" She giggled and handed over the baby.

"All right, take my hand. Go slow now."

He led her outside, the wind lifting her hair from her neck as she let him guide her off the porch and into the grass.

"Okay. Open your eyes," he said.

She opened her eyes and looked at the two boxes that were loaded in the bed of the truck. "What is it?" she asked.

"I thought you might like a present." He rubbed his hand over the back of his neck and gestured toward the boxes. "You've not quite been yourself lately, and I know it's hard with the baby and all. And since you wouldn't let me get you a nanny, I thought this would help make things easier. The salesman said they could do double the clothes in half the time."

"A new washer and dryer," she whispered, and he hugged her to him even as the baby squalled. A strange heat had woken in her chest, and it clawed up into her throat.

"But we already have one."

"Not anything like this. This has all the bells and whistles. The salesman says you can even put those new miracle fabrics in there, and it won't mess them up."

Her body refused to move, her cheeks pulling her mouth into a rictus of a smile. She learned long ago how to mold herself into what people expected of her. Painted, practiced smiles and graceful, demure head nods. Like a corpse dolled up and ready for viewing, the strings pulling her forehead smooth and eyes up at the corners to give the appearance of life. The murmured voices passing over her cold skin: *Isn't she pretty?*

"Honey. Your nose is bleeding." Robert pulled his handkerchief from his pocket—the one she gave him when they were married, his initials embroidered by her careful hand in the corner—and blotted her face.

"Oh," she said, her hands dropping limply to her sides as the baby reached for her, its tiny face scrunched in fury.

"Well, hold on to the handkerchief, Mary. Don't just stand there. And tip your head back."

She tried to move, to take the handkerchief from him, but her body would not respond, and the white fabric slipped through her fingers as the blood crept over her lips and chin. The baby caught at her hair and tugged, and a thick heat bloomed in her chest. Her blood tasted of summer. Of grass after it's mown. Of rain. Of the deep acid that burned in her throat those first few months of pregnancy. Abnormal and *wrong*. As if whatever hand had stitched her had not been God's but something darker. She shivered, and the tightness in her chest broke as the first sob crested over her, and then the next and the next, and her body was a thing separate from her. She knelt, the gravel digging into her knees as she retched, the emptiness in her stomach mixing with the blood as she spat. It was almost beautiful. A light pink that made her think of the smooth interiors of shells, or those early morning skies when she'd been a girl and risen before the house had come awake, just so she could pretend she was the only person in the world.

"The hell?" Robert stepped backward, and she could have laughed. He wouldn't want to get any of it on his shoes. But if he did, she would be the one to clean it, so what did it really matter? She'd spend the rest of her life shining his shoes and fetching his dinners—an endless line of casseroles and puckered fingers from washing dishes.

She gasped, the air burning in her lungs as the words she wasn't supposed to say fell out of her. "Take them back. I don't want them."

"What do you mean, you don't want them? They're top of the line, Mary." There was confusion in his voice. And a hesitation. He didn't understand her like this. His role as a husband suddenly cast as something he'd not rehearsed.

She curled her fingers into the gravel and stared up at him. At her baby. At love and duty and boredom all tangled together in the dying sunlight. She wanted to scream until her throat went raw.

"I said I don't want the damn things," she hissed. "Take them back."

"Don't curse." He recoiled, his face pinching as if the word was some foul-smelling thing.

She did laugh then, and his face went slack, as if he couldn't decide which emotion was the right one. "I'm dying in there, Robert. Every day inside that house. It's like there's broken glass shoved inside me. Every time I move, I bleed, and then I mop it up and start all over again."

"You're not talking sense."

It would be better to force her breathing to slow. To settle herself, fix her face, smile at him, and tell him she was thrilled. How lucky she was to have such a thoughtful husband. How blessed by God. To take the baby and go back into the house and serve their dinner. She'd heard the stories of what happened to women who left their babies crying in the crib, the roasts to burn in the oven as they stared drooling out a window. Doctors and small rooms and medications.

But she couldn't do it. What had come apart inside her could not be put together again. It had been three years of marriage making Robert's breakfasts and kissing him goodbye and telling herself not to look at her magazines. Another two of trying for a baby, each month another disappointment when she'd go to the restroom and see that rusted red on her underwear. A slow progression that stretched into a future made up of washers and dryers that made her want to walk into the closest body of water with stones in her pockets. Her mother would be so disappointed.

"Come on. Up you go." Robert grasped her arm and hauled her upright, the baby still wailing as he guided her toward the house. Inside, the air was stale and smelled of the carrots she'd boiled earlier. Her stomach heaved again, but she swallowed and kept moving.

"Sit there," he said before plopping the baby in the playpen and vanishing into the kitchen. She tipped her head back and closed her eyes, listening to the tap turn on, the tinkle of ice in a glass, and then Robert was before her, a damp washcloth in one hand and a glass of brandy in the other.

"Drink this. It'll make you feel better."

She sipped slowly while he wiped at her face with a delicacy she hadn't known he possessed. As if he understood to go slowly so he wouldn't frighten her, so she wouldn't run like prey.

"I'll take them back if that's what you want." Robert cupped her cheek as he went to his knees before her. "But that wasn't just about the washer and dryer."

"I have to get out of this house. I feel like I'm losing my mind."

"Is it the baby? I can get my mother to come and stay for a bit—"

"No. The baby is wonderful. *You're* wonderful."

"Then what's this all about, Mary?"

"I made three loaves of bread today. Three. No one needs that much bread. It's obscene to have that much bread. I ironed your shirts that I already ironed yesterday. I rescrubbed the breakfast dishes."

"You don't have to make that much bread, honey."

Her mother would have had a fit if she saw her. These were secrets meant only for wives and mothers. You did not share the trials of domestic life with your husband. To do so was to be an abject failure. They were daughters of Hawthorne Springs, after all. Born to a set of unspoken expectations. Of what it meant to be a good Christian wife and mother. As much as her mother's antiquated ideals grated on her, she found herself falling into the rhythm of them.

"That's not what I mean."

He gripped her face between his hands, firmer now than the previous gentle touches he'd given her. "What do you mean?"

"I don't know." She sobbed again, but there was no rawness in it. Only a sort of defeat as she realized he would never fully understand the extent of the tedium that dominated her daily life. Her world would never belong to him. It was too small, too insular, for the bulk of him.

"I can't help you if you don't talk."

She drew in a ragged breath and let the fear flood out of her. Robert was a good man. Kind and understanding. He would not condemn her. He was not her mother or any of her mother's like-minded friends. "I know I should be happy. And I am. I *am*. But . . . it's like I'm stuck in a spider's web, and I'm fighting and fighting, and I know I can't get out."

"Oh, sweetheart," he chuckled, and drew her into his chest. She breathed in his cologne—vetiver and saffron and the darker note of his sweat. "That's all?"

She stiffened, and he tugged her closer. "I'll call my mother. She can come and watch the baby a few days a week. She's been practically begging me anyway. And you remember John Letting? He's looking for typists. You studied that for a bit, right? He doesn't normally hire married women, but I can put in a word. Just a couple days a week out of the house, and you'll be right as rain."

"But the baby—" Panic froze the words in her throat. She couldn't admit to wanting time away from her child and to what that meant about the sort of mother she was. What it would look like to any of the other women in Hawthorne Springs.

"Momma will be ecstatic. Don't you worry about the baby. She'll be just fine. The house isn't going to fall apart without you. At least not for two days a week."

She should be melting. All that ice she'd been carrying around in her heart and chest pooling at her feet because Robert had swooped in and saved her. A knight in a three-piece suit come bearing a new washer and dryer and a dim promise of salvation as a typist in Atlanta. She reminded herself that she was away from her mother's influence. A married woman with a child and her own house. She could do as she pleased, and it had been Robert, after all, who had suggested it. Even in the truth of all those reassurances, the anxiety running in her blood did not ease in the way she'd hoped it would.

Maybe it wasn't the house or the expectations of being a wife and mother at all. Maybe it was her.

She pushed the thought away. She had to try.

"You'll see, darling. Everything will be just fine," Robert said and turned to the baby, who'd finally quieted down and was cooing from the playpen. "And you, my beauty, will be the most spoiled girl in all of Hawthorne Springs. Your grandmother has been waiting for the chance."

"Yes." Mary delicately wiped away the tears that still stained her face. "Just fine."

"So it's definite then? He said he'd hire you?"

Vera Stephens placed a teacup in front of Mary and poured before offering the sugar bowl, which Mary waved away.

"I start next Monday." Mary took a Lorna Doone cookie from the bone china Vera used for company regardless of whether they were close friends or not and nibbled at the edge, wishing all the while she could shove three into her mouth at once. And take two teaspoons of sugar in her tea. The still-present tightness at her waistline kept her from it.

"It'll be good for you. To have some time to yourself."

"It's a job, not a vacation," she said, unable to keep the smile from her face. She had never thought it was possible for work to feel like freedom, but every breath felt lighter than the last.

"Did your mother have an absolute fit?" Vera settled across from her and took a sip of her tea.

Mary grinned. "You should have seen how red she got. I thought her head was going to pop clean off."

"What I would give to have been a fly on the wall." Vera settled her teacup in her saucer. "I've thought about it, you know? Getting work in the city. I don't know where I'd find the time."

"Just you wait until you have a little one of your own. You'll learn an entirely new definition of not having time."

Vera cleared her throat and stood, the lacy napkin across her lap falling to the floor. "I should get more cookies."

Mary glanced at the table with its plate of cookies still half-full, but Vera was already gone. Mary lifted the napkin and folded it neatly before placing it next to Vera's saucer. Vera had never been like Mary and the other young, married women—their discussions filled with baby talk and unabashed longing for houses filled with children—but as of late, she'd begun to blatantly avoid it. Yes, her own domestic ennui was a thorn in her side, but she wouldn't trade her daughter for the world.

"Did you hear Pauline Johnson is sick?" Vera held another plate of cookies, and Mary inwardly groaned. Vera would force her to eat at least two.

"I hadn't. That same virus that's been going around?"

"More than likely. A couple of us went out to visit her the other day, and she said the doctor told her she just needed lots of rest, but she told us she'd been sleeping nonstop. Didn't look it though. Her skin was practically gray, and she looked like she hadn't eaten anything in weeks. It's no wonder with those sores in her mouth. Bless her heart."

"I'm just glad I haven't gotten it. Evelyn Manley was out with it for weeks, and even once she came back, she looked terrible. My mother went on and on about how if she'd just put on a little lipstick, it'd go a long way to at least making her look better. What a shame how women let themselves go nowadays. You know how she is." She sighed, picked up a cookie, and took a bite. Good Lord, she missed sugar.

"You'll have to call the second you get home from your first day and tell me all about it," Vera said.

Mary brushed cookie crumbs from the edges of her mouth, careful to avoid smudging her lipstick. "I should be getting back. Any longer and Mother will have turned the baby into a tiny version of herself."

"Take a cookie with you. You only ate one." Vera thrust the plate at Mary, and she shook her head. She'd conceded enough of her willpower for one day. She smoothed her skirt and stood.

"I'll call you Monday once the baby's asleep," she said, and Vera reached for her hand and squeezed.

"You're going to be wonderful. I just know it."

FOR TWO WEEKS, it *was* wonderful. The mornings breaking over her in glorious bursts of pale pink and orange as she drove into the city. The buildings rising around her—monolithic and commanding and filled with purpose. The quiet of her drive had become a sort of invocation—an offering of holy tongues unfolding as she let the windows down just enough to feel the wind lift her hair from her shoulders. The subtle rise and fall of sound in the office as fingers flew over keys and low voices murmured back and forth. The delicate chatter of female voices so much younger seeming than her own over finger sandwiches and tea before the lunch bell rang.

And the baby seemed happy. She squealed whenever Mary walked through the door, her tiny arms dancing as Mary gathered her up and dropped kisses all over her blessed face. The house was still clean as a pin, and Robert still kissed her every night and called her his little dove and didn't grumble over his dinner if she was a few minutes late. She was able to push her thoughts into some dim corner of her mind, and she'd not looked once at the new issue of *Vogue* even if she desperately longed to press her cheek against the slim contours of the model's waist in the spread on beach dresses. It remained unopened on the coffee table—a testament to this step forward into the woman she should be. In the most secret parts of her heart, she knew her longing had nothing to do with wanting whatever dress the model wore or whatever hairstyle she had. But she could not speak anything of it aloud. The thoughts themselves may have damned her soul according to The Path, but to act on them meant losing her husband, her home, her daughter. Everything.

For those two weeks, Mr. Letting, her boss, came and went without incident. He took his coffee in his office and remained there until he emerged for a three-martini lunch. Then back into his office to smoke cigarette after cigarette as he yelled into his phone long after the typing pool had placed the dust covers over their typewriters and gathered their purses. He'd introduced himself on the first day, his eyes traveling over her body in a way that made her skin creep, but since then, she'd seen him only enough times to count on her fingers.

But one of the girls asked if she could cover her that Friday: she was *certain* her boyfriend was finally going to propose, and she needed the time to find the perfect dress. Mary smiled and agreed. Her mother-in-law told her at the start she was happy to keep the baby any time, and an extra day here and there wouldn't hurt.

What Mary hadn't realized was that on Fridays, the office ran on a skeleton staff, and the normal bustle that filled her hours was a vacuum of silence punctuated now and then by someone clearing their throat or a solitary phone ringing only to be answered in hushed tones meant not to shatter the cathedral quiet.

Mr. Letting was already enshrined in his office when Mary arrived, but he emerged shortly after and asked her to come in and take a letter. He closed the door behind them. It was only wood—a small divider between herself and the world outside it—but she was small, and he was large, and she was suddenly aware of the acrid scent of his sweat as he waved her toward the typewriter that sat in the corner. As she typed, he rested a meaty hand on her shoulder. She felt the weight of his gaze on her chest. She wished she'd thought to drape her sweater over her shoulders before she followed him into this godforsaken man den with its leather chair and oversized desk and stuffed quails and foxes that proved he knew how to shoot a gun and kill something that had no intention of attacking him.

His hand drifted down her arm, and he squeezed the extra flesh she still carried there. She froze under him, her fingers hovering over the keys as sweat trickled down her lower back and into the waistband of her slip. She wondered if he could smell her fear. If it smelled of the forest where he hunted. Of something small caught in a trap.

"I can appreciate a woman who doesn't worry too much about losing the baby weight. A woman should be soft," he said, and his voice filled the room, filled her chest, and she wanted to bring her fingers to her collarbone and crack herself open so she could tear out the sound.

"My husband is very happy," she said. Her body burned and burned, and still, he didn't draw away from her.

He chuckled, his hand dropping lower. "I just bet he is."

Behind her, the door slammed open, and she startled, Mr. Letting's hand falling away as if it was the most casual thing in the world.

"You tell those Darlington assholes— Oops. Didn't mean to interrupt." The man in the doorway darted a worming, pink tongue along the bottom of his neatly trimmed moustache and grinned.

"Is that all, Mr. Letting?" she said and stood, her hands itching to tug her skirt down and her blouse up. He'd not finished his dictation, but if she was forced to stay any longer in that chair, his fingers creeping farther and farther down, she was afraid she would scream. Or gouge out his eyes. Her body felt like something beyond her control.

"Mmm. What do you say, Bruce? Figure we should let this pretty kitty scurry on back to her hidey-hole?" Together, they laughed, and she ducked her head, hoping they would not see the heat she knew colored her neck and face.

Mr. Letting sighed. "Darlington, you said? That'll be all, Mary." He caught her hand and planted a wet kiss directly over her wedding ring. "For now."

She hurried out, the men still chuckling to themselves before the door swung shut. Her sweater still hung over the back of her chair, her purse still tucked away in the drawer beside the typewriter. Her neat, orderly world seemed to mock her racing heart. Like so many other moments in her life, she had found herself on the other side of the illusion. She blinked furiously at the tears forming. She would not cry. She would not allow him any sort of triumph. Even if he wasn't there to see it.

Instead, she snatched up her things—forcing her body to move quickly before her mind made her a coward—and dropped the dust cover over her typewriter. It was only a quarter after eleven, but the room was too small, the air like thick dust in her lungs. She could not stay there. If Mr. Letting's door were to open once more, she would pitch herself out a window.

She kept her eyes trained on the floor as she walked to the elevator, her fingers trembling as she pressed the button and then again because her touch had been too light the first time.

Perhaps Mr. Letting would come out of his office, see that she'd gone, and fire her. Perhaps he would remain there, closed behind that awful door, drinking Scotch and laughing until he forgot about her completely in the way he forgot about every woman for whom he had no immediate use. Perhaps he would come out now and order her back inside, and the afternoon would unfold into a slow-moving nightmare.

But she stepped into the empty elevator, her stomach lurching as it carried her down and away, and the breath she held flooded out of her. The doors opened onto the lobby, and she pushed herself toward the main entrance, her heels echoing through the open space, and then she was out and blinking against the glare of the late morning sun.

Her car was in the lot to her left, but she veered right. She couldn't go home this early. Her mother-in-law would tell Robert, and Robert would ask her what happened, and she wouldn't be able to lie to him. Wouldn't be able to make up a fake excuse. She didn't want him to know she was a failure. That she'd bolted at the first sign of trouble.

And had it even been trouble? What had Mr. Letting done after all? Touched her arm? Done some harmless flirting? Her head spun.

No. She would find something to do in the meantime. Rich's was only a few blocks away, and she'd been thinking of a new hat. She would shop. Get some lunch. And unless Mr. Letting did fire her, Robert would be none the wiser.

Only once she passed under the Crystal Bridge and entered the revolving door, the air scented with delicate florals and leather, did the tightness in her chest finally unstitch itself. She drifted toward the women's section, her hands passing over the slick coolness of silk blouses and delicately spun softness of cashmere as she let the sensation bring her back to her body. This was a world she understood. A golden, jeweled, rose-scented universe with which she was intimately acquainted. A world that spoke the language of her girlhood, and she sank into it like warm water.

She drifted toward the hats, the displays feathered and tulled and shining with promise. Lifted a pillbox from its stand, the brilliant peacock tones set against a cream silk and a pop of sapphire netting.

"Gorgeous, isn't it? It'll bring out the green in your eyes." The shopgirl appeared at her elbow, a gilded mirror in her hand. Mary sucked in a sharp breath as she stared. The woman smiled, her mouth a perfect, scarlet-painted bow made even brighter by the golden cascade of curling hair. Her dress clung at the hips and matched the color of her mouth. A brilliant, burning thing amid so much beige.

"Here. Let me," the woman said, and handed the mirror to Mary before placing the hat atop her head. She grasped Mary's arms and peeked over her shoulder into the mirror, eyes the color of ice meeting Mary's hazel ones.

"See? Lovely." The woman pulled Mary's hair away from her face, cool fingers brushing her neck. She felt herself begin to flush, and she silently begged her body to not give in to such an act of betrayal. "Everyone should have a hat like this, don't you think?"

"I'm certain you say that to all the ladies," Mary said, and almost clapped her hand over her mouth. She was not one to make jokes. To play at being coy. And yet here she was, a smile creeping over her own face as she arched an eyebrow.

"Only the ones I like."

Mary *did* flush then, and she brought an ineffective hand to her chest in the hopes the woman wouldn't notice.

"But we've never met. I could be terrible," she said. The woman shook her head, that golden hair flying.

"That's where you're wrong. Want to know how I know?" She leaned forward, her whisper sending a delicious shiver up Mary's spine. "It's because you *glow*."

Mary's hand fell to the side as the heat she felt unfurled beneath her skin. No one had ever been so forward with her. Not even Robert during their courtship. Everything with him was a stoic set of expectations. Romantic only in that it checked off a series of boxes set by some other person's definition of tame flirtations. But she wanted to glow. To be seen in the way this woman had seen her.

"I'm Sharon. Sharon Hutchins," the woman said, pressing her hand into Mary's.

"Mary Shephard," she said, and something like grief stole over her as Sharon dropped her hand.

If she had been a good girl, the girl her mother had raised her to be, Mary would have turned away then. As her mother always told her, such things wore attractive wrappings but hid a serpent's tongue.

Instead, she opened her pocketbook and withdrew her checkbook. Her heart fluttering, she looked directly into the deep blue of Sharon's eyes and told herself not to look away. To be decisive for once. "Have you had lunch? And I'll take the hat."

Sharon did not hesitate. "There's a café just down the street that does a beautiful chicken salad sandwich. Can you wait? I take my lunch at twelve fifteen."

Mary nodded. It was almost noon. The afternoon sparkled with possibility. She would have waited hours if it meant even twenty minutes with Sharon Hutchins. Being in her presence was like sunlight after a long, gray winter. A warmth she hadn't realized she was missing.

Sharon rang up the sale and boxed the hat, her delicate fingers tying a thick cream bow across the top. Mary's skin prickled as she watched Sharon's hands and wondered what it would be like to feel them, soft and cool against her skin. She pushed the thought away. Focused on the sounds of the other shopgirls and their customers, the quiet murmur of wealth being transferred, as she wandered toward the children's section to wait for Sharon.

"There you are." Sharon materialized at her elbow. "You'll have to come back wearing the hat, so I can get the full effect."

"I'll do that. I work just around the corner. I can pop in any time." Even as the words spilled out of her mouth, Mary could hardly believe her own bravado. That mousy, mincing girl she'd always been suddenly flowering and daring. Smiling back at this woman she didn't know but desperately wanted to. Pushing away all thoughts of what this meant on any level deeper than the want of friendship. She could not think about the unread magazines she'd thrown in the trash or the reasons she'd done it. Doing so would mean having to face why she was now waiting for Sharon amid a charming display of baby clothes, her hands blindly passing over frothy lace in a pantomime of interest. Right now, her child, the daughter she loved beyond reason and logic, was a faraway memory.

"That's pretty." Sharon came to stand beside her, a bland tan handbag tucked under her arm. "A little girl?"

"Oh." Dumbly, Mary looked down at the tiny periwinkle dress she held. "Sweet, isn't it?"

Sharon tilted her head, clearly waiting for something else from Mary, and she blushed. Of course. A little girl. Her daughter.

"Yes, a girl." She put the dress back in its place as blood rushed her ears. "She'll be six months on the fifteenth."

Sharon's gaze traveled to her left hand, pausing to take in her diamond engagement ring and the gold wedding band. It could have been the lighting or a momentary shadow cast from the sun that filtered through the large windows, but Mary imagined she saw Sharon's smile fall just a bit. The moment passed, however, and even though Mary twitched her hand away, determined that these next hours not be filled with conversation about her husband and daughter, she felt as if something between her and Sharon had already been lost. She wondered if it was possible to grieve for a thing she never had.

"Shall we?" Sharon asked, and Mary nodded, blissfully allowing Sharon to lead her through the labyrinthine displays and then out onto Broad Street, where Sharon turned left, her heels a pleasant clattering along the pavement.

"Have you worked here long?" Mary asked, suddenly realizing she knew nothing about the woman who walked beside her. That she'd somehow invited her to lunch for a reason she could not yet even admit to herself much less put into words. Sharon stepped smartly ahead of her, and Mary quickened her pace so she would not lose Sharon's response in the general commotion of the other pedestrians.

"A little over a year. It's not much, but I have my own apartment over on Irwin Street. Food on the table. A little cat named Radish." She smiled. "What's your daughter's name?"

"Ada." Again, she felt the urge to change the subject, to lead Sharon away from anything related to Ada or Robert. Toward something safe. Something innocuous. "We're in Hawthorne Springs."

Sharon paused, and Mary had to draw herself up so she wouldn't slam into her. She turned to face Mary, squinting against the sunlight. "So, you're a member of that big church then? The Path?"

Her tone was light. Breezy. But something flitted across Sharon's face. A momentary darkness or confusion Mary couldn't completely identify but which was obvious. She suddenly had the urge to apologize or to tell Sharon she misheard, and she didn't live in Hawthorne Springs at all, but it would have only made things more confusing.

"Yes. I grew up there," she offered, but she had no way of knowing if that lessened or intensified whatever emotion it was that crossed Sharon's face. Looking at her now, at the slight smile that spoke only of interest, Mary wondered if she imagined it. If it was her nerves twisting every reaction, every word, into something harsher rather than anything Sharon had actually done or said.

"Every girl I grew up with dreamed about marrying someone from Hawthorne Springs. The whole Cinderella fantasy." Sharon resumed their walk, her voice dreamy. Mary fell in beside her as she did her best to dispel the lingering memory of what she thought she saw pass over Sharon's face. "It was the talk of the town when Tracy Manning was invited to some party out there, but nothing ever came of it. She married Bob Crandell and that was that. Here we are."

She stopped in front of a plate glass window framed by a navy-and-white-striped awning. A large orange tabby cat sat blinking back at them from behind the window.

"That's Bobby. Hope you don't mind. He's not the owner, but don't tell him so." Sharon winked and then stepped neatly inside. Bobby narrowed his eyes and yawned, dismissive of these newcomers to his café. Charmed, Mary followed.

The café wasn't a place Mary would have picked on her own. White and spare, it was, outside of Bobby's presence, unromantic and efficient. But it smelled of coffee and fresh bread, and there was a warmth there that reduced her snobbery to a quick investigation of the silverware as they tucked themselves onto stools at the single counter that stretched the café's length. All clean.

Fifteen minutes later, the women sat beside each other at one end of the single counter, two of the aforementioned chicken salad sandwiches and glasses of sweet tea sitting before them. Around them, the noise of the other diners seemed to drop away, the space they occupied untouched by the controlled chaos of orders placed and lunches delivered.

Sharon had been right. The chicken salad looked divine. For once, Mary was going to allow herself to enjoy the meal. To eat the entire thing without worrying about her waistline.

The waitress refilled their teas and then moved down the counter as Mary dipped her head in silent prayer.

Sharon watched her, a slight smirk playing at her lips, and then did the same.

"Goddess Mother, whose abundant gifts I now receive, accept my gratitude and bless all living creatures, great and small.

"I hope you don't mind," Sharon said as she lifted her sandwich. "I'm still a decent, praying girl. Just to a slightly different god." She tilted her head and winked, and Mary wanted to lean in and breathe the air Sharon had just exhaled. Sitting with this woman was a dangerous act of rebellion, and it thrilled her in all the ways her mother and The Path told her it shouldn't. She should be excusing herself, should be fleeing such a blatant display of blasphemy, but she felt herself resisting. Felt herself wanting to stay.

"You're a witch," Mary said, and immediately wished she could pull the words back into her.

"I've been called worse," Sharon said and popped a cherry tomato into her still somehow perfect bloom of a mouth.

"I'm so sorry. I didn't mean to—"

Sharon reached across the counter and laid her hand over the top of Mary's. "Don't worry, darling. I'm not going to hex you, if that's what you're thinking."

"No. Of course not. I suppose I just . . ." She searched for what it was she truly wanted to say, but the words had evaporated on her tongue like smoke.

Sharon bit into her sandwich and chewed as she considered Mary. Her voice softened. A clear effort to lessen her prior brazenness. "If it helps, I don't believe in any sort of divine evil. Channeling it for selfish purposes. There's too much beauty in the world to spend my time trying to darken it. What I *do* believe in is nature. The ebb and flow of energy secreted inside all things. How we might channel it outward. I have no desire to find myself on the receiving end of such negativity. No matter how much someone might irritate me."

Mary did lean forward then, Sharon's scent falling over them like a veil. Bergamot and rosemary unfolding over something darker. Like walking barefoot through the woods after rain, the moss cool beneath her feet. The chatter of the café fell away, the patrons vanishing into the ether, and they were simply two wild creatures staring at each other and waiting for the other to move.

"So you do magic? Spells?" Mary asked.

Sharon danced her fingers over Mary's hand. "You can call it that. If you like. It's funny..." Sharon sank back, taking her hand with her, and Mary fought to keep the disappointment from showing on her face. "I don't usually discuss my beliefs the first time I meet someone. People are quick to judge, and they tend to find the violence they're looking for. The Burning Times aren't that long gone, and even so, those ignorant assholes in their white sheets just found a new thing to persecute. So it keeps me fairly quiet with strangers. But I feel like I've known you my entire life. Like I can tell you all my secrets, and you'll keep them."

"I understand. About the judgment. My mother would lose her mind if she knew I was here right now. Disown me, get me kicked out of the church, the whole song and dance," Mary said.

"Well, we just won't tell her, will we?" Sharon smirked, and it was a quiet devastation. Beside her, Bobby materialized and stretched, his tail wrapping around Sharon's leg as she leaned down to pet him. "Look at you, you glorious beast! Think you can keep our secret?"

The cat stared back at them, gave a blink, and wandered on.

"I think that means yes," Mary said.

"I think so, too." Sharon dropped into a whisper. "I had a feeling something wonderful would happen today. And here you are."

"Like magic," Mary said. She was giving in to this warmth, this acceptance, and it felt so much better than pushing it away in shame.

"Yes. Exactly like magic."

INTERLUDE: 1750

I took care not to stain my apron as I gobbled down the heart. I would be able to rinse my hands and arms at the well, but there would be no time to change before Benjamin's arrival. Nowhere to hide a bloodstained garment where Florence would not find it. If Florence asked after the missing hen, a fox would serve as justification, but I hoped we would be gone by then. That all threads binding us here would be dissolved and our freedom growing with every step.

By the time I cleaned myself and buried that small, broken lump of feathers, the day's shadows had lengthened into afternoon, and I knew well that the bitter taste that lingered on my tongue had naught to do with the blood but more to do with guilt. Even though I hurried, my steps back to our cottage felt weighted, as if my feet wanted to root themselves into the very earth I dared to flee.

There were a few things yet to pack, but I found myself unable to focus as I settled once more before the hearth, a bit of stitching in my hand as an illusion of industriousness. My attention focused only on listening for the sound of Benjamin's horse and the gate's squeak.

But when the clatter of hooves finally sounded there was little relief in it. Only a sense of duty and a bright rush of heat in my throat. A reminder of the blood I'd taken. The oath I'd given. And beneath it all, the steadying rush of my own yet-beating heart. That ancient cadence that had carried me and my daughter this far and, I hoped, would carry us so much further.

I waited, eyes closed, and then rose and went to the door.

"Benjamin! You are good to come," I called as Benjamin dismounted and looped his reins across the garden gate.

"No trouble. I only hope I can be of some service." He strode lightly, his hand cupped over his brow to block the sun's glare. "Florence has not yet found her, I trust?"

"She has not. She's still out, even now. But come in, come in. I cannot send you off without some refreshment." I waved him inside, a spider to a fly, and he came easily. Eyes open and bright as I let the door swing closed behind him.

"There is fresh bread. Pickled egg and butter," I said.

"I would not turn down fresh bread." He removed his hat and held it before him, and I could see a spot on his jaw that still bled. He'd shaved then. An effort to make himself presentable for Florence. I hardened myself against that sweetness and focused on the bread. How, in the cutting of it, it did not bleed. For, in that moment, it seemed it was not the loaf I baked the day before lying before me but instead the hen with its rotting neck.

I spoke with a joviality I did not feel. "I cannot think of many who would." I cut two large slices and spread them thickly with butter. I could afford to be wanton. There was no need for any stinginess when I knew whatever remained of our larder would only go to waste.

He finished the first slice in three bites, his eyes closed as his jaw worked. "If Florence is half as good a baker as her mother, I am a lucky man indeed."

I did what was expected and flushed with pleasure. "That is kind."

"This is a bread that will keep a babe hearty. Grow him into a strapping lad. Poor Florence will have her work cut out for her keeping them fed!" He laughed and bit into the second slice.

There should be no ice in the air, but I felt it curling against me.

Felt it knitting itself to my bones as I let my body drift into stillness. As I let the blood do its work.

I did not bother keeping my voice light. It was necessary that Benjamin feel the weight behind it. "Keeping *them* fed?"

He paused, his brow wrinkling, but then went back to the bread. "Of course. A house full of sons. Though I would not be opposed to a girl or two." He laughed, but I did not meet it. Rather, I held every part of my body still. Soft. As if it pained me beyond measure to speak what came next.

"Oh, Benjamin. I thought you knew." I laid a hand over his arm and squeezed in maternal sympathy. "Florence cannot bear a child."

The lie, aided by the heart I'd eaten, slipped from me easily, and I watched as the devastation took Benjamin apart. His face twisted into first confusion, then anger, then grief, as I hoped beyond measure this dishonesty would hold. That it would break apart what had been promised in whispers so I might still save not only myself but Florence from certain persecution and death.

"I cannot think why she would not have told you. She took ill as a girl. The doctor said that with her fever..." There was no need to offer any further details or legitimizing evidence of Florence's falsified illness. Benjamin wouldn't question them. Not with the shock and betrayal of Florence's secret still roiling through him. No respectable man would question anything related to the mysterious inner workings of a woman's childbearing organs. Even the most tolerant among them found other things to do when the midwife came calling. He would only hear what he wanted, and I would take advantage while I could.

"It is certain then? She cannot provide a child?" He clenched his fists, the tendons along his forearm corded as he looked up with a hopefulness that almost broke me. I touched my tongue to the back of my teeth, a reminder of the blood I'd taken, and let it settle my aching heart. I was stronger than their bond, and this was the only way. Florence would not leave so long as there was any remaining tie to Benjamin.

"I'm so sorry, Benjamin. It was not my place to tell. It would be better if Florence did not know I spoke of it."

He rose and wiped a hand over his mouth, ridding himself of any lingering crumbs from the bread and forced a tight smile. "It is a natural thing to speak honest. No good man would find fault in it." He turned to the door. "Thank you. For the bread. I should get searching before the day is out. Perhaps I'll find the red cow and Florence both. Bring them each back home to you."

I heard the finality in his voice. An underlying truth he was only coming to understand. That Florence would not belong to him. She could not. She was not the woman he thought her to be. Not the woman he wanted. The future he'd planned so fully for himself was an illusion. One he believed my daughter purposely kept from him.

It would be exactly as I planned. He would speak with her. Tell her he could not take her as a wife. Even if it hurt him, even if he still loved her, the betrayal was too great. The vision he'd crafted for himself could not die for something as simple as a woman.

I could have wept with relief, but I followed him to the door and watched as he settled himself back into the saddle. We would be safe. We would leave that night, if possible, and see the next morning in a place where we could build a new life. Watch the sun chase away the shadows.

"If I don't see Florence, tell her I'll call on her tomorrow," he said, and lifted a hand in farewell.

"I will. Keep well, Benjamin."

Nodding, he clicked his tongue, the horse moving easily under him, and once more, the yard was empty.

I had no way of knowing then, but in town, a noose had already been formed. A room with three men who wore their holiness as something sharp held my name and Florence's on their tongues. It did not matter how many I helped with my knowledge. Their wives and children all kept from sickness with what I made with my own hands and the earth's offerings. The beginning of all I feared unfurled rapidly even as Benjamin came upon Florence just outside the main road, her cheeks flushing prettily as she offered a smile he did not return.

Already, he'd hardened his heart. Already, he saw her as something worthy of dismissal. Perhaps, if he had been in that room among those covenanted men, he would have found the same wickedness within the woman who not even two hours prior had been his betrothed.

But I would not know those things until later. How, when Florence stumbled home along the main road, her vision blurred from weeping, Phillip Franklin spat at her as she went past, a mumbled "witch" tossed at her retreating back. How fear grew to overtake sorrow in Florence's heart as she pressed to go more quickly, the ground blurring beneath her feet as her breath caught in her chest with a pain she'd never known. Hers was not a body made for running, but she would grow used to it. I would be there to see to it.

I was seated once more beside the hearth when Florence came in. Despite her running, she came in softly, with a quiet that spoke of shame and regret. She did not close the door behind her but stood there, trembling, in the dying light.

I stood; my arms extended as I went to meet my daughter in feigned ignorance. "Florence? What's happened?"

"Benjamin has ended our engagement. He would not look at me. Would offer no reason no matter how I begged him for one. Said it was as God willed it. And then, on the road home—" She broke into a sob, her hand over her mouth as if she could hold the sound inside. As if by doing so, it could erase what was happening to us. "He called me 'witch.' Phillip Franklin did. As I passed by him."

I gathered her to me and pressed my lips to her hair. Soothed her, in the way only I could. I wished, as I had since she was a child, I could take it all, her pain and worry and doubts. Absorb them and let her be absolved. Let them scar me instead of her. But this was a necessary cut. I could not save her from this.

"We cannot stay, Florence. You understand. Once that word is spoken, death is the only thing that can follow."

She gasped against my shoulder. "I cannot. It is the only life I've known. All that I have."

I gripped her, pulled her backward so she could look nowhere but my eyes. "You have no choice. There is nothing left for you here. I would not speak ill of the man you love, but he has cast you aside for a reason. Even if he did not speak it, you must see it for what it is. They have spoken an accusation. Such a thing will not keep quiet. It will spread. It already has."

Her face was swollen with crying, but she was still lovely. My daughter. This woman who stood in the place a girl once did. I saw all versions of her in that moment; remembered how she saved me after her father died. Her very presence a tether to the earth I wanted to leave so I might follow after my husband. The only man who'd not seen me as wicked and worthy of crushing beneath his boot. The only man I would ever love.

All those years ago, I whispered to her that I would stay alive. For her. I would keep that promise no matter how it filled me with a hurt I knew would never fully abandon me. No matter the lies I told, the life she longed for lost because I willed it so in the name of saving her life. I would see us out.

"I have only ever wanted happiness for you. To see you live fully. But it cannot be here." I took her hand and squeezed it. "We will find a place where that can happen. I swear it. By any god that will hear, I swear it."

Florence looked back at me, her eyes gone dull. "It is a ghost that leaves this place. Not myself."

Once more, I hugged her to me. "We will wait for dark and go. We cannot take much, and even then, I fear taking the wagon. The noise of it. But we will need food. The chickens will do for now. And I have packed enough seeds and roots to see us through. The earth will provide."

As the night came on, the dark of it reaching for us, looking for something to place between its teeth, Florence aided me in packing the wagon. It was she who remembered the ax. The rifle her father left behind. She who settled the chickens in their baskets, their clucking finally quieting when she covered them. She who hitched the horse to the wagon, staying her with a soft hand and softer words. I added a single heavy-lidded cast-iron pot. The roots and seeds. What clothing we would need, and my sewing kit. Bottles and mortar and pestle.

I would have preferred to go on foot, but we would not have been able to carry what was necessary on our own. I could only hope we'd gotten ahead of the risk. Already gone by the time Reverend Brenton and his men came looking for us. It was a blessing we were already so isolated. There was smaller opportunity for any enterprising neighbor to spy our escape and send up the alert.

Above us, the sky was dark. A new moon. Auspicious. A time for new beginnings. For cutting away the dead and rotted and looking toward the blank face of what may come.

Together, we went through the house in that dark. Room by room. Touched what remained and then moved on. Those rooms and what lay within those walls no longer belonged to us, but it felt right to try to memorize their shapes. To take even the smallest memory with us. A remembrance of the women we once were.

We came back into the front room. The hearth had burned down to embers, but we would not be there to stoke them back into life. "It is time," I said.

Florence did not speak but nodded. When she went through the door, she did not look back.

There was no manner of fully disguising our path, but we did what little we could. We entered the woods in several places only to trace our path out and then reenter at a separate point. It would grant us some time should anyone attempt to follow us, and with any luck, they would tire quickly of looking and assume we would meet our own deaths regardless. Starvation. Wolves. The natives they feared because they did not understand them. The devil himself with his book of names stamped in blood. So many ways a woman could die that did not involve the rope or the flame.

Finally, we set off in earnest, the forest closing over our heads as we pushed into the trees. It would be a slow, arduous journey, for there were no roads or paths. What our horse could not push through would have to be circumnavigated, and it was always possible we would have to go on foot in the end should the terrain become too steep or impassable. But I could not think of that. There was only room for moving forward, and the quiet hush of the nocturnal creatures moving about us.

"Where will we go? We have no map. No shelter," Florence said.

"The earth will provide. It always does."

She looked askance at me; her face hardened. "It is God who will grant whatever blessing He sees fit."

I kept silent, unwilling to introduce an argument into the start of this new life. I would not begrudge Florence the god she had chosen. I had not before. Even as I tried to teach her the old ways. It only pushed her further from me. But perhaps we could find a new path together. A common ground built from a necessary intimacy with the natural cycle of things. The earth and its growing. The wind and water and sun and all that was nourished by those things. The power that slept there. Perhaps, without the influence of Reverend Brenton, my daughter and I could live as I'd always wanted. Simply, in accordance with the natural order. My heart glowed with the possibility of it.

Exhausted as we were, the gentle rock of the wagon finally pulled us into slumber. Somehow, the horse carried on, Florence and I drifting somewhere in the twilight world between sleeping and waking. It was a stupid thing to let myself sleep when there was so much danger still around us, but I had grown tired of fighting, and so I slept, comforted by the warmth of Florence's body beside mine.

I was not sure how long we wandered or how far we'd gone into the heart of the forest. If it had been days or only hours, and if the morning stole upon us, I could not remember its light. I only remembered when we stopped, and the sudden, insistent pull that seemed to travel to the very center of my being.

I'd spent my entire life with my hands in the dirt. Learning from what grew there and the creatures that drew life from it. The chorus of my girlhood was learning the steady hum that lay at the core of the world. A power so many people could not sense because they would not take the time to do so or feared it meant there was no use for their god. Those who would shy away from blood or death because they saw it as evil rather than the natural order of things. They labeled me "witch" because of it. I could not wear such a name there. But perhaps, with such a power perfuming the very air, I could wear it here. There was a power in naming, and I'd been running from my own name for too long.

The horse came to rest, dropping his head to crop at the grass, and I felt as if I could do nothing other than stare. A black walnut tree in full flower sat in the center of an impossibly open space. Its branches twisted into the sky, and leaves of full, verdant green buzzed with the drunk stumble of bees. Around it, the air seemed to expand and contract like some great, living creature drawing breath. It was as if some transparent eye had turned itself upon me, left me exposed and trembling and aware of how in the face of something so infinite, I was immaterial.

It struck me that the tree had always been there, biding its time, casting deep roots that drank from pools that were older than any man could comprehend. There were spaces in this world that held an ancient power, and this was one. I stumbled out of the wagon, not minding when my legs buckled from lack of use. I needed to touch it, run my hands over its bark and breathe in the magic it held. I wanted to hold that power inside me and feel it blossom into something that would let Florence and me flourish.

I expected something to stop me, to keep me away from the tree and what it contained, but I approached without opposition. As in all things, the tree held a beauty that served as a thin veil for grotesqueries the common eye would not see. I held my breath as I ran my hands over the rough bark. It traced outward in a series of bulbous growths that bent and shifted in the light so they resembled screaming mouths and bloated heads lopped off at the neck. My skin prickled, each part of me suddenly longing to feel the velvet touch of leaves, to sprout roots and drink deep from the hidden darkness that fed the tree and take into myself that same power.

"I do not like the look of it." Florence appeared at my shoulder, and I startled and dropped my hands.

Florence pointed at the tree. The bark with its strange markings. "It is the mark of the devil."

I shook my head. "No. The natural world could not be so befouled. The devil resides only in the hearts of men."

"It frightens me."

I clasped Florence's hand, pressed it to the tree, and smiled. This was only the beginning of a reintroduction to what I had always hoped she would understand. "There is nothing to fear in power. Can you not feel it?"

She withdrew her hand and let it drop to her side where it twitched spiderlike over her skirts. She'd smoothed the lines of her face, but her gaze was still fearful, her eyes damp as she looked up at the tree.

"Here. On this ground. In this place. We will live well. I feel it in my very bones," I said.

Florence said nothing and turned away.

I ignored the sinking in my heart and looked at the tree. Only at the tree.

CHAPTER III
2007

"I'm going to talk to Henry. I can't let her go, Vera. I can't." Her mother's voice sharpened with a resolution Camilla had learned meant she would not change her mind.

Camilla wanted out. Out of the basement, out of the house, out of the entire compound. She didn't want to think her mother had kept her from participating in the Purity Ball all because of some childish memory. That she would keep her from it *again*. As she pushed herself back from the door and toward the stairs, the apprehension she'd felt at first settled into a sharper frustration, and then anger.

For years, Camilla had been the punch line of every joke. Openly laughed at because she was the preacher's daughter, and still, even after high school graduation and turning eighteen, not allowed to participate. Most of the girls were twelve or thirteen at the most when they attended their Ball. She would be the oldest by far. She would look ridiculous standing next to those little girls. Even Noah and Brianna regularly joined in, laughing hysterically as they asked if Camilla planned to wear white tights and Mary Janes with her gown. It didn't matter if they were joking. The whole thing was humiliating.

And all for what? Some long-ago neuroticism her mother still clung to while Camilla bore the brunt of the teasing?

Her bare feet sank into the runner's plush carpet as she pushed herself up the stairs. Her mother wouldn't notice she'd not come down for Pilates. Not with Vera there offering a shoulder to snivel on. And her father would likely be in his study the rest of the day. No one would be looking for her, and she wanted it that way. The last thing she needed right now was any semblance of trouble because someone caught her sneaking out.

Grabbing a pair of shoes from her bedroom, she slipped back down the main stairs and breathed a sigh of relief when no one saw her grab the keys to the Jeep. Staff used it to shuttle equipment back and forth across the property on days they hosted luncheons, so no one would miss it.

She kept to the edges of the house, darting past the windows as she hoped no one was inside to see. Or, if they did, they would think she was a squirrel or a leaf caught on the wind. There and gone and not worthy of their attention. She'd learned the external security camera blind spots a long time ago and avoided them, but their house was never quiet. Never still. Housekeepers and chef staff and visitors and security . . . it seemed as if there was someone always there. Someone more than willing to report her to her father. Because it didn't matter that she was an adult. She was his daughter. A representative of him in all things. And she would be kidding herself if she thought he wasn't capable of punishing her anymore. The threat of his sending her on Retreat was ever present. It was his money. His power. There was no question of her falling in line. What else did she have but the life he provided her?

But what she had planned, she would keep secret. There would be no risk of her father finding out. Not if she did everything correctly.

As she crept toward the barn where they stored the Jeep, she couldn't help but hold her breath. An old habit left over from girlhood. A need to create some sort of ache inside her, a penance for her rebellion. There were other moments—holding ice in her hand until its winter burn was too much; yanking a few strands of hair from the back of her head where no one would see; a safety pin on the soft flesh of her inner arm. A sum of all her small sins laid bare on the altar of her body.

The barn was quiet, the main doors opening on silent, well-oiled rollers, and she slid into the cool dark. The air tasted as it always did, of oil and dust and hay and things put away from lack of use, and she pulled it into her, relishing the sudden fullness in her chest. The air she denied herself flooded into her with a delicious sting.

The Jeep started easily, and she let the windows down, wanting the sensation of the wind in her hair. Wanting to believe, even for a moment, she had some semblance of control over her life. That she could choose to do something on her own without the ever-present threat of Jesus and her father. Without her mother pretending she was still a little girl. She swung the Jeep wide and then guided it onto the gravel road that led behind the house and then back to the main entrance.

It took twelve minutes to get to Noah's house. She parked at the entrance gate with its ivy-covered iron filigree, and then ducked behind the strangling vines, her hands searching for the secret entrance Noah cut when they were fourteen. It had been a while since she needed to use it, but it was still there, and she pushed through, hoping he'd be out at the dog pens like he always was.

The Whitten family was known for its impeccably bred and trained German shepherds, sold to families intent on security. There were nights Noah slept out in the pens, surrounded by the dogs his father told him not to love. He'd never been able to help himself.

She crested the first hill, and then another, before she heard the dogs and then the sound of Noah's voice calling out a series of commands. The pens opened before her, a series of intricate gates and chain link, and there was Noah surrounded by his dogs, their tails beating frantically against the dirt as he held up his hand. She brought her fingers to her mouth and whistled the way he'd taught her, and his head snapped up in alarm, his body tensing and then relaxing when he saw her.

"You scared the hell out of me," he called as she trotted down to the pens. "What are you even doing here? You could have just texted me."

"Didn't want to risk anyone seeing anything they don't need to."

He arched an eyebrow. "I'm listening."

"There's a few people I want you to text."

He pulled his phone out of his pocket. "About?"

She grinned. The word that came to mind was "wicked." She wondered how long it would take for the shame to settle into her blood like it always did. For her father's voice to overthrow her own. "This Friday night. We're having a party."

SOMEONE BROUGHT KEROSENE, and the bonfire Camilla, Noah, and Brianna built at the start of the evening was now an inferno. The flames licked at the sky, sparks falling around them in a way a now fairly drunk Camilla found beautiful. Behind them, a massive tree cast strange shadows, painted them all in dark that turned their faces angular. Hungry.

Camilla's parents were out for the night—a dinner party with the Deans. They would come home Scotch tipsy and stumble up to bed without worrying whether their daughter was safely asleep in her room. Camilla would be home before they woke the next morning to nurse their hangovers with black coffee and ibuprofen.

Noah stood before the bonfire with Brianna as they chatted with Sam Rickard. Camilla glanced back at the tree, looking for the only face she hoped to see, but he wasn't there. They all came—Noah and Brianna and Sam and Ariana and Rachel and Michael—but Grant Pemberton had not. She should have known he wouldn't bother with some fresh-out-of-high-schooler's party, but it stung all the same. Whatever significance she thought passed between them was clearly a product of her imagination. Or her desire. Likely her desire. Wishful thinking had led her down yet another dead end.

Camilla stood and stretched her arms overhead, her cup balanced so she wouldn't spill, and then made her way over to Noah and Brianna and Sam before settling on the grass in front of them.

Sam ran his hands through a perfectly unkempt swoop of blond hair and nudged her with the tip of his impractical leather loafer. "Can't believe you pulled all this off, Camilla." He gestured toward the bonfire with the flask he brought. "Figured you'd be locked up inside your house, scared the Dark Sisters were coming for you."

Noah laughed and grabbed at Brianna, his best approximation of ghost noises coming out in a garbled wail that sounded more like a dying cat.

"Stop it. Someone is actually sick," Brianna hissed, and sidestepped Noah. Her body shrank into itself. Closed off. Angry. Signs he should have easily read but didn't.

"Oh, calm down, Brianna. Learn to take a joke," Sam said. The boys' laughter increased, the alcohol making them blind to the silence that had fallen over the girls. They fell into Michael, their wails choked beneath their idiotic glee as they contorted their faces into gaping, crooked mouths.

"It's not fucking funny," Brianna said, but they didn't hear her. There was only enough space for their laughter. Their dismissal.

But the girls. They all knew. The fear. How it didn't matter that the Sisters weren't real. They'd all grown up in The Path. They knew better than anyone how belief was more powerful than sight or logic. Sight meant so little in the face of something as formidable as a little girl's fear and belief. But even if they shared the same Sunday school classes, heard the same platitudes week after week, Noah and Sam and Michael would never fully understand the depth to which the girls could believe in monsters.

Camilla turned away. Looked at the tree and wondered if she could forget what was happening behind her. Focus on the bark and its great looping twists. Breathe and pretend she didn't want to rip

Noah's head off particularly. He wasn't like the rest of them. Wasn't posturing or condescending. He was supposed to be better.

Her fingers itched toward her scalp. It would be so easy to tear a piece of herself away. A tiny scab. Something no one would think to look for. Something no one would miss. Every part of her vibrated in anticipation of the relief that would move like a great tremor down her spine.

She lifted her hand as if to tuck her fingers behind her ears. Pretense on display. The summation of her life made small.

And then there was the first scream.

It seemed to begin in the chest. Guttural and halting. As if the person couldn't understand why they were making such a noise. It pitched upward into something raw. Panicked.

The guys' laughter, as quickly as it had come, died away.

Without wanting to, Camilla's body turned back toward the bonfire. The fear had become part of her, too. It drew on her in small sips. Taking her belly. Her chest. Her tongue. Bit by bit devouring her until she could do nothing but tremble and look where Sam lay twitching in the dirt.

He screamed again and clawed at his throat, his back arched and mouth opening so wide Camilla worried his jaw would crack open. "Please. Oh, please." His teeth bit off the edges of the words, and his head jerked back and forth as a thin line of drool crept from his lips.

"What's happening?" Ariana asked. No one responded. No one moved. Shock held them in too tight a grip. It was as if they were held under a great dome, the air gone still as whatever watched them kept them pinned beneath its watchful eye.

Finally, Noah knelt beside Sam, his hands hovering over his chest as if the act of movement could suddenly conjure the right thing to do.

He'll ruin his jeans, Camilla thought, dimly aware what a stupid thing it was to worry over.

"Someone call 911," Brianna said, and took a step forward, her own cell phone forgotten in the limp grip of her palm.

Michael held out a hand. "No cops. Just give me a second to think."

Over and over, Sam gagged, the sound deepening and lengthening as it grew into something that sounded more animal than human.

What if Sam swallowed his tongue? Was that even possible? Or what if he'd hit his head when he fell and what they'd all just seen was a seizure and now they were all standing around watching him die?

The bonfire leapt behind them, a draft of wind seizing at the sparks and casting them upward. Camilla followed their trajectory and wondered if she would spend the rest of her life categorizing her future self around this night. What she had and had not done and what that meant about her. If it meant she was as empty as she sometimes felt. A carcass built of rot.

She closed her eyes, and the sparks followed her into the dark. In the world outside, Sam still choked, but Camilla felt removed. As if she'd slipped out of the skin of this world and into some strange in-between place.

In the distance, the wind caught at the trees. Buried within it, she imagined she heard her name. The barest of whispers.

Camilla.

Her throat burned with the need to respond, but her tongue sat useless behind her teeth. She could have torn it out for the want of movement. Just to know she still had some semblance of control over her body instead of this woozy lethargy. To see it there in her hand and know that it belonged to her alone, and she held the power of its use.

"Camilla."

Her eyes snapped open. Sam stared at her, his voice ragged as he called her name again. "Camilla."

Garbled sounds leaked from between his fingers as he sat up, and then there was another terrible groan as he opened his hands and showed her the pale, fleshy mound in his grip.

A tongue. He was holding a tongue.

Camilla screamed and scrambled backward, her hands scraping against the dirt as his mouth gaped open, dark blood spilling over his chin. He crawled toward her, the tongue held before him in one hand.

He lifted it to her, and Camilla closed her eyes. She could not bring herself to process that he'd bitten or torn off his own tongue. Everything was confusion and fear and so much screaming, the world around her crashing down as they all scrabbled away from Sam and what he held in his hands. He made another sound in his throat—a strange ticking that grew louder as he drew closer to her.

But the sound changed. Another hitch, and then another, and her eyes flew open because she recognized what it was Sam was doing.

He was laughing. And then Michael, too. And then, because her body was suddenly empty of its adrenaline or because the relief was too great or because she didn't know what else to do and was still confused and woozy and a little drunk, Camilla laughed as well.

Noah did not laugh. He looked at Brianna.

"What the *fuck?*" Brianna advanced on them, her body trembling, fists clenched at her sides. Her rage was incandescent. A shimmering aura that threatened to consume anything that dared to draw near.

"Cow tongue. And a fake blood capsule," Sam said, and then dangled the organ over his mouth and lewdly waggled his own tongue at it. He turned and faced Noah, blood still streaming down his chin. "You nailed it, dude. Way more realistic than the fake one. Thanks again for bringing it."

"Noah?" Brianna did not face him but kept her gaze leveled on a still-grinning Sam.

Noah reached for her. Thought better of it and dropped his hands. "We keep them for the dogs. It was just a joke."

Brianna nodded once. "A joke. Sure."

She looked at Camilla, and Camilla felt the chill in her gaze. She wished she had not laughed. She couldn't remember why she had. None of what was happening was funny. Tucked in a faraway part of her, there was only the sensation of the release it brought. How the laughter had been the only thing that could drive away the feeling of free-falling into an abyss.

"You're all a fucking joke." Brianna turned on her heel, her fists still tucked at her sides as she strode away.

"Brianna," Noah called as he stumbled to his feet and made to follow her.

She did not pause. Did not choose to wait for him or to let him come to her. Camilla watched as the defeat moved through Noah—his body loosening with that failure.

Brianna's voice carried back to them in hard, angry syllables. "Don't you dare."

"Here, Brianna." Sam hoisted the tongue overhead before tossing it after her retreating back. "Don't forget your treat. I heard it's good for bitches," he said.

Camilla didn't see Noah move, but she heard the punch connect. The meaty slap of skin against skin. The shouting as the others tried to pull them apart, Sam's nose bleeding as he went after Noah, who ducked low and tackled Sam to the ground.

The firelight glinted against the blood spattered in the grass. Hard to tell what was animal and what was human, but Camilla stepped past it and hurried after Brianna. She would be able to calm her down and bring her back. Explain that Noah hadn't meant it, that *she* hadn't meant it; he had only wanted to make them all laugh, and it had all been so confusing.

"Brianna, wait!" she called. Brianna was already to the tree line, following the path that led through those massive, arching branches and back out to the Shaw's unused field, where they parked their vehicles.

They were beneath the trees, Camilla stumbling over roots that threaded themselves near the earth's surface, when Brianna finally stopped. Her body gone so still it seemed unnatural. As if she'd surrendered herself to the forest around them, and it held her suspended there in stasis until it commanded her to move.

"You know," Brianna began, the words dying off between them as Camilla slowed, "I should have known better."

"Sam's an asshole. And Noah's an idiot. But he didn't mean it."

"I should have known you were no better than them. Everything's a joke, right? Nothing matters to you because it doesn't *have* to."

Camilla shook her head. She tried to throw off the sting of what Brianna had said, but it sank into her like venom. "That's not true."

"Except that it is. You get to flit around. Act out your little make-believe rebellion with absolutely no consequences. And the fucked-up thing is, you don't even see it. You get to laugh at the Dark Sisters because nothing like that would ever touch you."

"The Dark Sisters aren't real." Camilla felt as if she was nine again. Back in Tricia Allman's pool house, telling herself she didn't believe.

"That's not the point!" Brianna's voice pitched upward.

In the four years of their friendship, Brianna had never looked at Camilla with such disgust. The hurt of it lodged in Camilla's chest and made it hard to take a full breath. If she could go back, she would swallow her laughter. She would erase the entire night.

"You get to laugh because you get to *choose*." Brianna stared into the trees, the moon catching at her face and illuminating the tears on her cheeks. "You get to choose to ignore it all. The Sisters. What they symbolize. Those expectations. I don't get to do that, Camilla. I never have. So no, they aren't real, but what they stand for is."

"You really think I don't feel that pressure, too? That my entire childhood wasn't a parade of being a godly example?" She began ticking off on her fingers, the sting she felt turning to anger that Brianna would ever think she didn't feel those same demands. "Of cultivating a meek and quiet spirit, of being modest, of being obedient, of being virtuous, of keeping out the world's temptations, of arming myself with the word of God." It felt as if her father's words were pouring out of her, his voice merging with hers as she let that never-ending list die out. "As if people haven't been waiting for me to mess up since I was old enough to form half a thought."

"You don't get it, Camilla. Even if you did mess up. What then? A slap on the wrist? A few days on Retreat, and then you get to come back, and Daddy tells everyone how he brought you back to God, and now you're this magic, perfect example of exactly the sort of woman we're all supposed to be. The epitome of everything the Sisters aren't. The whole reason he tells the story. And then you get back to doing exactly what you want. Getting what you want. Lather, rinse, repeat."

Camilla's hands shook. With humiliation. With anger. With a cold acceptance she didn't want to own. Because Brianna was right. Her role in life was to serve as her father's paragon. Forever falling and being lifted back up by the tenets he preached. Hellfire forever licking at her back without tasting its cold burn. A wife. A mother. The angel in the house.

"And what about me?" Brianna dropped her voice to a whisper. "If I make a mistake? Make a choice that's just for me and not for God, or my future husband, or the kids I'm not even sure I want?" She drew in a shaky breath and wiped at her face. "No one asked if I wanted to go to college after we graduated. No one asked what I wanted to do with my life. Not even you, Camilla. No one asked if I wanted to go to law school and then go into practice in the city. None of that is an option for me because my father wouldn't allow it. There's no backup plan. No coming home again. No redemption. In this world, I marry Wendell Crampton because he's from the only other Black family in Hawthorne Springs and *God forbid* anyone ends up with mixed grandbabies. In this world I go to Bible study and try my best not to land myself on Retreat and die wondering if I could have been anything more."

Above them, the trees groaned in the wind. An otherworldly cry that set Camilla's skin prickling as she tried to take in everything Brianna said. As she tried to see Brianna's life as one set on a trajectory any different from her own. The limitations and demands as any more than what was her own birthright. The scales demanded to be tipped one way or the other, and she was blind in her anger. Limited in her ability to understand. She could not see beyond her perception of their sameness. Even if it was not and never would be.

"Do you honestly think I don't feel the exact same way? I don't have options either. None of us do. They made it like this."

"Oh, fuck you, Camilla. Fuck you and your pretty, white, blond-girl mentality in your pretty, white, blond-girl town. Let's just see how equal it is." She whirled, pushed herself into the forest, and was gone.

Camilla watched her go. She waited for her frustration to cool, but there had been too many years of it. Too many days had passed with no reasonable outlet. There was no space for Brianna's accusations even if they warranted examination. Even if in the depths of her heart she knew they were true.

Behind her, everyone was still fighting, but she wanted nothing to do with it. Let Noah and Sam pound each other into pulped piles of skin. They deserved it for what they'd done. They didn't live under the long shadow cast by the Dark Sisters. The threat they posed for every girl born in Hawthorne Springs and then baptized into The Path. She hoped at least one of them had gotten his nose broken.

She waited for a moment, letting the wind push her hair off her shoulders, and then walked back to her car. Brianna's Audi was already gone, but she'd expected it to be. Even if there was a part of her that hoped when she came through the trees, she'd see Brianna waiting for her there. But there was only the other cars and the wind, and she drove home without turning on the radio.

The house was still dark when she let herself in, and she trudged up the stairs in the velvet quiet, the night settling over her like a veil. She showered quickly, the water almost scalding because she wanted to feel the sting of it, a reminder she was still inside her own skin and not floating somewhere in the ether. Her phone set to silent, she crawled into bed with her hair still damp and her body heavy. Sleep hovered somewhere just beyond her, and she settled into that liminal space where her thoughts tilted into an almost recognizable strangeness. Buried somewhere beneath those dim shapes came the sound of her parents stumbling upstairs, their laughter punctuated by the low rumble of her father's voice, and then silence once more. She sank further down and then she was asleep.

SHE'D EXPECTED A hangover. At least a headache or a general queasiness that only coffee and something dripping grease could cure, but she woke feeling as if she'd spent the previous night sipping chamomile tea and reading her Bible. She burrowed further under the duvet as the rush of all that happened came flooding back. The tongue. Noah and Sam. Brianna. And buried beneath it all, her mother's renewed intentions to keep Camilla away from the Purity Ball. Even if her body felt fine, she decidedly was not.

Tomorrow was Sunday, which meant her father would spend the day locked in his office preparing his sermon, and her mother would head into the city to spend hours at Phipps Plaza only to return with complaints that the service at the Chanel store wasn't what it used to be and maybe a bag or three. Then another dinner at yet another church leader's house that Camilla would not be invited to. Same shit, different week.

She didn't want to bother with her makeup or hair, but she did it anyway because she knew if her father did venture out of his study, he would immediately notice and begin questioning her reasons for falling out of her usual routine. So, she lined her eyes, straightened and curled her hair, and then padded downstairs, her phone in hand.

The kitchen smelled of coffee and roses. A crystal bowl on the island overflowed with expertly arranged white blooms, and the coffee pot was wonderfully full.

She'd not bothered to check her phone yet, not quite ready to deal with the realities Brianna set before her, but woke the home screen as she took down a mug and then shuffled to the coffee pot.

Seven missed calls from Noah. Four texts.

Call me as soon as you can.

It's important.

Camilla?

CALL ME. EMERGENCY.

She paused, the coffee splashing over the edge of the mug and burning her hand as worry pooled in her belly. She leaned against the sink, the vigor she felt that morning draining away as she turned on the water and thrust her hand beneath. Around the burn her skin was freezing, and her guilt rose up hard and fast.

What if the fight had been worse than she thought, and Noah or Sam was in the hospital? What if something happened to Brianna? A car crash or she'd never made it home? Her imagination spun through the possibilities, each one somehow worse than the last. Nausea rose up her throat, thick and hard, and she fought against the urge to vomit. Inhaled through her nose and exhaled through her mouth as she pulled up Noah's number and brought the phone to her ear.

Not even a full ring sounded before the call connected, and Noah's voice came through.

"Did she call you? Did Brianna call you?"

Her heart seized. In the multiple calls and texts from Noah, there'd been nothing from Brianna. If anything had happened, she would never forgive herself for how they left things between them.

"No. What's wrong?"

"She's on Retreat, Camilla. They took her this morning."

The words swept over her, but she could not process them. Her mind had gone dull, the burn the only thing that connected her to the world.

"What?"

"She wasn't answering her phone, so I went over to her house, and they were loading her up in one of those Range Rovers. You know the ones. Her parents wouldn't talk to me, but they took her, and I don't know for how long, but you could find out, yeah?" His voice wavered and went gentle. The way it did when he was training a nervous dog. All soft words and softer hands. "Ask your dad how long she'll be there?"

Again and again, her mind tried to process what he'd told her, but the reality of it slipped away. If Brianna's parents sent her on Retreat, that meant they knew about the party. And if they knew about the party, they knew Camilla had been there, too. And Brianna had been so *angry*—they both had been. It was only a matter of time before the accusation and punishment fell on Camilla, too. Everything Brianna said last night would become a fulfilled prophecy. Her last words still rang in Camilla's ear.

Let's just see how equal it is.

"I have to go," she said.

"Camilla, don't—" Noah began, but she disconnected the call and slid her phone onto the counter as a headache stole through her temples. Brianna was making a point. Sacrificing herself in the name of exposing a truth Camilla refused to admit. And now, they would both suffer. The only question left was how long until they came for Camilla?

All there was to do was wait.

Her father's office door was still closed and the house quiet as she let herself back into her bedroom and crawled under the duvet. When they came for her, she would be here. She settled and let the waves of pain emanating down her body carry her into unconsciousness.

SHE WOKE DISORIENTED, her limbs heavy. Her dream tugged at her, pulled her back down, but her head was a bloated, disconnected thing, and she could not fall back into that hallucinatory world.

Her body felt damp and cold. Her lethargy like a weight on her chest as she tried to untangle herself from the snarled remainders of sleep until, finally, they fell away, and she was gasping and staring into a teeming dark she didn't understand. Above her, the sky was a hollowed-out reminder of the bedroom where she was supposed to be.

She was outside, knelt before the tree where they had the party. Confused, she stared up at it, her fingers reaching to trace over the bark as a reminder she was awake. That this was real, and she'd been sleepwalking.

The bark ran in discordant lines, looping back in on themselves before scattering. It looked like heads hacked off at the neck. Like mouths opening wide to scream. A hellscape wrought in wood. Shuddering, she withdrew her hand, but she still felt the sensation of the bark against her fingers, the outline of those yawning mouths that could draw her in and swallow her bit by bit.

Some animal part told her to run, to leave this place, but her body remained inert, her lips parting as she tipped her head back and looked up at the tree like a supplicant come to beg for the unspoken things in her heart. As if it could hear and ease her guilt over what happened with Brianna. The branches splintered outward, the leaves glistening darkly, and she suddenly wanted to take them in her mouth and bite down, their juices coating her tongue.

She listened as the night fell down around her, watched as the tree bent and shifted in the wind, and then opened, parted its shaded veil so she might see what it hid. There, among the branches, the amorphous outline of two faces stared down at her.

Her heart stuttered, a strange, terrible heat running over her skin, and she moaned—low and guttural—but still she could do nothing more than look up as the faces dipped toward her. Their mouths were dark, awful smears against pale faces, the jaws distended and stretched as their eyes gleamed with a viscous, milkish sheen.

"It's just a story," Camilla whispered, but it didn't matter. If this was a nightmare, she was awake inside it. She could not move. Could not scream. Could do nothing more than stare up at those blank eyes. At the tangled braid that connected the Dark Sisters and made them one body. At the blank hollow of their mouths. Their broken, missing teeth. They were the monsters. Camilla was the thing that was supposed to run.

She cried because she could not scream. Terror mixed with fascination as she gulped air and wondered if her heart would stop just from looking at them. If she would carry this image into heaven and be cast out because God would not bear to have even the memory of such a horrific thing enter into His kingdom.

The leaves shook, those pallid eyes blinking as they saw into the meat of her. Their eyes slid over every inch of her skin, and she hated it. The torture of their gaze, how hungry it was. Surely, they would swallow her whole, those jagged teeth tearing at her skin bit by bit until she was nothing more than a smear of blood and bone. It would be a righteous punishment. The pastor's daughter gobbled up like some wicked child in a fairy tale.

Overhead, a branch cracked, and the Sisters reached for her, their mouths open in a desperate, hungry plea.

Camilla's body lurched backward as her muscles came to life, her lungs expanding painfully as she drew in air and then, finally, blessedly, screamed.

CHAPTER IV

1953

The following Monday came and went, and if Mr. Letting remembered anything about what happened between them in his office, he didn't let on. Still, Mary jumped every time his office door opened. So much so that the other girls teased her for it, asking if she had ants in her pants. She smiled back at them and told them she had too much coffee and it had been a long night with the baby.

They made sympathetic sounds but didn't question her further. Their worlds were filled with the office and dinners and dates, not babies. They wouldn't want to sit together at lunch and talk nappies and colic and diaper rash, and for that, she was grateful.

For lunch each day, she wandered out of the building, but rather than eating, she spent the hour back inside Rich's hoping she'd see Sharon again. But every day, a different gray-faced woman stood behind the hat counter, and every day, Mary's heart sank a little further.

That Saturday night, her mother came for dinner, and Mary spent the evening tugging at her dress and fussing over the pork roast as her mother pursed her lips in the way that clearly meant she would hold her tongue while they were in front of Robert, but once they were alone, she had an earful of criticisms to offer her daughter. After her mother left and Robert and the baby were asleep, she slipped outside, the hem of her nightgown growing damp as she walked farther and then farther still into the woods. It didn't matter she could barely see or that she stumbled three times. She walked on until she was certain she wouldn't be heard, and she screamed until her throat felt raw.

Around her, the nocturnal creatures sent back their own cries, and she felt like one of them. A wild sister locked in a lovely domestic cage.

For two more mornings, she rose and went through the motions of her day. Feeding the baby, rocking the baby, cooking, cleaning, waiting for Robert to finish moving over her body while she floated somewhere above—a distant, disconnected thing as he grunted and rooted against her like an animal.

And then, like some miracle, Sharon was finally there. Leaning against the counter, her hair falling over her shoulder in rippling gold as she laughed at whatever the man standing before her had just said. Mary's heart squeezed painfully, and she wished she had been the one to make Sharon laugh like that.

The man leaned forward, his hand creeping across the counter to where Sharon's rested, and Mary ducked behind a display, suddenly ashamed. Why had she come here? It was likely Sharon would find it strange, off-putting even, that Mary came back specifically to see her. Maybe the connection Mary felt over their lunch was only on her part, and Sharon flitted from person to person, always effervescent but never settling.

From her hiding spot, Mary watched as Sharon straightened, her hand casually trailing along the counter and away from the man's before she lifted it to her mouth to stifle another laugh. Mary could have laughed herself. How many times had she done something similar in the hopes of ending a man's advances? A subtle maneuvering of the shoulders, a quick pivot of the hip or the chin, so there was no certain path for him to access any part of her body he might have deemed in desperate need of touching.

Emboldened, Mary lifted the first hat she touched, stepped out, and cleared her throat. "Ma'am? I was wondering if you could tell me if this comes in navy? If you're helping this gentleman with a purchase, I'm happy to wait, but I really am in a hurry."

"Of course! If you'll excuse me," Sharon said, and stepped out from behind the counter and hurried to Mary's side.

Confusion creased the man's brow, but he ducked his head in assent and backed away from the counter. Even as he left the women to their business, his eyes burned against them, and Mary held her breath until he was well and truly gone. Only then did the stitch in her side come undone.

"You've no idea how much I was hoping for someone to come along and save me," Sharon said.

Mary flushed, her newfound confidence draining away. "I shouldn't have interrupted—"

"Nonsense." Sharon waved a hand in Mary's direction. "He was a creep, and the fact that it was a friend scaring him off and not just any old customer was the cherry on the sundae."

"A friend?"

"Of course, you goose. I felt like I knew you so well after last time I assumed I had your telephone number, but then I realized I didn't. So, I couldn't call and ask you, but I was so hoping we could do lunch again. That is, if you'd like to." Sharon looked up through her lashes, and Mary wondered if everyone she did that to felt as if they were melting.

"Can I tell you a secret?" Mary asked.

Sharon looped her arm through Mary's. "I'd die if you didn't."

"That's why I came."

Sharon squeezed Mary tighter. "I knew it. I felt it in my heart. Can you wait ten minutes? I'm not due off the floor until then."

"Sure," Mary said, but she knew she would have waited twenty or thirty minutes if it meant sharing a tiny table with Sharon Hutchins again. Even if it meant Mr. Letting would fire her for being late. None of that mattered.

But exactly ten minutes later, Sharon hurried toward her, and they swept out of the store, and Mary wondered if she wasn't floating just a bit. If whatever magic lived inside Sharon hadn't somehow also found its way into her.

The remaining minutes of her lunch hour passed far too quickly, and Mary only realized later she hadn't actually eaten at all—only poked at the salad on her plate while she and Sharon talked without seeming to need to draw breath. They talked about Shirley Jackson's *Hangsaman*, which Mary didn't believe anyone other than herself had read. The dark magic of her prose bewitched both of them, held them breathless and transfixed. Reading her books was like looking into the sun before an apocalyptic devastation.

Sharon explained more of her beliefs—the transmutable energy in nature. Those natural cycles that flowed through and supported every living thing. No good. No evil. Only an equality of desire and, should she will it, a practice that allowed her to fix and alter such energies to her liking.

Had anyone from The Path heard their conversations, they would have called such things blasphemous, but Mary was fascinated. There was nothing wicked about Sharon. She was kind. Gentle. And funny. Mary hadn't laughed so much in years. There was a comfort in their conversations she'd never found with anyone. With Sharon, she was able to forget the need to say or do the right thing. With Sharon, anything Mary said or did *was* the right thing.

They met again the next day. And then the next, and the next, and soon, it had been three weeks, and Mary found herself coming back to the office later and later. Why would she want to return to the predictability of her life when she could let Sharon dazzle her?

The girls raised their eyebrows as she settled back at her typewriter, but they said nothing, and Mr. Letting had not yet noticed because his own lunches stretched for two, sometimes three hours. There were still mornings he hovered over Mary's shoulder, his gaze fixed on her chest, but she was just one of many, and he didn't seem to notice her unless she was directly before him.

Even though there was no need, Sharon was a secret she kept.

She told no one she'd made a new friend in the city, not even Vera. A part of her knew she should feel guilty, but it felt important for a reason she couldn't quite identify. So when Sharon asked her over lunch if she'd like to have a cocktail with her after work, Mary knew it was yet another secret she would keep.

Lunch with a new friend, even one she'd not talked about, was explainable. No one would have reason to suspect she was behaving as anything other than the good, Christian wife and mother she was expected to be, but such dismissal did not extend to cocktails in the city with an unknown woman who was not a member of The Path. Despite her worry, Mary couldn't help but anticipate their meeting. This was a new direction in their friendship. One that brought them closer.

She phoned her mother-in-law and told her she had to stay late to catch up on a project, and for a moment, a bubble of guilt lodged itself in her throat. Lying was a sin. She grew up knowing that. But her excitement was powerful, and the thought of a shadowed corner and the sound of glasses clinking overrode any sort of Christian guilt she should feel.

Mary chose the restaurant, but she let Sharon order—two sloe gin fizzes—and she sipped the drink slowly, warmth flooding her cheeks as the alcohol took hold. Around them, the crystal on the tables glittered as the daylight faded into candlelight. The booths slipped into shadow as waiters drifted here and there like pale ghosts, their smiles pasted on as they poured wine and then vanished. Mary had asked the girls around the office for recommendations for a quiet, tucked-away spot, and she'd chosen this one for the privacy it afforded. It was the sort of enchanted place where it was easy to get lost. To lose yourself, if you chose.

"Is this real silver?" Sharon held a fork up to the flickering light and squinted.

Mary smothered a smile. "Probably."

"If I had two more of these"—Sharon rattled what remained of her drink—"I might decide to accidentally take a couple of them home with me."

Mary laughed and let herself lean into Sharon—the space between them shortening as Sharon made no effort to pull herself away.

"My sister says I'm like a raven. Distracted by shiny things. But I can't help it. Who wouldn't want to surround themselves with beauty if they could?" Sharon's eyes seemed to go darker—the color of a deep ocean—and Mary forced herself to look away.

"Your sister?"

"Older sister. She's married. Two beautiful babies who I could just eat, they're so delicious. Big house in the country. The golden daughter who did everything right and is my parents' pride and joy. Not like their heathen daughter living alone in Atlanta." Her tone deepened. "They conveniently forget to mention me whenever company comes." She lifted her glass to her lips and drained it.

"I'm sorry," Mary said, even as her face burned from humiliation instead of the alcohol. In describing her sister who never strayed from the straight-and-narrow expectations set for her, Sharon had inadvertently described Mary as well. Maybe she'd deluded herself. Maybe Sharon didn't see something special in her at all, but instead, a substitute for the sister who served as a guide for everything they were supposed to be. Mothers. Wives. Homemakers.

Sharon shook her head, her face lightening. The shining girl once more. "Don't be sorry. I wouldn't trade places with her for all the money in the world. I quite like where I am. Especially right now." Sharon reached across what little space remained between them and stroked the back of Mary's hand. "You should only be lit in candlelight. You look like a goddess." She reached up and tucked a wayward strand behind Mary's ear, her touch lingering and then dipping to trace along her jaw, her neck, her bottom lip.

Mary's head swam, her heart a living, frantic thing. Untamable and wild. She was a married woman. A good woman. A good mother. She repeated these things, but none of it mattered. None of it had ever mattered. For so long, she'd hidden herself because there was always someone watching. For once, no one was looking.

She let herself lean in. Let herself take one more breath before she pressed her mouth to Sharon's, her hair falling over them like a veil.

Sharon's mouth tasted of honey. Of rosemary. Of a lovely thing Mary had not known she was thirsty for. And oh, God, she wanted to drown in it. To let herself die and be reborn in the way baptism had never allowed. She knew then what she was. What she'd denied for so long because of what it meant. Of how she would suffer for the truth of it.

She thought of Robert. Of the baby. Of her mother's tight, disapproving face. Of judgment and punishment and damnation.

With a gasp, she pulled herself away, the tears already hot on her cheeks.

"I can't. It's not . . ." Mary began, the words she wanted to say tangling impossibly inside her.

"Oh, Mary. I'm so sorry. I thought that we—"

"It's not that. Not at all. It's Robert. And the baby. And it's all so confusing, and you're so . . . so *wonderful*, but I can't. Please understand."

Sharon bit her lip and turned away, but Mary could see the tears glittering at the corners of her eyes. It broke her heart.

"I hoped I wasn't fooling myself. That it wasn't my imagination telling me we were . . . *more*."

"It's not," Mary whispered. "But I have a duty. To my husband. To my daughter. My church."

"And what about to yourself?"

Mary shook her head. Weighed out, was her soul worth such denial? How long could she bury herself before an unwilling resurrection?

"It's a sin." Even as she repeated the words she learned as a girl, she hated herself for them.

Sharon's gaze sharpened. No longer saddened, but angry. Defiant. "Not to me it isn't."

"I can't. I'm sorry." Mary's breath caught in her chest, and her voice broke as she said it again and again. *I'm sorry. I'm sorry.*

Sharon reached out once more and caught up Mary's hand. Squeezed it and then brought it to her lips. A lovely, burning reminder of what Mary would lose. Sharon's eyes had softened, but the anger was still there, glittering behind the regret.

"Want me to put a spell on them that will make them forget who you are?" She grinned, and it cut like a knife even as Mary burst into teary laughter.

"Can we still be friends?" Mary asked.

"You want to be friends with a broken-hearted sad sack like me?"

Mary could hear how forced her attempt at humor was. How her voice strained to find a lightness she didn't feel. Hearing it hurt even more.

"Two peas in a pod."

"I'll try not to kiss you again. Cross my heart." Sharon drew an x over her left breast, and Mary laughed again and dabbed at her face with a napkin.

"I'm a mess."

"No. You're not." Sharon's whisper shattered what remained of her heart. Mary bit down on her lip to keep from crying again.

They finished their drinks, and Mary knew ordering another would be dangerous. To stay any longer in this twilight world would be inviting temptation that would not be so easily shaken.

They left together, the space between them carrying the weight of everything Mary could not say, and when they stepped out into the early evening, she wished there were so many things she had done differently. If only she'd been born somewhere else, to someone else. In a different time period or place. Her life had amounted to a series of limitations specifically meant to keep her from existing as her truest self. She could have screamed at the lack of fairness of it all.

"I—" Mary began, but Sharon drew her into a hug.

"Don't. I'll see you soon. I promise," she said, and brushed her lips across the thin space between Mary's mouth and cheek.

Before Mary could respond, Sharon turned and then was gone.

Mary's eyes burned once more, and she held her fingers beneath them, counting her breaths until the threat of tears faded. She shook out her hair and pulled her compact from her purse. It wouldn't do to walk back to her car looking as if she'd been to a funeral.

Thankfully her eyes had not swollen, but her lipstick was smudged in the corners, and she quickly wiped it away before snapping the compact closed with a sigh. If she hurried, she could make it home before the baby's bedtime.

Across the street, a door opened to reveal the waiting room of a doctor's office, and a woman stepped out, a small paper bag clutched at her side. She paused, her eyes adjusting to the dimmed light, and then her gaze settled on Mary with a shock of recognition.

Mary lifted her hand in a wave. "Vera!" she called, and then waved again. She could certainly use a friend right now. There was no need to tell Vera about Sharon, certainly not about what happened between them, but it would be nice to have a distraction. If Vera asked, she would offer the same excuse she gave her mother-in-law—she stayed after hours to work on a project.

Vera did not acknowledge her even though Mary was certain she saw her. Strange to have such a late doctor's appointment—she didn't know of any private doctor who took patients in the evening—but Mary supposed it was a special after-hours visit. Perhaps Vera's husband, Gerry, arranged for it.

"Do you need a ride back?" Mary asked, stepping out into the street to cross. Vera paused, her eyes still locked on Mary, and then, the paper bag still tucked to her side, hurried away from her best friend.

The truth of it all fell over Mary, and she almost collapsed.
She'd seen. Somehow, Vera had seen.

INTERLUDE: 1750

The sun rose and set, but for me, there was only my muscles' dull burn and an exhaustion that lingered no matter how I slept.

But I was content.

Our home was not the steadfast one my husband built, but it was secure from the elements. A crude dwelling crafted of angled branches and mud and more than a few drops of my own blood, it kept us mostly dry, and every day either I or Florence made small improvements, our meager skills growing as we learned from our errors.

During the day, I would gather what I could—water from a nearby stream, herbs, mushrooms—and tend to the garden I started. Florence took to her father's rifle quite well, and by the end of the second week, we had a rabbit skinned and roasting over the fire. She did not speak of Benjamin. I could not fault her if she thought of him, but for her silence, I was thankful. The daily reminder of my betrayal would only serve as yet another weight on my back.

In the evenings, I would visit the tree. Sit in the quiet as the night fell around me, my fingers tracing the bark, longing for the power it held. The earth hummed with its magnitude; the very air shimmered with the intensity of it. It did not matter where it came from, if it had been some deity or unknown entity from the cosmos who brought it there, I yearned to know and carry that ancient magic within myself. To take back a portion of all I had been denied and heal myself of all those hurts. To show others there was another path that did not involve judgment and bloodshed wrought by the pale representation of a vengeful god. There had been years with only the taste of silence on my tongue, but this was a new world born of my hands. Creation was an act worthy not only of gods and men.

Florence did not come with me when I visited the tree. When the dark fell, thick and soft over our dwelling, exhaustion carried her with it, and she slept hard until the morning light stole over us.

But my worship was not her worship. The tree would not have recognized her as its own no matter how I hoped the scales would finally fall away from her eyes and she would understand such things. Perhaps, in time, she would feel the power as I felt it, but for now, I was alone with my need.

It was when Florence developed a persistent cough that I felt the first sting of worry. It rattled deep in her chest, thick with phlegm, her skin glowing with fever as I boiled the small onions my garden produced for a poultice.

I sat up with her in the night, spooning what little remained of the elderberry syrup I made into her mouth, squeezing her hand as I listened to the labored rise and fall of her breath.

Fury held me in its grip, and I gave in to it on the nights I managed to bring myself to leave Florence resting and go to the tree where I would scream and scream until it seemed as if there had never been any sound in the world other than that of my own anguish. If the power the tree contained heard me, it gave no sign.

For the first time in my life, I cursed the natural world. To have escaped our hangings only to witness my daughter's death at the hand of such a small thing was too cruel a fate. The truth of it was that I was a feckless woman. The confidence I had in my knowledge of herbs and roots and blood—the salvation tucked within those roots and leaves and small bodies—was nothing in the face of watching as life drained out of my girl.

I took no food. No water. There was only Florence and the cough that had so reduced her she looked more like a child than a woman.

When Florence's breath became no more than a wheeze, I took up the curved blade I used for herb gathering and a bucket and set out for the tree. Intuition guided me, the power sleeping beneath the tree a constant tug that led me to kneel and dig my fingers against the bark.

"Give it to me," I said. "Even a part. If only to save her." Sobbing, I brought the blade to the bark and cut deep. Above me, the moon cast its dim light, a shining crown about my head, as the tree offered up its sap. It flowed over my fingers, warm as blood, and I brought that sweetness to my lips as the earth beneath me shuddered. Once. Twice. As if a great eye had opened to look upon my insignificant body and then closed in indifference.

With the knife, I cut my hand. The blood came quickly, and I pressed my palm to the cut I'd left on the tree. The magic would give. It would take. It was the nature of all things, and the power held within the tree obeyed the same laws. With it, there was no intention for good or for evil. No benevolent god or scheming devil at the helm. There was only the request and the action. The wielder of that power decided its use. And I saw only to save my daughter's life.

"Thank you," I whispered, and then held the bucket beneath to catch the sap that continued to flow. Around me the earth trembled, but I did not fear it. It was only the way of things.

By the time I returned, Florence's lips had gone blue. I didn't bother with a spoon, but dipped my fingers into the sap and placed them into Florence's mouth as I had when she was a babe and would not nurse. In this way, I fed her.

Through the night, I sat with Florence, every muscle flooded with a burning pain, but I did not leave her. Did not alter the repetition of my movements as I brought my hand again and again to her mouth.

I measured the rise and fall of her chest. Counted the seconds between one breath and the next. Waited and watched until, as the night broke and morning stole in, I saw her lips had once more gone pink, and the fever that had darkened her cheeks for the better part of a week fell away.

I laid my head against her chest and listened. The wheeze, while not gone completely, had quieted, and I wept, my arms around my darling girl. Only then, as I listened to her strengthening lungs, did I grant myself sleep. Tucked against her, I fell into it quickly. I did not dream.

I woke the moment she stirred.

"Mama?" Florence's voice was hoarse from lack of use, but it was hers, and hearing it brought more joy than anything I'd yet experienced in this life.

"I'm here." I crushed her to me, my nose buried in her hair as I breathed in her scent. I would forever know it as hers. I would carry it into death as a cord tying me to her.

"Thirsty," she said.

I brought her cup after cup of water, going twice to the stream to fetch more to boil and cool. I mixed the remaining sap into it and watched as she gulped it down, marveling at her increased heartiness. By evening, she was up and moving about as if she'd never fallen ill at all.

A lightness settled over me. Joy unbound. A golden shimmer that left me wanting to laugh and run and jump and bend myself before the tree and let the power within wash over me like a wave.

"Do not tire yourself," I said as Florence bent to stir the fire.

"I am quite well. Providence has made it so." Her eyes gleamed in the light. "A miracle."

It did not matter she deemed her recovery the work of God. Telling her otherwise would do little more than affirm what she already believed. That God saved her. She was well. All the rest would come in time.

A fortnight passed. Florence's illness became a memory I could not quite forget but could tuck away. Our garden flourished. Everything lush and green and ripening with a quickness that was a marvel. Florence smiled again and hummed as she went about her work. Twice more, I tapped the tree, the syrup sweetening our meals as summer flowered, thick and heavy.

FLORENCE WAS GATHERING peas when they came, her basket left to the dirt as she rose slowly and backed away.

"Mother," she called, but I'd heard them already and was at the door, my grip tight on the ax. Fear, keen and quick, settled within me, but I kept my face even. My back straight. If they'd come to drag us back or to kill us, I would do my best to make it difficult. To give Florence the opportunity to flee.

There were seven of them. Two men on horseback, two women, and three small girls, the oldest no more than six or seven, and the youngest still carried by her mother. I remembered their faces. Their names. Their children's ailments and the tinctures I'd made and administered. If the men came for violence, they would not have brought their women and children. My fear eased, but I kept hold of the ax all the same.

They held up their hands as they approached, the women bowing their heads but peeking up from under their caps.

"We mean no harm." Isaac Hatcher dismounted, removed his hat, and came to stand beside his wife, Hope, who was now openly staring. "It took some time to find you. What with all the false trails." He grinned. "A smart trick. We thought we'd lost it completely until Lewis found this one."

Lewis Indicott shifted his gaze to his wife. "It was Joan who found it. I cannot take credit for that." She smiled shyly and bounced the babe she carried.

Isaac went to take a step forward, thought better of it, and planted his feet where he stood.

"They did not look for you—Reverend Brenton and his men—if it's troubled you. Said you were a pestilence that burned itself out."

He frowned, his jaw set in a hard line. "Even as they were the ones who did the burning."

Lewis turned away from his wife and spat. "Hypocrites."

A dim hope flared in my heart, but I tamped it down. Better to remain wary. "We have very little here. What would you ask of us?"

Isaac dropped his gaze to the hat he carried between his hands. "My Rebecca." He lifted his chin toward the eldest child. A girl with a tangle of dark waist-length hair. I remembered the pox on her body. Her fever. The paste of marigold flowers and witch hazel I gave her mother. The burdock root and rosemary. "She would have died had you not . . ." He cleared his throat and looked away.

Hope placed a steady hand on his arm and looked to me, her gaze clear and determined. "Wherever you go, we will follow."

"We swear it," Lewis said.

I glanced at Florence, who swayed on her feet, overwhelmed as I was with astonishment. Unsteady and unsure of the magnitude of such a blessing and the gratitude now filling my heart near to bursting. These people saw the world as I did and chose the same path no matter the difficulty. No matter the danger to themselves. I could not help but smile, my own tears coming quick as the children and their parents smiled back.

I dropped the ax and held out my hands to them. "Then you are all welcome."

I showed Hope and Joan and Florence how to tap the tree. They all wondered at the taste, sweet with a delicate note of greenery and soil. Like drinking from a spring never touched by man.

They came to the tree reverently, stricken by the same sense of immense power I felt. Their hands were the lightest touch against the bark even as they cut into it. There was a duality in this cutting, as was the way in all things. To come with such softness to enact a violence that did not carry the intention to harm.

"Touched by God," Florence said as she sat beneath its branches, her head tipped toward the sky. She clung yet to the ways she'd learned as a girl, but neither Hope nor Joan faulted her for it. They themselves were not so far removed from Reverend Brenton's indoctrinations to be so harsh. They would not name the power they felt at the tree God, but they saw it as greater than themselves. A mutable force that bent based only on what it was rather than what others wished it to be.

"Lewis has found another town not far from here. Says there is a man there who will sell him a heifer and a bull. We have some coin left, and we would have milk. Butter," Joan said as she wiped a sticky hand against her apron.

I froze, the bucket I was filling suddenly heavy in my grip. I knew we were isolated here, but our number had grown, and it would be impossible to remain completely hidden. Florence and I could have lived on our garden and what we caught, but it would have been a meager existence. There were others now. Children. They would need more.

"He was careful and said nothing of this place. Only that he was readying a new homestead and was in need," Joan said, and placed a reassuring hand on my shoulder. "We would not flee persecution only to endanger our place here."

I bowed my head, grateful for this gesture. Their families were at as much risk as Florence and I. My fear would be hard erased, but I knew it would lessen in time.

Together, Lewis and Isaac tilled the earth by hand and planted what seeds they'd brought with them. Wheat. Corn. Barley. They cleared a separate pasture and raised a fence where the cows Lewis purchased happily grazed. They cut wood, smoothing the logs so they could build their own small cabins, plus another for Florence and me.

"It is too much," I said when they led me to it, pride shining in their eyes as they watched me take it in. Eyes damp with tears, I touched the walls one by one and marveled at their kindness. They said nothing but stole away so I might revel in their gift without their eyes on me.

There, in the doorway, I wept. To taste such joy after so many years of darkness. It was a gift.

The crops grew with a swiftness none of us had ever seen. Their first yield overfilled our baskets, and the men clapped each other on the back as they looked upon their reward. The heifer gave up bucket after bucket of milk, thick as cream, and the children drank it down, their cheeks flushed with good health as their mothers looked on with pride. The chickens laid eggs with yolks the deep orange of sunset. The air was golden-tinted and filled with the sounds of children's laughter as their fathers chased them about, scattering the chickens as they roared with their own mirth. If ever there was a utopia on this earth, we had found it.

WITH OUR SURPLUS crops and milk and butter in tow, Isaac and Lewis returned to the neighboring town. The next day they came home, their pockets full of coins and another heifer trailing behind them. The trade between men inspired no queries or accusations, and while we were part of the world, we did not live within its sphere of influence.

But Florence grew ever distant. Sullen as she worked alongside me. She no longer visited the tree, and I watched her face darken each night I returned, my bucket filled with sap.

Finally, one night, as we settled in for sleep, she spoke. "It is a false god. Your tree."

"Perhaps there is something of a god in it. Perhaps it is only as nature intended it. But it has served us well. I would not deny my gratitude."

She turned over on her pallet so I could no longer see her face. "It is only a tree. Set down by God's hand."

I opened my mouth to tell her the tree's power had saved her life, but I had no energy to give voice to the words. Florence's beliefs in opposition to mine had been a long, bloody war, and I was tired of fighting. Tired of waiting for her to understand. To become the woman I'd raised rather than the one she'd become.

She did not have to believe in the power, or the tree, or that the sap we took from it ensured we would thrive in this new land. I and Hope and Joan had enough belief for all of us. We would live well here. We would thrive.

I spent many nights thinking of the tree, of the magic that fed it, and how we might further channel it. A sacred rite for the good of each of us. Our children and their children after them. A fulfillment of all that Reverend Brenton had suspected of me. A witch born of a deeper magic than his god. I smiled at the thought of it.

The following night, we met as we always did at the tree. Three women. Three mothers. We who had given up so much in the names of our children and would continue to do so if it meant they would know comfort.

"Sisters." I called them such for that is what I felt they were. They circled about me, eyes keen in the moonlight. I could only hope they would listen and understand what I was about to ask of them. I passed my hands over their mouths, their cheeks, the earth beneath a warm, trembling thing that waited for an offering. For what I would ask it.

"Together, we have seen such blessings. Together, we have watched our families flourish." I pointed to the tree, to its spreading branches and its strange bark I had come to know as a second skin.

I felt no fear, only a growing sense of joyful anticipation as I withdrew the curved knife from my apron, brought it to my palm, and closed my hand around it. "You all know the power here. You have sensed how it casts a golden light over all that we touch. I gave the sap to Florence when she fell ill, and it saved her. For everything we have asked, it has heard and granted our wishes. We wanted to flourish. To see our children grow strong and happy. And we have. Do you not agree?"

Their heads nodded as one.

Wincing, I drew the knife through the soft flesh of my hand, the pain both lovely and sharp, and then extended the weapon.

"Join me, sisters. We know of the power in blood. How it is sacrifice and sacrament. Let us give an offering so our bloodline, our daughters, will know good fortune forever." I stepped toward the tree, its exposed interior still weeping from earlier taps, and pressed my hand against it, the blood melding with the thick, dark sap.

I had always felt set apart. I moved through the world aware of the energies around me and how they ebbed and flowed. Not a vessel that created its own magic but one that could channel it. Make use of it. But now, as my blood soaked into the tree, I could feel it spark against whatever more ancient magic existed there. That same hum we'd felt since we'd first come to this land found root in me—an oath wrought in blood that every woman born of our line would live richly.

Hope and then Joan stepped forward. "For our daughters," they whispered as they pressed their bloodied hands to the tree. We stood, arms linked, tears streaming down our faces, as we let the magic move through us in gentle waves.

"Florence! Thou art come!" Joan stared over my shoulder, and I turned to look, desperate in my hope I would see my daughter walking toward us.

When I saw her striding through the grass, her nightshift under her cloak a pale bloom, my knees buckled. I opened my arms to my daughter and let out a ragged sob. Florence made no move to come to me. It did not matter. My girl was here, and it was enough.

Her gaze fell to our hands. The thin lines of blood still staining our wrists. "What have you done?"

Joan caught at Florence's shoulders, spinning her like a child, and laughed. "It is a wonderful feeling! To have such magic flowing through you. Like capturing sunshine." She held out the knife. "Will you join us?"

Florence did not look at the blade offered her, but only at me, her gaze heavy with judgment. With accusation. "I will not."

"Oh, Florence." Joan chattered on, unconcerned with my daughter's denial, drunk on the power coursing through her. "I cannot tell you how pleased I was to see you happy in your place here. Benjamin would be glad to know you are content. He never felt any malice toward you, only a sadness you could not be what he wanted."

I felt the precipice then. The world tipping toward an end I could no longer hold at bay. I'd thought myself safe from discovery, but I could not keep Joan from speaking. Could not keep Florence from hearing. Any attempt to do so would only be further damnation.

"He has married happily and well. His wife was newly with child before we left. It is as he wanted, to have children, but I did wish it would have been you despite your not being able to bear children. I always found the two of you well matched."

A deep chill settled over my skin, nausea worming its way up my throat as I watched my daughter's face go pale.

"Cannot bear children?" Florence said.

"Yes," Joan mumbled, her brow creasing with confusion. "I visited her shortly after they married, and she said Benjamin had mentioned it. It bothered her that he still spoke of you, so imprinted upon him as you were that even she could not erase your memory."

"Strange that he would think such a thing was true when it isn't. I cannot help but wonder how such an idea was planted in his head." Her tone was restrained. A measured cadence that could not hide her rage. Her sorrow. As her mother, I heard what lay hidden beneath the words. Each syllable was a small death.

"Florence, I only meant to keep you safe." I had nothing else to offer. Nothing that would serve as a balm for the wound I dealt her. I could have opened myself up, my ribs pried apart so she might see the heart that bled for her since she came screaming into the world, but it would have done no good.

Florence moved so quickly I saw only the knife's glint as she snatched it from Joan. When she drew the blade over her palm, she did not cry out, but held her hand steady as she approached the tree.

She paused, her hand hovering over the spot where we'd offered our blood, and then pressed it to the bark. Only then did she look at me, her lip lifted in a sneer.

"You will live to regret this sacrilege. Whether in this life or the next."

CHAPTER V

2007

Away. Get away. Camilla's thighs, her calves, burned with the need for escape as she ran blindly through the trees. Greenbrier lashed her arms and ankles, the forest taking her blood into itself as sustenance as if it could hold and keep her still, but she kept running until she burst through the trees and onto the main road.

Sobbing, she turned opposite of what would lead her back to the house. She couldn't go home. Couldn't let her parents see her tear-streaked face or the blood on her arms and legs and then rationally try to explain she saw the Dark Sisters. There was nothing rational in a haunting. Nothing logical in the monstrous.

Her bare feet slapped against the asphalt, and she ignored the sting and pushed on. Vera's house was close. Going there would delay the inevitable questions her parents would ask. It would give her time to keep herself from spilling what she saw and ensuring herself a place on Retreat. If Brianna hadn't already done exactly that.

Camilla was thankful for the late hour despite the terrible dark, thankful that no one would see her—a bloodied, wide-eyed girl running as if something would devour her if she stopped.

Vera's house was dark except for a dim glow coming from an upper window, and Camilla almost collapsed in gratitude. Vera would listen; she would clean the cuts on her arms and feet and then bandage them with gentle hands. She would give Camilla the time to think and figure out how she was going to explain.

She stumbled onto the small porch with its wicker rockers and sage-green cushions and wind chimes where she'd spent countless hours drinking sweet tea and eating Lorna Doone cookies because there was no one there to tell her there were too many calories.

Vera's house was smaller than the others in Hawthorne Springs. There was no need for some ostentatious Tudor obscenity. She was widowed, and there were no children to care for. She didn't need all that house only for her. Her little bungalow with its stained glass windows and rose garden was more than enough, so she lived without the extravagances the rest of the town insisted upon. Had she not been a dear friend of Pastor Burson's wife, Camilla imagined she would have been dismissed by Hawthorne Springs' elite. It stung as she realized this was exactly the same thing Brianna felt every day. The same thing she'd tried to explain that night at the tree.

"Vera." She felt the urge to scream again, but her voice was little more than a croak, and she slammed her palm against the door.

Already, Camilla could hear the sound of hurrying footsteps, and her throat went thick as her eyes flooded with fresh tears. When Vera threw open the door, her face a mask of panic, Camilla's knees buckled, and she collapsed into Vera's waiting arms.

"Camilla? It's the middle of the night. What in the world are you doing here?" she asked.

The words flowed out of her unchecked—a stream she could not control once it began. "I was sleepwalking, and I woke up in the woods in front of this tree. It had heads. On the bark. Like they'd been cut off, and they were screaming, and there were mouths, and they were open so wide. Too wide."

"Slow down. You're talking crazy. Here—" She stepped back and guided Camilla inside the foyer. "Let's get you off your feet. Why aren't you wearing shoes? Oh, honey. You're bleeding."

Vera settled Camilla on the overstuffed faded-blue couch and tugged a throw blanket over her. "Let me get something for those cuts. Don't move."

Camilla let her eyes drift closed, fatigue washing over her even though she'd slept for all those lost hours before the tree. From the kitchen came the sound of running water, and she sank into it as relief overcame her.

Safe. You're safe.

She kept her eyes closed as Vera shuffled back into the room. "Let me see," she said, and lifted the blanket before sucking in a hissed breath. "Lord have mercy, girl. What did you get into?" She drew Camilla's feet onto her lap, her fingers gently probing as she inspected the injuries.

"I was asleep, and then I woke up in the woods," Camilla said, and winced as Vera drew a damp cloth over her feet. "I was at this tree. We had a party there. And then Sam started talking about the Dark Sisters and pretended to have a fit or something. I thought he'd bitten off his tongue. It was so awful, and there was blood, only it wasn't his. It was a cow tongue. Brianna was so mad, and she said—" Her breath caught in her throat, her voice hitching as she heaved out another sob.

"Just breathe. In and out. There you go. Slow it down."

Camilla nodded and let the air fill her lungs, focused on the rise and fall of her chest so she would not remember the moon-pale reflection of the Dark Sisters' eyes. Vera continued her work, moving from Camilla's feet to her arms.

"It was a joke. He was trying to scare us," Camilla said. "And it's just a story, right?" Her voice pitched upward.

Vera paused, her hands hovering, the cloth still tight in her grip. "What's just a story, Camilla?"

"The Dark Sisters," she whispered. "And then tonight. I saw them—saw something—in the tree."

Vera dropped the cloth, and it fell to the floor with a wet slap. "You saw them?"

Camilla nodded, and Vera leaned forward, her gaze sharp.

"Have you ever seen them before?" she asked.

"No. It's just a story. I was dreaming. Right? I had a bad dream?" She desperately wanted it to be true, and if Vera would only tell her that yes, she'd had a nightmare, she could forget the entire night.

"Have you ever dreamed about them before? The Sisters?"

"No."

"Think back. Not even once? Not even when you were little?"

"Never." She would have remembered if she had. They would have burned themselves into her memory. Even the sleepover at Tricia Allman's, as imprinted in her mind as it was, held no memory of a dream. And if the Sisters were just a story, she didn't understand why Vera needed any sort of confirmation that Camilla had seen them.

"You're certain?"

Camilla's skin crawled into gooseflesh. "Absolutely sure. Why?"

Vera bent to gather the cloth, but not before Camilla saw the frown spreading across her face. "I should get you home. Ada's probably sick with worry," she said, and then stood and offered her hand to Camilla. Camilla couldn't bring herself to mention her feet were still bleeding.

Vera asked no further questions as she drove, and the silence filled up with all the things Camilla wanted to say but didn't dare speak aloud. She worried if she did, it would only make what she saw real.

If the Sisters were only a story, why had Vera asked such pointed questions? Questions that made it seem Camilla had actually seen them? And then why had she dismissed it so quickly?

She rested her head against the window, the glass cool against her cheek. She was still confused, her brain scrambling to process everything around her. It was likely Vera hadn't meant anything at all, and that she'd only been checking to see if Camilla was lucid. Or, if Camilla had dreamed of the Sisters before, it was likely she had again. Maybe she'd been locked inside some kind of sleep paralysis at the tree, and none of it had been real. But then why the dismissal and the frown when Camilla had tried to question her further? Her head swam.

The security lights came on as Vera guided the car down Camilla's driveway. The front door opened, and her mother came running out, her father framed in the doorway behind her.

Camilla opened the car door and slowly stood. Her back and legs were stiff, and she wanted a shower and to go back to bed. Preferably with someone guarding her bedroom to make sure she didn't sleepwalk again.

Already her mother was at the car, and she opened her arms and crushed Camilla to her. "Where have you been? We got home, and you weren't here. No one had seen you or knew where you were. There was nothing on the cameras. We were terrified something happened, and you didn't have your phone. You can't just take off without telling us."

"I'm so sorry, Ada. I should have called and told you she came over, but we got to talking and completely lost track of time," Vera said. Camilla darted a glance at Vera over her mother's shoulder, but Vera looked calmly up at Henry and lifted her hand in a wave. "We didn't mean to worry y'all."

Camilla fought to keep the bewilderment from her face. Why was Vera covering for her? Why not tell her parents about the sleepwalking? About the Dark Sisters? Unless Vera had her own secrets to hide. Unless Vera knew something more about the Dark Sisters than she was letting on.

So her parents wouldn't see her confusion, Camilla leaned into her mother and breathed in the mimosa and rose and lily scent of her perfume—one of the many Hermès bottles she kept in her bathroom. She didn't have to feign the exhaustion she felt. In the morning, she'd have to be dressed and polished, her scratches covered with concealer, and ready to face another Sunday. She just wanted to go to sleep.

Ada finally released Camilla and reached for Vera's hand and squeezed it. "Thank you for bringing her home. We're just so relieved," she said, and turned to smile at Henry.

Camilla's father had not moved from the doorway. He observed them silently, his eyes narrowing as he took in her bare feet. Camilla had seen that look far too often to know it as anything other than suspicion. Her mother may have believed Vera, but her father clearly had other ideas. Camilla understood he'd call her into his office the next day and interrogate her about exactly what she'd been doing at Vera's house. And if Brianna had accused her of planning the party, she'd be dealing with that, too. But she wouldn't tell him about the Dark Sisters. If Vera had reasons to keep quiet, Camilla would follow her lead.

"I trust we'll see you at service tomorrow, Vera," her father said.

"Of course," Vera said.

"You be safe," her mother said, touching Vera's shoulder one final time before drifting toward the stairs as she tightened her cream dressing gown about her waist.

Camilla took a step toward the house, but Vera reached out and wrapped her in yet another hug. For a long moment, Vera simply held her, their hearts beating an incongruous rhythm, and then she put her mouth against Camilla's ear.

"If you see them again—the Sisters—tell me."

FOR THE REST of the night, Camilla slept without dreaming. In the dim morning hours, she heard her father moving through the house, his voice an urgent rumble as doors opened and closed and then silence fell.

Later, she woke to her alarm clock. Did her makeup. Her hair. Dressed slowly, each movement painful. She had more cuts than she'd imagined, and a bruise, already darkening, spread down her right hip. She tugged on a pair of dark pantyhose, not caring it wasn't appropriate for the season. Better for everyone to gossip about her lack of fashion sense than for them to start wondering aloud how she'd gotten so banged up.

Her mother was already in the car, the driver standing sentry, when Camilla descended, ready as she could be to face another Sunday pretending everything was fine.

"Your father's already at the church. Some emergency," she said as Camilla slid onto the seat beside her.

They rode without speaking, the hum of the tires on the asphalt the only sound. The Purity Ball and her mother's insistence that Camilla not attend—all those concerns felt far away. She'd not dreamed of the Sisters again, but even in the bright cheer of sunlight, Camilla felt as if they were hidden in the trees flashing past the car. Waiting for her to look. To see.

She curved into herself and willed the vision away, focusing instead on the clock on the dash, the steady flip of one minute to the next.

"I thought we were early," her mother said as they pulled into the church. She craned forward in the seat to look at the number of cars already in the parking lot. A few people—mostly church leaders—milled about outside, their faces grave as they talked. Pulled conspicuously to the curb was a single, empty police cruiser. At the sight of it, Camilla's heart accelerated.

"Did something happen?" her mother asked, and the driver glanced up into the rearview.

"Not sure, ma'am. All I know is Pastor Burson requested I drive you two this morning. Said he was needed here and wouldn't be able to do it himself."

Her mother drummed her fingers along the seat as they pulled up to the front. Immediately, the leaders turned to watch, their conversations abandoned as Camilla and her mother stepped out.

"Good morning, Mrs. Burson." Trent Glover, youth pastor extraordinaire, stepped forward. He fidgeted with his tie. Smiled. Dropped his hands and the smile. Smiled again. Camilla had the sudden urge to kick him directly in the shin and tell him if he had something to say, to spit it out.

"Is there something happening, Trent?" her mother asked.

"You'll have to ask Pastor Burson about that."

"And where might I find *Pastor* Burson?"

Trent did the proper thing and blushed, his cheeks mottling as his hands went back to fussing with his tie. "He's in his office."

"Thank you." Her mother swept past Trent and the other men, who'd all developed a sudden fascination with their feet. Camilla rushed to follow.

As the entry doors closed behind them, the men resumed their hushed conversations.

"Idiots," her mother said as she walked toward the hall that led to her father's offices.

"Why would there be a police officer here?" Camilla tried to keep her tone light. Her question one of curiosity rather than alarm.

Her mother inclined her head toward the sanctuary. "Go inside and sit."

"What if something happened?"

"I said go." Her mother's voice echoed through the empty vestibule, and she waited, arms crossed, until Camilla was inside the sanctuary before she turned and made her way toward *Pastor Burson's* office.

The sanctuary was dim. A reminder that any who entered that space should do so with a stillness born of humility. A quiet soundtrack of worship music played through the speakers as Camilla drifted down the aisle and took her seat in the family pew. Often, the most devout of her father's congregation would come early to pray. Knelt in their pew, they would remain there, heads bowed and eyes closed, until the lights slowly came up. They would rise, bleary-eyed and rumpled, and wait for her father to appear. Sometimes they would cry when they saw him. It made Camilla want to peel off her skin every time it happened.

But there was no one in the pews other than her. It was the stillness of the sanctuary and the absence of those who came to pray that let Camilla know there was something very wrong.

She pulled her phone from her purse, but she had no missed calls. No texts. She pulled up Noah's last text message to her and typed quickly.

> Police at the church. Did you hear anything?

She kept her phone in her hand, willed it to vibrate, to light up, to do anything other than nothing, but five minutes passed, then seven, and still no response from Noah. Sighing, she tucked her phone back into her purse and looked up at the pulpit. Her father's domain. His seat of power and influence all crafted from a few pieces of polished wood. If she took a match to it, it would burn like any other thing. She wondered how hot a fire would have to be to melt the glass windows and leave the entire building a smoldering pile of ash.

By the time the first few people began filtering into the sanctuary, she'd checked her phone twice more. Still no response from Noah. Worry fluttered in her gut. Had he not responded because whatever happened had to do with him? Or Brianna?

She picked at a loose cuticle, sighing when it finally tore away, the thin line of blood an iron tang in her mouth.

The hush she found earlier fell away. Whatever semblance of piety the congregation typically wore on Sundays was abandoned in favor of gossip. There was no pretense of whispering. The police officer's car out front had seen an end to that.

Camilla shifted in the pew so she was closer to the edge and better able to hear without actively appearing to eavesdrop. The voices surged around her, but she focused in and managed to untangle one of the conversations nearest her.

"Tania Fullerton is who I heard. I didn't even know she was sick."

"Plenty of people get sick, but I've never seen the police get involved before."

"Plenty of women get sick, you mean."

"Some virus, that's all. Men have stronger immune systems. That's why we don't catch it."

There was a collective but discreet rolling of eyes from the women. "Her husband reported her missing two days ago. Figured she ran off with that contractor she was fooling around with. She told him she was in love with him."

"But she was sick. It doesn't make sense that she would have even been able to do something like that."

Camilla shifted in the pew as she remembered. Tania Fullerton. The woman with the Cartier bracelets who made such a point of asking Camilla to tell her father how wonderful the service had been. Tania Fullerton who had an affair and was sent on Retreat and returned to her husband, who likely kept chiding her about her weight under the guise of joking or being concerned for her health. Tania Fullerton who now was missing and the most likely reason for her father's emergency call and the police presence at the church.

She scooted closer, hoping to hear more, but the house lights came up as the worship leader took his place on stage, the musicians following behind. Camilla saw her mother working her way down the aisle and pushed herself back into her rightful spot, her eyes trained up front.

"What happened?" Camilla whispered when her mother took her place beside her.

"The police wanted to ask your father some questions."

"About Tania Fullerton?"

Her mother said nothing but picked up Camilla's hand and examined the ragged wound she'd left, her brow lifted.

Her body heated in shame. For years she'd managed to keep the small hurts she committed a secret. But now, it felt like there was a spotlight on her. A focus she was not going to be able to escape. The Purity Ball. Brianna and Retreat. The sleepwalking. The Dark Sisters. All of it felt tied to her and pulled her toward something she couldn't yet name but could feel. Like a slow strangulation.

When the service began, she rose on cue and went through the motions. A bowed head as the worship leader started a prayer—an opening act before the singing and her father's appearance. When the worship service began, she mouthed the lyrics even as she swept her gaze over the rear pews, looking for Brianna. An ache traveled the length of her body as she remembered that Brianna would not be there, and that she didn't know how long Brianna would not be there.

At least Noah was in his place in the Whitten family pew. He was a little rumpled—his hair uncombed, his shirt in need of ironing, and his eyes red-rimmed—but relief settled over her at the sight of him. Even if nothing else felt solid, Noah was there.

Together—the congregation, her mother, Camilla—they waited for her father. For Pastor Burson.

When her father finally appeared, it was without the usual accompanying music. He strode to the pulpit, his Bible in hand, immaculate in his navy suit. The silence thick as he stared down at them.

"Before we begin, I need to share something with all of you. Our sister Tania Fullerton has gone to be with the Lord. Many of you have already heard, but she was found this morning." He waited as the news rippled through the congregation; his head bowed as they whispered.

Camilla's eyes burned, and she resisted the urge to rub them. So not missing then. Tania Fullerton was dead.

She felt her mother go rigid, her muscles drawing up tight as her breath hitched. Tiny sips of air that kept her back straight and gaze forward. Stalwart. Steady. The responsibility of the preacher's wife.

Camilla had never considered how her mother might struggle under such a burden. She slipped her hand into her mother's. Squeezed and felt the smallest bit of anxiety dissolve when her mother squeezed back.

"I've already told the police they have our full cooperation. If anyone has any information, I urge you to speak with them."

There were no more whispers. No more exclamations. Only a shocked silence as the reality of what happened to Tania Fullerton settled over them. Investigation meant it had not been a natural death. Investigation meant something terrible had happened.

"Let us pray," her father said.

But Camilla could not pray. The room was too hot. Too close. The crush of bodies around her pressed in as nausea rolled through her. She stood and pushed past her mother, stumbling as she exited the pew. She kept her head down so she would not see anyone staring at her, and hurried to the restroom, which was, thankfully, empty of anyone to hear her puke her guts out.

She was still in the stall, her knees aching against the tiles, when the door to the restroom creaked open.

"Camilla?"

She could have wept with relief. It was one of the only voices she wanted to hear.

"This is the ladies' room, you know," she replied.

Noah gave the stall door a single knock. "I'm willing to take my chances." She swung the door open, and he held out his hand. "Well, I've seen you in worse shape, but I'm not going to lie, Burson, this is pretty bad." He chuckled, but it was a hollow imitation of his typical exuberance. His voice softened. "You okay?"

She shook her head as the tears she'd managed to keep at bay finally spilled over.

"Come over here." He guided her to the sink, where he turned on the tap, dampened a paper towel, and pressed it to her face. "It's okay. Just take a breath."

"Someone could come in," she said, and tried to stop his hands, but he just kept wiping at her tears, his touch gentle.

"That's their problem. Right now, I'm helping my friend." He paused, the paper towel still pressed to her face. "I'm sorry about the other night. It was stupid. I was stupid. It shouldn't have happened."

She let his words hang for a moment, knowing it had been difficult for him to say them but glad he did. That he hadn't dismissed what he'd done as just a joke. It didn't erase everything, but it was a step forward.

"I hope you'll tell Brianna that, too. Once she gets home," she said.

A pained look crossed his face, and Camilla wondered if this was the closest he'd ever come to grief. "Absolutely. A million times."

Sighing, she took the paper towel from him and dabbed at the tender skin beneath her eyes. "Did you see my text?"

"I wasn't supposed to say anything. My dad would have killed me. Anthony Frazier called this morning while we were out at the pens. He had it on speaker."

She twisted the paper towel, watching as the water dripped toward the sink. The question she wanted to ask lodged in her throat.

"What happened?"

He considered her. She hated it. How he was measuring her ability to handle whatever it was he already knew. It didn't matter she'd forgiven him only moments before. Her frustration momentarily overrode it.

"I'm not a fucking child, Noah," she snapped.

"I know. It's just . . ." He swallowed. "It's a lot."

"Tell me."

"There were some officers searching last night. They found her in the clearing around six this morning. Where we were the other night for the party. She was up in that big tree—the one with the weird bark." He grimaced, his face gone ashen. "They don't know if she did it to herself because she was sick and confused or in pain or if someone put her there, but she was impaled. On one of the branches."

She waited to be sick again. For the room to tilt beneath her feet, her body careening toward the floor and unconsciousness, but she stayed upright. Breathing. An obscene reaction given the panic that wanted to take hold of her. She could feel it, coiled in her belly.

Her mind replayed the previous night. The sleepwalking. The Sisters. The tree. The same place where Tania Fullerton's body was found only hours after Camilla had been there.

"I was there last night. At the tree. I was sleepwalking, and I saw them. The Dark Sisters." She hadn't meant to tell him, but she couldn't keep the truth from spilling out. She couldn't carry it anymore. Not without it breaking her apart.

"It's just a story, Camilla. You've been stressed. With everything that happened at the party and then Brianna, it makes sense you would dream about it. You freaked yourself out. That's all. Tania Fullerton was sick. It was probably just an accident." There was pity in his voice. A tender denial of what she'd told him.

Exasperated, she pushed away from the sink as her heart and breathing accelerated. "But they don't die from it, Noah. Not like this. Not on some fucking tree."

"Stop it, Camilla. Listen to me. You can't do this to yourself. There is no such thing as the Dark Sisters. What happened to Tania is awful, but it didn't have anything to do with them. She was sick. That's all."

She let her breathing slow, forced herself to go still. Noah wouldn't believe her. He hadn't seen what she had. She would let herself tumble into feigned calm and bury the truth of that night until she could go back to the tree. Until she could try to find out what she actually saw, and if what happened to Tania Fullerton had anything to do with it.

She turned back to him and softened her face. Forced a sheepish smile and wondered how often Brianna or her mother had done exactly the same. "You're right. I'm sorry. It's just . . . a shock," she said.

"I know." He rubbed her back, and even though she knew he meant well, she wanted to scream at him. To tear her nails across his face for placating her instead of believing her. But she kept her hands still. If the roles were reversed, it was likely she'd be doing exactly what he was. Noah wasn't one to pat her on the head and tell her what a silly girl she was being, but this wasn't something she could share fully with him. It made her miss Brianna all the more.

It cut at her knowing this would be the first time he couldn't be fully by her side. He hadn't seen. He wouldn't believe. For him and the other boys and men of Hawthorne Springs, the Dark Sisters were nothing more than a scary story, but it was different for the girls. For them, the Sisters were a visceral reality that served as a warning of what could happen if a woman strayed too far from God's will and the teachings of The Path. Punishment. Pain. A hell crafted from all their shortcomings.

She needed to go back to the tree and, despite her fear, confront what she saw there. Those twisted bodies, hair bound together like a rope. She needed to see if there was anything still hidden among the branches that would reveal the truth of what the Dark Sisters really were. What role, if any, they played in the death of Tania Fullerton. Why Camilla was the one seeing them after all this time.

"We should get back," she said, that dumb smile still plastered to her face as she shook her hair off her shoulders.

"Sure you're okay?" His face held genuine concern, but she waved him off.

"Yeah." She made for the door. Shocked as she was no one had come in and found them together in the women's restroom, she couldn't help but feel the smallest tinge of worry someone would see them coming out. Together. Alone.

She creaked the door open and peeked out into an empty vestibule. "I'll text you later," she said, and then made her way back to the sanctuary.

She would go that night. After the house was quiet, and her parents asleep. Back to the tree.

As she hurried to her seat under the watchful eye of her father, her skin prickled. Later, he would ask her where she'd gone, and she would offer up a partial truth. She would not tell him she had seen the ghosts or demons that were the Dark Sisters. She would not tell him she knew about Tania Fullerton and the tree branch that ran through her.

She wondered how long it would take him to see her for what she was.

Sinful. A bad daughter. A bad woman.

HER PARENTS SPENT the rest of the day at the church. Her father there to counsel anyone who came to him in their shock and grief.

Her mother there as a show of support. The calm, beautiful face of The Path's divine leader.

They sent Camilla home with the driver.

"Stay inside," her mother said before crushing her in a hug. Her father had already turned away, his hand extended to the next church leader with something to say about Tania Fullerton. How very sorry they all were. How awful, how *selfish* it was for someone to take their own life, if that's what happened. What a burden this illness was. What other specialists could they possibly find who would finally provide some answers? What could they do to protect their wives and daughters?

Camilla had heard it all before, and it was no less tiresome. She leaned against the window, eyes closed, until the driver told her they'd arrived.

The house was quiet when she let herself inside, but she knew she was not alone. She could sense the heat of them, tucked away in their hidey-holes, doing the work Pastor Burson had the goodwill of providing them. The silent eye of the outside cameras watching to make certain she did not venture past those opulent walls.

Among them, someone was tasked with watching her. Making sure she stayed inside, doing as she was told. Camilla was sure of it. She wandered into the kitchen, but she wasn't really hungry. She ate four grapes. A string cheese. A handful of dark chocolate–covered almonds. And then, because the kitchen was empty and no one was there to tell her not to, she poured a chilled glass of sauvignon blanc and carried it up to her bedroom.

Settled on her bed, she sipped at the wine as she pulled up her text messages and stared at Brianna's name. Before she could think, she typed.

I saw them. The Dark Sisters. At least, I think I did. It could have been a dream, but it felt so real. She stopped. Exhaled. Typed again. I'm sorry. I miss you.

Her finger hovered over the send button. It would be pointless to send it. There were no phones allowed while on Retreat. Brianna wouldn't even see it. Or, even worse, her parents had her phone, and they would see it instead. With a sigh, she tossed the phone and took another sip, wishing she'd brought the bottle with her.

Back down the stairs she went into the unnatural stillness of the house, where she filled her glass and grabbed the bottle.

She paused on the landing, unnerved by the emptiness of the house and called out, "Angela?"

Normally, the housekeeper would pop out from wherever she was scrubbing or dusting something, an affable smile on her face as she asked what she could do for Camilla. But the house remained still, and Camilla felt the emptiness of all those rooms pressing down on her. Maybe she'd been wrong. Maybe she was alone. The news of Tania Fullerton sending everyone scuttling back to their own houses, doors shut against whatever terrible thing had killed her. Or influenced her to do it herself. Camilla shivered and went back to her room and locked herself in.

The hours melted away in a wine haze, and by four, Camilla emerged from her bedroom and searched the house, room by room, but there was nothing to find. Each door led to more emptiness. More silence. She'd been alone the entire time. It was a surreal feeling to know she imagined she wasn't. It made her feel as if she couldn't trust her own instincts. To have sensed a presence in the house even though she was alone.

Her stomach churned with indecision. She could go to the tree now, before her parents returned. Take a quick look around and come right back. But they'd been at the church all day. They could come home while she was gone, and how would she explain it if they found an empty house?

But did any of it really matter? It was likely only a matter of time before her father sent her on Retreat anyway. Brianna's theory proven correct but delayed because of Tania Fullerton's death. Why not risk it and go out with a bang?

"Just a story," she whispered to herself—Noah's words offered her no comfort—and then opened the door and stepped outside, tracing her typical path that led her past the cameras' watch. Walking would take longer, but she didn't want to chance the drive. It would be more conspicuous than approaching on foot.

Within minutes, she was sweating. Attracted to her warmth, mosquitoes found the exposed bits of skin and drank deeply.

It felt like a dream. Her feet retracing the same steps she took only the night before, carrying her toward death even as her body wanted to turn around and go home. Screamed for it. But she had to see. Had to know if what she saw was real.

With each step, the smell of wood rot and damp moss rose around her, the forest itself staining her clothes and skin so she could not forget she'd been inside it. Later, she could scrub it away. Once she saw the tree, she could bury her fear and go back to being the girl she used to be. A girl excited for the Purity Ball. A girl who believed the Sisters were only a story.

She slowed as she approached the clearing where the tree stood, her breath catching, and then pushed through.

The earth was still blackened from where they set up the fire, and the tree arched above. If she wasn't shivering, if there wasn't the police tape's accusatory yellow around the tree, she might have found it beautiful. Everything tranquil.

If there had been blood, some officer had washed it away. Heart pounding, she ducked under the tape.

She did not look at the bark, at those twisted mouths forever locked in a scream, but her fingers traced over it as if she could memorize the patterns beneath, her skin absorbing whatever sort of terrible heart might beat at its center.

Even in the day's heat, her body felt cold. Lethargic. Birdsong filled the air, and it should have reassured her. A haunting could not happen in the daylight. Monsters were reserved for dark closets, not open fields and trees.

She searched the branches, the leaves a green blur opening to reveal the sky beyond, but there was nothing there. No braided hair or gaping mouths. No Dark Sisters.

"Where the fuck are you?" she said. The wind swallowed her voice and whipped it away from her. What had she hoped for in coming out here? That the women she saw would crawl out of the tree and tell her there was nothing to worry about? Just devils here, keep it moving.

Still, her body held an unnatural chill, her bones moving under her skin in a way that made it feel as if there were wasps trapped there, a buzzing that made her want to dig her fingers into her thighs and tear them out, and she turned from the tree.

Her hand was still pressed to its bark when she heard something sigh. Such a small sound—the lightest exhalation—but it fixed her in place and left every muscle trembling against the need to turn and see what it was.

Slowly, so slowly, she let her head turn, let herself look up into the branches that tasted Tania's blood and once held something that was supposed to only be a story. A nightmare spun out of gossamer thread.

Two sets of eyes stared down at her, the bodies unnaturally bent as they leaned toward Camilla, their hair bound together so they moved as a single entity. Together they opened their bleeding mouths, those pale eyes taking in every part of her as if weighing out what to eat first, and she could not move, could not even so much as breathe as those mouths twisted, their fingers skittering over the bark as they reached for her.

Every inch of Camilla's body screamed at her to run, to move, to do something other than stand there stupidly staring up at the Dark Sisters, at this nocturnal hallucination she'd brought to life, but she couldn't. Couldn't do anything but watch as they crept closer, as they buried broken, bleeding fingers into the bark and crawled down the tree.

"No," she whispered. "No, no." There were no other words. Nothing inside her that was worthy of the terror she felt. Only a desperate need to keep them from reaching her and sinking their fingers and teeth into her, ripping and tearing until she was just another offering to the Sisters. Gored through on the tree's branches like Tania Fullerton as they lapped at her blood. Reduced her to a pile of skin.

Finally, her body responded, and she ran. There was no sense of direction, only a blind need to get away, get away, *get away*, and she wondered if this would be her life now. A series of terrible discoveries followed by her body trying to escape something that should not exist. Because they *shouldn't* exist. The Sisters. But they were here. There was no denying it any longer. She'd seen them now for the second time.

It didn't matter that her parents might be home, it didn't matter that her hair had come undone, her face reddened and sweaty, her dress torn. There was only movement, the tree line receding behind her as she stumbled over an exposed root and then kept going.

The rear of her house rose up before her, and she flung herself toward it and then through the first door she saw, not caring if the cameras saw. The house closed around her—walls, ceilings, doors—all illusions of safety that should make her feel better but didn't. She spun wildly, trying to orient herself in the house she'd grown up in, but the shadows, the room she stood in, were foreign, and she bit down on her tongue so she would not scream.

"Camilla? What are you doing?"

She whipped around, and the walls around her finally settled into their familiar forms. The kitchen island with its gleaming marble countertop stretching outward, the chef's range and copper pots hanging above, the chandelier catching the sunlight and casting it back in a dizzying explosion.

Her mother and Vera sat at the island, two glasses and a bottle of cabernet between them, their mouths burgundy stains fallen slightly open in shock.

"They're in the woods. At the tree where Tania . . . where Tania died," Camilla said, the frenetic tumble of her mind unable to keep her tongue in check. Her terror was too great. Vera's face remained neutral, but her eyes narrowed.

"What in the world are you talking about?" her mother asked, but Camilla looked only at Vera.

"You told me to tell you. If I saw them again."

"Saw who? Vera, what on earth is going on?" her mother said, but Vera ignored her.

"Where?" Vera asked.

"At the tree. The *tree*. Like I already fucking said!"

"Camilla! Language!" her mother said.

"Where in the tree?" Vera leaned forward, her tone urgent.

"In the branches. It was like they were reaching for me. And their mouths . . . There was blood, and they opened them, and I could see . . ." Her voice dropped into a whisper, and she drew breath into her lungs, but it wasn't enough to ease the deep ache that bloomed there. It would never be enough. "I needed to go back, to see if there was anything that would prove the Dark Sisters were real. That I hadn't imagined it."

At the mention of the Dark Sisters, her mother froze. "What did you say?"

"I saw them," Camilla began, but her mother pushed back from the island. Her glass toppled, the wine spilling over the pale marble. So much like blood. It made Camilla nauseated to look at it.

"Stop it. The both of you," her mother hissed, and Vera's eyebrows rose in surprise. "This is my house, and I won't allow it. I didn't know any better when I was a girl, but I'm not doing this anymore."

"Ada. Honey, you know—"

"Don't 'honey' me," her mother said, and Camilla watched in confusion as the two women argued. She'd never known any friction between them. They so rarely disagreed, and even then, it was over silly, inconsequential things. Whether a shade of lipstick was slightly too bright a pink. Whether Bottega Veneta was better before or after Gucci bought the brand and ushered in the stealth wealth style.

"You can't keep ignoring the truth, Ada. Not anymore. You can't keep pretending it didn't happen."

"Except that's not true, is it? None of it. I thought I saw them, too. All those years ago, and I told you about it, but it wasn't real. It doesn't matter what you say, Vera, it wasn't. And I won't let you do this to Camilla."

Around her, the room seemed to expand and contract as if they were caught in the belly of some terrible beast. Camilla opened her mouth, ready to ask what it was they meant, what it was her mother had seen and was trying to keep her from, but her father's voice cut through the quiet. So calm. So measured.

"Camilla. Where were you?"

She swallowed the bile rising slick and hot in her throat, unsure how to respond, unsure how long he'd been there. How much he'd heard. "I needed to know, so I went back to the tree."

Her father held up his hand. "I know about the party. That Brianna wasn't the only one there. That you planned it." He lifted his lip, disgust clearly written across his face. "And now there's . . . this absurdity about the Dark Sisters." He spat the final words as if he found them distasteful.

"I've looked the other way for far too long. Told myself it was just girlish impulse. But I was wrong. You aren't a child anymore. And it's time to rectify those mistakes." He paused and adjusted his tie. "Paul and Gordon are here. They'll escort you. I think it's best you spend some time on Retreat."

Out of the gloom the men came and stood at her father's side, their faces emotionless as they looked at the three women still clustered around the kitchen island in an ironic domestic tableau. As if they'd merely found their way into the kitchen while the women prepared the nightly meal.

Camilla stumbled backward, her legs useless beneath her. It was finally happening. Everything Brianna said. Punished so she might be reformed and held up as an example. Nothing more than her father's pawn. And looming over all were the Dark Sisters.

"You don't understand. They're real, Daddy, please. Mama's seen them, too," Camilla said, but the men gripped her arms and began pulling her forward.

"Ada?" her father asked.

Her mother remained at the island, unmoving, her gaze focused on the wine still spreading over the counter.

"Camilla's upset, Henry. Give it a night. Let everyone cool down," Vera said.

"It's for her own good," he said to Vera, and then to the men, "Take her out."

Vera sagged against the island even as her eyes darted between Ada and Camilla.

"Daddy, please just listen." Camilla stared at her mother, who still hadn't looked up. "Mom, tell him you saw them, too. Tell him!" Her voice rose into a shout, but her mother sat silent, and Camilla tried to pull herself out of the men's grip to get to her mother, but they dragged her backward.

"Camilla," her father warned. She kicked, her vision blurring with tears as the men pulled her out of the kitchen. As if she was nothing at all. Something they knew would not fight back.

"You coward," she whispered, and hoped even as the men half carried, half dragged her toward the door, her mother could somehow hear her. Hoped she could feel her words like a blade in the gut. "You fucking *coward*."

CHAPTER VI

1953

Mary adjusted her dress and then peeked again at the pineapple upside-down cake in its basket. She never took anything more than a bottle of wine with her whenever she went to visit Vera, but she couldn't sleep the night before and found herself in the kitchen at five, the flour and sugar scattered across the countertop as she baked.

Her mother-in-law agreed to watch the baby for an extra day, and Mary dressed herself carefully, discarding dress after dress as if she was going to a ball rather than her oldest friend's home.

She hadn't called. She feared if she did, Vera would find a reason to keep her away or not answer the phone at all, and she couldn't sit still inside her house knowing Vera had seen her with Sharon.

She stood on Vera's front porch, her finger on the doorbell as she tried to still her trembling hands. Even now, Vera could refuse to speak to her, could leave the door closed on their friendship. Sin did not account for love, and what Vera had seen surpassed whatever small indiscretions made up their daily lives. It would be easy to turn her in. To tell Robert she saw his wife kissing another woman. He would divorce her. Deem her unfit. Take the baby from her. There would be no place for her back home with her parents either. She would lose everything.

Again, she checked the cake, and then the door swung open.

"Mary." Vera's voice was quiet but not surprised.

Mary lifted the basket. "I brought a cake."

Vera stepped backward, the door opening further, and Mary could have wept with relief as she followed Vera inside. Vera led her to the kitchen, where she took down two plates.

"There's coffee if you like."

"No. Thank you. I'm already so jumpy."

Vera set the plates down gently, her fingers tracing over the pattern she and Mary had spent hours discussing.

"Mary, I—"

"No. Please. Let me tell it. All of it." She took a breath and held it, weighed it out against the jumble of words pressing against her lips. "What you saw . . ." She held the lie there, ready to place it before Vera as truth, but she couldn't. It was too much of a betrayal to what she felt for Sharon. Too much of a betrayal for herself.

"Her name is Sharon. I never meant for it to go as far as it did, but she kissed me, and it was like . . . like the entire world had turned itself inside out, and I couldn't breathe or think or remember where I was."

Vera froze, her gaze still fixed on the plates before her. "What I saw?"

Mary felt her heart and stomach churning into something monstrous. "I think I'm in love with her." The words fell out of her, and she knew she couldn't call them back even if she wanted to. She needed to say it. To hear it finally spoken aloud. Even if it felt like flaying herself open.

"Oh, honey," Vera said, and then her arms were around Mary, her hands smoothing her hair as Mary let herself cry for all the things she could not have.

"I can't see her again. If Robert found out—"

"He's not going to find out." With gentle fingers, Vera wiped Mary's tears and gave her a small smile.

"But—"

"No one saw. I was so focused on myself, I didn't see, even if you thought I did. And it's not mine to tell."

"It's a *sin*, Vera."

"Fuck sin. This is you. Your heart. We can be afraid of what it means to live in this world. Of the judgment. But it isn't who we are. And those secrets are worth keeping."

Mary leaned into Vera and let herself go still. Even if there was safety only in this small moment, tucked away inside Vera's kitchen, Mary allowed herself this sweetness.

Together, they sat in the silence, knowing there would come a time when it would be broken, but it would have to be enough. They had learned to expect so little, but it ached all the same.

"There's a doctor in the city. He doesn't advertise. You have to come in the evening only, and getting the appointment is practically impossible. I waited for months, but I finally got the call last week."

"A doctor?" A cold rush of fear flooded through Mary. She hadn't even known Vera was sick.

"He fitted me for a diaphragm. I was picking it up."

"A diaphragm," she said, the confusion in her voice clear even as her anxiety fled. She would not judge Vera's secret, but she didn't understand it. Since she was a girl, Mary longed to be a mother. To be all the things her own mother had not. The family unit—the father and mother and children—was a commandment The Path's followers were meant to keep. Even if she was an abomination in their eyes for what she felt toward Sharon, she had at least fulfilled that singular duty. And her daughter was such a *joy*. But if Vera did not see her future as one with a child, Mary would support her in that. She reached for Vera's hand and held it.

Vera kept her eyes cast down. "Gerry doesn't know. It's all he talks about lately. A house full of babies. But I don't . . . I never wanted it. I tried to make myself believe I did. But then it happened, and oh, God, it was like someone was squeezing and squeezing, and I woke up every morning wondering if that was the day I'd finally stop breathing. And it was a relief. The thought that I might die and not have to push it out of me. All the blood and milk and screaming that comes after."

"You were pregnant," Mary said, and Vera nodded.

"It was a different doctor that did it. European. I could barely understand him, but he was gentle. He held my hand. Told me I would cramp. That even after he'd finished, I would bleed. And all I could think about while he was scraping it out of me was that if I died, I wouldn't have to worry about this again. No one expects motherhood from a dead woman. And there are so many of us. So many women who've tried to escape only to bleed out. Senseless. All of it. These shouldn't be the only choices. We shouldn't have to feel this way."

Vera paused and touched her mouth, her hair. "But I didn't die. And I knew I couldn't let it happen again." Her breath came in short gasps, and she drooped over the counter, her face wet with tears as she buried it in her hands.

"Oh, Vera," Mary said, and put her arms around her friend.

"Please don't tell anyone. I would lose Gerry. Everything. Please."

"We both would." She felt the truth of her words stir an anger within her. They would be forced to wear the mask. To deny their very selves. It felt like willingly swallowing poison. But they had no choice. They were trapped.

"Neither of us will tell anyone then," Vera said.

Mary pulled Vera in closer and stroked her back. "No. I wouldn't do that."

INTERLUDE: 1750

By the next full moon, an illness I'd never before seen took hold of me. I could feel it unfolding. It crept slowly, leaching away the soft meat it could find. My throat. My gums. My tongue. Soft boils that burned when I spoke, their hot, foul fluid flooding my mouth if I dared to eat anything other than the softest foods.

Again and again, I tapped the tree, intent that the syrup infused with its power would heal me as it had Florence, but another fortnight passed, and I was no better. I wet the bark with my blood, swearing fealty as I had before, but whatever slept beneath did not hear. My teeth began to rot away, and my mouth filled constantly with a dark blood that carried the sweet odor of death.

Florence was not there to see it. After the night at the tree, she requested that Isaac build a small dwelling for her, and until it was finished, she went back to the hovel we first built. I did not know how she spent her days but would spy her from time to time heading into town, a basket filled with butter at her side. I doubted seeing me so reduced would have troubled her. More likely she would have seen it as triumphant proof of God's punishment. Any omen can be bent in one's favor, whether ill or good, so long as the belief is strong enough. She would have deemed it a swift and just penance for how I had stolen away her only happiness in life and brought her to this godless country.

It was a truth she would not be denied no matter how I tried to speak reason with her and tell her I only wanted her safe no matter the cost. I had damned her almost as certainly as I had saved her life.

Joan and Hope ministered in what ways they could. They had learned a great amount in their short time with me, but the sickness far surpassed our collective efforts.

"How can we help?" Hope asked, her skirts tucked beneath her as she held a warm compress to my gums.

I shook my head. There was nothing to do but help ease the pain. White willow bark. Feverfew. Blue vervain for sleep.

"Florence goes most days now to town," Joan said as she took down the kettle and set it over the fire. "Lewis says she sells her butter and then goes directly to the meetinghouse. She spent all of last Sabbath there."

"I do not like it. There will be questions. An unmarried girl. Unaccompanied in a covenanted town. Mark me, there will be eyes upon us. Judgment." Hope removed the compress and turned resolutely away to rinse the blood in the bowl of water at her feet.

Exhaustion kept me to the pallet. Another boil burst anew as I spoke, and I spat and carried on. "We are protected. We swore an oath and marked it with blood. Such things are not so easily broken."

Joan and Hope cast doubtful glances at one another and fell back to their tasks. Unease worked its way through my limbs, my very skin twitching with it. There was no certainty in what I told them. We asked for abundance and have been granted it, but there were many ways to live well. Many ways to see our children flourish. Whether they thrived under our teachings or another's.

I pushed the thoughts away. Such things would lead to despair, and I had no room for it. There was only this disease that pushed at the insides of my wasting throat as if it could claw its way into the world, laying waste to all it touched.

Three days later, Hope's oldest girl spat out a tooth. Neither she nor Isaac thought much of it. She was of an age when children lose teeth, the larger ones pushing through and leaving their smiles crooked.

But she woke in the night crying and feverish, her gums raw as she sobbed that she could feel something sharp in her throat. Like an animal tearing at her each time she drew breath.

By morning, she would take no water, and there were boils on the insides of her cheeks.

They brought her to me, her tiny body folded inside Isaac's cloak as he laid her gently before the fire.

"I cannot break her fever. She talks of devils. A delirium, but she tries to scream, frightened as she is." Hope wrung her hands as Isaac paced, his brow furrowed as he took in the hanging herbs and bottles and the curved knife on the table as if truly seeing them all for the first time.

"You can cure her? As you have done before?" he asked.

My own mouth wept blood, the pain so great I thought I would faint, but I forced myself to respond. "I will do all I can."

He bowed his head and nodded. "Then do it."

As we worked, Isaac stood outside, his face turned toward the sun. The last good thing he could look upon. He could not turn and face the darkness at his back as it devoured his daughter bit by bit.

Hope set the water to boiling, and I bent to the mortar and pestle, the pain an almost searing point at the base of my tongue. I ground dried mullein and mixed it with the tree's syrup and spread the paste over the child's gums, her little heart fluttering like a bird beneath my hand.

"It will help if there is any infection and to open her lungs so she might breathe easier," I said. In truth, I did not know what to do. I'd not been able to heal myself. I did not think I would be able to heal their daughter.

Sobbing, Hope sank to the floor beside her daughter and gripped her hand. Such despair only a parent can understand. I knew it well.

Blinking away tears, I readied the kettle. If nothing else, I could help the girl sleep.

Hours passed, each of us locked in stasis as we waited and watched. Isaac seated near the hearth, his gaze far away. Hope beside her daughter. I on my own pallet, a small bowl filled with blood at my feet.

I did not know when we fell into sleep, only that for me, it was deep. Dreamless. An endless, dark sea of pain that followed me without regard for my unconsciousness.

It was Hope's scream that woke me.

"Where is she?"

I startled awake, blood pooling in my mouth as I choked and then spat. Whatever had come loose in my mouth fell with a thick plop, and I looked down in horror at the rotted portion of my tongue lying beneath me.

"Where is she?" Hope shrieked again.

I blinked at the gloom; the fire had died down to nothing but coals that left the room in shadow. Hope clawed at Isaac's cloak, desperation sending her into a frenzy, but the girl who was supposed to be wrapped within was gone.

"She can't have gone far," Isaac said, and pushed past his wife and out into the gathering night as he called his daughter's name, his voice raw-edged and pleading.

"She'll be cold," Hope said, her hands still locked on the fabric of Isaac's cloak.

"Come. Sit here," I told her as I stoked the coals, urging them back toward flame and warmth. "He will find her."

It was a necessary dishonesty. With all my knowledge of the earth and its magic, I had never been one granted the ability to see the future. But I spoke to her then as if I could.

A chill wind settled over us as we waited for Isaac's voice. His relief as he stumbled back inside, his arms around their little girl.

But there was only silence, and in it I felt the beginning swell of dread.

It was Isaac who found her. Exhausted and shivering from the long hours spent searching in the cold, he finally went to the tree, remembering how his daughter loved it. How beautiful she found it. Perhaps she'd gone there, seeking some kind of comfort or had stumbled there in her fevered delirium.

He did not speak when he returned but trembled like a man haunted.

Hope leapt from her place by the fire. "You found her?"

"I cannot reach her. My girl. I cannot reach—" He brought his hands to his face and covered his eyes. "She is on the tree. Run through on the branches. Hanging there like . . . my God."

His wail was that of a wounded animal. Grief and rage and horror given voice and let loose upon the world because he could not raise the dead. Not even I, with the tree's magic coursing through my blood, had that power. In my diminished state, I assumed I would soon join her. I was of no use to them other than to bear witness to their grief.

They held each other, salting the earth with their tears. I held quiet vigil, unable to speak any words of comfort as I swallowed the blood in my mouth, so they would not be forced to see such horrors. They had already seen enough.

When the morning came, they went, and with Lewis's help, took their daughter from the branch wrapped round her heart.

That evening, we met under the tree. All but Florence. I waited for the sadness at her absence. She might disagree with our way of life, but this was a child. An innocent taken from the world too soon. Instead, I felt the dark edges of my anger rising. It was not right she chose not to join us. She abandoned us to our grief and confusion in favor of her pious judgment. If she had appeared before me, I would have slapped her for such lack of compassion.

The sun warmed our backs even as the wind chilled us, and with gentle hands, the men buried Isaac and Hope's daughter beneath the black walnut's branches.

Isaac had not wanted to bury her there, but Hope insisted. "She loved it so. I would have her go into the next life surrounded by the things she cherished. The things she found beautiful."

After we finished, Joan came to stand beside me and offered her arm as support. I had lost no more of my tongue, but it took all my strength to stand, and the handkerchief in my pocket was dark with blood.

"We have found abundance here," she said, her gaze focused on the small mound of earth that should not exist. "But I worry at what cost."

CHAPTER VII
2007

Before her father's goons loaded her into the back of a black Range Rover, they tugged a blindfold over her eyes.

"Sorry, Miss Burson. It's protocol. We can't have everyone knowing exactly where Retreat is. Would defeat the whole purpose," the taller one said, his voice sheepish.

"Fuck you," Camilla said, and the other one chuckled.

"You got a smart mouth on you, girlie. Seems like Daddy was just in time with getting you on Retreat," he said.

She heard the car door opening as he pulled her forward, his hands under her bent arms as he lifted her like a doll and shoved her inside.

She tumbled against the leather seat, and her skirt rode up her hips. She fought to pull herself upright and keep them from getting a full view of her underwear. Once she heard the front doors close and them settle into their seats, she pushed herself backward, drew her legs up, and kicked both feet directly into what she hoped was Mr. Smart Mouth's kidneys.

"Aw, kitten's got claws," he said, the engine turning over. "I'd buckle up if I were you. Never know if I'll have to slam on the brakes. Hate to see that pretty face get messed up."

As they began to move, she settled back and gave the seat another kick for good measure, seething as he laughed even louder. But, in all their forethought and planning, they forgot one thing. Her hands were still free.

Gouging out his eyes would be unsafe even though she could practically feel the soft pop of them in her hands. Instead, she sank lower in the seat, her legs extended as far as possible in front of her so her back rested mostly on the bottom seat. If either of the men looked in the rearview, they would see her scrunched up like a petulant child, roll their eyes, and go back to watching the road. What they wouldn't see was her quick swipe at the blindfold. It was not enough to be noticeable but enough to give her a blurred sight line of where they were going. She wasn't sure why yet, but it felt important to know exactly where they took the women sent on Retreat. To know how to get there. Or how to get out.

She anticipated a long ride. Some time on 75 South as they drove her a few exits away from home. A more rural, open area good for containing wayward Christian women. But they followed Crestwood past the church and then turned off onto what didn't look like a road at all. The vehicle rolled to a stop so the more sympathetic of the two men could hop out and clear the brush that concealed a metal gate. A camera observed from above as he punched a code into the access box, and the gate opened on well-oiled wheels.

It was all hidden in plain sight then. Not some great secret like she always imagined.

They rolled through the gate, and it closed behind them. She tried not to panic as she felt the finality of it. How cut off she was from anything other than the constructed world of the Retreat.

Women come home all the time, she told herself as a thick screen of trees swallowed the Range Rover. *Nothing to get scared about.*

She couldn't help it though. She was scared. They could lock her in a cell. Starve her. Make her kneel for hours while atoning for every sin she ever committed. Keep her sleep deprived and memorizing Bible verses until she collapsed. All in the name of reforming her.

A number of minutes passed, the road rough beneath them, and then the vehicle lurched to a sudden, violent stop. Camilla flew forward, her face crushed against the back of the driver's seat.

"I tried to tell you about that seat belt," the driver said, his laughter filling the car. "Too bad."

They pulled her out with the same roughness and hustled her along. She tried to look around and get her bearings, but it was dark, and the blindfold had partially slipped back into place. The only things she could make out were flashes of a mulched path, a gray building that looked like a service shed, and the thick cover of trees. Enough trees to make anyone believe there was nothing on that land at all.

"Home sweet home," Mr. Smart Mouth said.

A door creaked, and then there were softer hands that guided her forward. The air that enveloped her was jasmine scented. Warm. The carpet beneath her an opulent thickness that made her want to lie down. Her exhaustion slammed back into her with enough force to make her stumble.

"Easy, darling. You're okay now." A woman's voice. "You'll have to excuse Paul. He's rougher than the others, but he doesn't mean anything by it. It's just his way. And sometimes it needs doing." She sighed and patted Camilla's forearm.

"He slammed on the brakes so I rammed my face into the seat, but sure. Whatever you need to tell yourself."

The woman tutted and then paused, the high-pitched beeps of her punching in a key code making Camilla wince. Her nose throbbed, and she felt the phantom beginnings of a headache. She wondered if she could ask for ibuprofen or if Jesus would frown on that, too.

"I'm Barbara. I'll be doing all your intake, and then if you have any questions at all during your visit, you can ask me." She guided them gently into a right turn. "You're just down here. Pastor Burson made certain you had one of the nicest rooms," she said.

"How kind of him," she said, her sarcasm bleeding through.

The woman breezed right past Camilla's comment. "And here we are!" Another series of beeps, and Camilla felt the air change as the door opened. Together, they shuffled inside.

"Oh! Sorry, I always forget I can take these off once y'all are officially inside," Barbara said, and lifted the blindfold.

Blinking, Camilla took in the room. *Her* room.

She'd expected concrete floors. A yellowed, urine-scented cot shoved into a corner. Bare walls and a single nightstand with a Bible. What they gave her was something more akin to the Four Seasons with a dash of the Ritz.

A king-size bed dominated the center of the room, a Persian rug spread beneath it to protect the gleaming hardwoods. The cream duvet reflected a luxuriant shimmer in the warm light cast from a tasteful scattering of floor lamps. Two nightstands flanked the bed, and a large dresser stood at the far side of the room, its drawers inlaid with impossibly delicate floral carvings in the sorts of neutrals every woman in Hawthorne Springs determined was the must-have palette for the year. To the left stood a chaise lounge in the same cream as the duvet, and then the room opened into a private bathroom with a rainfall shower and sunken tub.

French paneling covered the walls, the edges gilded in the most subtle traces of gold. There were no windows. Of course, there weren't. They wouldn't want their guests making a jump for it.

"Now. Let's go over a few things, and then I can get out of your hair." Barbara settled a pair of glasses on her nose and peered down at the binder she was holding. "Daily menus are delivered the night before. Mark off your selections and leave it on the table next to the door." She pointed to a tiny round table Camilla hadn't seen during her initial examination. "I'm afraid you've missed it for tonight, so you'll get the standard selections. Tomorrow is . . ." She flipped through the binder. "Spinach omelet. Salmon with spring pea puree and baby lettuces with a champagne vinaigrette. And for dinner, scallops with white asparagus and a lemon foam. Chef Goddard says no carbs this week. Helps with inflammation and focus. And we need you all focused. Otherwise, the work we're doing here would take much longer. And nobody wants that, right?" Barbara smiled, two rows of tiny teeth that seemed to vanish into her gums.

"All toiletries are in the bathroom. The closet is full. All your size, but you let me know if there's something else you need. Let's see..." Barbara flipped more pages. "Morning prayer and breakfast is at six. You get an hour to clean up and dress back in your room, and then individual sessions start at eight. That will take you through lunch. Group sessions are at four. Bible study at six. Dr. Worthington is on staff this week. Botox, if you're interested. Oh! And Pilates at eight after dinner. Lights out at nine."

Fucking Pilates. Of course, there was Pilates.

Camilla's head pounded. They kept the women here busy the entire day. An onslaught of prayer and Bible study and sessions that kept them from talking to each other. Kept them from *thinking*. Nothing beyond what they did wrong and how they could fix it.

"Lights out? Is that when you lock us in our rooms?"

Barbara pursed her lips. "Oh, sweetheart. This isn't a *prison*. I think you'll find all the women enjoy their time here. The whole point of Retreat is to draw y'all back to God and the path you should be walking. To remind you of how blessed you are."

"Didn't answer the question," Camilla said under her breath, but Barbara moved back toward the door, the binder at her side.

"I'll have them bring a little something up since you're just getting your legs underneath you. Any requests? We can't do *everything*, but we're able to accommodate most."

"Doesn't matter," she said, sinking onto the chaise lounge. All she wanted right now was silence and to figure out how she was going to make it through the coming days without completely losing her mind, but first, she wanted to sit in the dark and hope sleep took her before the headache turned fierce. She sat up. "Actually, could I get some ibuprofen? And some water?"

"I'll see what I can do." Barbara smiled, and then let herself out, the lock sliding into place behind her with a final beep.

"Wonder where they hide the cameras?" Camilla said as she stared at the walls, every nook and cranny another possibility for concealed surveillance. She had a feeling that even when she was alone, someone was watching. Making sure she was being good. Praying or sleeping or otherwise engaged in some sort of activity that would make God proud. Or, at the bare minimum, not trying to burn the place down.

Ten minutes later, a knock sounded at the door. Even with the headache bearing down on her, she almost laughed at the irony of it. Such theater of privacy was absurd when every door required a key code and every minute of every day was accounted for.

The door swung open and Barbara reappeared, a silver dome-topped tray in hand. "Here we are," she said, and placed it carefully on the little table beside the door. She withdrew the lid with a flourish. "Ibuprofen, water, a Greek yogurt, some almonds, and a banana." She pointed to each item in turn, that same tiny-toothed smile stuck to her face.

Camilla grabbed the two pills on the tray and the water with a mumbled "Thanks," and swallowed.

"I suggest you get some sleep. Remember, morning prayer starts promptly at—"

"Six," Camilla interrupted. "Yeah, I got it."

"Very good. See you in the morning, Miss Burson," she said, and slipped out.

Camilla left the yogurt and the banana but ate a few of the almonds and then made her way over to the bed. The day was crashing in on her, making it impossible to keep her eyes open.

Tomorrow, she would figure out what to do. See if she could find Brianna and talk with her and get to the bottom of the Dark Sisters and the fact that her mother had seen them but was trying to hide it.

She fell into the bed with her clothes still on and wondered how a place so regimented could be this comfortable and luxurious. Within minutes, she was asleep.

IT WAS ANOTHER knock at the door that woke her, the sharp rap startling her so she sat up gasping in the dark, a scream dying at the back of her throat as Barbara opened the door and stepped neatly inside.

"I thought you might want a wake-up call this morning. Since it's your first day," she said, advancing into the room until she stood over Camilla like a mother waking her daughter for school. She held another glass of water and a small white ramekin, which she offered Camilla.

Whatever was inside rattled as Camilla took the ramekin. "What's this?" she asked.

"Vitamins," Barbara said.

Camilla peered down at the two white pills. "I'm not taking those."

"I would advise you do."

"Or what?"

"It's harder the other way," Barbara said, holding out the glass of water. Camilla could only imagine that the man who drove her there would love to be the one to pin her and force the pills down her throat.

Begrudgingly, she lifted the ramekin to her lips. "Cheers," she said. At least they weren't trying to hide that they were keeping the women happy by drugging them to the gills. No wonder all the women found their way back to God. Take enough drugs, and you could see him in person.

"Open," Barbara said, and Camilla rolled her eyes as the woman checked under her tongue to be certain she had, in fact, swallowed the pills. "Good girl. I trust you'll want to take a moment to freshen up before morning prayer?" She glanced at Camilla's rumpled clothing—the same she wore the day before—and wrinkled her nose.

Camilla didn't give a shit if she wasn't perfectly coiffed for the duration of her time on Retreat, but she didn't think Barbara would follow her into the bathroom. If she had a minute alone, she could try to get rid of the pills. She could only hope she was able to get the pills up before they fully broke down and flooded her bloodstream, leaving her in a pliable mental fog.

"Sure," she said, and turned toward the bathroom.

"You'll want to hurry though. Wouldn't want to be late on your first day."

Camilla didn't bother asking the consequences this time. She had a feeling it would be another variation of "it's harder the other way."

She tugged the door to the bathroom closed behind her, relieved when Barbara didn't tell her to leave it open, and then turned on the sink, so the noise would cover the sound of her puking.

She would have to be quick.

She knelt and angled her fingers toward the back of her throat, hoping it would actually work rather than leaving her gagging as tears ran down her face.

She was lucky. Three tries, and she flushed the mess away, hoping the pills were gone. Avoiding the mirror, she brushed her teeth and gargled with the mouthwash they'd left on the counter with the assortment of other toiletries. She dragged a brush through her hair without bothering with the curling iron and hairspray and makeup also set out on the counter. As if this wasn't a gilded cage meant for pampered animals at all but an extension of your own home. Maybe better than your own home. Because it was there that you'd learned all your nasty, secret habits.

Behind her, a walk-in closet opened, lined with racks of clothing, wrinkle free and ready to wear as if they'd been expecting her. She tugged a pair of cropped cream linen pants from the hanger to go with the turquoise and chartreuse Pucci top she already held, marveling that they would stock the closet with such a *loud* designer. She'd pictured the women at Retreat in all neutrals—a sea of white and oatmeal and dusty pinks. Instead, her closet looked like a peacock's wet dream. Probably in case she ran. She'd be easier to spot in bright colors.

A chill worked its way up her back. Nothing on Retreat was done by accident. Every decision was tactical. Everything planned down to the smallest detail to give the illusion of freedom when, really, this was a prison built on their sins.

She went slowly back into the bedroom, feeling unseen eyes itching at her skin, and closed the door.

"See? Isn't that much better?" Barbara stood and smoothed her skirt.

Camilla forced herself to nod. She'd taken pills—whatever they were meant to do for her, she knew they weren't vitamins. They were expecting her to be compliant. As much as she hated it, she would have to play along.

"I'll show you to morning prayer and breakfast, but after today, we'll expect you to get yourself there." She opened the door, the hallway's light flooding into the still dark of the bedroom. "On time," she added, and held the door open for Camilla to pass through.

Camilla blinked as she took in everything she'd not seen the night before. The hallway stretched to her left, brushed metal sconces accenting the other doorways. Only then did she realize how large the rooms must be. The hallway seemed interminable, but there were only four other doors. Four other women who could be down this hallway, and even still, Camilla realized it was entirely possible she was alone. That her father had ensured she would be isolated, unable to even make small talk with the women also staying on her hall.

"This hallway will lead you directly to the main atrium," Barbara said, and handed her a small map. "From there you can find the worship room for Sunday services, the dining room, and the Bible study room." She tapped the glossy surface of the map. "All individual sessions are here, in Wing A. You'll get your assignment after breakfast. You'll see each room is numbered, and you'll report there promptly at eight. Group sessions are in Wing B."

Barbara picked up her pace, the click of her heels muffled by the thick carpeting, and Camilla hurried to keep up. She only processed every other word out of Barbara's mouth, and she anticipated getting in trouble for not following her schedule sooner rather than later.

"The Annex is where you'll find the amenities. The spa, Pilates studio, pool—indoor *and* heated—and salon. You have one free hour on Saturdays to schedule anything at the spa or salon—you'll check in and check out for your appointment—and the pool and studio are open daily. You may be advised during individual sessions to visit either. Again, you'll check in and out."

Finally, they reached the end of the hallway and turned, the atrium opening around them like a flower. The ceiling vaulted upward in the center, all glass and arched wooden beams, the first glow of morning casting lavender shadows through the vast space. In the center, a water feature trickled through lush greenery before settling into a pool where gold and orange koi flitted back and forth. The air was cool and had the damp, chlorinated scent of all hotels. The one they tried to cover with lemongrass or green tea but that lingered no matter how many chemicals they pumped through the air. Beyond, the atrium branched into further hallways—the wings and Annex Barbara had mentioned. Somewhere in the distance, a woman laughed and another answered, her voice a low murmur.

Barbara glanced down at the watch on her wrist. Van Cleef & Arpels. Of course. Even the people who worked here were wealthy, in service of The Path because they didn't need the money. Only the prestige of being close to her father. A vestigial bit of power meant to sustain them. Another illusion. She wondered just how far she would have to scratch to understand the full truth of her father's influence.

"Just in time. Dining room is this way," Barbara said.

Camilla followed, remembering to keep her steps slow and shuffling so there was no suspicion she hadn't taken her pills. A set of French doors stood open, and beyond that, the dining room.

The tables were small. Round. Each set for a full service. Silver and crystal and linen napkins and porcelain cups for their French-press coffees. There were a few women at the other tables, their hands folded primly in their laps as they stared at their plates but not each other. Each one wore an almost identical smile, their pupils so dilated she wondered how it didn't hurt them just to keep their eyes open.

"Camilla, this will be your seat. You'll sit here every day during your stay with us," Barbara said, and moved to pull out her chair.

Camilla nodded and sank into it, folding her hands as well. Better to fit in, but even as she darted glances at the women around her, she doubted that would be possible. She was Pastor Burson's daughter. She might as well have run in screaming and wearing nothing but twinkle lights.

"We start with morning prayer. I'll be back later with your individual and group assignments. Enjoy your breakfast!" Barbara retreated with quick steps, taking her own seat at a long table stretching across the back of the room. Camilla dared a glance at what she could only assume were other Retreat staff members. She recognized most of the women and men sitting there. She'd seen their faces among the sea of others on Sundays. Each one gazed at their folded hands or straight ahead. They looked smoothed over. Glazed. As if they had been told to smile and then pressed flat.

Camilla flicked her eyes back to the front where the dais stood, and a cold sense of dread gripped her. A morning prayer. She could only hope her father wouldn't be the one leading it. It would be too complete of a humiliation.

The dining room filled quickly. The only sounds were chairs scraping and throats clearing as the women settled into their seats. She dared one more quick sweep of the room, but she didn't see Brianna. It was likely she hadn't come in yet, but still, her heart sunk. Her hopes of talking with Brianna and telling her about the Dark Sisters slipped further away as she forced herself to mimic the perfect, drugged stillness of the women around her.

Camilla stared at her empty coffee cup with longing. She'd hoped they would at least have given them caffeine first, but she should have known better. There was other sustenance that was a higher priority.

She was considering taking a chance and asking the woman beside her how long morning prayer lasted when the lights dimmed. Automatically, the women turned their attention to the dais and the man now striding toward it. The slightest sense of relief washed over Camilla even as she inwardly groaned. The man standing at the front might not have been her father, but Youth Pastor Trent wasn't much better.

He flashed a perfectly whitened smile. "Good morning, ladies."

"Good morning, Pastor Trent," the women repeated in unison.

"It is truly a blessing to be among you today. Both those of you in the midst of your journeys, and those of you who have just begun." He stared out, his gaze immediately landing on Camilla. He smirked. "How privileged you are to be given this opportunity to turn away from that which keeps you from Christ. From pride. From disobedience. From discontent. From envy. From dishonesty. It is a wonderful thing to humble oneself before God, and we are happy to welcome Camilla Burson. I hope you'll all encourage her as she finds her way back to the path the Lord intends for her."

Seething, Camilla gripped the sides of her chair as the women around her clapped. She wanted to tear out his throat, use his trachea as a fucking straw, but she forced a pleasant smile to her face, nodding her gratitude as the room quieted.

"Let us pray as we always do, for the peace of restoration and the contentment we find in humbling ourselves before the Lord."

Automatically, the women bowed their heads, and Camilla followed. It didn't matter that Pastor Trent had humiliated her and would likely make it his personal mission to continue doing so. She had to play the part. Even if it meant swallowing her anger at every turn.

With her teeth pressed to the insides of her cheeks, Camilla let the prayer wash over her, the words passing through her as if she were a ghost. Insubstantial as air. Her body went numb as Trent droned on and on, the totality of what she would endure on Retreat dawning on her. Hours of exactly this same bullshit while her brain slowly liquified and dribbled out of her ears.

Her heart surged, her eyes fluttering open as panic robbed whatever control she had over her body. As the need to run grew larger than logic.

Everyone else was still. Quiet. Absorbed in Pastor Trent's prayer. She craned her neck, looking for the exit in the hope just seeing it would calm her.

From the back of the room, another woman lifted her head, any pretense of prayer dismissed as she locked eyes with Camilla.

Camilla choked back a sob. The woman looking back at her was Brianna.

CHAPTER VIII

1953

Mary traced the very tips of her fingers over Sharon's skin. She imagined patterns swirling beneath. Patterns only she could root out. Notes only she could play. A series of strings to be plucked, the sound echoing through her before nesting in her heart.

She did so well those initial months after the kiss. She threw herself into cooking dinners with ingredients that required trips to multiple stores and sharpened knives. Slabs of meat, all deep red and sinewy, laid out and ready to carve. Vegetables and gelatin and carved radishes. Her table expertly set. The china, the crystal, the silver all glimmering and perfect as she served her husband in the Jacques Fath dresses she bought for their plunging necklines, his eyes traveling the length of her body as she bent to offer him more pork roast and mushroom gravy. The baby tucked away in her crib, full of formula and happy as Robert cupped a hand at the curve behind her knee and slid it up and up, her thigh burning and throat tightening as she forced her body to respond to this touch that wasn't the one she wanted. She knew she had loved him. In her way. She had forced her body to give in because it was what was expected of her. But Sharon had usurped everything.

She let him fuck her. It was a word she never used, but that's what it was. Fucking. His animal need destroyed again and again with the small movements of her body. Her hands touching the quilt, her hair, anything if it meant she wouldn't have to touch the male coarseness that was his back and shoulders.

None of it worked. Sharon was a wound she couldn't stop touching. Her dreams burst with Sharon's scent and the burn that was their mouths coming together. The memory of that night was a ghost she couldn't shed no matter how she tried to bury it beneath the dinners and the sex.

Eventually, she found herself outside Rich's, the pale pink polish chipped off her middle and index finger as she stared at the watery outline of her reflection in the shop window. It was possible Sharon wasn't inside, that it was her day off, and maybe she hadn't thought of Mary once since that night. It could be that Sharon discounted her as just another housewife and moved on. A cord so easily broken.

Before she could remember she had told Sharon they could never be, she pushed herself through the revolving doors and toward the women's department.

There were a handful of other shoppers milling about the hats, and Mary slowed, her heart surging as she scanned the counter.

But there were no golden-haired shopgirls. Disappointment threatened to topple her, and she turned, blinking away tears she could not allow. It was idiotic to have come here. What had she intended? What would she have said? Even if Sharon was there, what Mary was hoping for was still an impossibility. Something other people would see and want to rip apart. Either with condemnation or with violence.

She'd taken three steps when she felt a hand on her shoulder. "Mary?"

Mary felt herself there, suspended in that moment. Shame and want and fear held her in place and tied her, forever, to this moment. This was a precipice that would certainly rise up to swallow her the moment she turned to face Sharon.

But there had never been any choice for her. This was who she was. No matter how she might try to run from it. How she might try to bury herself in homemaking. In being a wife. In being a mother. And so, she let herself turn and look at Sharon.

"I wasn't sure you'd be here, and when I didn't see you . . ." Mary dropped her hands to her sides, the words she wanted to say a chaos of unspoken need.

"I was just leaving. Quentin had too many of us on the floor, and I have the least seniority, so off I go." Her face was bright. Open. As if there had never been any difficulty between them. As if hope and possibility might still exist in their world.

She took a step, closing the distance between them so Mary could smell her perfume. Rose. Bergamot. A woody touch of cedar. "I was headed home, but if you're free . . ."

Mary could have laughed at the mimicry. How Sharon let her sentence drift toward an implied ending that neither was able to speak. She was not free. Neither of them truly was.

"I'm free," she said, and it was like taking a final breath before drowning. She knew the danger, knew what there was to lose, but with Sharon standing there, the sun on her hair as she smiled, none of it mattered.

The hours would be stolen, but if she didn't take them, she would go to her death knowing she lived a lie. It was like Vera told her. This wasn't sin. This was *her*. The truth of who she was. Her nature. How could anything about that be bad?

"I make a martini that'll knock your socks off," Sharon said, her voice dropping into a shyness Mary hadn't heard before.

Mary's cheeks heated. They both knew this wasn't going to be a simple lunch at a café or a cocktail at a dimly lit restaurant.

"I would love that."

The walk was quick, both women aware of how limited their time was. Neither spoke, but Sharon gripped Mary's hand as they crossed the street. Lost in the throng, they were invisible, but Mary could not keep herself from trembling. Anxiety and anticipation both flooding her senses so that by the time they reached Sharon's building, she was panting.

"There's no elevator. I'm on the third floor," Sharon said. In the stairwell, she again took Mary's hand, but this was not the protective touch Mary had felt on the street. This was soft. The stroke of her thumb across the back of Mary's hand spoke of something greater.

But as they came out of the stairwell, Sharon dropped her hand. Even though Mary understood, had, in fact, been readying herself to do exactly the same, disappointment flashed through her.

"I'm number three-three-three. They're called angel numbers when they repeat like that. Feels fortuitous somehow," Sharon said, and withdrew a set of keys from her purse. "But this is it. Home sweet home."

She held the door open, and Mary stepped inside, struck by the heady scent of rosemary and some darker, more earthy scent she couldn't place. Suddenly, she felt as if she couldn't move. As if she were a child in a museum, afraid to touch anything, her body clumsy and stupid and capable only of destruction.

Something furred brushed past her ankles, and she yelped and sprang forward.

"Radish, you naughty thing." Sharon bent and scooped up a longhaired tabby cat and nuzzled her face in its fur. "Don't frighten our guest. She might not come back, and I wouldn't like that at all."

"I didn't mean to scream. She startled me, that's all," Mary said, reaching to stroke the cat's head.

"How did you know Radish was a she?"

"I didn't. It just seemed that she was."

Sharon dropped a kiss on Radish's cheek and placed her back on the floor. "There may be some magic in you yet," she said, winking. "Come in, come in. Make yourself comfortable."

Sharon made her way to the window and threw open the curtains, afternoon sunlight painting the room in amber, and Mary gasped. Outside of a library, she had never seen so many books.

Several bookcases lined the back wall of the small living room, each one crammed with row after row of hardcovers and paperbacks alike. A small tan leather couch sat facing the window, and to the left, a record player cabinet complete with a towering stack of records.

Another set of bookcases dominated the opposite wall, and several vibrant houseplants sat along the top, their vines trailing over the shelves in a show of good health and obvious care. A pastel watercolor hung on the wall—abstract imitations of flowers blooming over the canvas.

"My sister painted that," Sharon said from the kitchen, her focus on pouring gin into a shaker. "She could have gone to art school, but she met a boy, and well, you know the rest."

Mary nodded. She knew all too well. How the expectation and want of marriage could swallow everything that once defined you. You were told your entire life to want it. Finding the man. The romance. The storybook wedding. It was only after, in the quiet of your new domestic life, that the cracks started to show, and the voice you muzzled suddenly learned how to scream.

Mary stepped farther into the living room, her fingers trailing over the book spines as she absorbed the titles. The collected poems of Percy Bysshe Shelley. Thoreau. Emerson. Whitman. Camus' *The Stranger*. Richard Wright's *Native Son*. Carson McCullers and Betty Smith. Two books by someone named Gerald Gardner.

At the end of the shelves, tucked into the corner beside the window, a tiny table hid in the shadows. On it, a spread of butter-colored cloth with a scattering of dried flower petals. Two heavy silver candlesticks with half-melted yellow candles stood on each side of a chalice placed at the center. On the right side, a knife, the heavy handle carved with leaves. A large roseate crystal lay at the bottom. Mary had the urge to pick it up and feel the weight of it in her palm.

"You found my altar," Sharon said, and stepped beside her. She handed one of the martinis she held to Mary and took a sip of her own.

With her free hand, Mary traced the rough surface of the crystal. "I'm surprised I haven't burst into flames."

Sharon threw her head back and laughed. "Wait until you see my bedroom. That's where I keep the good stuff."

Desire coiled in Mary's stomach. She took a deep swallow of her drink, the olive brine the perfect counter to the gin's bite. The delicious burn of it drew a path down her throat and bloomed across her chest. Her shoulders relaxed a little.

"What's it all for?" Mary inclined her head toward the altar.

"The cloth is for the season. Ostara is the next Sabbat. You call it Easter. The renewal of life. The balance between light and dark restored. New beginnings. And the yellow... it reminded me of spring. Of the sun. Same thing for the flower petals."

Her words came more rapidly. "There's honey in the chalice. A touch of sweetness for abundance and transformation." She took a step closer, their shoulders touching. Mary could feel the heat of her, and she leaned into it ever so slightly. "Candles for ritual practice and meditation. The knife is called an athame. It guides energy. Sometimes I use it for herbs during rituals. And the crystal." She set her drink on the altar, lifted the crystal, and placed it in Mary's hand, wrapping both of hers around it so they both held the stone.

Mary could feel the flutter of her heart in her throat as Sharon tipped her head closer, her breath warm against Mary's neck.

"Rose quartz. It can be used for so many things, but I put it here not that long ago because I wanted something. Even though I thought I couldn't have it."

With her free hand, Mary also set her drink down next to Sharon's. Another offering for what they both wanted.

"Isn't it pretty?" Sharon tipped their hands toward the sunlight, the light pink of the crystal sparkling. "I tried to forget. I swear I did, Mary. But I couldn't. I put it here only with the intention that it was reciprocal. I never want you to do anything you don't want to." Her voice wavered, and she drew in a breath. "I put it here to attract and encourage love."

Before Sharon could say another word, before she could remember all the reasons not to, Mary turned her head and pressed her lips to Sharon's.

Sharon crushed her body to Mary's, a small sigh escaping her lips that set Mary burning. She couldn't think. Couldn't control the surge of her mind. There was only the heavy ache in her lower abdomen, and Sharon's mouth and tongue. Sharon's hands now in her hair, on her jaw, and then on the zipper on the back of her dress.

In a sudden panic, Mary wrenched herself away. It was an automatic movement that had nothing to do with her desire. She stood, panting and hating herself, as she watched the shock and confusion pass over Sharon's face.

"I'm sorry. I thought—"

"No, it's not that. I do. I want . . ." Mary flushed with embarrassment, her voice dropping to a whisper. "I don't know how."

She understood the mechanics of a man. How their bodies came together and apart. The rough, almost violent nature of it. But this was different. With Sharon there would be a hidden softness she had never even truly understood about her own body. There had been moments, alone in her bedroom, where she thought she was on the edge of understanding, but her mind would drift, reminding her that such things were indecent, and the sensation would recede, and she would spend another day learning to tamp down yet another frustration.

"It's okay," Sharon said, and traced her fingers down Mary's neck. Her collarbone. "I'll show you."

An hour later, Mary sat cross-legged before Sharon wearing only her slip as Sharon marked a symbol on her chest with ash and rose oil.

"A sigil. So you might know the truth of your heart and the courage to heed it," she said, before trailing her lips and tongue and teeth over the same spot.

There was not time that evening to learn everything about Sharon's body. The small moan she gave when Mary gripped the outside of her thigh. The birdlike sound she made when a kiss deepened. How she sometimes laughed during orgasm. How her hair reflected like burnt gold in the late afternoon light. All those stolen hours. Tiny bits of time here and there that weren't nearly enough to hold back the leviathan of their need. Always touching. Tasting. Learning. A lifetime wouldn't be enough. If Mary were to die before she had her fill, she would find a way to resurrection. A way to roll back the stone of her mortality if it meant even one more afternoon with Sharon.

A month passed. Then three, spring deepening into summer's dogged heat. Another afternoon of false appointments served as Mary's reason for lying beside Sharon, their legs tangled together.

"You should join The Path." Mary twirled a single lock of Sharon's hair and let it drop, watching how it held shape. Her own hair never held curl like that. Her mother always made a point of sighing each time she tried and failed to get Mary's hair to behave.

"I knew it. You've been trying to convert me all along," Sharon said. Mary pinched her arm, wishing she could take the skin between her teeth instead, feel the gentle give of it, before letting her mouth roam other places.

Mary sat up abruptly. She meant it as a joke, but as the idea took root, she realized it wasn't a joke at all. The levity in her voice dropped away. "I'm serious. We would have more time together. Wouldn't have to do all this sneaking around."

Sharon scoffed. "Somehow I very much doubt that."

"You know what I mean. We couldn't be public, but at least we could see each other more often." Mary settled onto her elbows, the idea taking flight. "It's so beautiful there. It really is. Like a storybook. Horses, and these gorgeous open pastures, and these ancient woods you can get lost in. You could still . . . worship. Is that even what you call it? You would just have to come to church on Thursday and Sunday. And the services are lovely."

Sharon waved her hand and laughed. "Slow down there, cowgirl.

So, I join The Path and then what? Move into a little house in the woods and wait for someone to finally call me a witch because I'm not married and having babies? That's what they would expect of me. The same they expected of you."

"It's not—"

"Isn't it?" Sharon leaned forward and pressed a gentle kiss to Mary's cheek. "I couldn't do it, Mary. Punish myself like that. Not even if it meant seeing you every single day. Living one secret is difficult enough. Pretending to be a happy housewife while you're doing the same thing a few houses down would be like dying over and over again."

Mary wanted to set fire to the truth of Sharon's words. Everyone in Hawthorne Springs looked askance at a woman who'd not managed to find a husband before she aged into a full crone at twenty-five.

"You're right." She sighed. "I wouldn't want to force that on you. It's not who you are. But maybe you could visit one day. We could take a walk in those woods. Get lost for a little while," Mary said.

"Just a little while?" Sharon slid her hand up Mary's thigh. "What if I want to take longer than that?"

Mary opened her mouth to respond, but Sharon had shifted her touch, and she gasped as her thoughts shattered under the pressure building with that sensation.

"I'll come," Sharon said, nipping at Mary's bottom lip. "But only if you do first."

It was the first Bible study Mary had been to since she went back to Rich's looking for Sharon. Her absence had been noted and commented on to the point that Robert brought it up over dinner.

She nodded and promised him she would go the following week. But now, standing outside Hester Carrington's house, she wished she was home with the baby, curled together under the quilt as she counted each miraculous finger and toe, their breath mingling in the way their blood had when Mary carried her safely inside her own body.

But Hester flung the door open and pressed a glass of red wine into her hand as she pulled her into the warm, yeast-scented kitchen.

"Look who I found!" Hester called as they entered. The group of women turned, their lips already stained burgundy from the wine as they exclaimed and then fell on her.

By her third glass of wine, Mary relaxed into the old patterns of church gossip, punctuated by the absence of any Bible talk, and realized she was having *fun*. With Sharon, it was different. A burning without relief. A need. There was ease in being with her, but there was nothing easy in it. Here, she knew her role. Understood it as inherently as breathing. Here, she didn't have to *try*.

She looked for Vera and found her in the center of a cluster of women, sipping her wine and smiling as she leaned forward to catch some salacious bit of chatter. She waved, and Vera waved back.

She wanted to barge in and pull Vera away. Politeness be damned. She hadn't seen her best friend in far too long, and she wanted a long talk between just the two of them, but there were already eyes on her. Suspicions over her absence she needed to mitigate. Instead, she let herself fall into conversation as Hester pressed yet another glass of wine into her hand. And then another.

The wine loosened her. It had been some time since she had this much to drink, but it felt good to let go and pretend, even for a moment, that she had nothing to hide. Nothing to worry about.

When Hester offered yet another glass, she didn't refuse. Halfway through it, she passed from tipsy to fully drunk.

"We've kept after Vera all the time. Asking about you." Hester pressed close, her eyes too wide and wine glazed. "She kept saying she didn't know. As if y'all haven't been thick as thieves since you were little girls." She gave a small hiccup and covered her mouth. "She's sly, that one. Keeping secrets. We were starting to wonder if there was a baby on the way."

"No. No babies. Doesn't want one."

The words bubbled out of her, her mind numbed and made stupid by the wine. It was only after she spoke that she realized what she had done. Her stomach twisted, and a heat crawled up her neck as she fought the urge to be sick right there on Hester's pristine kitchen floor.

Hester raised an eyebrow, her pink mouth forming a perfect circle. Theirs was a god that believed in babies. In good wives and hard-working husbands and a nursery that was always filled.

"Doesn't *want one*?" Hester's voice pitched upward into disbelief. "How could you not want a baby? It's not natural for a woman not to want a family. And how would you even go about making sure you didn't . . ." Hester inhaled a sharp intake of breath. "Oh."

"I didn't say. It's not . . ." Mary said, but her brain would not form a coherent thought. Her tongue felt swollen and clumsy, and she swallowed and swallowed, but it did nothing to ease the sensation that at any moment she was going to bring up what she'd eaten at lunch.

Another woman approached, squealing some exclamation in Mary's direction, but Mary could not hear over the roaring in her ears. A rush of blood and regret she tried to ignore as the room pitched around her.

Hester gestured toward Vera, and Mary could see it all unfolding. A fire eating until it was satiated. How every ear would turn, greedy for scandal, and she would watch it all because she could not move. She would be forced to watch this terrible mistake, and oh God, what had she done?

One by one, they fell. A gathering of Eves in the garden, infatuated with the promises of a serpent. They did not bother to hide behind their hands or false smiles. Did not bother to lower their voices to whispers. For this was a reaping of feminine failures, and they were the victors gathering their spoils.

Pink frosted lips lifted into sneers. Eyes narrowed and manicured fingers pointed in accusation.

Mary sagged against the countertop. "I think I'm going to be sick," she said, but no one heard. Every gaze was trained on Hester, who was making her way toward Vera, her wine sloshing over her hand so it dribbled down her wrist like blood.

"Vera," she said, her tone one of sisterly, Christian concern. "I was chatting with Mary and . . ."

Around Mary, the room hummed, Hester's words fading in and out. She caught at every other word, but she could piece together what Hester said. Suggestions for Bible verses that would lead Vera back to the path He'd chosen for her. A reminder that it was only His hand that could give or take away. How divine it was to raise up a family in His image. What an aberration to deny her womb what it was designed so lovingly for.

"Can we pray for you now, Vera? That you might find your way back to Him?"

Mary could not tell who said it. If it was Hester or all of them in one voice lifting their fallen sister up in prayer. The lights were too bright, their voices too loud.

Vera stood across the room, her gaze locked on Mary as the other women crowded around her. Mary wished she was dead. That God would reach His all-knowing hand down and smite her. Anything not to see the stricken expression on Vera's face, her eyes filling with tears she didn't bother blinking away. Anything not to be forced with witnessing her own betrayal. Mary hadn't meant it. Hadn't meant it at all. She was drunk and babbling, and Hester came to her own conclusions.

She had to apologize. Tell Vera it had all been a mistake. She would never betray Vera in such a way, and it had been the wine. She could tell Hester she'd been mistaken, that she'd misheard, if only her throat would open and let her talk reasonably.

She closed her eyes and took a settling breath. But when she opened her eyes, Vera had already fled.

INTERLUDE: 1751

For weeks, I coughed up no other fouled bits of my decaying body. No flecks of throat or lung or shreds of tongue brought up between my teeth. But the pain and the blood were ever present, and each day, I moved less and less. Until, finally, I saw both the sun and moon rise from my cot and wondered why I still lingered on this side of the living when the illness had taken Hope and Isaac's daughter so quickly.

I had not spoken to my daughter since the blood rite. Joan offered what little she knew on the days she checked in on me, her hands always patient as she passed a cool cloth over my brow or spooned broth into my mouth, taking care to avoid the open, weeping boils.

"She will marry." Joan settled beside me, her face hidden beneath her cap as she wiped her hands on her apron.

I'd lost track of the days. Couldn't remember how long it had been since we buried Hope and Isaac's girl. It couldn't have been long enough for a courtship. Such swiftness would be unseemly for a woman such as Florence, but I had forgotten Florence had made a habit of going into town long before that.

"Marry?" I sputtered, the blood warm against my lips as Joan wiped it away.

"A man from town. Gideon Dudley. He's been to see Lewis. Says there's good farmland here—the richest he's seen—and he would pay handsomely for it."

Laughter burbled in my throat, but my lungs would not allow it so what emerged was a harsh scrape of a cough. "And who is it he would pay? There are none among us who own it. It is land. It belongs only to itself."

Joan averted her gaze, and I knew then whose pockets the gold would find. "Ah. I see."

"Lewis would like an ox for plowing. The coin Gideon has offered him would be of great help." Her voice was meek, but I heard the resolve in her words. The hard edge of a decision made.

She continued. "It would bring Florence back. If they made their home here. It would be as you wished. To have her here. Away from suspicion. Happy."

Inside my throat, something slid free, and I gagged against it, my eyes tearing as I retched again and again. I felt it settle in my stomach, thick and viscous, and I brought my hands to the soft flesh there, wishing I could cut it out of me. Peel back the skin, the muscle and fat, until I could dig that foulness out. Throw it on the fire and watch it burn.

Joan held a basin to my lips, her hand making smooth circles along my back.

"Thank you," I rasped, and gazed up at her. Her cap had come loose and fallen backward, and she quickly removed her hand from my back and tugged it into place.

But I had seen. The boil on her mouth gone milky pink with fluid and blood.

I grasped her arm. "How long?"

She pulled away from me. "It's nothing."

"How long, Joan?" I forced the words out, the anger and fear and confusion impossible to hide despite not wanting to frighten her.

"A few days. But it has not worsened. And there's been nothing else. No fever. No other symptoms."

I sank back into my cot and evaluated her. There was a possibility it had nothing to do with the illness that had made an infestation of my tongue, and mouth, and lungs. It could be little more than a coincidence, and within weeks, she would heal, the entire ordeal forgotten.

My heart longed for such a thing, but even as I reached for her hand as reassurance, I guessed at the truth of it.

I did not bother to hide my tears. "You are a good woman, Joan."

"As are you. And whatever comes, I do not fear it."

We sat together in the dying light, our hands pressed together until I could no longer tell where her flesh left off and my own began. We were not sisters. I was not her mother, and she not my daughter, but in those final moments, I felt as if there were blood running between us. A force that bound us together in an eternal, unbreakable connection.

Lewis found Joan the following week, her body made small by the tree where it hung, impaled on a branch. Her hair's dark curl made darker by the blood marring her broken flesh. The lovely arch of her body made offensive by the branch running through her chest. She was an impossible sight. A polluted thing made in the image of a woman. His wife reduced to skin and bone and blood and bark.

It was Hope who came and told me, the morning barely born as she spoke, her voice laden with grief.

"Lewis will bury her this afternoon. But not at the tree. He sees only evil in it now."

"It can only be what it is," I whispered, but it had become a useless refrain.

Hope furrowed her brow but said nothing.

"And what about you? Is that what you think?" I asked.

"It does not matter what I think. Nothing I think, nothing I do, nothing I say . . . none of it will bring my girl back." She turned and left without another word.

When the sun began its descent, I dragged myself from the cot.

Whatever power still lived within me burned low, but it was enough to force me outside and toward the broken ground where Lewis would bury Joan.

I went slowly, the pain in my chest an unending fire, and I coughed, the cloth I carried spattered with blood and another darker, thicker substance I could not name.

As I approached, Lewis paused his digging, his eyes flashing as he threw down the shovel and advanced on me, his pace quickening as he drew nearer.

"Lewis, don't," Hope called after him, but Isaac remained where he was, his arms crossed and face stoic.

"We came here because of you." Lewis's hands shook as he pointed at me, and spittle flew from his mouth. "Blinded as we were in our debt to you and then taken in by the shiny promise of gold. We came bearing grace in our hearts, but there is only so long we can turn our faces from such abominations."

An old fear spread cold fingers around my heart. His anger was not so far from an accusation, and the threat of violence came not far after that. I had survived it once, and I knew I would not survive it again. The illness would not allow for escape this time.

"You brought this sickness into our houses, and yet, you still live. Why is that? What deal have you struck?" He lifted his lip in a sneer. "It is as they said. Marked by the devil himself. We should have carried you back when we found you and let you hang."

Isaac stepped forward then and clapped a hand on Lewis's back. "That's enough. There's work to be done yet."

With a sob, Lewis turned away, his shoulders drooping as he made his way back to the hole he'd begun.

"It would be best if you left us, Anne," Isaac said. There was no pretense of softness in his voice.

I forced my chin up in a small show of defiance even as blood dripped down it. "She was my friend."

"And she was his wife. You may pay your respects some other time, but it will not be today." His hands clenched into fists at his side. "I'll toss you out myself if I see so much as the edge of your cloak before Lewis has mourned her properly."

Through a veil of tears, I nodded once. Lewis would grieve as Isaac and Hope had. As much as it pained me, I would not serve as an impediment to that grief. I feared the implications of their words, but I could only hope that, with time, they would come to understand I had nothing to do with those terrible deaths. Whatever stole away their daughter and wife also afflicted me. I would not wish it upon anyone. I turned and readied myself for the journey home.

"Anne! Wait." At the sound of Hope's voice, I faltered. I did not want her to suffer at Isaac's hand for me, but she was my friend, too. I paused, but I did not look back.

When she reached my elbow, she took it and bent her head, her voice low in my ear. "Florence has returned. Her new husband has already purchased the land and is readying himself to come, but she is home and alone for a few days yet."

"Thank you," I said, and she hurried away.

My body was weary and longed for home, but I did not go there. Instead, my feet carried me down a different path. One that led to a door that was closed to me. One I knew I would have to try to open.

Suspicion lodged itself in my heart, but I could not bear to give voice to it. To do so would be to grapple with the truth of what happened the night we offered our blood to the tree. There would be no turning away from that awful knowledge. No pretending. Because there was something that spoke of ritual in the torn bodies impaled on the tree. Of an offering that hinted at a desire for punishment of the wicked. Dark magic. A curse rather than a blessing.

And there was only one person who longed for such a thing.

A single candle burned in Florence's window, the door already opened as if to welcome in the evening. A cool wind rose around me, the leaves scratching at the earth as I stepped into the doorway.

"I wondered when you might find me," Florence said. She sat beside the hearth, her hands occupied with needle and thread.

I drew in a silent breath as I observed my daughter. Even in the shadows, the swell in Florence's abdomen was obvious.

"You are—" I said as shock radiated through every limb. She was too far along, married so little time ago. Not enough days between her vows and this child quickening in her belly. A laugh built between my lips and burst outward. I could not help it. I was proud of her. My daughter, finally striving against such stringent, ridiculous rules. Her hypocrisy drowned because she gave in to her body's heat paired with another. "Oh, Florence. The covenant means so little in the face of love. It would take a madman to argue."

"Say what you will and then leave this house."

I gathered myself. My momentary happiness fading as I remembered what I came to ask. "You've seen this illness and what it has taken. The deaths. They go back to the tree where we offered our blood in exchange for abundance. The very source of our power and fortune. Hang themselves from it like some damned ornament." She looked back at me, her eyes glittering. "That night at the tree. You cut your hand as well. Offered your blood. What bargain did you make?"

"There is no bargaining in what is godly. What is right. Whatever punishment our Lord gives out is His alone to determine."

"And yet you've taken it upon yourself to be God's finger." I dropped my voice to a hiss. "I will ask again. What bargain have you made?"

She smiled then, her face transformed into something I did not recognize as my daughter. It held something akin to what I saw in Reverend Brenton's face when he looked at me. Something made of sharp teeth. Something hungry. It left my blood cold.

"I asked for punishment." She rose, her embroidery dropping to her feet. "I asked that those who pledged themselves to that tree, that those carrying betrayal in their hearts might suffer. I asked that they would choke on their treacherous tongues. That every word would be like a thorn in their throats. That every duplicity would rot them from the inside out until their hearts could beat no longer." She stepped toward me, her face twisted with hatred. "And I asked that you see it all. That you should suffer through every bit of it. That you should linger, death taking longer to grant you peace, so you might finally understand the same betrayal, the same suffering as you have given to *me*."

I stared at her, the door at my back slamming closed as the wind whined past the cabin and through the trees. Sorrow and rage and regret all came to rest uneasily inside me as I took full measure of what Florence told me.

A curse. In her desire for vengeance, Florence had cursed us all.

My eyes were dry. I could cry no more. No matter how I wanted to weep for my daughter. For all of us. My body was wrung out of all but blood. Of that, I still held plenty.

"You cannot understand what it is you've done." I spoke the rest through clenched teeth. "You have damned us all in the name of your god."

"Utter but one more word of blasphemy—"

"What else can you do?" I withdrew the bloodied handkerchief from my pocket and cast it at Florence's feet. "There. Look upon your justice and see it for the curse it is. How many more of us will it kill in the name of holiness? This illness that would drive us to madness and force our bodies back on the same tree that was once our nourishment? A child, Florence. Consider that. You have killed a child on the altar of your god. Tell me what justice there is in that!"

Florence did not flinch but looked upon the handkerchief, her brow lifted in disdain. "Leave my house."

The anger that heated my bones only moments before fled, and I reached for my daughter in supplication. "Please, Florence. There is time yet to undo this brutality. I can help you. Think of the child you carry. Your daughter. My granddaughter." The words spilled from my lips before I could call them back. I'd smelled it the second I stepped into the room. The child sleeping in Florence's womb would be a girl.

"You have no granddaughter. No daughter." Her voice was cold. Unfeeling.

"All that we have built. You would see it laid to waste. Would prefer a life of meetinghouses filled with meek little wives carrying the scent of their men's viciousness. Their fear and the yoke they would make you wear."

"I would prefer a life I *chose*. A life that lets me rest my head upon my pillow each night with ease in my heart because I know I lived according to God's laws. I have that now with Gideon. At least you cannot rob me of that as well."

"I only ever wanted you to see the glory that is our world. To know its treasures and how you might hold them in the palm of your hand. To be your mother in all ways. The good and the flawed." I felt the last of my strength leaving me, but I fought against it, fought to keep myself standing. "Please, Florence. Help me undo this. As your mother, I'm begging you to help me remove this curse."

"I have no mother," she said, and turned her back.

CHAPTER IX
2007

The day moved with a slowness Camilla never imagined possible. A day of small rooms made smaller by the eyes on her and lack of windows. Other than the main atrium, Retreat was a place of no sunlight. By the time she made her way back to the dining room for a pathetically tiny lunch, she felt positively vampiric.

After breakfast, she'd not had the time to look for Brianna. Barbara swooped in the moment the staff removed the dishes from the table, Camilla's assignments for the day in hand, the supposed allotted hour to return to her room to shower or dress or curl her hair and eyelashes forgotten.

"The Gospel and Women's Identity," Barbara read from the pages in her hand, and then handed them to Camilla. "That's a great one for your first group session! Pastor Wade will serve as your individual counselor. He's tough, but by the end, you'll be grateful for how he's held you accountable."

By the time Camilla swept her eyes over the women being herded toward their individual sessions, Brianna was already gone. She fought against her disappointment. Even if Brianna were standing right in front of her, they wouldn't be able to speak freely, and there were no opportunities for sneaking off. Every moment of every day was accounted for, and even though the nights belonged to the women, they were locked away in their rooms and probably under the watchful eye of a hidden security camera.

Barbara led her down another hallway, the doors closing as other women shuffled inside.

"I'll leave you here." She paused and rapped lightly on the door labeled as Pastor Wade's office. "But you'll see me throughout the day. I won't ever be far, so don't feel like you can't find me to ask any question you may have."

Even though she presented her last sentence as helpful, Camilla heard it for the threat it was. *Someone is always watching.*

"Come in, Miss Burson," Pastor Wade called, and Barbara nodded, smiled, and made her exit.

Camilla drew in a breath, a reminder to keep her face placid, and stepped into the office.

"Have a seat." Pastor Wade smiled from behind his desk, a knockoff version of her father. Blond highlights so perfectly placed they clearly came from a salon. Strong, square jawline. Bleached teeth. Handsome in all the textbook ways, but as he smiled at her, she saw the cruelty threaded in his expression. How clearly he enjoyed this position of power.

He flipped open a folder in front of him and pulled a pen from the holder on the desk. "Now. Why don't you tell me a bit about why you're here."

Camilla froze. What a stupid question. They both knew why she was there. Because her father demanded it.

But she dropped her head. Made sure her response came out slightly slurred. Sluggish as the drugs were supposed to be making her. "Dishonesty."

He made a mark on the paper in the folder. "Mm-hmm. When the devil first tempted Eve, don't you think she understood what it was he was doing? She knew the sin. Had been warned against it. And yet she made a choice of her flesh. One with the intent only of pleasing her body."

Camilla kept her head down so he would not see if she inadvertently rolled her eyes. He didn't need to go over this Sunday school minutia with her. If she was on the other side of the desk, she could outlecture him without even really trying.

For the next hour, Pastor Wade droned on about every woman in the Bible guilty of dishonesty. Delilah and her betrayal of Samson. Salome and her request for the head of John the Baptist. Potiphar's wife and her lust for the young prophet Joseph.

Every now and then, she would blink up at him in a fake show of attention, until finally, another knock sounded at the door. Another woman come for her hour-long personal session.

"See you tomorrow, Miss Burson," he said, his hand along her lower back as he guided her out. It made her skin crawl. Only once the door was closed behind her did she scratch at the place where his hand rested, wishing she could peel back the skin there, the raw meat beneath unblemished and clear of his touch.

The hours crawled as she went from room to room, each one containing another Pastor Somebody channeling his very best version of her father. An endless stream of prayers and Bible verses and platitudes and reminders of all the ways they'd failed not just as Christians but as women. The only thing keeping her mind from unraveling was her continued search for Brianna, but as the day wore on, she'd not seen her. Not even at lunch, the meal so quick and focused that she dared not sneak a peek at the table where she'd seen her earlier.

By the time the women all shambled back to the dining room for dinner, Camilla's entire body ached from the hours spent either sitting or kneeling in prayer, and her mind was numb from boredom.

As she walked, she glanced at the table where she'd seen Brianna, but the seat was empty. Part of her wondered if she'd seen Brianna at all. If, in her desperation, she'd imagined it. She sank into her designated seat and lifted her napkin. As she unfolded it, a small piece of paper fell into her lap. Quickly, she draped the cloth over her thighs so it covered the paper and scanned the room. Had anyone seen? She took stock of each bland face, each blank stare, all focused on either their plates or the dais or their hands. Even the staff members were distracted with their own murmured conversations, the weight of the day lessening their focus on the women they monitored. She made a show of rolling her neck.

She placed a hand under the napkin and grazed her fingertips over the thick, glossy paper, wishing she could read what it said just by touch. The rest of her table had not yet arrived; women still trickled in from their various sessions. Her closest neighbor sat a few feet to her left, her back to Camilla.

There were only a few moments before the others seated themselves at the table. Before there was the possibility of other eyes, drugged, perhaps, but still eager to report any indiscretion from the preacher's daughter. Anything to gain whatever favor they could in this hellhole.

Smoothing the paper flat, she slid it out from beneath the napkin, her pulse fluttering at her throat as she tried to make sense of what she was looking at.

It was a torn section of the map Barbara had shown her earlier. Both Wing A and the Annex unfolded before her, the room numbers blending together as she tried to process faster.

Slow down. Breathe.

She forced herself to go slower, to look more deliberately, and then she saw it. A tiny x marked over one of the rooms in the Annex. When she saw what the room was, she stifled a laugh.

A restroom. Of course. The staff members couldn't keep them from needing the restroom, and she could only hope, as she had earlier back in her own room, there were no cameras. She flipped the map over, and there, scrawled in faint pencil that would be easy to miss, a single directive.

Go B-4 prayer

At the sight of Brianna's looping handwriting, she felt tears gather, and she blinked rapidly. She couldn't cry. Not if she didn't want anyone asking questions or following her to "check in."

The room grew more crowded, the waitstaff appearing at the tables to fill water glasses in preparation for the start of dinner. If she was going to take the chance, it would have to be now.

Pushing herself backward, she rose, her palm still cupped around the map as she approached the back table where Barbara and her staff cronies sat.

"Restroom?" she asked.

Barbara barely glanced up at her. "Prayer is about to start. You should have gone earlier."

"It's an emergency," Camilla pressed.

Barbara lifted her glasses and rubbed at the indentations left on her nose. "Fine. Make it quick."

Camilla nodded, and in what she hoped was a good show of faith, jogged from the dining room and back out into the muted gold light of the atrium. Sweat pooled against her lower back as she crossed the massive open space, the rush of her blood in her ears muffling her footsteps as she turned in the Annex's direction.

If there were cameras on her, she could claim she got turned around. That she didn't know where the closest bathroom was and was glad to have finally found one in the labyrinth of hallways and doors. Even still, she hurried. Of course, the bathroom on Brianna's map had to be at the very end of the hallway.

As she approached the door, she slowed. What if Brianna was still angry with her? What if the only reason she hid the shred of map in Camilla's napkin was to draw her here and get her in trouble? It would only further prove the point she made the night of the party. That she was a tool for her father. That everything about Camilla was fake.

She shook her head. Brianna was her friend. Even if she was still angry, she had to talk with her. To apologize and tell her everything that happened with Tania Fullerton and her mother and Vera and the Dark Sisters. With a deep breath, she pushed open the door and stepped inside.

A mirror reflected back at her, the light catching as she stepped farther in and swept her gaze over the sinks and handful of stalls.

Empty. No Brianna leaning against the sink. No Brianna checking her hair in the mirror.

Her heart sank, fresh tears stinging her eyes as she went to the sink, turned the tap to cold, and placed her hands beneath the water. She ran her wet hands over her face, and pressed the heels of her palms against her eyes, the coolness a temporary relief. Brianna's absence pressed in, the force of it threatening to crush her. Every heartbeat was a painful reminder that it still animated her. A reminder she would have to go back to the dining room and spend however many days her father deemed it necessary pretending to reform herself in the image he expected.

Her shoulders hitched as she tried to push her sobs into some subterranean part of her.

"Get it together," she whispered to her reflection. Later, in the supposed privacy of her bedroom, she could break down, but not yet. Not when there was dinner and Pilates still to get through. If she wanted out of this place, she had to play along.

She was scrubbing at her face with a paper towel when the restroom door creaked open. Camilla paused, her brain tripping over her excuse for being in such an out-of-the-way restroom.

"You're here. You're actually here." Brianna stood in the door, a shy, tight-lipped smile on her face.

She took a single step forward, and then Camilla closed the distance between them, not caring what had happened between them, not caring that Brianna was the reason she was here. She threw her arms around her friend.

"I'm so sorry. I just wanted you to understand. Sometimes I feel like I'm going crazy. It's like I'm the only one who sees it. How differently they treat us. How they treat me. It's like I'm completely alone," Brianna said into her hair. Camilla held her tighter.

"I should have listened to you. It was shitty not to. You were trying to tell me how you felt, and I wasn't listening." She pulled away and waved her hand at the room. "And, I mean, you were right after all. Here I am."

Brianna laughed and wiped at the tears on her own face and then Camilla's. "I didn't think you would get the note. You remember Robin Chatsworth? She was a year ahead of us in school." Camilla shook her head, and Brianna continued. "She was in my Brit Lit class, and we made friends. She's here, too. Well, not *here*, but she works here. Robin said she would sneak it into your napkin, but leadership watches her, too, so I didn't know if she could pull it off. Even though she works for them, they don't trust her. I mean, they probably shouldn't because she does things like help me sneak notes into napkins and tell me where the cameras can't see everything."

Camilla wanted to keep talking. Hours and hours of just the two of them, chattering on about nothing and everything, but there would be eyes looking for them soon, and there was still so much she needed to explain.

"I saw them. The Dark Sisters," she blurted. Brianna's face went serious. "Twice now. The first time I was sleepwalking, so I thought maybe it was a dream, but the second time, I was awake."

"Where?"

"At that weird tree. Where we had the party. The one that looks like it has chopped-off heads all over the bark. The same place they found Tania Fullerton."

"They told us about that. Used it as an example for what happens when we falter in our walk with Christ." Brianna shook her head, her lip lifted in disgust. "As if she was a lesson instead of a person."

"My mom has seen them, too. She says she just imagined it, but Vera was trying to get her to admit it," Camilla barreled on, not caring if any of it made sense. She needed to get all of it out. "I think it has something to do with why she doesn't want me to go to the Purity Ball. I overheard her talking to Vera about that, too. She's convinced something bad happened, and that it will happen again. It's all . . ." She tried to order her thoughts, organize them into some semblance of logic, but they shifted and bent, one idea bleeding into the next, and she looked hopelessly at Brianna. "I'm not explaining it right."

"Okay. Tania Fullerton died at the same tree where you saw the Dark Sisters. Your mom saw them too but doesn't want to talk about it. Not even with Vera. So the Sisters—whatever they are—are real, and maybe they're the reason the women in Hawthorne Springs get sick. And the Purity Ball. I don't know. It doesn't make sense. It's just a ceremony, right?"

Camilla flushed. She'd forgotten she wasn't the only girl who hadn't participated in the Purity Ball. Brianna technically hadn't either. She'd moved to Hawthorne Springs after most girls usually participated, so maybe her parents didn't see the point in having their teenage daughter involved with something meant for twelve-year-old girls. Or maybe there was some unspoken rule that kept her from it in the same way it kept her family in that back pew.

"Right."

Suddenly, Brianna grimaced, her hand flying to her chin as a thin line of blood trickled from her mouth. She shouldered past Camilla to the sink where she bent and spat, the spray a delicate pink.

Camilla listened to the sound of something clattering against the sink's porcelain. She took a step forward, concern forcing her into movement. "Brianna?" Another step. "Should I find someone to help?"

Brianna did not move. Her hands gripped the edges of the sink, her head dipping toward the basin as she shuddered once. Twice.

Shuffling forward, Camilla looked past Brianna and into the sink. There, nestled against the drain, was a single molar.

Throughout her life, Camilla had known fear. The bend and shape of its many forms. The childish fear of the dark; the monster lurking under her bed, ready to snatch her ankles if she didn't jump far enough. The fear of being caught doing something she shouldn't and the punishment that came as a result of it. And then the Dark Sisters. This new awareness that the nightmare from which they came had somehow found its way into the waking world. Looking at Brianna's drooping form, at her bloodied tooth in the sink, she came to know fear in a different way. Loss had never truly touched her life, but she felt the vast finality of that fear. She did not think she would survive it.

Grasping Brianna's shoulder, Camilla pulled her backward. With her left hand, she gripped Brianna's chin. "Let me see," she said.

"Don't." Brianna tried to pull away, but Camilla held her firm, the blood now as much a part of her as it was of Brianna.

"Damn it, Brianna. Let me see." Her voice shook, but she tightened her hold. She needed to see it. To confirm what she already knew was true. Even if it meant more pain than she'd ever known. Fresh tears spilled down Brianna's face, her gaze locked on Camilla's as she opened her mouth.

Sores covered the insides of her cheeks. Her gums and tongue swollen with the weeping, blood-filled sacs. The tooth's empty socket was blackened, and whatever rot had taken hold spread upward in thin strands.

Camilla dropped her hands. "How long have you been sick?"

"Since I got here. I've been able to hide it because it's inside my mouth, but I don't feel right, Camilla. And I didn't want you to know. Didn't want you to be scared, but I knew I couldn't keep hiding it." She drew in a shuddering breath. "At nighttime, I can feel it. Something inside me. Eating. And I keep thinking about Tania Fullerton. What if what happened to her, happens to—"

Camilla crushed Brianna to her. She didn't want to hear the rest. Brianna couldn't die. There was no world without her best friend in it.

"You're going to be fine. We're going to figure this all out, and you'll get better, and you'll get out of Hawthorne Springs and go to law school, and one day, when you're a big hotshot lawyer, I'll hire you to be the divorce attorney for my first marriage."

Brianna hiccupped a laugh into Camilla's chest. "I'll charge you double my fee." They stood there, locked together, the stolen minutes slipping by too quickly as Camilla let herself ignore the truth for a bit longer.

Her father may have used the Dark Sisters as a parable—a warning for girls and women of Hawthorne Springs to stay on the straight and narrow—but now, Camilla understood they were much more than that. Demons. Ghosts. Witches. Whatever they were, they were the source of the illnesses in Hawthorne Springs. The reason Tania Fullerton had impaled herself on that same tree. The reason Brianna was sick as well.

Resolve settled, hard and insistent in her chest. They had to get out. She had to get them out. She wasn't going to let what happened to Tania Fullerton happen to Brianna.

"Listen, we're going to get out of here, and I'll get my mom to talk to me and tell me what she saw. If the Dark Sisters are real, if they're the reason for this sickness, we can figure out a way to stop them," Camilla said.

Brianna lifted her head and gestured to the room around them. "This place is locked down. There's no getting out of here."

Camilla cocked an eyebrow and grinned. "Sure there is. We'll just do what we do best." She stepped back to the sink, lifted Brianna's tooth, and tossed it in the trash. "We'll be *good*."

CHAPTER X

1953

"The Purity Ball. It's perfect."

Sharon quirked her mouth to the side—a poor attempt to keep herself from laughing. "The Purity Ball? What's that, some sort of debutante ball for virgins?" She pretended to bring a monocle to her eye. "Oh, look darling, it's the Morrison girl. I've heard she's never even seen her own breasts, isn't that smashing?"

Mary tugged a strand of that curling blond hair and tried not to lose herself in the sight of Sharon's neck arching. "Don't joke. It's actually very sweet. It's a ceremony where girls promise their fathers to stay pure until marriage. And fathers promise their daughters to protect them until they find their husbands. I did mine when I was eleven. Someone spiked the punch, and my father said he never laughed so hard as he did watching me fall all over myself that night."

Sharon wrinkled her nose. "Eleven? It sounds a little creepy."

Mary rolled her eyes. "You won't have to participate. This is my chance to show you Hawthorne Springs at the height of glamour. Besides"—she tugged Sharon's hair tighter—"everyone is distracted that night. The ladies trot out their daughters, and everyone gossips about which designers did everyone's dresses. There's a little reception with canapés and champagne before the actual ceremony that's just for the fathers and daughters. Once the ceremony starts, all the women head home to drink more champagne and gossip some more. And while they're wagging their tongues hard enough to drop out of their heads, I could give you my own personal tour."

"I dream about you in moonlight. Crowned in stars. Like a goddess. Hecate incarnate."

"Don't you talk poetry to me, Sharon Hutchins. Say you'll come. Please?" Mary dropped her gaze and batted her eyelashes.

Sharon offered her an indulgent smile. "Fine, but only if you promise not to sell me off to the highest-bidding bachelor."

"He'd have to outbid me first."

This was how they navigated their world. Normalcy hidden behind walls and doors. Pretending as if the freedom they found away from prying eyes was the same freedom they could have in public. As if judgment couldn't touch them.

The weeks passed quickly, and Mary distracted herself with work and planning her gown for the Purity Ball reception and the baby. She'd not seen or heard from Vera since the night of the Bible study. She tried to call, but the phone rang and rang, and the two times she dared to actually show up at Vera's door, her knocks went unanswered. Then the letter she mailed was returned, and she didn't know what else to do. She felt Vera's absence keenly, a sharp edge that would not dull.

But Vera would be at the Purity Ball. It was practically a sin not to be there. Mary would talk to her then. Apologize until her throat went sore.

By the night of the Purity Ball, Mary couldn't bring herself to eat anything more than a bite or two of whatever meal she placed on the table. Her mother would marvel at her devotion if she'd seen her anxiety disguised as restraint. Would tell her how lovely she looked in her emerald taffeta, her waist cinched over the full skirt.

Even Robert noticed, his hands cupping her rib cage as he brushed his lips over her cheek. "My tiny girl. Try not to float away from me tonight," he said.

Out of nervousness, she waited until the last possible moment to tell him she'd invited a friend from work. Over breakfast, she mentioned in passing she had a friend interested in The Path and she had invited her to the reception. Absorbed in his coffee and paper, he asked her no questions. Outside of an initial introduction, she wouldn't have to worry too much about him. He'd have his own diversions during the Ball. Talk of work and golf and money as the women spoke of whatever frothy things they spoke of at parties.

Sharon agreed to drive up from the city since it was the only thing that would guarantee she could leave whenever she wanted. "No slumber parties for me. I refuse to sleep on some trundle bed while your husband snores next to you," she said with a wry smile. It rankled, how every joke was a hurtful truth.

They left the baby at home with Robert's mother, silence stretching between them as Robert fiddled with the radio and complained they would be late.

"We won't miss anything. They've never started the reception on time," she reassured him. He frowned and punched the accelerator.

By the time they came careening into the lot, there were still groups milling about outside. Pastel gatherings of organza and tulle with their suited, gel-slicked husbands.

"See?" she said, smiling, and Robert slid out to open her door.

She'd told Sharon to come late. Ten minutes, fifteen, if possible. Easier to have her come after everyone had already downed their first few sips of champagne, the mood looser and easier than the initial, sober evaluations that came with everyone's arrival. Easier to sneak away and find a quiet spot where she could learn what Sharon's bare skin looked like pressed against the earth.

By the time they finally filed inside, Mary felt as if she might crawl out of her own body. She accepted a glass of champagne as she scanned the faces of those around her, hoping to catch Vera's eye, but she didn't see her. Didn't even see Gerry standing there with his chubby, flushed cheeks—embarrassed to be attending the Purity Ball without his wife.

She'll be here, she thought as she lowered her gaze and told herself not to gulp the champagne down in a single swallow. She squeezed Robert's hand, hoping he didn't notice how damp her palm was. "I left my lipstick in the car," she said. "I'll just run out and grab it before the reception gets in full swing."

"Can't have that, can we?" He stepped away from her, his arm already raised to call Montgomery Palmer over. He'd already forgotten her. Just another skirt among the others, caught up in the importance of her own appearance. A gilded plaything given permission to wander.

She hurried outside. What if Sharon decided not to come, after all? What if she decided it wasn't worth the trouble, that *Mary* wasn't worth the trouble, and left the dress she bought hanging in the closet, the tags still attached so she could return it the following week?

But Sharon was there, leaning against her car in a demure dress of cobalt blue with a matching pearled capelet draped over her shoulders.

"You look exactly like a girl waiting to be picked up for the dance," Mary said.

Sharon twirled. "You may kiss me on the cheek as good friends or sisters do."

Mary did so, her heart fluttering to know how near Sharon was to this other life. This other self she knew so intimately and had carried with her since girlhood, but Sharon had not seen. These two disparate selves suddenly thrown together. She wondered again if this all was a mistake.

"Right then." Sharon clapped her hands together. "Show me this glamorous church. And the virgins! Take me to the virgins!"

They passed the sanctuary, taking only a moment to peek inside at the glimmering altar before hurrying to the reception pavilion, where the light notes of restrained cocktail-hour jazz floated.

"No hymns?" Sharon pressed a hand to her chest. "How progressive."

"You're awful," Mary said, and then together, they stepped outside where the reception had already reached a volume that spoke of two, if not three, glasses of passed champagne. The women and their daughters gathered like swans here and there, their feathers fluffed and proudly on display as they cut their eyes at the others who stood nearby.

"Holy Mother. I've certainly never seen jewelry like this at any church I've been to before," Sharon said, jutting her chin at the nearest group of women.

"I've seen them all drunk. Bible study, if you can believe it," she said, even as she remembered that Vera should be standing with them. She'd been right then. Vera had not come.

Mary's face went hot, and she very much wanted to cry, but she bit down on her tongue. She could worry about Vera any other time. Tonight was for Sharon alone.

She led Sharon from group to group, the already tipsy women chattering over one another as they complimented Sharon's dress, her hair, the little golden ring she wore on her right hand.

"Utterly charming. I've never been able to wear gold, myself. And what a shame. Gary got me the most gorgeous necklace for our anniversary, and I simply cannot wear it without turning into a human pincushion. Tiny little pinpricks everywhere," Hester said before reaching out to squeeze Sharon's hands. "I'm so glad our Mary brought you tonight. What a blessing it is to lead those blinded by the world back to the righteous path."

Mary watched as Sharon stiffened, but her smile never faded. "Thank you. You've all been so lovely."

"Mary, you must trot her over by the canapés and introduce her to Clifton. I think I spied him over there." Hester threw a conspiratorial wink at Sharon. "A banker, you know, and single."

Sharon arched a brow, her mouth opening, but Mary tugged at her elbow. "Didn't you mention you needed to visit the powder room, Sharon?"

"I don't recall. Perhaps if I was married—"

"If you'll excuse us," Mary said, pulling Sharon away.

"Wonderful to meet you!" Sharon called over her shoulder. "Be sure to send Clifton my best!"

"I ought to pull your hair. You wicked, wicked thing," Mary said once they were safely out of earshot.

"It would certainly save Clifton the trouble, but I would much prefer if you pulled it." She leaned close, her mouth pressed against Mary's ear as if she was relating a secret. "I don't need the powder room, but I could use some air. It's gotten dark. And no one's looking."

Mary felt her blood heat as an aching heaviness built slowly in her abdomen.

Before she could convince herself she shouldn't, Mary took Sharon's hand and pulled her away from the candlelit glow of the pavilion and into the woods that slept beyond. No one saw them go.

"I used to sneak off and come back here when I was a little girl. There was this enormous tree. A black walnut. Branches stretching out every which way, and in the spring, when it bloomed, it smelled like oranges and pine. Almost like Christmas. I would tear the blooms off and rub them all over me. If the sermon got boring, I'd tell my mother I was going to the restroom and go stand underneath it instead. She whipped me when she realized what I was doing, but coming out here . . . it was better than church. Holier, somehow."

Sharon nodded. Of course she understood. It was what she worshipped. "Will you show it to me? The tree?"

Still holding Sharon's hand, Mary led her farther into the woods, the path coming back to her as if she'd never stopped walking it. As if, after all this time, it was still waiting for her.

When they stepped into the clearing where the tree stood, Sharon gasped and then laughed. "There's old magic here. No wonder you loved it. It's like a heart beating."

They made their way to the tree, hand in hand, and stood beneath it, crowned in its leaves as Sharon kissed Mary's palms, her eyes starry with tears.

"I would marry you here. If things weren't . . ." Sharon let the words die out. There was no need to say them. To bring such hurt into this sacred place.

Mary leaned her forehead against Sharon's. Let herself rest and pretend they were newly born. Free of expectation. Free of anything that was not cleaving to the other.

Sharon pulled the little gold ring from her finger and pushed it onto Mary's.

"I don't have anything to give you," she said, and Sharon pressed her fingers against Mary's heart.

"You already have."

They fell into each other then, all mouths and touch, and Mary wondered how they did not burst into flame. How the earth did not tremble beneath them.

Sharon pressed her against the tree, and Mary wished she could take it all into her. The tree, the earth, the sky, the cold burn of Sharon's touch. If only it would mean she never had to go without it.

"I love you. I love you," she said again and again. A prayer offered up to a faceless, ancient god as Sharon traced her tongue along her collarbone. And then a tight groan as her fingers slipped inside.

They did not see the dark form that entered the clearing. They forgot they were not the only ones who might want to be alone that night.

Vera paused as she watched Mary and Sharon. And then, still unseen, she stole back into the darkness.

INTERLUDE: 1751

I did not wait. Even though my body was failing. Even though I wanted to put myself into the earth and wait for the slow death Florence wished upon me. There was no time. If I meant to undo Florence's curse, to ensure death no longer plagued us, I knew I must act quickly.

I went to the tree that same night. The moon above me bore witness as I moved silently among the sleeping, grief-stricken houses.

By the time I reached it, my mouth was filled with blood brought up from my decaying lungs. My breath came in shuddering gasps, my heart used up and pumping worthlessly in my chest as I stared at the tree. I carried my knife beneath my cloak, and it weighed against me as if the blade understood the immensity of what I came to do.

In nature, there was harmony. Predator and prey. Birth and bloodletting in equal measure. I always understood that greed was a behavior learned by man. Their own meanness clouded by the belief God would hold them in esteem for their scant good deeds. So limited were they by their own wants and desires they had forgotten how simple it was to give and to be provided for in return.

We had given our blood. Had sworn ourselves to this land so our daughters and their daughters on into the future might know peace. Prosperity. But Florence, blinded with her anger at my betrayal, had made a request tinged darker by her need for what she called justice but I understood as vengeance. The magic bound within the tree did not understand the good or the ill of the requests made of it. It was of nature. It only responded in kind.

I took my share of the blame. I had interfered in Florence's happiness, if only to save her, but I could not turn my face against my own mistakes. I had not given her the words to curse us, but I had given her the knowledge of how to wield them. I had given her the anger that led her to them.

I was not the one who had completed the ritual, but perhaps, I could be the one to undo it.

"Grant us forgiveness," I said as the knife burned a deep cut across my hand. "Break the bonds of Florence's request that those with betrayal in their hearts might suffer. She saw only anger, and if you will not let it pass by, then I ask you to soften this plague. Let death pass over those who have spilled their blood here. Let death pass over their bloodline that will come after." I smeared my hand along the bark, squeezed it into a fist and let the drops fall onto the roots below.

The earth swallowed my blood, but I worried it would not be enough. Mine had not been the only offering. The only intention set. As in all things, there was a balance that must be struck. My request did not necessarily outweigh the other. The snake is not favored over the wolf in the natural world. They may differ, but they are only variations of a single, deadly beast. I could only wait and hope I had set right what Florence had seen as justice.

I bound my hand, my legs aching as I pushed myself to my feet and, with a weariness I'd never known, finally turned toward home.

———

WEEKS PASSED, BUT I lacked awareness of time. The sunrise and sunset meant nothing to me as I curled on my cot, my insides granted an intimacy with death not yet allowed my flesh-bound spirit. My teeth were gone, the gums so inflamed they split apart if I drew a deep breath. My tongue eaten through with sores, the deep pink meat of its interior ringed with a sickly yellow. Every day, I retched more and more chunks of tissue into my palm as I wondered how a body could sustain such loss and still live.

But it was as Florence had wished it. Her blood was a sigil that guaranteed my failing organs' continual work.

Hope came to see me once more. It could have been months since Joan's death or only weeks, but it was enough to have witnessed a transformation among those who'd once followed me.

"They plan to build a meetinghouse. Isaac and Gideon will see to it. Gideon has an eye toward the pulpit."

I watched her from my place on the cot. She did not advance past the doorway, her hands clasped in front of her as she gazed upon anything but my wasting body. I gave her a single nod. It was fitting that Florence married a man who felt himself anointed by God.

They would replicate the town we fled. They would build their meetinghouse and pray to their God and ignore the reason for their prosperity. The tree's magic and our devotion to it would die with me.

Hope wrung her hands. "I wanted to tell you ... I am sorry, Anne. This place, what it has become, it is not as we intended, but this world will not allow for it. He is my husband, and I will follow him." She took a step backward, the sun outlining her frame. "I will not come here again."

With a final glance back, she vanished.

It was as she said. I did not see her again.

THE LAST PERSON to darken my door was Florence.

She came to me, both palms cut, the wounds ragged and still bleeding as she stumbled over the threshold.

"How do I take it back? How do I take back what I asked of the tree?" She stood over me, her face reddened, the hair escaping her cap windblown and wild. Her belly had grown heavier, the apron she wore stretched taut. And there, on her mouth, the tell-tale ring of boils.

Florence was sick.

I wanted to weep. To scream. To pound my fists against the tree and earth and demand even a small measure of grace. My own attempt at a reversal had no effect. The request could not be taken back no matter what I did. If only this curse would pass over Florence, I would gladly take it all. Would go into death without fear or regret if it would not touch her and the child she carried.

"You must know of something else. Some other thing to offer. I have given the tree my blood twice now, and still, this sickness lingers." She moaned, her hand creeping to her belly. "Tell me what to do."

Around us the lamplight cast shadows against the wall. Strange devils that had frightened Florence as a girl even as I told her there was nothing to fear in the exchange between light and dark. One was counterpart to the other.

A new understanding grew within me as I watched the shadows, the balance between them. I forced my rotted tongue to speak. "I didn't understand, but I think I do now." My breathing was thick. Liquid. But my voice was firm. "I'm so close to the darkness, and my eyes are opened. I wanted only the good. For all of us. But I'd forgotten." I gulped at the air. "There is no light without the dark. They are sisters, born of the same mother. When we knelt there and gave of our blood to the tree, there were darker gods. And they also listen when granted an offering.

"They mirror the wild chaos of our hearts. They give back what is asked of them in the same way any god might. Even the wickedness we try to hide. With our good deeds. With our faith."

Florence made a strangled noise in her throat but said nothing.

"But we should not fear such things. There is nothing to fear in the untamed chaos of nature. The rabbit eats the clover. The fox eats the rabbit. There is no iniquity in it. Nothing but nature doing as it will. And we . . . *you*"—I reached for Florence's hand then, her palm fever hot from the cut she made—"must not deny the shadowed portions of yourself."

Florence attempted to shake off my grip, but I held firm. I would never know for certain, but this new awareness held a truth in it I hoped would serve as some sort of salvation for my daughter. For my granddaughter. For Hope. For all the women who would be born and die here.

"You asked for punishment for those with betrayal in their hearts. You cannot let that shadow swallow you. Jealousy. Duplicity. These are such petty, dangerous things to plant in an earth that hears and accepts all." I drew Florence closer. "It does not have to be as such. One does not have to snuff out the other. We can hold all parts of ourselves without denial or shame or bitterness. The light and the dark. Refusal is ruin. Disease. Death. You have seen it firsthand. This sickness.

"It is this refusal to accept all parts of the self that has undone us, Florence. You must see. What you asked of the tree cannot be willed away in the same way one cannot extinguish the dark in favor of the light. There is no amount of bloodshed that will undo this sickness. What is enacted cannot be stopped. We can only adapt to its parameters." My breathing grew more labored, my lungs exhausted from drawing enough air to speak, and I clawed at Florence's arm. "Tell Hope. Tell the women who will come to live here. Tell your daughter. Tell them to accept it all. Tell them not to hide their darkness, their shadow selves, for it is only another part of them. If they do not, it will bring further harm."

With a final tug, Florence wrenched her hand from me, and I felt its absence as a keen pain. "These are the ravings of a mad woman. If you will not tell me what to do, I will find a way to stop it myself."

"I cannot stop it. There is nothing to tell. Please, Florence, you must listen—"

"I hope you can feel the hellfire licking at your feet even now." She straightened her skirt and, without another glance at me, left the house that held all that had once been her mother.

CHAPTER XI
2007

For two weeks, Camilla and Brianna were very, very good. Model representatives of the Retreat's tenets. Devout women who embodied everything The Path taught. Chaste. Modest. Quiet. Humble. Servile.

Camilla grew used to waking every morning grateful for the necessary, pill-eliminating vomit because she felt completely filled with bullshit and the need to rid herself of it. She hated doing it, but psychologically, it helped her hold on for another day because it felt like she was purging more than just the pills. Like an ejection of a poison intent on making her a pod person.

She and Brianna had not had another opportunity to talk in private, but they saw each other in the dining room. Quick glimpses so they drew no suspicion. And while Brianna did not seem to get any worse, she also didn't seem to get any better. It didn't matter that there seemed to be a temporary stasis in Brianna's illness; each day, Camilla grew more and more desperate.

On the morning Barbara came to tell her she was going home, it took every ounce of her newly practiced reserve to keep herself from bolting out of the building. Such joyous intent to leave Retreat would likely lead to them locking her right back in her room. Instead, she allowed Barbara to lead her back down the main hallway and then, after a series of beeps and clicks from several keypads and locked doors, outside into cool damp of early morning.

The same Range Rover that brought her there sat out front, and Barbara opened the door for her and waved her inside. "Your father has been so pleased with your progress, Camilla. He's looking forward to having you home." Barbara stood back, her hand still on the Range Rover's door, as she looked in at Camilla.

"I'll be glad to see him. And glad to show him what a blessing it was he sent me here." She lifted her voice into a higher pitch, the lilt so syrupy sweet it made her sick.

Barbara stepped away and lifted a hand in farewell. Camilla returned the wave, and then held herself still as the driver fastened the blindfold over her eyes. She kept her smile even as they pulled away since it was likely her father had instructed the driver to report any and all abnormalities.

She directed her thoughts to the questions she would ask her mother. Every night, she'd run through them in her head as if they were a lullaby that would soothe her into sleep.

When did you see the Dark Sisters? What do you think they are? Are they what's causing this sickness? Why are you afraid of me going to the Purity Ball? What aren't you telling me?

Her driver stayed silent as he drove, and she was thankful her father sent a different man than the ones who brought her. She could have acted her way through his comments, forced herself to play nice even as he tried to rile her up, but she was glad she didn't have to.

She remembered the ride wouldn't take long, but as the car rolled to a stop, she was surprised at how quickly it had gone. She settled herself. She had a role to play, and she'd practiced for it. She'd spent those long hours of silence after Pilates and lights out locked in her room with only her thoughts and intentions, training herself to keep her composure no matter how she wanted to bite a chunk out of Pastor Wade's face or take a fistful of Barbara's hair and pull until it tore wetly away from her scalp.

Folding her hands in her lap, she listened as the car door opened and closed, shutting her inside still wearing the blindfold. She knew if she tried the handle, she would find it locked, but she didn't dare move. Not until she'd been given the permission to do so. It would be too easy for her father to take one look and decide to send her back.

From outside came the muffled voices of the driver and her father, the latter providing the expected update on her behavior following her dismissal. She'd done perfectly. No issues. She did not hear her mother's voice, and her heart sank. She knew she would have to wait until her father was gone to talk with her mother, but she'd at least hoped to see her when she got home. To hug her and tell her she loved her.

And then the car door opened.

"Oh, honey." Her father's voice was all tenderness. The voice he'd used when she was little and scraped her knee. "Let's get this thing off you."

With gentle hands, he removed the blindfold, and she made a show of blinking against the sunlight as she took his hand and let him help her down.

"That'll be all, Kevin," he said to the driver, who nodded and then vanished back into the front seat, the engine humming to life before he pulled away and left them standing alone in front of the house.

She'd been right. Her mother wasn't there. She took a breath, feeling the disappointment, but holding it at bay. She'd practiced this, and even though it hurt, she knew she could do it. She stared past her father's shoulder at a distant spot of greenery, focusing on trying to see every individual leaf and twig rather than on her mother's absence. It settled her, and she was able to look back at him and offer up a tentative smile.

"Let me get a look at you." He held her at arm's length, his gaze traveling the length of her body, before pulling her into a hug. It made her feel like a rag doll, keeping her body still so she could be manipulated, but she let him hold her. Let him grip her face between his hands and inspect her like she was something he'd purchased and was trying to decide whether he wanted to keep.

"I'm so proud of you, Camilla. You know that?"

She nodded, a slight dip of her head that spoke of humility. Any shred of enthusiasm over such praise would be construed as pride. A lesson Pastor Wade taught her. She was nothing if not an excellent student. An actress born of necessity.

"I know it wasn't easy, but nothing worthy of His grace is. It's the struggle back to Him that makes us shine. God laid that on my heart for service tomorrow. Planned my whole sermon around this entire *experience*." He lingered on the final word so she might understand his purposeful euphemism, then squeezed her again, and with his arm around her shoulder, turned her toward the house. "Let's get you inside."

She fell into step with him as they ascended the front stairs. The question she wanted to ask hovered at the back of her throat, her resolve wavering because it was innocent enough, but he might find some offense in it. Some reason to see it as a fault. But she couldn't help it. She blurted it out as soon he closed the front door behind them, the house's perfumed air invading her lungs.

"Where's Mom?"

He frowned. Her heart stuttered, but she kept her gaze downcast. Soft and respectful. The frown dropped from his face, and he cleared his throat as he pasted on an expression of concern. The one she'd seen him use whenever someone seeking his guidance came to the house unannounced. She knew then she wasn't the only one acting.

"She hasn't been feeling well. Went to bed early. Said to tell you she's missed you and to give all her love."

"Everything okay?"

"Dr. Morgan's come out to see her. Just a nasty virus. She'll be fine in a week or two."

"That's good."

He would tell Camilla if her mother was sick with the illness. Certainly, he would. It would make too much of an impact, keeping a secret like that. Her father might have sent her on Retreat, but he wouldn't keep something like that from her.

They stared at each other, both waiting for the other to make a move that would decide the path forward. Her father out of confusion, she out of necessity.

"Well." He clapped his hands together. "I have some work to finish before tomorrow's service, but Angela is here. She can bring you something up if you're hungry. Chef left a wonderful Niçoise salad."

"I think I'll just rest. I got plenty of sleep while I was there, but it's always nice to be home."

"Of course. I'll be in my office," he said, and made his way to the stairs.

Dutifully, she followed, glad to know he would be busy. Tucked away behind his door that he always kept closed, that inner sanctum a place he'd long forbidden her from entering. There was an order to that room. A peace meant only for him and his connection to God. Any sort of intrusion would disturb that tenuous thread. If they needed him, they could dial in to his line, but even that was unwelcome. She could count on one hand the number of times her mother had done it—once because Camilla had a nosebleed that would not stop and she panicked. Even that caused problems, the two of them fighting as he asked why her mother hadn't just called their driver or for an ambulance. She didn't need him to get Camilla to a hospital. Not when he was in the middle of sermon preparation, every nerve attuned to whatever holy missive he was meant to deliver. There was no time for something as inconsequential as his daughter's nosebleed.

Outside her bedroom, she lingered, listening for the click of her father's office door closing. Her heartbeat surging in her ears, she counted to one hundred and then another hundred for good measure, her ears pricked for any sound that would indicate her father had decided not to stay in his office after all. But the hall remained quiet, and the door closed against her.

Quickly, she tiptoed past the office, holding her breath as she did so. Her parents' room was at the other end of the long hallway, and she hurried toward it, hoping she would find her mother. Even if it was just a few minutes. She'd learned to be grateful for stolen time.

But the door, like her father's, was closed. Her heart sank as she approached, her hand coming to rest on the handle, the shift under her grip gentle so it made no sound.

Locked.

She placed her palm against the door, her fingers curled into the wood, a bright irritation itching at her throat as she swallowed and forced herself to whisper rather than scream.

She brought her lips close to the door. "Mom?" Waited for a breath and then another, but there was no response.

She lightly scratched her fingers over the wood, fairy tale lines ringing in her head. *Little pig, little pig, let me in.*

She glanced over her shoulder, expecting to find her father looming over her, his face a calm mask, but the hallway was still empty.

Maybe it was as her father told her. Maybe her mom did have a cold and was resting, the door locked to ensure Angela wouldn't come barging in to complete some chore. But Angela had never done that. She watched each member of the Burson family carefully, noting their comings and goings to ensure whatever cleaning took place in their private rooms did so without their knowledge. Quiet and unobtrusive as a mouse. It was the reason she'd lasted as long as she had as their housekeeper. She blended in. An invisible hand that did all their dirty work and kept silent.

"Mom?" she hissed, daring to jiggle the handle, but her mother did not respond. Could be she was asleep. Could be she was too sick to get up. Too sick to even respond, her mouth and tongue covered in sores. But her father wouldn't have lied to her about that, would he?

She couldn't help thinking it though. Her mind kept drifting to that diseased thought as she went slowly back down the hallway, hoping she would hear the door opening behind her.

It didn't.

She wanted to call Brianna, who had gone home two days before. To check in on her and see if she was any worse. To ask her how it went with her family when she got home. To tell her that her mother was sick with a cold and she hadn't been able to talk with her. To hear her voice. To tell her they were still in this together.

But her phone was likely locked away in her father's office. Looking for it would only get her in trouble, and the landline wasn't an option. Too easy for someone to listen in, and she and Brianna had never been the sort of friends to come up with a secret language for just the two of them. Theirs was a language of pointed glances and lifted eyebrows paired with knowing smirks, not some bastardized version of Pig Latin.

Instead, she took a shower hot enough to leave her skin red and blotchy. Scrubbed her face. Her legs and arms and back. Shaved everything that needed it. Skin care. Body cream. The need to make everything slick and smooth a momentary distraction from that closed door at the end of the hall and what lay behind it.

For a long while, she did not sleep. When it finally came, an insistent pull, she dreamed of a sudden, sharp pain. Of blood in her mouth.

When she woke, she still tasted it. The bright tang of blood.

She'd bitten her tongue.

Wincing, she rose and stumbled to the mirror to examine the wound, tears springing to her eyes when she ran a finger over the raw flesh. She grabbed a washcloth from the closet in her bathroom and held it there, waiting for the bleeding to stop as she examined her face in the mirror.

She'd lost weight. Her cheeks gaunt in the way she once wished for. The supermodel look every woman in Hawthorne Springs starved for. She turned away from the mirror in disgust. She hated it. It made her look like a corpse. Like the Dark Sisters.

Finally, the bleeding slowed, and she tossed the washcloth into the hamper and glanced at the clock on her bedside table. Six fifteen. Enough time to get ready for church. Primped and polished and ready for her father to preach all about how Retreat had saved his wayward daughter. Just in time for Purity Ball, too! Praise the Lord!

She turned, ready to plop herself in front of her vanity, the makeup brushes scattered before her, a mockery of her attempts at beauty, when she heard her father's voice. And then her mother's, raised to a volume Camilla had only heard a few times in her life.

She crept toward her door and opened it the tiniest bit. Just enough to see the length of the hallway, the door at the end thrown open. Her mother stood in the doorway, the black silk dressing gown she so loved gaping open to reveal her sunken chest, the ribs visible beneath the skin and flexing as she panted, eyes wild as she pushed against Henry.

"We've talked about this, Ada." His voice was stern, the voice he used when there was no room for argument, no room for anything but strict obedience. But Ada did not meekly nod and retreat back into the depths of her sickroom. She balled her fists at her sides, the cords at her neck straining.

Camilla forced herself to stay hidden even though she wanted to rush down the hallway and throw her arms around her mother. Sometimes learning what you wanted to know meant staying quiet.

"I'm fine. I can cover it with makeup. It's my duty to be there. With you," she said.

"No, you'll stay here and get some rest. Dr. Morgan said—"

"I don't care what Dr. Morgan said!" Her mother slammed her hands against the doorframe.

Camilla tried to open the door just a bit further, an attempt to see her mother more fully, to see if those telltale sores ringed her mouth, but she'd stepped backward, the still-darkened room wrapping her in shadow.

"You have to understand, Ada. Camilla's just come home from

Retreat, and I've barely managed to pass that off as a momentary lapse of faith. The struggle we all go through but can correct with the right guidance. But if the congregation were to see you in your ... *condition*, they'd take it as a sign from the Lord. As a punishment for sin."

Ada's voice sharpened. "Sin?"

"Ada—"

"No. Tell me, Henry. I want you to tell me all the ways I've disappointed you as a wife. All the ways I've managed to sin."

Camilla swallowed against the knot in her throat as she let what her father said settle over her. *Condition. Punishment for sin.*

She moved as if in a dream. Her hand pushing the door fully open before she stepped into the hallway, her gaze locked on her mother. Her impossibly beautiful mother whose mouth was a seeping mess of sores.

"Mom? Are you sick?"

In the same moment her mother took a stumbling step forward, her father pushed her back, his right hand clamping on her wrist as her mother cried out in pain.

"You're hurting her." Tears fell over Camilla's cheeks, her vision going blurry as she hurried toward them. She didn't know what she would do when she got there. Didn't know what she could do. He was so much bigger than her. It didn't matter that he was her father. She wanted to hurt him. To slap him or bite his arm until the skin tore. Anything to get him to stop.

Her father turned to her even as he backed her mother farther into the bedroom. "Get ready for church and wait for me downstairs, Camilla."

"You lied to me. You said it was a cold." She pushed forward, ready to shove him aside, to beat him with her fists until she was inside that room with her mother.

"Camilla." Her mother's voice wavered, but she spoke clearly. With authority. "Listen to your father. We don't know if it's contagious."

Camilla forced herself to stop and to settle back into her body. Furiously, she swiped at the tears on her cheeks and nodded. She would do what was asked of her. Not out of devotion to her father but because her mother had asked. She would do this, for now, under the pretense of obedience. She needed her father to think she was the good, reformed girl he expected. To give her, if not the trust, then the time and space to be able to talk with her mother in private.

But Brianna was sick. Her mother was sick. There was no more time. She needed to know what her mother knew about the Dark Sisters. They were connected somehow. They had to be. She needed to understand their connection to this illness, to the women of Hawthorne Springs, so she could try to stop it. To save them.

She dropped her head. "Yes, sir. Yes, ma'am," she said and turned back to her room. She could have screamed even as the door closed silently behind her.

Two hours later, Camilla sat alone in the backseat, her fingers curled against her thighs as she kept her gaze trained straight ahead. Her father had gone ahead. He had not come out of the bedroom at all before a driver had come to collect her, saying that Pastor Burson would meet her at the church.

He'd never intended to have a conversation with her. To admit he'd lied and try to apologize with some lame excuse like he hadn't wanted to worry her. Especially with her only just back from Retreat, still so fresh on her renewed path and liable to stumble over the slightest provocation. She could practically hear his voice in her head. He was handling it. He had the best doctors. The best staff. The best team. And God was on their side.

She couldn't do it. Couldn't go and sit through an hour and a half of service, her father smiling down at them from the pulpit while he pretended everything was just fine, his hands on the puppet strings as he dangled Camilla's time at Retreat over them like some sort of perfect story of redemption. Her acting was good, but she wasn't that good.

But for what she had in mind, she didn't need to be *that* good. It was an old story, one she'd used to get out of countless P.E. classes. She knew it well, and she knew that it worked. Even better was that her father would believe it, too. He would be angry, but he wouldn't be suspicious. He might be ashamed of the potential sin hidden inside her body, but even he couldn't deny its functions.

And it would mean time alone with her mother.

She leaned forward in the seat and tapped the driver. "I'm so sorry, but could you turn around? I need to go back to the house."

He shifted uncomfortably in his seat. "Pastor Burson says I'm supposed to take you to church. We're almost there. If you forgot something, I can call and have Angela bring it."

"It's not that. It's just that . . . well . . . I'm having"—she dropped her voice into an embarrassed whisper—"a lady problem."

"Oh." His face flushed a mottled crimson. "I see." He put on his indicator and shifted to the left lane, the opposite lane clear as he completed what was likely an illegal U-turn. Anything to keep him from sharing space with a bleeding woman.

He took the curves a bit too fast, but within minutes, they were pulling back down the long driveway, and Camilla didn't wait for him to open her door, making a show of holding her purse over her backside as she did so.

"No need to wait. I wouldn't want you to be late for service, and I'll need to change. Maybe even shower. I'll call my dad and let him know I can drive myself back."

He flushed again and kept his eyes trained on the steering wheel instead of having the decency to look at her as if she was an actual person and not a walking, talking she-devil.

"Thank you, Miss Burson."

She closed the door and backed up a few steps with her hands and purse still behind her as the car pulled away. Only when it was a distant speck on the horizon did she allow herself to turn and make her way into the house.

She hoped Angela was already gone. She never left before the rest of the Burson family, always staying behind to ensure she was there to provide for any last-minute request. She wouldn't linger though. Wouldn't want to be late for service herself, so while Camilla had left no more than twenty minutes ago, the house was likely empty.

Empty of everyone except her mother.

She knew she should call her father and feed him her excuse for not being front and center in the family pew for her grand return to righteousness. Her explanation would only mildly calm his fury over her absence, and offering it sooner rather than later would work in her favor.

But it would have to wait. She didn't know how long she would have alone with her mother. If her father would send Angela or the driver back to check on her. If he would foist today's sermon off on one of his many assistant pastors and show up himself.

She kicked off her heels and ran up the stairs, skipping the last one and hauling herself up by the banister. If only her legs would move *faster*.

The door was as she saw it last: closed against her. A barrier meant to serve as a reminder to keep away, but she rushed toward it and then slammed her palm against the wood.

"Mom? It's me." She jiggled the handle, knowing it was locked but hoping her father had forgotten or left without locking it behind him, assuming the house would be empty of anyone who wanted to get inside.

"Open the door. I don't care if it's contagious, you have to open the door." Her voice grew thick, tears pooling in her eyes so that she blinked furiously, the world around her a blurred smear of light and color.

But there was no movement. No sounds of her mother pulling herself out of bed and shuffling toward the door, her voice soothing as she called out for Camilla and told her not to worry, she was coming.

She leaned her head against the door and heaved a sob. She was going to lose them. Brianna and her mother. They were going to get sicker and sicker, and she couldn't stop it. Tania Fullerton hadn't been able to stop it. It was foolish to think she would be any different.

From behind the door came the smallest sound. An exhale or a sigh, Camilla didn't know, but it was enough to know there was someone there. Her mother heard her.

The handle turned, and the door opened. Her mother stood there, illuminated by the dim glow of a single lamp. The curtains were closed, and the room had the stale odor of unwashed bodies. A sickroom that opened now for Camilla as her mother reached for her and drew her inside.

"You shouldn't have come back."

"I needed to talk to you. Without him here. And I couldn't sit through that service and pretend like everything is okay. Not with..." She let her gaze drift to her mother's mouth. The sores. "How long have you known?"

Her mother squeezed her hand. "Not long. I found the first one right after you left. I used every makeup trick I know, but not even I could hide it." She chuckled, but it was a loose, wet sound. As if some integral part of her throat had shaken free.

"He lied to me. He said you had a cold."

Her mother closed her eyes and drew in a deep breath. "I know."

"He should have told me."

"I know." Her mother let silence fall between them. She did not try to fill it with justifications for her father's lie. That he did it to protect her, to keep her from being upset. Camilla was grateful she didn't. He wasn't here. There was no reason to lie for him.

Camilla had only ever known her mother's body as gracefully poised, an embodiment of all things lithe and flowing, but the illness had collapsed those elegant lines. Her shoulders hunched. Her chin fell toward her chest. It was the first time Camilla had ever seen the potential that one day her mother would grow old.

"You should lie down," she said, but her mother waved her away.

"I'm so tired of lying down. Every hour I think about setting that mattress on fire. Or climbing out the window." She glanced toward the windows as if she was considering it right then.

"Mom." Camilla covered both her hands with her own and gently tugged, relieved when her mother's gaze finally slid from the windows and back to her. "I have to ask you something." She licked her lips, suddenly nervous.

"What is it?"

"Before. The night I went on Retreat. You said you'd seen them. The Dark Sisters."

She watched as her mother's lips creased into a frown, the sores cracking as they opened and blood seeped onto her chin. A beauty queen born into a nightmare.

"They aren't real. I'm not doing this. Not with you." She tried to turn away, but Camilla held her, the bones of her mother's hands flexing beneath her grip, the skin gone so thin, Camilla worried it might tear.

"I saw them, Mom. The first time, I thought it was a dream. The night I was sleepwalking. But then I saw them again, and I knew it was real. They're real."

Her mother groaned as yet another sore stretched and popped, her lips pulled back from her teeth as she spoke. "I told Vera then that it was wrong. To stop asking about them because it was a story. A bad dream I'd had. But she kept on and on, and my father . . . if he knew I'd even considered the possibility of what I'd seen as anything other than some delusion, my entire life would have been ruined. Everything I wanted just *poof*. He used to say, 'The Lord giveth, but I'm the one who taketh away.'" She snorted and used the hem of her robe to dab away the blood on her chin. "What an asshole."

"Listen to me. Brianna's sick, too. And Tania Fullerton—the tree where they found her body—that's where I saw them." She spoke more rapidly now, urgency forcing her to bypass the script she mapped out in her head during Retreat. "I think it's all connected. The Sisters. That tree. The reason why you and Brianna are sick. It has something to do with them. So if you know something, you have to tell me. Okay?"

Her mother's eyes went glassy. Her gaze unfocused, her hands going limp beneath Camilla's as she lifted them toward her face. Her mouth.

"I can feel it. Inside. How it's making everything loose."

"Mom?"

"They're not real," her mother said, pinching her front canine tooth between two fingers. "Not real," she repeated, and tugged.

The tooth came away easily, blood oozing from the opening where it had once been. The decaying root dangled from its bottom. With it came the smell of spoiled meat. Of sun-heated carrion. Camilla fought against her desire to retch and tried to pull her mother's hands away, but they were slippery with blood.

"Mom, stop!"

But her mother did not stop, and Camilla looked on in horror as her mother pulled two more teeth and tossed them to the floor.

"Not real," she repeated. "Not real."

CHAPTER XII
1953

"We've been gone too long," Mary said. They were still tangled together, and she buried her face in Sharon's hair and wished, as she always did, that any construct of time would fall away and grant them an infinity of moments like this. She wanted to go into death with the taste of Sharon's sweat on her tongue.

"Mmm," Sharon mumbled. "What if I want to stay here?"

Mary tugged at her. "Come on you. Up, up, up. The reception is probably winding down. They'll be starting the ceremony soon, and Robert will be looking for me. Only leadership stays for the actual ceremony." She brushed off the bits of bark that clung to Sharon's skirt and pushed the tendrils of hair that had escaped back into place. "There. Pretty as a picture."

"You'll want to fix your lipstick. It's all smeared. I wonder how that happened." Sharon smirked—the cat who ate the canary—and Mary swatted at her.

"I should have worn something less bright," she said, pulling her compact from her handbag and reapplying another layer of Helena Rubinstein's Dark Red.

"The better to see you with, my dear," Sharon said, and gave her shoulder a gentle nip.

"You said see, not eat."

"Why not both?"

Mary snapped the compact closed. The glow she felt after their coupling was rapidly fading. Neither of them wore a watch, and the twilight they set off in had grown to full dark. If they hurried, they might make it back just as the ceremony was starting, and Robert would not have started to wonder where she had disappeared to. She could wander in, cool as a cucumber, and ask if he'd had quite enough talk of business and golf, and was he ready to go home?

"Be careful," Mary said as they began to make their way back the way they came. "High heels and the outdoors don't play well together."

She kept her tone light. Playful. It would do no good to worry Sharon unnecessarily. She came to Hawthorne Springs because Mary asked her to. She didn't want to soil the memory before it was complete.

Still, she found herself wanting to run. The dark at her back pressed in, lapping at her with a hungry mouth, and she wanted to go faster and faster. Anything to get them back more quickly, but her dress was too tight. Her heels too high.

When they finally came through the trees, the lights from the church and the parking lot casting an amber glow, the sight didn't calm her in the way she hoped.

"We're back. See? It's okay," Sharon said, but Mary did not respond. They weren't close enough yet. She couldn't see the parking lot and if it was still full, the drivers still at the reception, distracted with the champagne and the anticipation of the start of the Purity Ball.

The path bent, the church vanishing behind yet another line of trees, and then they emerged on the other side, the parking lot in full view.

Other than a handful of cars, it was empty.

"Oh," Sharon said, and Mary's mouth went dry.

The ceremony had already begun. The cars left in the lot belonged to leadership and the fathers participating in the ceremony.

Two figures stood in the lot, illuminated by the lights. Mary registered each of their faces, one with a quiet acceptance, and the other with shock.

Robert and Vera.

Mary spoke quietly, hoping Sharon could hear without her needing to turn around. "We'll say you needed some air. That the champagne got to you, and I went along to make sure you were all right. We'll say goodbye, and you'll tell Robert you're so sorry for stealing me away, but champagne has always gone right to your head, and you'll get in your car and go."

"Mary—"

"Tell me you'll do it. Exactly as I said."

Silence stretched between them, and still, Mary did not let herself turn back to look. Instead, she looked only at Robert, a smile painted on her face because he would expect it. His expression was impassive as he watched her. Beside him, Vera fidgeted, her gaze fixed on her feet. She didn't know why Vera would be there, alone with Robert after everyone else had gone home. Maybe she'd come late, and Robert asked to help him look for her, and they'd come out of the woods right as they were about to start their search.

"I'll do it," Sharon replied.

She could feel the flutter of her pulse at her throat as they stepped into full view, their heels clicking against the parking lot's asphalt as they made their way toward Robert and Vera. She opened her mouth, the lie ready on her tongue, but Robert spoke before she could.

"Well look what the cat dragged in. Thought I'd lost you. Thank goodness Vera saw you two, otherwise, I wouldn't have known where to even start looking."

For so many years, Mary had thought she'd known terror. Living under her mother's rule, always at fault for some indiscretion and terrified someone might finally see who she really was, she'd grown intimately acquainted with it. But as Robert watched her, the realization Vera saw her and Sharon in the woods sank in, and she knew then she had never understood true terror. She wanted to bolt or to curl into the soft parts of herself and wish for death. Even as her body trembled, adrenaline she would not use spiking in her bloodstream, she kept the emotion from her face and hoped it was dark enough to hide her reddened cheeks.

There was no way to know what Vera saw and what she'd told Robert, but she felt the weight of Robert's scrutiny. His eyes crawled over her body as he waited for her to speak. It felt like a trap.

Beside him, Vera had gone completely still. Her own animal instinct left her frozen in place. Mary wanted to look at her, to see in her eyes the extent of what Robert knew, but she couldn't. If she did, Robert would know.

"The champagne," she began. Already the words began to dissolve, soft as snow on her tongue. Her panic and fear like a bridle between her teeth. She waved her hand at Sharon, who still stood behind her, and forced herself to speak. "Poor Sharon. It went right to her head."

Robert stepped forward and caught Mary's hand. "Well, look at that." He held her hand up to the light as she tried to keep herself from gasping. Her head swam, tiny pinpricks of stars crowding the edge of her vision as Robert examined the ring Sharon gave her. "Where'd you get this little thing?"

Was it possible that even as Judas betrayed Christ he understood the gravity of that moment? There would be years to come, his body crumbling into dust, and there would be no undoing it. Or had he only seen himself? His immediate need for silver. For the semblance of safety it could provide.

"I bought it last week. I thought it would work with the dress."

Behind her Sharon drew in a breath. If devastation had a sound, it was this. A drawing in of air to keep the heart from withering. Mary had denied her. She had denied the intimacy of everything between them. Denied that union made symbolic, made magical, by the gold band on her finger.

"Hmm." Robert glanced up from the ring with a smirk, his eyes flashing. He didn't believe her.

She waited for him to say what he knew. For him to tell it all. That Vera had seen them together, and he was going to burn every part of her carefully constructed little world and leave her behind to molder in the ashes.

He would take their daughter. He would take her because he could. And she would die. She loved Sharon, but without her daughter, she would die.

Instead, he clasped her hand, tender as the first day he came courting, and extended his other hand to Sharon.

"I'm Robert Shephard," he said.

Blinking in confusion, Sharon allowed Robert to shake her hand. "Sharon Hutchins."

"You know what's funny, Sharon?"

He tipped his head to the side, the boyish grin Mary once found so attractive plastered over his face. She saw it now for what it was. Condescension.

"That somehow, you and my wife seem to be thick as thieves, and I've never even heard your name before today. Isn't that something?" He barked out a laugh. "About the only friend's name I ever hear is Vera here, and even she doesn't seem to know you very well. Isn't that right, Vera?"

Vera darted a glance at Robert and let out a wavery "No."

"In fact, I'm starting to wonder if maybe you aren't a very good influence on my Mary." He took a step toward Sharon, Mary's hand still tight inside his as he looked down on them. His body so much larger than theirs. His power on display and meant to shrink them down, make them less than. A reminder of his ownership over her. A reminder of their *place*.

But Sharon lifted her chin and held his gaze. Self-possessed. Defiant. "I suppose that would depend on your definition of a good influence."

Robert's grip tightened, and Mary felt the weak give of her bones. A bit more pressure, and they would snap. "Everyone was asking where you'd disappeared, Mary. Imagine my surprise when

I found out you went for a walk in the woods with a woman I've never met."

She'd never known Vera to seek vengeance. Had only ever known her as kind. Compassionate. If she was making use of that vengeance now, she was justified in it, but it hurt all the same. Still she held to the dim hope that Vera had not told Robert. That he saw her and asked if she'd seen Mary, and she'd lied for them. Lied for Mary. If only Vera would look at her, she might be able to understand what she told him.

"The champagne. We needed some air." She shifted her hand beneath his and tried, ineffectually, to flex her fingers. "Robert, you're hurting me."

"I'm sorry, love. Guess I don't know my own strength." He let off the pressure, but only slightly, and her fingers throbbed as the blood rushed back in. "I think it's best we all got ourselves home. Call it a night. And I think it's best, Sharon, if you left Hawthorne Springs altogether and found several reasons to stay away. I can offer a few if you need."

"Mary is my friend," Sharon said, her voice clear and strong.

"'Be ye not unequally yoked together with unbelievers. What Communion hath light with darkness?' You remember that passage, don't you, Mary? Pastor Brighton preached on it not that long ago."

She did not answer. Did not nod. Her own pathetic rebellion.

"Mary?" Sharon asked, and Mary heard the crack in her voice. She'd tried to stay strong but was crumbling under the pressure of what they were both going to lose. And the awareness that Mary was going to let it happen.

If it were another life, she would pick Sharon. Again and again and again. Tears pricked at the corners of her eyes, but she would not let them fall. Would not let Robert see how her heart was breaking. She did not speak but willed Sharon to hear all she could not say.

Please understand. He would take everything. Everything.

"You should go home," she said. Mary did not want to watch

her world break apart, Sharon's lovely face stoic even as her eyes betrayed her, but she forced herself to. It was what she deserved. Her cowardice laid bare.

Sharon clamped her mouth shut. There was nothing left to say. They'd said it all back at the tree. Not even Robert could take that from them. Mary knew she would hold those moments close until her body went back into the dirt. A single, shining moment in the dull expanse of her life.

Robert clenched her hand, he and Mary and Vera watching as Sharon made her way back to her car. She paused only once to look back at Mary, but then set her shoulders, a small smile on her mouth as she lifted her hand in farewell.

"Honestly, Mary." Robert pulled her hand upward once more and pulled the gold band from her finger. He turned it over in his palm and laughed. "What a cheap piece of junk. I can't believe you bought it." He reared back and threw the ring in the same direction Mary and Sharon had come; the dark swallowed it almost instantly.

Mary stifled a cry. Wherever it landed, that was where she was also buried. She would leave that woman behind. The woman who loved Sharon. The woman who'd finally tasted happiness but had everything to lose. After all, she knew so much about dishonesty; it would be simple to become that other woman again. The happy housewife. The content mother.

But how long would it be until she could not exist inside that person anymore? How long until she cut her body open to let her true self out? Until everything she'd chosen out of weakness killed her?

Robert wrapped his arm around her waist and tugged her to him. That space where she'd learned to shrink herself to fit. "Don't worry, love. I'll buy you something nicer. You are my wife, after all. A husband should see to it that his wife has nice things." He turned, and she followed, her body responding to his even as she wanted to bite and scratch like some feral animal.

"Vera, I'll give you a ride home," he said.

Vera had not moved. It was as if some outside force struck her down. Some great, unseen, malevolent hand descended to render her motionless. A curse brought to life. But Robert's voice startled her, and she blinked. Shivered as if some many-legged thing crept over her skin.

"That's okay. I was out for a walk. I can get back on my own," Vera said.

"Nonsense. Gerry would kill me if he knew I let you walk home alone in the dark like this." He opened both the passenger and back doors.

"I couldn't impose—"

His voice dropped into what Mary knew was a warning. "Get in the car, Vera."

Vera scuttled forward, and both women let Robert guide them into the seats. It felt so foreign to Mary. To sit in the same seat she occupied hours earlier, the excitement and anticipation she'd felt now so foreign. A ghost from some forgotten time.

As he drove, Robert fiddled with the radio dial, but all Mary heard was static. She was keenly aware of Vera in the backseat. The sudden shift of her body against the leather as Robert took the turns too quickly. The damp, earthy smell of her sweat. It made Mary wonder what *she* smelled like. If she smelled like Sharon. If Robert tried to kiss her, would he taste Sharon on her mouth and tongue?

Every light was blazing when they pulled up Vera's drive. Gerry sat on the top porch step and stood when he saw them, his arms folded as he watched the car come to a stop.

"You stay put, Mary. I'm going to have a quick word with Gerry," Robert said. He opened the door and crossed in front of the car.

From the backseat came Vera's harsh whisper. "I didn't tell him. Just that you were with her. I'm so sorry, Mary."

And then Robert opened the door, and Vera was gone.

Her vision blurred. She wanted to weep hysterically. To scream and kick and break every window, the glass sharp beneath her palm, her blood bright under the moonlight. There was so little relief in what Vera told her. There'd been no real threat. Only a dim sort of doubt on Robert's part. Perhaps a touch of jealousy that the attention his wife should be paying him was being given to another woman. Robert might not know the full truth about her and Sharon, but Mary had still lost so much.

They looked unnatural. Robert and Gerry. Their faces blurred through the windshield and Mary's screen of tears as they talked about their wives. Their suspicions. They were not bad men. They did not dream of the give of their wives' flesh under their hands. But they lived in a world of male expectations, and their wives had found aberrant paths. They required correction.

When Robert got back into the car, Mary's face was dry.

"I talked to Mother this afternoon. She said she's not going to be able to keep the baby anymore. It's too much for her. I'll call John in the morning. Let him know you'll need to quit without two weeks' notice. Can't be helped. He'll find someone else, I'm sure."

She would be a caged animal with no teeth. No claws. Forever hungry and haunted by a memory of a life that could never belong to her.

But there was her daughter. If for nothing else, she would try to live for her.

She heard her own voice as if from some impossible depth. "Of course, darling."

Days passed like hours. Hours passed like days.

She became a blank space. A projection of wifely duty. A routine sleepwalking through childcare and homecare and church that left her fatigued and listless.

Robert tried to cheer her up. He really did. Brought her flowers. A cashmere twinset. Another ring to replace the one he'd thrown—the center sapphire so large she had difficulty lifting her finger when she wore it. He came home from work on time and spent an appropriate amount of time cooing over the baby. On Saturdays, he rose before she did and made breakfast. Eggs. Toast. Brought her coffee in bed and told her she was the most beautiful woman he'd ever seen. He would have made an excellent husband to some other woman.

At night, she dreamed of Sharon, and it was only then, in the quiet dark of their bedroom when she woke from the dreams with Robert snoring softly beside her, that she would allow herself to cry.

Every morning, Robert kissed her and the baby goodbye. She would wait exactly seventeen minutes after she heard his car leave the drive and then torture herself by sitting beside the telephone, wondering if that day would be the day she would find the courage to pick up the phone and call Sharon.

She never did. She felt that somehow Robert would find out, and she had no reason for doing it other than her own desperation. His suspicions had been put to bed but not completely undone. He would see how transparent she was, how he had been tricked. But she liked the smooth weight of it in her hand. The click it made as she settled the receiver back into its cradle. The operator on the other end must have hated her.

When she woke to the first chilly day in October, her mouth ached as if she'd bitten her cheek in the night. But when she craned her head before the mirror, she saw nothing but pink, spongy tissue. She swished her mouth with antiseptic, wincing at the sting, and spat, the sink a pink spatter she rinsed away.

By the end of the day, there were two sores on her mouth and another tickling at the back of her throat.

She was not afraid. Women in Hawthorne Springs were sick from time to time. Some strange virus that came and went with varying degrees of intensity. When she was a girl, a woman had died from it—some scandal that no one would talk about but involved a tree—but there'd been nothing like that since.

And there were still mornings when she woke, warm and soft and coated in sleep, that she forgot Sharon was absent from her life, the realization slamming into her with a force that took her breath away. It was on those mornings she wished for the clean simplicity of death.

Robert called doctors suggested to him by other husbands. One by one they came out to the house or Robert drove her to their clinics and held her hand as they examined her and told her they'd not seen anything like this before, and would she like an antibiotic? Painkiller? Perhaps a sedative?

"Don't worry. We'll get you fixed up. Right as rain," Robert would say after each appointment, the worry in his face more and more apparent.

"I'm not worried," she told him, and swallowed. Something inside her throat had worked itself free. It tasted gamy. Like something wild that had been hunted and left too long in the sun.

When she lost a molar, she hid it from Robert. Wrapped it in a handkerchief and buried it in the back of the drawer that held her underwear. Somehow, it felt important to keep this from him. Her disintegration.

In the quiet moments throughout the day when the baby slept, she could close her eyes and let herself go still. In that silence she felt as if there was a warm, hungry mouth buried somewhere in the depths of her chest, worming its way through her tissue, intent only on consumption. When it was finished with her, she wondered where it would go. That unending hunger. If it would find another body to inhabit—a carrion devil hunting its next meal—or if it would die with her.

THE NIGHT BEFORE Mary went to the tree, she dreamed of hair in her throat. She woke gagging and reached into the raw emptiness of her mouth and pulled and pulled. Long strings of hair dragged over her tongue and teeth. It clung to her hands, those damp, sticky coils like a second skin she could not peel away no matter how she tried.

She flushed the clump of hair down the toilet and washed the blood from her hands from where her teeth had scratched her skin.

She took the baby, her thought being they could both use the fresh air. She could not shake the sensation of that hair lodged in her throat, and she wanted out of the house. Out of that stale air that tasted like dust and her confinement. She wanted to feel the sun on her skin. To know the possibility of a freedom not granted to her.

And so, with her daughter sleeping in her arms, she left the front door open behind her and walked into the woods.

The sun she'd hoped for was absent. The day overcast, the clouds dark and heavy. The air held a thickness that spoke of rain, but she did not hurry. Her muscles ached from lack of use. Her body had gone soft from the limitations of her wifely movements, so she trod slowly, her gaze fixed firmly on the ground. She didn't want to trip and fall while holding the baby.

It took longer to get to the tree than she'd expected. Nothing in Hawthorne Springs was very far apart, but by the time she came through the clearing, she was panting, her shirtwaist damp with sweat. But she couldn't stop and rest. Some part of her was compelled to go to the tree. To stand beneath it, the memory of her skin pressed against its bark alive and burning inside her once more. As she drew closer, the desire to see it, to touch it, became a primal need. Her mouth and throat burned, and she gasped against the sudden onslaught of pain. The sores on her lips burst. She didn't bother to wipe the blood away as she told herself not to run no matter how she wanted to. She would wake the baby.

Even as she stepped up to the tree and pressed her forehead against the bark, those many screaming mouths impressing themselves on her skin, she was not satiated. She could not smell Sharon's perfume. The bark was not the gentle give of Sharon's waist and thighs. The ghosts they'd been here had long fled, exorcised to some other, kinder dimension.

The baby shifted in her arms and let out a tiny wail.

"Shhh. It's okay, little one." Mary bounced her, and she settled back into that deep sleep only babies are capable of.

She stared up into the canopy. So much green it was if the leaves had remade the sky into something alien. Those endless branches, some bare, but most heavily laden, so plentiful it made her dizzy.

So many of the bare branches were sharp. The beauty of the leaves a disguise against something far more insidious. A trap set for an unsuspecting creature.

She wondered what it would be like to hang herself from one of them. To pierce her heart with one of those sharp ends and leave her body to rot. Food for the scavengers. If she would finally find some sort of peace or just another form of hell.

Something shifted in the branches, and she startled. Some animal. A movement too quick to track, but she felt a presence there. The sensation of something looking back at her.

Another burst of movement. Dark fur. The quick flash of an eye.

She peered upward at the fur in confusion. It was too dark to be a squirrel. She knew there were other sorts, but she'd only ever seen gray squirrels, and the fur was too plentiful, too smooth to identify as any other animal she could think of.

If only it wasn't so green, she would be able to see better. She squinted and shaded her eyes as she watched whatever it was in the tree unfold, and she realized then, it wasn't fur she was looking at. Not fur at all.

It was hair.

Two women looked back at her, their hair bound into a single braid. Forever joined in waking death. And she knew who they were. What they were. She'd known the parable Pastor Brighton told since she was a girl, but she'd always dismissed it as a childish story.

The Dark Sisters.

She wanted to scream. To tuck the baby tight against her and run. But the same thing that compelled her to come to the tree locked her in place, and wasn't there a part of her that wanted what was about to happen? That had seen those sharpened branches and wondered about it only moments before? To know the sensation of pushing herself onto one of those branches, her skin breaking open to let it in?

"This is a dream," she said. But she knew it wasn't.

Gently, she laid the baby on the ground and kissed her forehead.

"Mama loves you, Ada. So much," she said, and turned back to the tree.

And then, she began to climb.

INTERLUDE: 1751

It was spite that still animated my body as one season gradually faded into the next. The wheel of the year ever turning onward as Florence's rage tethered me to the living world. It ate of me even as I wondered what there could have possibly been left to take.

The illness took me apart in small bits and found pleasure in that gradual decline. It was exactly as Florence had asked, so when I woke in the night, my very blood humming with the desire to go to the tree, I was astonished. I had thought this illness would carry on until I was a living corpse. A stretch of desiccated skin over stinking bones. A heart shriveled and black but pumping still because *she* had willed it so.

I had never imagined any sort of salvation for myself. The acceptance I spoke of with Florence would not be granted to me, and I knew it as surely as I knew my daughter's loathing.

Even as the need grew, I went to the tree slowly. My body could not withstand the strain, and I found the need to rest and to spit the blood from my mouth frequently. I'd long forgotten any pretense of civility and spat like a man. I would carry this small, carnal pleasure with me into death.

There was no moon. I'd long lost track of its cycle. Whether it was new or simply hidden by clouds, I did not know. Yet another thing to grieve. Her cold light gave me such comfort throughout my life. It felt like a betrayal to leave this world without her pale touch on my skin.

As I passed through the final group of trees and into the clearing, I knew, somehow, that she would be waiting for me. Florence, beneath the tree, her once lovely mouth covered in those sores I'd come to know so well. The pain they wrought become such an intimate bedfellow, I wondered what sort of woman I was before. If I had ever known life without that deep ache.

"I felt it would be tonight," she said, stepping out from the shadows. I could barely make out her face, but I could see how gaunt she had grown. The space under her cheekbones sunken, and the sockets of her eyes hollow. Her belly withered. She'd had the baby then. My granddaughter. In that moment, I desperately wanted to see the child. To hold her in my arms and bless her with what magic still lingered in my wasting bones.

Florence continued. "I wanted to be here. When you came to the tree. I wanted to see it happen."

I bowed my head. The exhaustion of having come so far pulled me toward the earth. "You found me a hard mother. Unyielding. Believed I foisted my beliefs upon you and then frowned in disapproval when you turned elsewhere. That I schemed to turn you from the life you so desired. The god you wished to worship. I cannot plead innocence in that. I have been fallible, and those faults are my own. Whatever anger you have for me, cast it aside. Even if for a moment. I do not want to take your hatred with me, Florence. You are a mother now. You must understand that."

"Do not speak of my daughter." She barked a deep, wet cough.

"Are you also afraid, Florence? That soon enough it will be your turn to come to the tree?"

She did not answer, but I saw the fear in her face. The shadow that passed over her countenance.

"I may be damned, but there is still time yet for you. To accept the darkness in yourself as well as the light. To not draw away from it. If nothing else, to *try*. To see your daughter grown, wouldn't it be worth it?"

I wanted to face her, my daughter, but the tree's pull was too great. The curse called me home, and there would be no allowance for me. Florence had made sure. I took a step toward it.

"I will not condemn my soul to hell. No matter the cost. I am no witch. I have not signed my name in the devil's book," she said.

"Oh, Florence. You would be so willfully blind. Even now." I was at the tree, my hand on the bark that held the sap that gave us so much. "You've seen what its magic can do. The sap and then our blood. Yours and mine. How it brought us riches. Plenty. Good health. But we must take the good with the bad. You must accept it all, and only then will this illness recede."

"I gave it my blood, but I am no witch," she shouted. Her voice echoed back, an endless litany of denial.

I began to climb the tree, my body hungry for its branch. I wept, the tears obscuring my vision, but I did not need to see. My body knew where to go, and I would not need to go far.

"Perhaps you will not claim it in name, but you offered it your blood in exchange for what you called justice. You carry the tree's magic in your veins. As do I and Hope. As did Joan. As will all our daughters. Yours included. They will prosper even as they suffer unless you tell them what I've said. They must accept all parts of themselves. The light and the dark."

I stopped climbing, my feet steady against the branch as I stepped forward. It extended over a shorter branch, the leaves stripped away to reveal a sharp point. Seeing it, I felt myself let go. Whatever fear I felt vanished as I studied the branch. With what strength I had left, I would be able to grasp the upper branch and let my body swing down and onto the lower. This way, I would be looking at Florence. It felt right I leave this world looking at the only thing that ever made me want to keep living in it.

When I reached the end of the lower, pointed branch, I turned to face the trunk, pressed my body flat, wrapped my arms around the bark, and then pushed myself backward until my legs dropped over the branch's edge. Never in my life had I contained such strength, but I knew there was an outside force making certain its end of the bargain was held. Another push, and I swung, the final inches dropping away as my chest went over the edge and only my arms circled the upper branch.

Beneath me, Florence let out a garbled cry, and I gazed down at her, wanting to see her eyes one final time.

But she was not looking at me. Instead, she stared past me, her face stricken.

"Gideon," she said.

Once more, my body swung, the branch rising to meet it. As it pierced my chest, the skin tearing away, my arms and chest blood slick, I watched as my daughter fell to the ground, her hand covering her mouth as her husband advanced on her.

"A pity. I had hoped there was nothing of your mother in you. That her influence had been torn out by the root." He cocked his head as he looked at his wife. At my daughter. "But it is not as I hoped. You are your mother's daughter after all. Engaged in the very practices you claimed to refuse. Marked by Satan's finger," he said.

The world around me grew dim, as if I observed everything beneath me from a great distance. I could not cry out. Could not tell Florence to run. Death was fast approaching, and it would allow me no voice.

"I have not—"

"I have heard all, Florence. That you have engaged in a blood ritual at this tree. That you have participated in witchcraft. There is no denying it." He gripped her by the shoulders and pulled her to her feet.

"Gideon. Please. Think of our daughter. Think of Felicity."

"I will raise her in the way she should be. Without your poisonous influence, she will grow into a good, Christian woman." He lifted her easily. She'd grown so thin; it couldn't have taken much effort.

He looked on her with disgust and turned to face the tree. "You know the Bible verse as well as I do, dear wife."

As the blood leaked from my body, he smiled.

"'Thou shalt not suffer a witch to live.'"

CHAPTER XIII

2007

It took less than an hour for Camilla to clean her mother up. To help her into the shower, gently rinse the blood from her chin and neck, and help her change into a clean nightgown before settling her back into bed. Her mother said nothing else after she pulled the final tooth from her gums, but allowed Camilla to manipulate her body like a catatonic, brunette Barbie.

Somehow, she managed to find a single bottle of disinfectant squirreled away in a secondary pantry. Angela's organization system was designed so the Burson family lived in a fantasy world where cleaning supplies didn't have to be seen, but with the disinfectant and a roll of paper towels, Camilla picked up the teeth and cleaned the blood from the floor.

It was a relief to let herself fall into such simple actions. The act of cleaning kept her from thinking about her mother's insistence that the Dark Sisters weren't real. It kept her from sobbing because if Camilla couldn't make the connection between the tree and the Sisters and the illness, her mother and Brianna were going to die.

She was burying the last bloodied paper towel at the bottom of the trash when she heard a knock at the kitchen entrance's door.

She shrieked and stumbled backward before she dropped to the floor, her hand over her mouth.

She wasn't supposed to be here. She could only hope that whoever was at the door hadn't heard her.

She crept forward on hands and knees until she was safely behind the kitchen island and then tucked her knees into her chest. If it was her father sending someone back to check on her, he would have sent Angela or someone who had a key. If he wanted to catch her in the act, he wouldn't have sent someone who announced themself by knocking.

Another knock, this one louder, as if the person on the other side was hammering the door with their fist, and then, two voices she knew almost as well as she knew her own. Noah and Brianna.

"Camilla, it's just us."

"Open the door."

Her body unfolded, the tension in her muscles draining away. She pushed herself to her knees, stood, and, on trembling legs, made her way to the door and opened it.

"Oh, thank God." Brianna pulled her in for a hug. "Noah texted and said your dad was at the church, but you and your mom weren't. I was worried something was wrong. We didn't have a way to call you. Figured you didn't have your phone back yet and calling the house phone didn't seem like a great idea either."

"Y'all shouldn't be here. They'll be looking for you," Camilla said.

"Noah's the only one who's supposed to be at church right now. I'm under strict orders to stay inside the house." Brianna pointed to a small sore in the right corner of her mouth. "This popped up last night. Mom and Dad don't want anyone to see. Apparently, they don't care that I feel better. It only matters what it looks like. If anyone knew I was sick, things would be even worse for us. As if we weren't already practically the roadkill of Hawthorne Springs."

"And, it doesn't matter if *I'm* not there. No one's going to be looking for me. And we know how to get past the cameras just as well as you do," Noah said.

"How'd you even get back home?" Brianna asked.

"Told the driver I had lady problems."

Noah crinkled his nose. "Ew."

"See? It's a classic for a reason. Works on you idiots every time," Brianna said. Her face grew serious as she reached out, her hand hovering over Camilla's sleeve. "You have blood on you."

"My mom," Camilla began, but her chest went tight, and she couldn't breathe. The words snarled in her chest like barbed wire, and she gasped for air as Noah and Brianna supported her between them and guided her inside.

"It's okay. Just focus on feeling the air in your lungs. It's there, I promise," Noah said as he settled her onto the couch in their sitting room.

Brianna sank onto the couch beside her and took her hand. "We're here. You're safe."

They sat with her until her chest unlocked, her breath finally slowing as her lungs expanded.

It was Brianna who finally broke the silence. "If you don't want to talk about it, you don't have to."

"No. It's okay," she said, and drew in another steadying breath.

She told it all. Her mother was sick, and her father had lied about it. He was keeping her hidden away. Her mother still wouldn't admit that she'd seen the Dark Sisters. She'd pulled out several teeth and was now catatonic upstairs while her father was preaching a sermon at the church, his fury likely mounting each moment he glanced at their empty family pew.

"Where's the phone?" Brianna said when Camilla finally reached the end.

"In the kitchen. Why?"

Brianna rose, her strides long and purposeful as she went into the kitchen and then made her way back. "You need to call your dad. Now."

"He's in the middle of the service."

"Doesn't matter. Leave a message. Listen, you need to keep

your story consistent. You got your period. You had to come home. Shower. Change. You were going to come back, but you felt awful and just couldn't." Brianna thrust the cordless into Camilla's hand.

"He won't believe me."

"Maybe he will, maybe he won't, but saying nothing will only make things worse. At least this way, he might doubt the story, but he won't outright reject the possibility it might be true. Also, Noah, care to demonstrate your reaction to the mention of 'lady problems' again?"

He screwed up his face in mock horror. "Eww!"

"Exactly. Call him. Leave a message. And then we can figure out the rest."

Camilla dialed her father's cell number. As it rang, she put her free hand in her hair and dug a nail into the scab she knew was there. Brianna swatted her hand away and whispered, "Stop that."

She did as Brianna told her. She dropped her hand and left the message, taking care she did not rush or seem panicked, and then hung up, pressing the end button three times and then checking for the dial tone to be certain the call disconnected.

"Okay. You're going to need a cell phone. So you have a way of reaching the outside world without anyone knowing," Brianna said, her gaze on Camilla.

"I can do that. A pay-as-you-go burner. No problem," Noah said.

Brianna squeezed his arm and smiled. "You'll have to keep it hidden. Your dad can't know you have it."

She rolled her eyes. "This isn't my first rodeo."

"I know it's not. Hey." Brianna took Camilla's face between her hands and leaned her forehead against Camilla's. "We're in this together, babe. All the way. We're going to figure it out."

"What if I'm wrong? What if none of this is connected at all?"

"We're not doing that, Camilla. Listen." She pulled backward, her eyes narrowing. "Didn't you say Vera was with your mom when she saw the Sisters? Or that she'd told Vera? And that Vera wanted to know if you saw them, too?"

Vera. Of course. How stupid she hadn't thought of it sooner. If her mother wouldn't explain what she'd seen, maybe Vera would.

"I need to talk to Vera," she said. Noah would have the cell phone for her soon, but she didn't know when he would be able to sneak it back to her. It could be a few days. It could be a few weeks. She wasn't sure she could wait that long, but she didn't know how she could get to Vera without her father knowing.

"In the meantime, we stick to the plan. Be good. Do everything right," Brianna stood, and with Noah following behind, made her way to the door.

"I'll get the phone to you as soon as I can," Noah said.

Camilla hugged both of them, her gratitude a painful lump in her chest as she watched them go. Somehow, she'd found two people who loved her fiercely and whom she loved back. It was more than she deserved. Such true friendship was more than anyone deserved.

She forced herself back upstairs. When her father came home to check on her, he needed to believe her story. Within ten minutes, Camilla was tucked into bed, her dress a tangle on the rug. Down the hall, her mother also lay quiet as the walls closed over them. Strange how such a large house could feel like a coffin.

It was almost as if she slept. Almost as if she dreamed.

When she finally came back into her body, her father sat at the foot of her bed with his head bowed. She didn't bother to sit up, only watched him and wondered if he doubted her. If he looked at her sleeping and saw a viper instead of his daughter. Regardless, she had to play the part.

"Hey," she said, her voice barely a scratch. Even still, he started, his head flying up so his carefully combed hair came tumbling over his brow.

"You're awake." He stood and then resettled next to her, his hands trembling as he reached to tuck her hair behind her ears like he had when she was little. Hope sparked in her blood, but she couldn't let herself fall into it completely. Not yet. There were still plenty of reasons to remain wary.

"How long have I been sleeping?"

"About six hours. You missed dinner, but I thought it best you get some rest." He cleared his throat and pointedly glanced away. "Since you aren't feeling well."

He smiled and patted her hand before closing his fingers around it. Such a small act, but she felt as if he'd swallowed her up—her body vanishing against the power that was his.

"I was thinking, now that you're home, and since you weren't in service today to hear the sermon, I want to throw a little dinner party. To celebrate how well you did on Retreat. A preparty before all the Purity Ball chaos."

"You don't have to do that," she said, forcing a shy smile. She'd known it would happen, that her father would trot her out like some prize pony, but she had not anticipated it in such an intimate setting as her own home. This party and her reaction to it was a test. Her father's voice was lighthearted but she knew the keenness in his gaze. Every movement was being measured against some metric only he understood.

"Already done. Invitations went out about an hour ago. I told Chef quail eggs and caviar to start. You went on and on about them at Christmas last year. Thought it would be a nice treat."

She didn't dare ask about her mother when she already knew he would keep her locked away. "When is it?"

"Tuesday night. I figured that'll give Chef enough time to prepare. And you time enough to get to feeling better."

Two days. Of course, he wouldn't want to wait any longer than necessary. She'd robbed him of his moment of triumph by skipping that day's sermon. If he could have pulled the party off that night, he would have done it.

She stretched her mouth further. A beauty queen smile. "Who's invited?"

"Darlin', I invited *everyone*."

She could only hope everyone also meant Noah and Brianna and Vera. If her father told the truth, it meant Noah would have an opportunity to bring her a phone, and, if she was lucky and very careful, she would be able to sneak away from the party and find a way to talk with Vera.

But when Camilla came down the stairs on her father's arm two nights later—her lungs aching against the corset top of her dress—Noah, and Brianna, and Vera were noticeably absent from the crowd in the foyer.

As expected, her mother was locked in her room, monitored by a nurse who looked less friendly bedside manner and more undercover assassin. Camilla had been allowed inside her room the night before to say goodnight, the watchful eyes of her father and the nurse preventing her from doing anything more than offering a whispered "I love you."

Her father placed his hand on her arm as he guided her down the steps. "You look lovely. I knew you weren't my little girl anymore, but I hadn't realized you'd become a woman." They reached the bottom, and a round of applause went up that made Camilla want to die even as she dipped her head in assumed humility.

She thought of her mother upstairs. Her teeth and her blood on the floor. She thought of her mother so she would not forget why she had to play the good girl.

"Thank you, Daddy."

He hugged her, and there was more clapping, and she wondered how much kerosene it would take to set the house on fire. After she got her mother out, of course.

Camilla drifted from group to group, dropping kisses on the women's cheeks and turning her body away from the men's hugs, their hands lingering at the small of her back as they told her what a good daughter she was. An inspiration. That she was a prize who would one day make someone a very lucky husband. She breathed through it. The good girl. She was temperate. She was submissive. She was gentle and hospitable. She could be all those things if it meant her father would believe them and turn his attention from her for even just a moment.

After Beau Fannin ignored propriety and let his liver-spotted hands rest firmly on her backside, she excused herself. "Enjoy the party," she said instead of kicking him in the crotch.

She closed herself in the downstairs powder room, locked the door behind her, and then checked it three times before she leaned against the sink.

"It's okay. You're okay," she said.

Two minutes. Then five. Outside, someone gave a delicate knock and then drifted away to find an unoccupied toilet.

She could do this. Even without Noah and Brianna. She'd hoped they would be there, but she should have known better. Her father never had any intention of inviting anyone who might serve as a negative influence on her, and Brianna's family was likely still keeping her hidden away. But it would be okay. They would help her, and she could figure out a way to talk with Vera. She blotted her face, touched up her lipstick, and forced herself to smile even if it looked more like she was snarling.

Already, the party's volume had risen, so when her father announced dinner was served, Camilla felt a rush of relief. At least her ass would be firmly planted in her seat and shielded from any wayward hands.

The dining room glowed. Candlelight caught at the china's cream-and-gold pattern, the table linen, the bowls of roses and lily of the valley all lit like holy relics, the crystal already filled with the dark jewel tones of her father's finest grand cru. A fairy tale breathed into life by wealth and prestige.

Heavy ecru place cards marked each setting, the calligraphy blurred in the golden light so that each guest leaned forward to read them, the women holding their hands to their chests to keep themselves modest. Each one of them quickly calculating their position within the church, how much esteem they held, based on their distance from the shepherd of their flock. The party might have been in Camilla's honor, but she held no power, even if she was the one seated at her father's right hand.

Her gaze drifted toward the seat beside her, her face growing hot as she read the name. *Ada Burson.* She turned away and dug her nails into her palm. She blinked back the tears that were threatening to form as she simultaneously willed herself not to reach over and tear the name card into ragged pieces.

Her father would have never allowed her mother to attend the party, not in her condition, but the name card was an act. A counterfeit demonstration meant to show his congregation the care he still showed his ailing wife. If Camilla was the good girl, he was the devoted husband.

After a prayer and the first and second course, Camilla managed to swallow two spoonfuls of beluga and a singular bite of endive, but she was on her second glass of red wine—fuck it, she'd get her teeth bleached before the Ball—when a voice interrupted what she hoped was the tingling beginning of drunkenness.

"Seems a shame that the person this entire party is for has somehow ended up sitting alone." The voice was a graveled sort of music. A warm depth that invited her to sink.

"You're never alone if you have a drink." Without bothering to look up and see who it was who'd spoken to her, she lifted her glass toward the voice and took another sip.

"May I?"

Camilla glanced again at the place card, at her mother's name, and then let her heart turn to stone. If she was going to make it through the night, she had to lock those emotions away. At least she had the wine.

"Knock yourself out," she said, tipped her glass again, and then frowned. Empty.

"Looks like I got here just in time. Could you bring her another?" The waiter standing at the head of the table dipped his head and, as if by magic, the bottle appeared in his hand, and he began to pour.

"My hero," she said, and then, finally, turned to take in the person who inserted himself in her mother's chair.

She bit down on her tongue, the sarcasm she called up vanishing as she tried not to gape at Grant Pemberton, who was grinning back at her.

His hair was longer than when she last saw him, and he wore it swept back from his face. A navy blazer made his eyes look darker, more gray than the blue she'd memorized at fifteen. He hadn't bothered with a tie and left the top button of his shirt undone; he smiled as he watched her gaze drift toward that bare skin.

She flushed and looked away, and not because she was playing the good girl.

At the very least she had the good sense to feel guilty. She couldn't sit here at a party thrown in the name of her virtue, in the same house as her sick mother, and flirt with Grant Pemberton. But it felt good to let herself lean toward him. To allow herself this small excitement, the wine warming her blood.

"Thank you."

"The very least I could do," he said.

"Thought you'd gone off to Connecticut for good."

"And leave all this behind?" He lifted his own glass in a sweeping motion. "Never. Besides, studying for the bar is a little easier at home. Fewer temptations."

She lifted an eyebrow, watching him over the rim of her glass. "You sure about that?"

He laughed then, and it set her body on fire because she knew it shouldn't. Because it wasn't pure or modest or chaste to want him. Because she wasn't fifteen anymore, and God, couldn't she just have this one thing? To feel wanted for this one night?

"Maybe not so sure. Can't hurt to find out," he said, and she wanted him to lean into her, to brush his hand against her thigh so she could burn, but he turned to Brian Stillman on the other side of him, who was slapping his back and saying something about how no one ever could find a decent woman north of the Mason–Dixon line like the shit heel he was.

She sipped her wine, but she'd lost the need she'd had for it only minutes before. She dipped a finger into the liquid and watched as a scarlet droplet traced its way to her wrist. Like blood against bark. Like one braid twisting into another.

With a quick, feral movement, she drew her tongue over the trickle and let her eyes drift closed. Maybe she would drink it, after all.

Something brushed against her leg, and her eyes snapped open. She looked down and watched as Grant poked her again. He reached for his glass, his body angled away from Brian Stillman, and mouthed *help me*.

She stifled a grin as he slowly turned back to the conversation. She lifted her glass to her lips, let the liquid flood her mouth before swallowing. No harm in making him wait.

She placed her hand on Grant's shoulder and leaned forward, "Grant, I meant to ask, when do you plan to take the bar exam?"

"In September. If I don't die of sleep deprivation before then."

Brian Stillman still hovered over Grant's shoulder, so she barreled on. "You'll be here for the Purity Ball then?"

"I will. A little birdie told me you're participating this year? I'd have thought you already went through it. Being the preacher's daughter and all."

Her scalp itched. She folded her hands in her lap so she would not scratch at it. No matter how the sensation of a scab tearing away, blood under her fingernails, would alleviate her embarrassment. "Better late than never."

He considered her. "Hmm. That's exactly how I felt about law school."

Her nerves were still fragile, capable of reducing her to the naïve, fifteen-year-old she'd once been, but she pushed her shoulders back and lifted her glass toward him. This, too, was an act of a different sort than the good girl. A variation born from her foundation. "To new friends," she said.

"And purity," he said, and winked before downing his glass and motioning for another.

For the rest of the night, Grant stayed beside her, and she forgot her worry. Her fear. Her mother upstairs and the Dark Sisters and the illness that connected them all like some insidious string of pearls.

In those moments with Grant, all she knew, all she could feel, was her own longing. Her desire to rake her teeth along Grant's throat and feel the give of flesh as she bit down. She imagined he would taste of ocean salt.

Once, she would have felt shame over such thoughts. She was a student of purity and modesty, and even entertaining such things was an immorality worthy of judgment. Of punishment. But she had seen how their punishment wasn't meant for the sinner at all. There was no real path back to holiness in it. It was a tool for their own use. So her father could throw his little parties or stand in the pulpit and remind everyone it was his divine connection to God that kept them from Satan's clutches, and wasn't it worth a bit more in the collection plate each Sunday? So she drank too much wine and let herself think about moving her body over Grant's and the press of his fingers on her hips, and when he smiled at her, she smiled back.

She didn't notice when the party began to die down or when her father began the slow process of seeing their final guests out. And then Grant was standing beside her father, his hand clasped over Grant's as Grant thanked him for the dinner.

"Hope to see more of you," her father said. "Much more."

Beside him, Camilla could do little more than focus on not tipping over in her heels, but she smiled, hoping she didn't have lipstick on her teeth or smeared mascara beside her eyes.

And then she was somehow upstairs, her dress on the floor as she stumbled toward her bed, the room floating under her feet because she'd drunk too much wine and had too little to eat. She sank onto the mattress, closed her eyes, and then immediately opened them. The room was too slippery, everything shifting around her as she took deep breaths through her nose and out through her mouth. She gazed about the room, trying to orient herself in space, to settle on something that would keep the room from spinning as violently as it was, but the edges of this room, of her things, blurred, and she could not hold on to any singular item for long enough.

She shifted uncomfortably. Maybe it would be better to stand and move instead of trying to fight against it. She leaned forward and placed her hand on the nightstand so she could push herself to standing and jumped at the sound of glass and porcelain rattling.

On her nightstand was a glass of water, a plate with a slice of buttered toast, two Advil, and a single, impossibly beautiful rose. A note lay beside the plate, and she picked it up, not daring to hope.

Grant's handwriting was a tight collision of letters, and she had to squint through her wine haze to make out the words.

> Thought you might need this and asked someone to bring it up for you. And the rose... well, that's from me. Here's to avoiding temptation and to purity!

Below, he'd drawn a cartoonish figure buried behind a book and then his name in looping cursive.

She giggled, gobbled the toast, drank the water, and took her pills like a good girl and then crawled under her duvet.

That night she dreamed of goblets filled not with wine but with blood. And of Grant, his crimson-stained mouth on hers and filling her with the sharp edge of his teeth. When he bit down, when she bled, they drank of her together, and it was the only Communion she would ever need again.

When she woke the next morning, there was the lingering sense of something lost and a faint nausea she knew would have been worse had Grant not been so thoughtful. She curled into herself, the duvet tucked tight, because even as the pleasant memories of the night came back to her, she knew they'd been a temporary distraction. She still needed to keep up the charade with her father. She still needed to talk to Vera. To figure out what she knew about the Dark Sisters and how they might be connected to the illnesses.

She showered and wandered downstairs, following the scent of coffee into the kitchen where her father sat with his Bible open before him. She paused in the entrance, but he'd already seen her and flipped his Bible closed.

"There she is. Have a nice time last night?"

"Mmm. Is there coffee?"

"In the pot." He watched as she pulled down a mug and poured. "Seems like you and Grant hit it off."

She busied herself with hunting for skim milk. "He's nice. Funny."

"He'll make some lucky girl a good husband one day. How's your luck feeling these days, darlin'?"

Heat built in her chest, burned its way up her throat, and she knew if she turned around, he would read the secret of how she felt there. And if he could read that secret, how good of an actress could she possibly be?

"I said he was nice, not that I wanted to marry him."

"Clock's ticking down there, hon. I married your mom when she was seventeen. An unattached woman without a husband's guidance is a danger to her brethren. To her community." His voice took on the cadence it did every Sunday. "You of all people understand the importance of that. Besides, you could do worse. I'm thinking of offering him a leadership position once he finishes law school. Not to mention the man looks like he was sculpted out of marble." He pushed his chair back from the island and gathered his Bible. "Got to run. Meeting with Brandon Thompson today to go over a few things for the Purity Ball. Oh! Speaking of the Ball . . ." He pulled his cell phone from his pocket and held it toward her.

She blinked down at the phone, her gaze blurring as she tried to make sense of what was on the screen. He laughed as she blinked stupidly.

"I made an appointment. At Dior. 30 Montaigne. In Paris. Told them it was a fashion emergency. You'll need a dress, and since your mom isn't feeling well, I figured I could help. We only have a week left. Most girls have had their dresses for months."

There was an ancient, deadened part of her that fluttered dimly awake. Once, she would have squealed and thrown herself at him without pretense. That part of her still existed in some small way, but she knew it would never be the same again. She'd buried that girl, and there had been no one there to mourn.

She acted it out though. Flung herself into her father's arms and ignored how it made her skin crawl to know how easily he'd tossed her aside the moment she didn't fit his expectations.

"Thank you, thank you. You have no idea."

"That's my girl." He pulled himself away and dropped a kiss on her forehead. She kept her gaze lowered, so she wouldn't be tempted to scrub it off in disgust like a child. "I'll be back soon, but the nurse is here if your mother needs anything. I expect you'll be here when I get back?"

He phrased it as a question, but she knew he meant it as a statement. A commandment she wouldn't dare break.

"Of course. Be careful," she said.

Back upstairs she went, coffee in hand, where her mother's door remained closed. She considered knocking, letting the nurse lie and say her mother was sleeping and couldn't be disturbed, but she turned and went back to her bedroom. Hearing the lie yet again would do nothing to change what was happening.

She would put on her makeup and do her hair, so when her father came home, he would see the effort she made and be pleased. Another step toward earning his trust.

She settled at her vanity and unzipped her makeup bag. Nestled on the top was a scrap of paper, meticulously folded. She smiled as she unfolded it, wondering how Grant could have possibly managed to sneak a note into her bathroom. Angela might have agreed to the water and toast and Advil, but this was a line she would not have crossed.

But it wasn't a note. It was a rushed sketch in the barest lines of pencil. What looked like a sink and a partially finished arrow pointing at its base.

She frowned. Was it supposed to mean something? Clearly, someone left it in a place they were certain she would find it but had taken care to hide it. She glanced over at the sink, the marble countertop with its crystal vase of pink roses gleaming, but there was nothing that caught her attention. Nothing out of place.

She glanced again at the drawing, wondering if she'd missed something. The arrow looked as if was a last-second addition, the pointed edge on the left side cut off as if the person drawing it had been interrupted while trying to add an important direction.

It hit her then. The drawing wasn't about the sink at all. It was what the arrow was pointing to. The cabinet under the sink.

She pushed back from her vanity, feeling more than a little stupid she hadn't immediately guessed at what the picture meant, knelt in front of the cabinet, and opened it. This was a singular space meant only for her, untouched by Angela and the other church members who comprised their cleaning staff, and it was filled with a variety of beauty products left there to die. She sank back on her heels and pulled out hairspray, self-tanner, body lotion that hadn't gotten rid of her cellulite like it promised, a series of eyeshadow palettes she'd forgotten she owned, three bottles of perfume gifted to her for white elephant parties, and a Lucite container with more bobby pins than should be legal.

She peered into the cabinet, past the bullshit detritus of her girlhood, thrust her hand into the very back, and swept everything out. Lip gloss, and nail polish, and hair clips, and maxi pads tumbled to the floor, and there, like a tiny, gift-wrapped miracle tucked behind the pipe she could never remember the name of, was a brick-shaped item wrapped in a dark cloth.

She pulled it out, testing the satisfying weight in her hand as she didn't bother to stifle her laugh. Noah had done it. Somehow, he'd gotten a phone inside her house.

"You absolute angel," she said as she unwrapped it. It was simple, no bells and whistles, but it would call and text, and that was all she needed.

She opened the home screen, where there was already a single text notification.

> It's me. Let me know when you find this. I paid Joel Franzen to sneak it into your dinner party since I wasn't invited, but he's an idiot, so . . . I pre-programmed the numbers for me and Brianna in case you're a normal person and don't have them memo-rized. And for Vera.

She typed a quick response. Got it. I hope Joel Franzen knows how to keep his mouth shut.

Noah replied almost instantly. He will. I paid him enough.

As she clicked away from the text messages, her hands shook. Her father was gone, and she was inside her locked bedroom. It would have to be now. She needed it to be now.

She pulled up the saved contacts and selected Vera's name.

Her throat went dry, and she wanted to stand, to run the tap and thrust her face under it and drink until her stomach ached, but she remained on the floor and waited as the phone rang three times. Four times.

"Pick up," she pleaded.

Five times. Six.

She dropped her head toward the floor, her body wilting. She could call again. Could call over and over, but it was possible Vera wouldn't pick up. Would assume it was a prank or a spam call and ignore it.

But the next ring didn't sound. There was only a slight crackling and then silence.

"Hello?" Camilla spoke into the silence, unwilling to let herself hope.

"Who is this?"

She let out a quiet sob.

"Vera, it's me. It's Camilla."

CHAPTER XIV

1953

"Mary? What are you doing?"

It was Vera's voice that broke through Mary's reverie, the confusion and fear in it pulling her back into her body. She'd cut her hand as she climbed, her blood a sticky smear against the bark.

"I ... I didn't ... I don't ..." She stared down at Vera and the screaming baby in her arms. There'd been something important. Something she came here to do, but she couldn't remember. And why was Vera holding a baby? She'd never had a child. She'd never wanted them.

The muscles in her limbs burned from the strain of pulling herself up the tree, but she felt the urge to go higher, to find a branch without leaves and bearing a pointed end.

"Mary, I think you should come down now," Vera said. She kept her tone light, but Mary could hear the edge in it. "Ada is upset. She needs you."

"Ada," she whispered. Above her the tree rustled, but she looked only at the baby. At *her* baby. Her baby who was crying and wanted her mother.

"I'm coming," she said. As she descended, it was almost as if the tree sighed, as if it pulled against her, reluctant to let her go, but she went carefully, holding her breath until her feet were fully planted on the ground.

She took Ada in her arms and breathed in the scent at the very top of her head. Ada flailed her tiny arms, still furious, and Mary shushed her.

"It's okay, love bunny. Mama's here."

"What were you doing?" Vera asked.

Mary startled. In that moment, even with Vera standing right there, she'd forgotten about her. She looked back at the tree, the leaves blurring. So much green. It was confusing. Her memories drifted like trails of smoke.

"I thought I saw something," she said, but that wasn't right. "No. Not something. Someone."

Vera looked past her and then turned slowly and took in the landscape around them. "I was out for a walk, and I haven't seen anyone. Other than you. There's no one else here."

Ada's skin was hot. Sticky. She clung to her mother, her cheeks flushed.

You could absorb her. Take her back into your body and finish what you started. Then she would be with you forever.

The thought was Mary's, but the voice belonged to someone else. She didn't want to have it. Awful thing. Vera looked at her expectantly. Had she asked her a question? Was there something she was supposed to say?

"What did you see?" Vera asked.

She remembered then. What she'd seen.

"Two women. In the tree. The Dark Sisters."

Vera glanced at the tree and back to Mary. Whatever was there had clearly gone.

"That's just a story."

Mary hummed. "I saw them. They were looking at me."

Vera took her arm and shifted away from the tree. "I think you're tired and need some rest. Let me help you back home."

"No." Mary tugged her arm from Vera as her muddled thoughts

cleared a bit more. "You told him. You told Robert. About Sharon. About me. And now he barely lets me out of the house. Watches me all the time. Keeps me locked up because he loves me and thinks if he just holds me a little tighter, I might love him back. The way he wants me to. That maybe if he fucks me enough, I'll learn to like it." She gulped at the air, but there were too many things she wanted to say. She could not draw enough breath to get them all out. "But all I think about is her. She's still alive, and she haunts me, and how do I love him instead, Vera? How do I love him instead?"

"Oh, honey." Vera pulled Mary in and hugged her, the baby wriggling between them in protest. "I'm so sorry. I should have never ... I was still so angry, and I saw him, and it all came out before I could even think."

Mary let Vera hold her. She was so tired, and there was a quieting part of her that still whispered she'd been so close. Just a few more inches and she could have rested. She could have closed her eyes and never bothered opening them again.

But Vera was here, and she was solid and real and good. They'd hurt each other. Secrets meant to sleep quietly, undisturbed in the dark, brought to light. There'd been no malice in it for either of them. Mary's heart softened, but it didn't change anything. She was still sick. Sharon was still gone. She could still not live the truth in her heart.

"It's okay," Mary said. Forgiving Vera would not erase her loss, but it was a lie worth telling. That everything would set itself right.

Her throat ached. It was as if someone was scratching at her from the inside. As if her throat had sprouted a full set of sharpened teeth and begun to consume itself. Something at the base of her spine spasmed, and she gagged against Vera's shoulder.

Vera stumbled backward as Mary coughed, her eyes widening as she watched Mary retch, her face turned away from the baby so it would not splatter against her perfect skin. The heated slick of the blood coating her teeth tasted foul, and she spat, but the taste lingered. She would never be rid of it.

"You're sick," Vera said.

"Yes."

"How long?"

"Long enough to know I'm not going to get better."

"Don't say that. There are doctors, and there have been other women who get better."

Mary shifted the baby, who watched the women with big, wet eyes and sucked noisily on two fingers. She'd not truly known until this moment, but she knew it with more certainty than she knew she loved Sharon. She was not going to get better.

The idea came to her all at once. If these were her last days, there was nothing left to fear. She could spend them as she wished. Could leave Hawthorne Springs, find Sharon, and live out her final hours in happiness.

But doing so would mean abandoning Ada. She could try to take her along, but she knew Robert would come looking for his daughter. He wouldn't rest until he found them, would involve the police if he had to, and he would bring, if not the both of them, then only Ada home, and Mary would die without ever seeing her daughter again.

No. She couldn't run. Besides, she had no money. No car. None of it had ever belonged to her. She was a bride of scarcity in all ways.

She would be happy with a single day. Even a few hours if that was all she could get. She knew it was wrong to ask Vera this favor—she didn't deserve it—but she had to.

"Would you help me, Vera?"

"If I can."

Again, her throat seemed to bloom into some malevolent, barbed organism, but she pushed past the need to cough, her eyes watering.

"Would you bring Sharon here? To your house?" She heaved a breath. "You could do it while Gerry is at work. Just a few hours, so I can see her one more time. Please."

Vera paled. "Mary. I—I can't. What if we got caught? Gerry is already suspicious. He hasn't said it outright, but I know he's heard the rumors about me. About why I haven't had any children yet. I think he wants to believe it's just gossip, but he watches me more closely now. Goes through my things. Listens in on the upstairs line whenever I get a phone call. I can hear him breathing." She reached out a hand and tucked Mary's hair behind her shoulders. "I love you, no matter what. But I can't help. Not with this."

Mary clutched her daughter to her chest. Her solid shape was the only thing keeping Mary from collapsing. She forced herself to nod. She understood. She did. Vera had as much to lose. As much to fear. Trapped by their station and lack of money independent of their husbands and limited education, they were not fit for the world outside Hawthorne Springs.

She looped her arm through Vera's. "Let's go home."

They went slowly, Ada babbling in Mary's arms even as the women kept silent.

It was only when they were standing at Mary's front door that Vera spoke again. "You'll call if you need anything?"

"Of course," Mary said. She shifted the baby to the other hip, hugged Vera, and then stepped into the house. "I love you, too," she said, and closed the door.

It was the last time Vera saw her alive.

INTERLUDE: 1751

Gideon cut her first. Before he put Florence on the tree. Perhaps he thought it a mercy. Perhaps he thought to spare his wife the agony of the branch piercing her chest even as he opened her throat, her blood wine dark against his hands.

I clung to life by the thinnest thread—a flimsy whisper born of the need to comfort Florence in the moment of our death. There was no final border I could cross that would prevent me from being her mother. I would hold to life until her final breath escaped.

Florence did not cry out. She did not scream. But I saw the silver glow of her tears. The shock on her face as he drew the knife over her skin, and then it was done. Blood leaked from her neck. Her lips. It coated her teeth as she opened and closed her mouth and stared up at him.

"You are blood bound to this tree. I heard you confess to it. It is only fitting that you go to your final judgment there. You and your witch mother." He grunted as he lifted her over his shoulder.

Rage gave me the strength to spit at his feet. To find my voice once more. "It is that bond that has provided your fortune. Your gold and bountiful land. I would not trust such a fool to understand such deep magic."

He threw back his head and laughed. "My fortune? You would

claim our providence here comes from this devilry? From some fealty you have sworn in blood to this... this *tree*?"

Against his shoulder, Florence gasped, the words she spoke a harsh rasp. "It is as she says. I have seen it."

"Well then." He pulled her from his shoulder and held her upright. "Let us see if it is as you say, or if it just the ravings of two godless whores."

He kissed her. Ran his tongue over her bloodied mouth and teeth and neck. Lapped at her blood as if she could quench his sanctimonious rage, and I sobbed because there was nothing I could do.

He pulled back, his mouth smeared with Florence's blood. He let Florence drop as he bent to the earth, swiped a finger through the blood I'd leaked there, and licked it clean. "If I should quickly acquire any more wealth, I'll be certain to look to hell and say a prayer of thanks to the one who made it so. The one true God and not the devil whose book you have signed."

He was tall. He did not have to climb as I had.

I have known death. Have looked it in the face. Seen its teeth and known its bite as natural rather than frightening. But as he placed Florence's body on the branch, as I listened to the wet gurgle of her flesh opening, the sharp intake of her breath that was the strangled sister to a scream, I felt fear's cold touch.

But that fear was not for Florence or myself. It belonged to her daughter. To the thought that she would live with such a man; that she would call him father, and he would raise her up as was his liking. Made in his image. To hate rather than to love. To see the world as cold and harsh and worthy of judgment rather than admired for its beauty. It was for her that I feared. For the daughters that would be born of her. Our bloodline forever tainted by brutality.

I reached for Florence. My daughter. This portion of my body I'd been granted for such a short time. I no longer felt any pain, and I pulled myself forward, the blood granting me purchase as I slid easily over the branch and wrapped my arms around Florence.

I knew her smell—the one she had since she was a child—and I took it in. Her scent would be all I knew of my last bit of air. I would have it no other way.

"I'm sorry, Mama," she whispered.

"Shh. I will love you always."

I felt the world tipping then. A great silence rising up to greet me at long last, close as an old friend.

Beneath us, Gideon watched, and for every bit of love I held for Florence, I held an equal amount of hatred for him.

"It seemed fitting to hang you from the same branch. You were sick, after all. Found your way here like all the others grown sick before you. No one will wonder when I tell them I found you together, joined in death as you were in life," he said, turned, and then left the clearing as quickly as he came.

I bared my teeth at his back, the tendons of my neck straining as my breath grew shallow. He should have taken it all. Taken our lips and tongues. Sliced our vocal cords so we could no longer make sound. He did not understand a woman's rage. How it manifests even as it stutters into death.

I held Florence, our blood mingling on the single branch of the tree that granted us power, my anger more powerful than any devil Gideon could imagine.

CHAPTER XV

2007

Vera's voice came through the phone as if through an immeasurable distance. "Camilla? Are you okay?"

Camilla weighed how to answer Vera's question. No, she wasn't okay. Nothing was. But there wasn't time to go into all the reasons why.

"I need you to tell me about the Dark Sisters."

The line went quiet, long enough to leave Camilla worried the call had disconnected or that Vera had hung up on her, but then came the distinct sound of Vera clearing her throat.

"Your mom wouldn't—"

"My mom is sick, Vera. She's sick, and my dad has her locked up. There's someone here watching her every hour of every day, and even if I could get in to talk to her, she would tell me they aren't real, or it was just a dream, so please." Her voice went ragged as she fought back tears. "Please. Tell me what you know."

Again, the line went quiet, and then Vera began. "You never met your grandmother. Mary. She died when your mom was just a baby. She was so beautiful. So funny and brave. She loved your mom. So, so much. She would have loved you just as much. And she—she trusted me. Told me a secret, and I was stupid and hurt and young and didn't understand that even hinting at something like that could ruin everything."

"What did she tell you?"

"She was in love with someone else. A woman named Sharon Hutchins. She didn't mean to hurt me. Even then I knew she hadn't done it intentionally, but she did all the same. And I was so angry. I wanted her to know what it felt like. That betrayal. We always think we're doing the right thing until it wounds us. If I could go back and change it, I would.

"It was my fault. What happened. I was the one who told Robert, your grandfather, about Sharon. Not outright, just that I'd seen them together, but it was enough to make him leery. He wouldn't let her go anywhere. Couldn't do anything other than clean his house and take care of your mom. And then she got sick. She asked me for help, and I wouldn't because I was too chickenshit, and it all fell apart anyway." Vera paused as she struggled to compose herself. "I was on Retreat when I realized I was sick, too. It wasn't like it is now. No antidepressants or beauty treatments or all the luxuries of home to accompany your brainwashing. And I swore then that I would do everything I could to make it right."

"You were sick? But you didn't—"

"I don't know why I lived when there are others who don't. When Mary didn't. If there's anything else in this life that's as unfair as that, I've yet to find it. But I told myself I would do anything to get out of Retreat so I could watch over your mother and make certain she was okay. I played the part. Read my Bible and went to prayer sessions and said all the right things. A good woman through and through."

Camilla nodded. She knew something about playing that role.

"Gerry did me the favor of dying not long after they let me go home. A car accident. I could have left Hawthorne Springs after that. There was plenty of money. No one would have questioned it if I did. But I couldn't leave Ada. So I stayed and did all the things expected of me so not even Robert had a reason to think I was anything other than a good, Christian woman. And I watched. Because

I owed a debt. Because what I'd done was unforgivable. Because I loved your grandmother, and maybe it wouldn't erase all I'd done, but it could be an atonement in its own way."

Camilla chewed on her lip. Vera's story was taking too long, and she'd still said nothing about the Dark Sisters.

"Your mom was thirteen when she told me she saw the Sisters. A dream, she said. Because that's what her daddy told her. It didn't matter that she'd woken up under the tree—sleepwalking even though she'd never done that in her life. And what reason did she have not to believe him? He was the sun in the dark. Her whole world revolved around him. It didn't matter I told her I'd seen them, too. That I'd thought it was a dream, too, but now, I wondered if they were something else. Something more important.

"But your mother was her father's daughter. He raised her in his image because he could. And she swore to me if I ever mentioned them again, she wouldn't speak to me for the rest of her life. That the Sisters were a story, and that was all. And then she married Henry. Became a preacher's wife. Even if she'd seen them, she couldn't talk about it. It would have been blasphemous to even hint at such a thing, and your mother is nothing if not devoted. A good, righteous woman."

Camilla could hear the fatigue in Vera's voice. Could sense the years and years she'd carried this story. Her regret and shame and confusion bound up in her sense of duty. She took each thing Vera told her, but all those truths fell through her hands. There was so little she could hold. She was just like her mother then. Her father's daughter. Naïve and willing to swallow whatever she was told, and hadn't she played the part of the spoiled, bratty preacher's daughter? Hadn't she grown into the woman they expected?

"Your daddy was never shy about letting me and your mom know he didn't like me hanging around. But I was good. Played along until you told me about the Sisters, that you saw them too, and well, you saw what the consequences were for that."

Around Camilla, the room seemed to swell. Both her mother

and Vera had seen the Sisters. She wondered how many women, how many girls, had seen them. Had woken, disoriented with sleep, to look up into those twisting branches, their fear damp and heavy in their mouths. But knowing Vera and her mom had seen them didn't answer any of her questions. Didn't tell her who they were or how they were related to her mother and Brianna's illness. If they even had anything to do with it at all.

To figure it out, she would have to go back to the tree. Sit in that great silence and make an invocation or an offering, whatever it was when one wanted to call forth a ghost or a demon.

A knock sounded at her door, and she jumped, fumbling the phone in her hands as she ended the call.

"Camilla? You decent?"

Her father. Already home from his planning session.

Hurriedly, she powered the phone off and shoved it and the box back under her sink and piled various bottles in front of it.

"Yes," she called, her heart racing as she looked at her improvised hiding spot and told herself he had no reason to look under the sink.

"There you are." He paused in the doorway and took in the scatter of cast-off beauty supplies around her with an indulgent smirk. "Doing a little reorganizing?"

She forced a smile. "I could have sworn I had this one moisturizer down here, and once I started looking, well . . ." She indicated the pile on the floor, and he chuckled.

"Let Angela take care of that. Come in here for a minute. I have something I want to show you."

Relief cooled the heat in her cheeks, and she closed the cabinet behind her and followed him.

"Talking about the Purity Ball got me thinking. Things have been tough around here lately. I think we both could use a little pick-me-up, and with the Ball being so soon, I don't think it's going to hurt anything." He pulled a small velvet box from his pocket. "Now, you can't wear it yet. Not until the ceremony is over, but I never could keep a secret for very long." He beamed at her as she crossed the room.

Nestled in the box was a platinum band, a spray of pear-cut diamonds that looked like a delicate cascade of water droplets. Her purity ring.

"Cartier." She let her fingers hover over the box like it was some sacred relic. Her father would want her to be impressed. Overwhelmed by this show of opulence. He would never imagine she saw how thin his gesture was. A distraction dressed in finery. Just like the Retreat, the money, the luxury, was meant to keep her happy and numb. Happy and numb didn't ask questions. Happy and numb didn't cause problems.

"The girl knows her diamonds," he said, snapped the box closed, and pulled her in for a hug. "I know you've been upset, hon. Given everything happening with Mom, it's hard not to be. I've had my own struggles with it. But there's comfort in giving that fear to God. In putting it all in His hands and knowing He's going to provide."

She nodded into his chest and made certain to keep her body soft. Open and receptive to his touch. "I know, Daddy."

"Good girl." He squeezed her shoulders as he released her. "I'll have Angela pack your bag and passport. You should be all set. Just make sure you get your beauty sleep tonight."

"Tonight?"

"We fly out tomorrow morning. Paris, remember?" He knocked his knuckles lightly against her forehead. "Seems like someone needs that rest more than she thought. Figured we could take a few days before your appointment. Take in the sights. Just you and me. A week in the most beautiful city in the world and then home just in time for the Ball."

She wanted to ask about her mother, if she'd remain behind, locked in her room while she and her father gallivanted around France, but she kept her jaw clamped shut so the words couldn't escape.

She smiled instead and wondered if it was possible to drop dead from smiling so much.

"I'm off then. I have a few things to button up myself before we leave." He waved the ring box at her as he opened her bedroom door. "See you bright and early."

A week. She would not be able to go to the tree until she returned, and even then, it would be difficult. Her father would still be watching her every move, intent on keeping her in the house or the church. She could have screamed in irritation, but it wouldn't have helped.

She went back into the bathroom, locked the door behind her, pulled the phone from its hiding place, and powered it on.

> Leaving for a week. Back next Friday.
> Need to get to the tree that night.
> Before the Purity Ball.

She waited as the text went through to Brianna and Noah, turned the phone off, and began the methodical process of putting everything back under her sink.

Only when the bathroom was put back in order, everything pristine and shining, did she close her eyes and offer up a prayer. To God or the Dark Sisters, she couldn't be sure, but it didn't matter anymore. Gods and devils weren't so very different. Each wore a beautiful skin.

"Please. Please don't let them die."

CHAPTER XVI

1953

Three days after Vera found Mary at the tree, Robert woke to an empty bed. He assumed Mary was already awake, downstairs making breakfast or in the nursery tending to Ada, but he went through the house room by room and could not find her. Still, he did not panic. It was possible she'd gone for a walk. That she'd not wanted to disturb the baby and, unable to sleep herself, wanted to tire herself out, but he walked the wooded paths near the house, his voice growing hoarse as he shouted her name, and he still couldn't find her.

He made phone calls to their neighbors, but no one had seen Mary. No one had any reason to think she would have run off of her own accord. She had a new, precious baby at home. A handsome, wealthy husband who practically worshipped the ground she walked on. What reason could she possibly have to disappear?

After a sleepless night of waiting for her to come home, he went to the police. The officer there listened to his story, a pinched expression on his face.

"Happens all the time. Either she'll turn up, or she won't, but I'll bet she'll be back in a week or two. Doesn't take long for them to realize they're better off at home."

"We have a baby. Mary wouldn't leave her," Robert said.

The officer heaved a sigh and pulled out a pen and pad of paper from his breast pocket. "Listen, if it makes you feel any better, I can get someone out there to take a look around. What's that address?"

Robert recited it faithfully, and the officer flipped the pad closed. "We'll let you know if anything turns up," he said.

"She had a friend, too. In the city. A Sharon Hutchins."

"Lots of women have friends."

"You're not hearing me. They were . . . close."

The officer's jaw tightened. "I see. Could be she's with her friend. You got a phone number for this Sharon Hutchins?"

"No. I only met her the one time. Mary never really talked about her, but apparently, they were thick as thieves."

The officer tapped his pen against the counter. "Like I said, Mr. Shephard, we'll take a look, but I bet dollars to doughnuts she's back soon enough."

Robert went home. His mother took the baby, claiming it would be easier. They would be out of his hair while he looked for Mary, and she wouldn't have to live out of a suitcase.

Each room felt haunted. Phantom reminders of the life he'd expected slept curled in the shadowed corners he never bothered to look in. The house was not his domain. It had never been worthy of his attention. His focus. But he felt it now. How it bore down on him. The teeth buried in the plaster and wood ready to take him apart piece by piece and hold him there forever.

That night he turned on every light—the house blazing in all that collected dark—and he slept in his truck. He woke periodically through the night, his gaze drifting toward the windows where he was certain he would see a dark figure watching him, but there was nothing there in all those rooms, and when the morning finally came, he knew he would never step foot inside it again.

So, when the phone call came, it was to his mother's house. Not from the police, but from Pastor Brighton.

"Robert, they've found her. I'm so sorry."

He held himself very still. "Where?"

"It was a group of hunters that found her. In the woods. Officers are already there, but they thought it best if I was the one to call."

He gripped the phone tighter, his hand tingling as the blood rushed from his fingers. *"Where?"*

"Are you at home? I'm coming to get you."

"I want to see her."

"I don't think that's wise. Given the . . . state they found her in."

"She's my wife, goddammit!" He brought his fist down on the phone table, the wood splintering.

"Stay there. I'm coming. You shouldn't be alone when you see her. We'll go together," Pastor Brighton said, and the call disconnected.

It took less than ten minutes for Pastor Brighton to arrive. Another fifteen for them to trek into the woods and then the clearing where a massive black walnut tree stood.

A group of three police officers clustered around a diminished form covered in a white sheet.

"Had to have swung herself onto that branch for it to have gone through her chest the way it did. You can't fall like that. It ain't natural," one of them said as he lit a cigarette and exhaled.

"Shut the hell up, Petey. That's the husband," one of the other officers hissed, but Robert didn't care. He fell to his knees in front of the draped body that had once been his wife. He felt no shame when a hysterical laugh scraped out of him. How absurd it was— this body before him. How reduced. He reached for it, his fingers catching at the edge of the sheet.

"Sir, we ask you not touch the body."

"Shut the hell up again, Petey."

He pulled, but what lay curled beneath the sheet was not his wife. It had her face. Her hair. But it was not her. Her eyes, gone clouded, held nothing of the woman he knew. Her mouth and its ravage of sores was not the one he kissed on their wedding day and so many times after.

The hole in her chest where she ran herself through, the lovely spill of her blood across the front of her dress, somehow these were the only things he recognized of his wife. Her desperation to be away from him. Her spite.

He curved his lip in disgust, his voice dropping to a whisper he hoped she could hear in hell. "You bitch. How dare you do this to me. *How dare you.*" He spat, the thick wet of it landing squarely on her pallid cheek.

"That's enough now." Pastor Brighton put a hand under Robert's shoulder and hauled him to his feet as the officers looked on in shocked silence. "Officers, I'm sure you'll call once the body is released back to the family?"

"Yes, sir. I wouldn't expect it to take long given the . . . nature of the death."

"Good. That's good. Mr. Shephard is in residence at his mother's home. I'll be certain you receive that information once I've gotten him settled. Unless you need his cooperation with something else?"

"No, sir. And our condolences, Mr. Shephard."

Robert laughed again and again, his sides aching, as Pastor Brighton dragged him away.

———

He let his and Mary's mothers handle the arrangements, let them place the obituary in the newspaper, and on the day of the funeral, he sat in the family pew, his gaze locked on the closed casket at the front of the church. Beside him, the baby slept in his mother's arms in her miniature mourning dress. Another absurdity. But he'd learned to control his laughter. Two tumblers of bourbon helped mightily with that need.

He did not hear the service—whether Pastor Brighton recited the Bible verses Mary's mother suggested or if the final prayer included a blessing for Ada as his mother wanted. All he knew was he was grateful when it ended.

He stood at the back of the church and accepted the gentle touches on his arms, the misty-eyed condolences of the other mourners. He nodded and thanked them and wondered why God had chosen not to smite the world a second time. A fire rather than a flood. As the congregants left the church, he envisioned each of them burning. The silver and gold of their jewelry melting to their skins. Their skulls peeling away, dripping redly against the sanctuary carpet. It made him feel better.

"Is that Vera Stephens?" His mother lifted her chin toward the front of the church.

He turned and looked at the woman standing beside the casket. She held a hand to the wood, her head bowed as her shoulders shook with the force of her tears.

"Yes," he said.

In that moment, Vera turned from the casket, her gaze locking with his. She narrowed her eyes, but her hatred was a paltry thing. Gerry stood to her right and offered her his arm, but she made no move to come down the center aisle and offer her condolences.

"Let's go," he said. With his daughter in his arms, they left the church.

INTERLUDE: 1751

Above us, the moon emerged from the clouds in full splendor. Our blood an offering. Perhaps the tree would grant us a final request.

I spoke into the void. "To the light and dark beneath the world, see us. Hear us." Black spots crowded my vision, but my heart beat with the need to punish. The need to be born again into something new. Something powerful.

"Let our daughters and those sworn in blood as we are see us. Let them know us. Let them open themselves so we may work through them and know the truth of who we are. Of *what* we are. So they may know their power and correct all that has been wronged. So we may taste their treacherous father's blood. So we may reclaim what he has stolen. The power that is rightfully ours."

"Hear us," Florence whispered, and I tightened my arms around her.

I felt as the words took root. A great shuddering I fed with my anger. My fear. I lifted my face to the moon so it might see the intent burning there. So I might see its light before I could not any longer. And I listened, joined as we were on the branch, as my and Florence's hearts slowed.

There was no wind when Florence and I stopped breathing. Nothing that would have lifted our hair from our bloodied faces and tangled it together in a single braid. Nothing that would have joined us in such a way. At least not in the common, unmagical world of men.

But it was so. We bound ourselves to this place in blood and death, and because of that action, the tree saw and claimed us as a singular entity. No longer mother and daughter existing as if across a great chasm, but joined, close as skin, and hair, and bone.

In life, I would have had no name for what Florence and I became. Ghosts. Spirits. Revenants. We were all and none of those things. Bound to the tree for eternity, we bore the appearances we had in death because the magic only saw things for what they were. It did not see the ugliness, nor did it know of the previous beauty. It only gave us back the faces it last saw us wearing, and left us, forever waiting for a daughter of our bloodline or one marked by our shared magic, to see us.

Of course, they learned to fear what they saw. With our gaping, bloodied mouths and death-clouded eyes, we were monstrous. The witch women of the wood.

But before their fear, we were alone. For several years, people came and went from the clearing, but no one came to tap the tree as we once had. No one approached in reverence, aware of the power beneath their feet as they placed their hand against the bark.

Our story, our legacy, died with us.

CHAPTER XVII

2007

The days in Paris passed like a fever dream. Glittering fragments of silk and lace and Pilates sweat and massages and glasses of champagne as Camilla trotted out her broken French. A fresh cut and color at one of the top salons, courtesy of her father. A facial. A spray tan. Her beauty laid out like a mechanism. So many moving parts that were the summation of her ability to attract a husband.

She let herself float somewhere above her father's attempts at conversation with her. His instructions of *No, the dress should be white*, and *I ordered the '96 blanc de blancs*, and *I've always thought the Beaubourg was the ugliest thing ever built* guided their days, and she was thankful he only truly saw her at dinner, and even then, she was able to distract herself with the champagne or the airy reminders of a meal he ordered.

"Don't want to bloat right before the Ball," he said, and nodded his approval when she didn't finish her plate.

In sleep and in daylight, she dreamed of the tree and the Sisters. The sharp scent of blood thick in the air as she prostrated herself before them. Her body and heart a blood offering if it meant they would absolve Brianna and her mother of their illness. There were daily check-in calls from the nurse, but if her mother spoke with her father or asked to talk with Camilla, he kept that to himself. She wouldn't let herself think her mother had already died, and her father was keeping it from her so it wouldn't spoil the trip. If she let herself, she would not be able to continue the farce that was her daily routine with her father.

On their last day, her hands trembled as she dressed for the trip home. Their bags were already packed and carried downstairs by the porter, and she listened to the faint rise and fall of her father's voice coming from the suite's living room. It was still too early to be rightfully considered morning, but he'd been on the phone for most of it, and she'd had coffee alone, relieved by his absence.

In less than twelve hours, she would be home. In less than twelve hours, she would go to the tree. She repeated it in her mind: a litany that soothed her.

"Bad news, hon." Her father appeared in the doorway, his phone clenched in his hand. "Our flight was cancelled. Some problem with the plane. I've called in every favor I have, but the earliest I could get us out was this evening. Good news is that I got us flatbed seats, so we can at least get some shut-eye."

Her skin went cold. They would not be home until the following day. She would not be home in time to go to the tree. Another delay. It was as if he had known what she planned. As if he were taunting her. She tucked her hands under her thighs so he would not see them tremble.

She would have no way of telling Brianna and Noah about the delay. She could only hope they would figure it out and not do anything stupid.

"Don't you worry though; your daddy will still get you home in time for the Purity Ball." He laughed and tweaked her nose. "You look like you've seen a ghost. We'll be fine. Everything is all set. We have the dress. Hair and makeup people all set. You just have to show up and look pretty."

After he left the room, she took his unused coffee cup, the porcelain so thin she could practically see through it, and wrapped it in a napkin. She waited to hear his voice again, another phone call among the many, and then made her way to the bathroom where she placed the wrapped mug on the floor and stomped on it, the porcelain shattering. A bloodless violence that did nothing to cool her frustration.

She spent the hours wandering the hotel shops in the effort of not being locked in a room with her father, and only once they were on the plane, her father once again distracted by his phone, did she feel the coiled nerves in her muscles relax the smallest amount.

Finally, they were ready to take off. The plane rumbled beneath them, a monster mimicking the anxiety that slept in Camilla's blood, and her father turned to her. "Try and get some beauty sleep, hon. Don't want to look tired at the Ball," he said, before tugging an eye mask on.

Sleep was an impossibility. Instead, she counted down the hours on her watch. She couldn't allow any more time to pass. After the Ball was over, once everyone was home and sleeping off the excess of champagne, she would go to the tree. Her father would be tired from the travel, from the business of the day, and his guard would be down. Still, she would have to be careful. She couldn't afford any more time lost to her father sending her on Retreat.

The drive home was a continuation of the flight. Her father alternately dozed between answering calls, and she kept her gaze trained on the passing trees as the driver carried them toward home.

She had barely stepped foot inside the house—no time to retrieve her hidden cell phone or see her mother—when the makeup artists descended on her with their brushes and sprays with the intent of a miraculous transfiguration. Everything pastel and pretty. Nothing that would give the implication of makeup. Nothing distasteful. They would make her into something holy. Something pure.

"We'll have to go heavier on the concealer," one of the artists said, patting beneath her eye. "Goodness gracious, did you sleep at all?"

She gave in to the push and pull of their hands, their intentional reshaping. An easy thing to float out of her body with the assurance that she only had to play this part for a few more hours. As she stepped into her dress, as they bound the yards of cream and ivory tulle tight enough to limit her breathing, she felt herself put on the mask. The pure, chaste supplicant. The good daughter.

"Look at you." Her father stood in her doorway, his suit a dark hunter green that only served to make his eyes brighter and his hair somehow more golden. He waved a finger in the air, and she obeyed, but the twirl was awkward and bumbling, the dress an uncomfortable weight against the insubstantiality of her body. "Breathtaking," he said, and she offered up a weak smile.

"Thank you, Daddy." She smoothed her hands over the voluminous skirt, hating how it limited her movement with its cinched waist and masses of pleated tulle. How like a fifties housewife it made her feel.

"I have another surprise." He paused for effect. "Your mother wants to see you."

Blood rushed through every part of her, leaving her arms and fingers tingling. "She's awake?"

"Go!" He chuckled as she struggled through the door, the dress catching at the frame, and then she was out, running as best she could in her four-inch heels, hoping her mother hadn't already faded back into sleep.

At the threshold of what had become her mother's sickroom, she slowed. Pulled herself in tight so she was small and then smaller. She would not bring anything other than calm into that space. She entered slowly. The nurse, thankfully, was nowhere to be seen.

Her mother sat upright, an enormous stack of overstuffed pillows behind her, but her head lolled, her eyes vacant as she gazed straight ahead.

"Mom?" Camilla's voice broke through the room's silent skin, and her mother's eyes snapped to her, her gaze traveling the length of her dress before finding their way back up. She took two steps forward and then another, but everything she wanted to say would have to remain locked behind her teeth. It made her want to weep, but she could sense her father's presence behind her, how he watched this orchestrated moment between mother and daughter.

Her mother reached for her, trembling as she tried to gather Camilla to her, but there wasn't enough strength in her arms. She let them drop, her fingers contorting painfully as she gripped the sheet.

"It's okay—" Camilla began, but her mother lurched forward, the sheet pushed aside to reveal her wasted body, the sores on her lips weeping a baby-pink fluid as she clawed at the mattress and tried to push herself out of bed. Her mouth gaped. A groan that descended into a rattle broke the stillness of the room; tears came hot and fast as her mother repeated the sound. Again, and then again, the pitch bending and changing into something that resembled a single word.

Don't.

"Don't what?" Camilla whispered. If her mother had anything to tell her, they only had seconds before her father was close enough to drag Camilla away.

Her mother's body twisted violently, and Camilla watched in horror as she pressed a hand to her throat and gagged. The skin there bulged around a solid, twitching mass.

"It's okay, honey." Camilla's father was suddenly there, his hands against her waist as he pulled her away. The nurse magically reappeared and held a basin to her mother's lips as she choked, the mass working its way up her throat like some great spider.

Camilla let out a sob as she struggled against her father's hold. "What is that? What's in her throat?"

Her mother coughed: a deep, wet tearing sound as the mass worked its way past her tongue and what remained of her teeth. Dark strands clung to her lips as she spat it into the basin, and Camilla felt her own throat grow thick as she tried to understand what she saw.

The mass in her mother's throat was a ball of hair.

CHAPTER XVIII

1953

Vera watched Robert go, her jaw clenched. There was nothing she could do. Whatever it was Mary saw at the tree—the Dark Sisters or some other presence—she'd gone to meet it. Mary was dead, and Vera was alone.

She was no prophet. She had no power to raise the dead.

She let Gerry take her home, and she went back to her routine of cooking and cleaning and pretending Gerry hadn't seen the truth of her.

For two days, she did it all perfectly, her mind locked away so she could float through her day without breaking into sobs. When the doorbell sounded just before lunch, she didn't peek through the curtains like she normally did. She had a pound cake in the oven and was worried she forgot to grease the pan. It would burn on the bottom, and Gerry would be disappointed there was no dessert with dinner, and so, distracted, she wiped her hands on her apron and threw open the door.

"Yes?" she said, before she even truly saw the woman standing on her porch.

She was dressed smartly—a turquoise twinset with a twist of pearls at the neck—and golden hair curled prettily around her face in the bubble cut that was so fashionable but Vera knew would only make her apple cheeks look rounder. She held a worn section of newspaper in her hands.

Vera's throat tightened, and she held herself very still. She'd not seen the woman standing on her porch since the night of the Purity Ball.

"Hello, Sharon."

"It took a while to find you. I knocked on at least four doors before someone even answered. And then another three to find anyone willing to tell me where you lived." She thrust the newspaper outward. "She's dead. Mary is *dead*, and this is how I find out? From a week-old newspaper?"

Vera closed the door behind her. Gerry had not gone into the office that morning. In fact, he'd not gone the past two mornings. He claimed a migraine, but she knew he wanted to keep an eye on her. After what happened with Mary, every husband in Hawthorne Springs was a touch more wary of their wives.

"I'm so sorry."

"Sorry?" Sharon's face crumpled. "You could have had the common decency to find me. It's not hard. After all, I found you, didn't I? Even a phone call." Her voice cracked, and she pressed a hand to her chest.

"I didn't think—"

"Did you tell him? That night at your stupid Ball, did you tell him about us?" Sharon stepped forward, close enough that Vera could see the vein fluttering in her neck.

"I didn't. I wouldn't."

"Oh." Sharon bent at the waist as her breath came in short, ragged gasps.

"Here, let me help you." Vera extended her hand, but Sharon slapped it away.

"Don't you touch me!"

Vera glanced nervously at the door behind her, and then back at Sharon. Her voice was too loud. She had to calm Sharon down or convince her to leave before Gerry heard, but she didn't know what to say or how to comfort this woman. Not when her own grief was still so raw.

"Was it him? Did he do it?" Sharon looked up at her, her teeth bared in a grimace.

Vera twisted her hands inside the folds of her apron. There'd been no details in the obituary. Sharon wouldn't know how Mary died.

Vera swallowed. She did not want to tell the rest, but she owed Sharon the truth. Even if she didn't know the right words to explain it. How to couch such violence in something that would soften it. There were no ways to make it easier, so she said it as simply as she could.

"She . . . she did it herself."

Sharon let out a wail, her body curling in on itself as she collapsed onto the porch. "She wouldn't have. She wouldn't have done that."

"She was sick. Confused," Vera said, and then listened in horror as the door behind her opened.

"Vera?" Gerry stepped out onto the porch, and Vera turned to him, a placating smile on her face as she tried to shoo him back inside.

"Everything's fine, honey. Just some lady troubles. Nothing for you to worry about."

"We loved each other. Did you know that? When you went and told her husband whatever you told him, did you know that Mary loved me? That you were hurting her even though you claim to be her friend?"

"Vera, who is this?" Gerry asked.

"You could have helped her. Could have helped *us*. Maybe if you had, she would still be alive."

Vera recoiled as if struck. She'd not been the one to push Mary onto that branch, but, in her selfishness, she abandoned her, and for that, there was blood on her hands.

Gerry advanced onto the porch, and he stooped, his hands under

Sharon's arms as he pulled her up. "I think it's time you were leaving, miss."

He hauled her toward the car Vera hadn't noticed when she answered the door and deposited her inside. Panting, he closed the door and backed away, but Sharon remained immobile and the engine quiet.

Gerry slammed a hand against the window, and Vera winced as she watched Sharon jump. "Lady, you have three minutes to get the hell off my property or I'm calling the cops. You hear me?"

Finally, the car's engine turned over, and Sharon sped away.

Drained, Vera leaned against a porch post and watched as her husband strode up the steps, his face darkened in anger. Without a word, he pushed past her and into the house, but he left the door open. A silent reminder she was meant to follow him.

She waited until the dust from Sharon's car settled, the evidence she'd ever been there vanished, and then she turned, ever the faithful wife, and followed Gerry into the house.

INTERLUDE: 1764

We knew her face the day Gideon brought her to the tree. So much of ourselves lay hidden within her features. The slope of my nose. The lovely quirk of Florence's mouth, and her wild, dark hair. Felicity, Florence's daughter, grown into a young woman of twelve, perhaps thirteen.

Felicity followed behind her father, her gaze lowered demurely, but we could see the vitality in her body. How she placed her feet as if she were dancing rather than walking, and how she twitched her mouth when she saw something that drew her interest. She was a rebellion covered in a veneer of obedience: brought up under her father's rule. Despite his rigidity, he was unable to stifle the glamour in her blood. We smiled to see it, Florence and I.

There were others—a few other men with young girls in tow—but we could look only at Felicity as she came to the tree and took her place beside her father as he turned and addressed the group.

"Blessed are these young women who have come among us. Those who would seek God in all things. They who pledge their hands to His works; their lips to His praises; their bodies to His glory." He smiled and withdrew a small flask from his breast pocket. "Let those who are pure in body and pure in heart come now in holiest Communion with the Lord."

We had no voice and could not scream. We could only watch as

Felicity stepped forward and drank from the flask her father offered, the scent so pungent I immediately knew it for what it was. Opium poppy.

One by one, the other girls also drank, but their fathers did not. Florence and I looked down from our place in the tree, our arms reaching, but the young women and Felicity did not look up. They did not see us.

"Let us pray," Gideon said, and the girls knelt before him, eyes closed, as he began to speak.

It did not take long for the opium poppy to take effect. The girls' heads lolled on their necks, and their bodies slumped to the earth as they gazed confusedly about them with heavy lids.

Gideon and the other fathers moved over them, eased them backward with gentle hands, and arranged their hair, their skirts and aprons, like lovely poppets left on the forest floor. Felicity groaned, and I felt our inanimate bodies stiffen when Gideon put a finger to her lips.

He produced a Bible and opened it, the inner leaf marked with letters I could not see clearly but recognized as names. My own and Florence's were written at the top.

"It will be as you said? And there will be no blasphemy in it?" one of the men asked.

Gideon looked at him sharply. "You would doubt the divine intercession of God? Did Abraham question when God commanded he kill his only son? No, sir. He did not. He has granted us blessings beyond compare. I myself have witnessed it as have each of you. It was a trial of the soul, but I obeyed the Lord's command and took my wife's blood in her untimely death. For that faith, He has granted me favor. And you would question His will?"

We opened our mouths, an endless well of rage, but we remained silent. Invisible. Locked behind the barrier of the tree's magic.

"No, Reverend Dudley. I only wish . . ." He looked at the girls beneath him, his breathing rapid. "I only wish not to see them hurt."

"Be still, man. They will not be hurt just as my own wife was not.

They will have the comfort of the poppy. They shall not remember their time here."

The knife Gideon withdrew from his cloak was small, but its edge was cruel. He knelt before Felicity, the Bible beside him, as he lifted her skirt past her stockings and garters, the pale strip of flesh at her thigh exposed.

The other men did not avert their eyes but watched as Gideon drew the knife over Felicity's skin, a scarlet pool of blood immediately forming.

Her eyes widened, tears forming at the corners, as she moaned. She tried to lift her hand and push him away, but the movement was clumsy, and her arm dropped back to the earth. With our broken, silent mouths, we pleaded with her to see us. To look up into the tree and recognize the features in her own face, but she squeezed her eyes shut and kept them closed.

"Brothers, as the heads of each of our houses, let us share in this glory that is rightfully ours. He has made unto us a feast. It would be sacrilege to discard it." He handed the knife to one of the others, who also knelt, lifted the girl's skirt, and cut a line across her thigh.

Gideon dipped his finger into the blood on Felicity's skin and lifted his hand. "And from their blood will we prosper. Join me in this harvest, brothers. Drink and know the treasures promised by God." He pressed the blood along the Bible's inner leaf, marking it as something that belonged to him. But it was not his. No matter how he claimed it.

Together, the men dipped their heads. Together, they placed their mouths along the delicate skin of the girls' thighs. And together, they drank.

CHAPTER XIX

2007

"What is that? *What is that?*" Camilla stared down at the wet clump of hair, shrieked, and slapped at her father's hands as he turned her face away. He'd been gentle with her, but he pinned her arms to her side, practically lifting her as he pulled her away. This was not as he intended. He'd made a mistake in letting Camilla see her mother. He would not let such a thing happen again.

"Camilla." He gripped her chin and forced her eyes to his. The authority in his voice offered no room for compromise. "You have to calm down. You hear me?"

She whimpered. He loosened his hold on her face, but not by much.

"I know, baby. I know. I can't imagine how scared you were." He pulled a handkerchief from his pocket and dabbed at her eyes. "Oh, darlin'. There. Pretty as a picture. Don't let this ruin your night. Your momma wouldn't want that. Not in a million years."

Camilla forced herself to nod through her panic and confusion. There was no more time. Whatever her mother had been trying to tell her was forgotten. She had to get back to the tree, and to do that, she had to get through the night without giving her father any reason to watch her closely. A few more hours and Hawthorne

Springs would go dark, tired from the revelry of the Ball, and she would go.

"That's a good girl." He offered her his arm. "Shall we?"

Together, they descended the stairs, and she let herself float beside him. Step after step that didn't seem to belong to her. Her body an entity grown separate. Her father watching over her in the same way that glorified babysitter he'd hired watched over her mother.

David Robinson stood in the driveway beside her father's new Mercedes GL 450, his white-gloved hand on the door as he grinned. He'd been assigned the honor of driving them to the Ball that night, and he was practically creaming his khakis over it.

Her father placed a hand on her back as he guided her into the car. "Easy now. Watch your toes and your nose." David practically fell over himself running to the other side to open the door for her father. She pictured him tripping, his perfectly pressed khaki slacks befouled with dirt, and sorrow ripped through her. It was the sort of thing she would tell Brianna and Noah, their shared laughter a momentary respite. But she was alone.

Her father settled himself before reaching beneath the seat to pull out a bottle of champagne and two glasses wrapped in towels. When he popped the cork, she winced.

"Drink this. It'll make you feel better." He handed her a glass and then filled his own before lifting it toward her. "I'm—*we're*—so proud of the woman you've become, and even more proud of the woman you're going to be."

She clinked her glass against his and took a dainty sip, the bubbles burning in her throat as she swallowed. Only once he buried himself in his phone did she down the rest of the glass, her head going light as the golden liquid settled in her empty stomach. She could almost hear Brianna's whispered laugh, and her heart twisted painfully. She would have seen the irony of it all. Her father happily drinking champagne with her immediately after witnessing something out of a horror movie.

The church shone like a beacon as David pulled into the parking lot—every light a sparkling reminder of the purity every girl participating in the Ball carried within her. Already, there were mothers lined up at the front directing their professional photographers as their daughters posed in their white dresses, their mouths a perfect rictus of a smile. But as her father climbed out, every head turned, and every eye narrowed as they waited to see what Pastor Burson's daughter had chosen to wear.

She took her father's hand as she stepped out, her dress trailing after her, and she saw the veiled hatred on their faces. Their daughters were lovely, perfect flowers, but they were not the preacher's daughter, and she drank down their disappointment like liquid fire. She wanted to scream at them. To tell them they'd all been tricked.

She went among them silently. Her hands pressed against theirs as they dropped kisses on her cheeks, their barbed tongues offering up sighed compliments. The little girls surged around her, their hands patting at her dress, their eyes sparkling as they stared at her.

"You look like a princess," one of them lisped, her tongue lodged in the space where she'd lost her two front teeth.

They did not know how she kept replaying the image of her mother. That mass of hair working its way up her throat. The sick plop it made when it fell into the basin. That even as she smiled and posed and stood beside her father, she could think only of the tree and the Sisters. Of what it would cost to save Brianna and her mother.

Another wave of fear clamped down on her. Brianna. She had no way of knowing if Brianna had also gotten worse since she'd last seen her. She scanned the crowd, looking for Noah, for anyone who might be able to tell her, but there were only the girls and their parents and the church leaders. Several of the mothers had already begun the process of kissing their daughters goodbye and telling them to be on their best behavior during the ceremony.

She clenched her hands into fists. A few hours. She could get through it.

Inside the church, Camilla stood beside the other girls and then knelt at the altar as her father blessed each of them. As he spoke on the importance of the task set before them, and their fathers in turn, to protect their chastity until marriage.

Camilla heard none of it—her father's voice a dull roar that did nothing to drown out her memory—but she rose and offered her hand when prompted, her eyes fluttering closed as her father slid the ring over her finger. The diamonds and platinum a lovely sort of prison.

The boning in her corset cut into her sides as she stood before the girls and their fathers and the church leaders like a flayed section of skin on display. Vivisected and held up for examination when she'd never asked for it. She smiled so she would not bare her teeth.

A final prayer, and the ceremony was over. The girls crowded together, their hands thrust outward as they examined each other's rings. Even the smallest among them wore a tiny band with a sprinkling of diamonds, and she smiled shyly as the older girls oohed and aahed appropriately.

The fathers clapped each other on the back as they led the way out of the sanctuary and then toward the pavilion where a million fairy lights sparkled. Jasmine and gardenia were mounded on tables heavy with charcuterie and roasted vegetables, and in the center of each, a cut crystal bowl filled with a pink punch Camilla knew was sweet enough to give her cavities. Music drifted from invisible speakers, and the girls blushed as the younger, eligible church leaders stepped forward to offer their arms as they swept into the pavilion.

"I see you survived." Grant appeared beside her as if emerging from the air.

She'd not seen him among the crowd earlier, but she'd been so intent on finding Noah, and she hadn't imagined he would be there. He had no other reason to attend, so she supposed her father had made good on his intentions to bring him into church leadership.

He pointed at the ring on her finger. "That's going to be hard to top."

She stared down at her hand, wondering how it came to be that she no longer recognized it as her own.

"It's Cartier."

He chuckled as he guided her to the punch bowl. "I may not be up to date on all the latest women's fashion, but I know Cartier when I see it." He took one of the heavy glasses from the table, filled it with punch, and offered it to her. "To purity," he said.

She knew it was rude, but she couldn't bring herself to respond. Instead, she lifted her glass and then drained it, the sickly sweet liquid coating her tongue like syrup. She coughed against the sudden thickness in her throat, thinking of her mother. The stretch of her skin around that matted lump of hair. She swallowed against a building nausea.

He took the glass from her and refilled it as he pointed his chin toward the girls moving across the dance floor. "How many of them will be married before Christmas, you reckon?"

"Counting the ones still in middle school? At least six," she said, and he chuckled.

He laughed, but she knew if the laws were different, there would be more weddings in Hawthorne Springs. She surveyed the clusters of girls giggling behind their hands as they darted glances at the church leaders milling about the food. She could almost see the collective visions dancing in their heads. The bridal gown and veil. The flowers. It was what they were raised for. What they were told to want from the time they were old enough to speak.

Several of the older girls were staring directly at her and Grant, not bothering to conceal their sneers. She wished she could pluck out their eyes, like grapes, and toss them in their drinks. Plop, plop, plop.

"Looks like we have an audience." He leaned into her, his voice dropping to a conspiratorial whisper. "They're jealous. You're the prettiest girl here."

Even with everything that happened that afternoon, her entire body flushed, heat working its way up her chest. It was a betrayal she hadn't known it was capable of. She gulped down more of the punch so he wouldn't see how her hands shook.

He gestured to the center of the room where a tiny group of the braver girls had kicked off their shoes and were dancing a formal "leave room for Jesus" waltz with a mixture of their fathers and some of the other leaders. "Let's make 'em burst into flames." He extended his hand with a flourish and bowed. "Dance with me."

She shook her head—the thought of dancing felt unbearably absurd, disrespectful even—but he took her hand and led her onto the floor. His hand went about her waist. It was warm and damp and made her think of pink earthworms squirming through dirt. Once, she'd dreamed about him touching her, but now, she felt the slightest sense of revulsion as the music began.

Around her, the room spun, the girls, the fathers, the dresses all becoming a sort of pale, glittering haze. The music swelled, the notes straining into a discordant harmony that made her shiver even as she held herself rigid in Grant's arms. Before the song came to a complete stop, another began, and again, Grant led her into the next step.

By the time the dance ended in a dizzying twirl, her breath came fast and shallow. She wasn't certain if the sound coming from her was laughter or some small, animal-like cry, but Grant smiled back at her, so surely he thought it was laughter falling from her lips like roses or precious jewels. In the distance, someone let out an exuberant whoop, and the music started up again, the tempo picking up speed as the dancers rushed the floor.

"You look like you need some air." Grant's mouth was tucked against her ear, and the rush of him was almost too much to bear. Every muscle loosened, and she felt her knees wanting to buckle. He looped her arm through his, and she let herself lean against him. Let him guide her away from the whirling dresses and laughter that had begun to sound more like a small creature being skinned alive. A tiny, squirming thing dropped into boiling water.

Others were drifting away from the pavilion and toward the

surrounding woods. Church leaders walked with the daughters as they offered them a glass of punch. The girls lowered their eyes and giggled, their fathers a distant memory and left behind.

It was a reminder of her own father. That he could be watching his newly pledged daughter walking with a man who wasn't anywhere near to being called her husband. "My father." Camilla twisted her head, but she could not find him. There were only lights and the sudden intrusion of the woods that covered the girls and their escorts in dim shadow.

"He's just there. Don't worry," Grant said, pointing at some amorphous shape that turned to her, its mouth widening and widening. A mouth meant to devour. A mouth of violence. She closed her eyes and swallowed.

"It's hot," she said. He led her farther into the woods. It had grown fully dark, her white dress the only source of light. The other girls had fallen away, and she stared up into the trees. How they stretched on and on, the canopy choking off the sounds of the reception. She let her head tip backward as she tried to make sense of all that dark. How it seemed to blossom into an unending series of patterns that confused the eye. It made her dizzy to look, but she couldn't move.

"You look like a ballerina, standing like that. Like the ghosts in *Swan Lake*," he said, and his voice came to her as if through water. Distended and warped.

"Hot," she said again, and pulled at the corset binding on her dress, not caring if Grant saw, but it was knotted, and she could not loosen it. Her fingers would not work, and her brain moved thickly, unable to work out exactly what tie to pull to undo the knot.

From some place deeper in the woods rose a ragged shriek that quickly dropped into a muffled sob. "Who's crying?" Camilla asked. Her skin had gone cold, the dim stirring of fear unable to fully unfold. She was too confused. Too woozy.

"No one. It's probably a coyote. Here." He guided her to a fallen tree. "Sit down for a bit and cool off. You'll feel better. I'll go and get you more punch."

"No. I heard—"

But he vanished into the gloom. Camilla ran her fingers over the crumbling bark beneath her. She could still hear the crying. Soft, soft, soft. Like someone trying very hard not to cry. Like a hand held over their mouth as they tried to stay silent.

And then, another sound. A wet squelching that droned on and on. Like a tongue lapping. Like teeth burrowing into meat. And still, threaded beneath it all, the crying that seemed as if it had always been with her.

She clamped her hands over her ears, but she could still hear it. She could scream until her throat went raw, and it would not erase it. It would burrow forever into her like a seed planted deep. There was no end to that sound, no end to the sky and the trees whirling above her. She sucked in air and tried to understand why the ground beneath her felt suddenly as if it had tipped on its side. Why it seemed she could hear the rush of blood moving through her heart's chambers.

She opened her mouth to tell the sounds to stop, to take a breath that wasn't tainted with heat, but a hand clamped over her mouth from behind and pulled her backward.

INTERLUDE

We would never forget the sound of their cries. All the girls the men brought to the tree, year after year, our descendants written in Gideon's Bible as he took their blood, their *birthright*, for himself and the other men. Their power, the wealth owed them by the promise we made to the tree, stolen as he carried out his bloodletting.

He thought he could drug them, and they would forget. He imagined he could keep them from the truth of what he and the others did, but the opium poppy's confusion did not fully erase the harm. The girls remembered in what small ways they could. In nightmares. In panic they could not explain. Their bodies carried that trauma, and they learned to live in fear of the woods and the tree that still held the blessing that belonged to them.

Years passed, Gideon's death marked only by the appearance of a new minister, but still, his tradition flourished as the town grew. Girls brought to the tree every year so the men of the newly christened Hawthorne Springs might lessen their daughters' power, that wealth and affluence, and take it as their own.

There was no endpoint to their greed.

At first, we were the witch women of the wood, but as with all things, our story changed. Generations were born and died, and the natural fear we inspired in the hearts of those who saw us became a warped parable of the virtues of goodness and the dangers of sin. Not mother and daughter, but sisters birthed from darkness.

Each time, the girls and women who saw us ran. Each time, they told themselves what they'd seen wasn't real.

And then there were the ones who came to the tree, their mouths and tongues bloodied, the illness Florence spoke into existence so long ago still alive. We did what we could, showed them our faces, but the women could not understand how we loved them. How we were not the source of their pain but only wanted to help them understand. They only knew their fear.

We continued to wait. For someone to see us.

So we might finally unleash our punishment.

CHAPTER XX

1953

Vera and Gerry spoke nothing else about what happened with Sharon, but Gerry took to calling home three times a day. To check in on her, he said. And there were a handful of times when she saw Robert's truck drive by the house in the afternoon even though he was on the opposite side of Hawthorne Springs now that he was staying with his mother and had no reason to find himself on Vera's street.

She found herself startling over the smallest things. The sound of the wind chimes hanging beside her kitchen window. The oven timer buzzing. The marked slap of the newspaper delivery in the mornings. The percolator once the coffee started to boil. Even without Gerry there, she felt eyes on her and a mounting sense of dread.

The men finally came for her on a Tuesday. She'd just finished mopping the kitchen, her cheeks flushed with effort, her hairline damp with sweat. She heard the cars in the driveway, the sound of doors slamming, and she straightened and went to the door because she'd been expecting it.

Gerry stood on the porch, his hat in his hand like it had been when he came to pick her up for their first date all those years ago. Pastor Brighton and a handful of the church leaders stood in a loose semicircle behind him. Robert was among them. She wondered if Pastor Brighton would make him a church leader as well.

"Let's take a ride, hon," Gerry said.

"To where exactly?"

"You'll see. You'll like it, I promise."

Gerry took a step forward, and she retreated into the cool depths of the house as if it wasn't his house, too. As if he couldn't come inside and toss her over his shoulder if he wanted and throw her into the back of the car like a rag doll.

He held out his hand, and she wondered if she had ever really loved him.

When she did not accept his hand, he took it anyway, his grip tight, and tugged her forward. "Come on," he said.

Gerry held her steady as he tugged her down the steps, and there was a part of her that wanted to bite, and kick, and scratch, but it would only make things more difficult for her. They'd not answered her unwillingness to cooperate with violence, but she saw the possibility of it in the muscle hidden under their button-downs and jackets. Robert opened the car door for her and guided her inside. Gerry took the driver's seat, while Pastor Brighton slid into the passenger seat. Robert and the other leaders followed behind.

Gerry drove slowly. Carefully. As if she was some breakable doll rendered beautifully mute as they made the turns Vera had known all her life. They were taking her to the church.

"I hope you'll see this as a blessing, Vera," Pastor Brighton said, and turned to give her knee a reassuring pat. "We've been working on this for quite some time."

She pulled her knee away, and he chuckled. "That's fine. That's just fine. Ah, here we are!" he said.

Again, Gerry opened her door and took her hand, but she wrestled it away. "I can walk just fine on my own," she said, and squared her shoulders. Gerry glanced at Pastor Brighton, who nodded, his eyes still twinkling with amusement.

"This way then," Pastor Brighton said.

With the men flanking her, Vera followed him inside. Down the long corridors that now felt haunted, their footsteps the only sound in all that sanctified quiet. They led her into a small room at the very back of the church that had clearly once been an office but now held a small cot, a dresser, and a single chair.

It was when Robert closed the door that she felt the first stirrings of fear.

Pastor Brighton gazed at her; whatever enjoyment he'd taken in her earlier rebellion was now absent. "Your husband has come to me with a heaviness on his heart, Vera. There have been . . . rumors. Rumors you have gone against God's will for your body, and that you have found means to prevent yourself from having a child. He believes these rumors to be true. An immoral man would have left you, Vera." His voice was dangerously quiet. "But God has commanded that a man cleave to his wife. *They shall be one flesh.*"

The other men muttered their assent—a chorus of *amen, brother* that left her feeling hollowed. As if Pastor Brighton had reached inside her and scooped her clean.

Gerry grasped her chin, his thumb stroking a line up her jaw. "We only want to help you, Vera. And all this business with Mary . . . it's confused you. We want to help you find your way back to your true self. Back to the woman God intended you to be."

"We've prayed on it, and God has put it on our hearts. What you need is quiet. Some time to find your way back without intrusions. Without influence," Pastor Brighton said.

"A place to rest and immerse yourself in His word." Gerry gestured to the room around them with its cot and scant furniture.

"A retreat, if you will," Robert added, and the men murmured their agreement.

"What if I don't want to go?" she asked.

Gerry threw his head back and laughed. "Now why wouldn't you want to go, you silly goose? Of course you want to go."

She glanced around the room. "There's no bathroom. Am I supposed to piss and shit in a bucket?"

Gerry's eyes widened at her profanity, but Pastor Brighton's face remained smooth.

"There'll be someone here to take you to the facilities when you feel the need to visit," Pastor Brighton said.

Robert called it a retreat, but this room was intended to be a prison.

Her heart accelerated. "I'll need to pack a bag," she said, hunting for any reason to delay.

"I'll make sure you have everything you need," Gerry said.

"We want you to be comfortable," Pastor Brighton added. "To remind you of how blessed you can be when you walk The Path."

"Could I at least visit the powder room to freshen up?" She swiped at her eyes, hoping for the first time in her life that her mascara was smeared. That they would fall back on their learned politeness. The expectations they carried that women should always look presentable.

"I'll take you," Gerry said.

She nodded and let him guide her back out into the hallway. No point in telling him she knew where it was. She needed him to think she was complacent. To think she was going to do exactly as she was told.

She wasn't going to let them lock her in that room. She would rather brave the outside world, would rather starve or find herself on the streets, than let them imprison her.

"It's only a week. Maybe two," he said, pausing at the entrance to the restrooms. "It really is all for the best. What happened with Mary was a horrible accident. But is it not God's will that we strike down wickedness before it takes root?"

"Of course," she whispered, and forced a gentle smile.

"Don't be long." He swung the door open for her, and she stepped inside.

Immediately, she turned on the tap, hoping the stream of water would cover any sounds that might give her away. The window was a thin transom near the ceiling. She would have to climb on top of the sink to reach it, and even then, she would have to haul herself up with only her arm strength. She kicked off her heels and set a knee on the sink. It might not work, but she had to try.

Balanced on the sink's edge, she reached for the window sash and ran her fingers along it. Her fingers bumped against raised metal, and she nearly cried out with relief. The lock was small and she had to push until her fingers hurt, but it finally gave way. She pushed against the window, but it did not budge. Her fingers were damp with sweat, and they slid across the glass.

"Come *on*," she whispered, darting a glance at the door. How much longer before Gerry realized she wasn't cleaning her face and burst through the door?

She shook her hair back and tried again, biting down on her lip so she would not grunt aloud, and inch by inch, the window opened. The air that swept against her face smelled of mown grass and earth, and she grasped each side of the window, braced one foot against the wall, and pulled herself upward. Her feet scrabbled against the wall, but then she was up, her torso through the window as she pushed herself through.

She heard her dress rip, and she grit her teeth, her hands clawing at the grass, at the dirt, anything that could help as the window edges bit into her lower back. The window was too small. She wasn't going to make it out. There was no more time.

Whimpering, she dug her elbows into the earth and heaved herself forward, biting down on a scream as the frame ripped the skin from her back. But she was out and scrambling on hands and knees and then on her feet and running because the door was opening behind her. Because she had minutes before they were on her.

She ran without any awareness of where she was going. There was only the need to get away. To find a place where she could hide and *think*. Of where she could possibly go. Once, Mary would have helped her, but Mary was gone, and it was her fault, and she didn't have family. Her mother and father were long gone, and she'd been an only child. No one in Hawthorne Springs would offer her sanctuary, and she had no money of her own. No car. She could go to the police, but they wouldn't believe her. She was just another hysterical woman.

It was cooler under the trees. She slowed and tried to orient herself as she shivered. She'd run for the woods that bordered the church, her subconscious knowing it would be easier to hide there, but now, she had no way of knowing where she was. There was blood on her back and feet. It fed the earth as she continued to walk, and she wondered what monstrous thing would scent her.

There was no one behind her, and the woods were quiet. Birdsong and a slight rustle as small creatures scurried about. Her body ached, screaming at her not to stop; the threat had not vanished simply because she was cocooned in the trees. There was no safety in the small distance she put between herself and the men. But she needed the stillness. Needed to pick apart the chaos in her mind and find a way past the limitations surrounding escape.

Leaning against a tree, she struggled to deepen her breaths, closed her eyes and focused on letting her lungs fill with air, on the raw, bloodied taste in her throat. A count of five and a slow exhale.

There was Sharon. Maybe Vera could find her in the city. Go to her and ask for her help. Even as she considered the possibility, Vera knew it wouldn't work. Sharon would not forgive her.

She sobbed through another breath. Held it in. Let it out. It was so quiet. As if a bell jar descended from some unknowable place in the sky. A suffocation meant only for her. And then, so delicate it might not have been a sound at all, a thin scrape. Another.

Opening her eyes would mean seeing whatever made that sound. Would mean facing the possibility that Gerry or Robert or any of the other men had caught up to her and were trying to move very carefully. Quietly. Easier to let her feel a false sense of safety. Easier to capture prey when it didn't hear you coming.

Her entire body tensed, every muscle burning, and she let her eyes open. Before her, there was only the tree. Immediately, she recognized it and pushed herself away. It was the tree where she'd last seen Mary. The tree where she killed herself.

She stared up at it, the bark all twisting, bifurcated lines that looped back on themselves. It made her dizzy. Like so many mouths opening, hungry or screaming, it didn't matter which.

The sound came again, that thin, soft scrape, and she let her gaze drift upward into the unending green that held it. Two sets of eyes stared back at her. A gnarled rope of braided hair swung, that soft sound suddenly filling Vera's head, so loud she didn't realize she'd begun to sob. She had not believed Mary, but she believed her now.

"I'm sorry," she whispered as she looked up at the Dark Sisters, at the stories she'd been told since she was a girl brought to life.

She dropped to her knees, her legs going damp as her bladder released.

That soft scrape sounded once more, and she screamed because it was the only thing she could do.

When the men found her, when they dragged her from the tree, she did not fight them. She hoped they would kill her.

They didn't.

CHAPTER XXI

2007

The bark tore at Camilla's dress as she flailed against the solid arms that bound her, her nails breaking as she tried to keep herself from being dragged into the further dark of the woods. But the arms were stronger than hers, and she was so, so dizzy. She was bleeding, and she had the dim thought it would ruin her dress.

"Shhh." A voice breathed into her ear. "It's just me."

If she'd not been so lightheaded, she would have whirled on Noah and slapped him as hard as she could.

"The *fuck*?" she shouted.

Again, he pressed his hand over her mouth. He darted a glance over her shoulder. "You have to stay quiet. Okay? I'm not supposed to be here, but we hadn't heard from you, and Brianna was worried. Hey." He snapped his fingers in front of her face. "You good?"

"I'm fine. You have to go. Grant went to get me punch. He's coming right back. He'll see you, and he'll tell my dad, and then he'll send me on Retreat, and I won't be able to get to the tree." She took a step away from him and stumbled.

"Are you drunk?"

She looked back at him, indignant. "No, I am not *drunk* at the Purity Ball. We flew in this morning, and I haven't slept."

Behind them, a branch cracked, and she stiffened. "You have to go. Now," she whispered.

"Text us when you're home. We'll help however we can." He paused to look back at her, his face twisted in concern, and then vanished.

She settled back onto the fallen tree where Grant left her. If he noticed her torn dress or the blood, she would tell him she'd scraped herself. She could not think of Noah or the sounds she'd heard. She had to focus on Grant. On getting through these next few hours. But the ground kept slipping out from under her. The world a shifting series of shadows.

Another branch cracked, and Grant emerged from the gloom.

"Here we are. Refreshment." He offered her the glass, and she tipped her head back and drank greedily.

She was still swallowing when she felt his hand on her throat—a single finger tracing a line toward her collarbone.

"You have the most beautiful neck. It's a shame it's too visible. He won't let me use it."

She couldn't breathe, couldn't think. There was only the dim sensation of movement as Grant slid his hand down her back, and her own heart beating, and the sky slipping itself inside out to show all the monsters hidden behind that thin skin that kept them contained. She bent at the waist—a bruised flower in her dress.

"Such a shame," he said, and then the world went hazy.

SOMEONE WAS CRYING again. She wondered if it was her.

Her eyes would not settle, the shapes around her blurring into a series of moving shadows and light. Her tongue lay dead in her mouth, but even if she could speak, how would she articulate what was happening?

There was a sharp line of pain on her inner thigh. The sensation of teeth. And that sound.

The wet sound of someone eating.

She struggled to lift her head, her vision snapping in and out of focus as she realized she was lying flat, her dress hiked up over her hips. She tried to push at it, to pull it down, but she couldn't move. Couldn't do anything other than try and make sense of what it was she was seeing.

She thought of her mother then. Of what she tried to tell Camilla earlier that evening.

Don't.

Her mother had never wanted her to participate in the Purity Ball, had carried some fear of it she couldn't trace, and now Camilla understood why.

Grant looked up at her from his place between her thighs, his mouth smeared with her blood. Her father knelt beside him, a Bible in one hand, the other on Grant's shoulder. His own mouth bloodied. They looked at her. And they smiled.

Once more, the world went dark.

CHAPTER XXII
2007

Camilla's mouth tasted of syrup. Like pink lemonade left too long in the sun. It coated her tongue, and she had the urge to spit. To scrape it with something sharp.

She was not yet awake. Not quite. But her awareness was there, lying quietly in wait for her to return to it.

But she was frightened. There was something waiting for her. She could feel its presence in the room. The slick sensation of its teeth working against her skin, its breath hot against her thigh.

If she held herself still, curled as she was in the depths of sleep, the monster wouldn't find her.

It was her father's voice that cut through that safety. "Camilla? Honey?"

She groaned and shifted, the animal smell of her body rising thick as she opened her eyes in thin slits. Everything ached. Her head. Her muscles. The vestigial reminders of a night spent drinking a too-sweet wine.

"There she is. Back from the dead." He rubbed her knee over the duvet, and she blinked, her bedroom swimming into focus. Someone had drawn the curtains over the windows, and the room was wonderfully dark.

She looked down at the t-shirt she wore. Oversized and clearly her father's.

She tried to think. To sort through the absence that was the night before, her memory thin and transparent. There was the ceremony, and the dance with Grant, his hand on her waist, but the rest of the night faded after that. She pushed the thoughts away because even trying to recall them made her head feel like it would explode.

"Wanted to check in on you. You were a mess last night, bless your heart. Tried to get you in the shower, but you weren't having it. Fought me like a wildcat. Took everything in me just to get you changed and into bed."

Under the t-shirt, she was wearing only her underwear.

She went cold, her teeth clamping down as she fought the urge to vomit. He had undressed her. Her father.

She drew the duvet up to her neck. "Why would you—"

"Oh, it ain't nothing I've never seen before. I changed your diapers, remember?"

She looked back at him. His amusement at her exposure so clear. The grin on his face. His teeth. An image from the night before floated to the surface. His mouth streaked with blood. Smiling. Grant between her legs. That sharp sting that was now a dull throb.

She ran a hand over her thighs, expecting to find a cut, but instead found the smooth surface of a bandage about the size of her palm. She drew in a breath she hoped would keep her voice calm.

"Did I cut myself?"

"Sure did. Got tangled up in some greenbrier. Tore your dress, too. Might want to hit it with some Neosporin. Looked pretty nasty last night."

She remembered then. Noah had come to check on her, and she'd shooed him away so Grant wouldn't see him. So he wouldn't tell her father. Grant had brought her punch, and she'd been so tired. She'd been afraid.

And the sound. The sound of a tongue on meat.

"I had the weirdest dream." She watched him carefully. It's what he would tell her. That what she'd seen—Grant and his bloodied mouth—was a dream. But she knew it wasn't no matter how hazy her memory felt. "I heard someone crying, but I couldn't see who it was. Couldn't move. Grant was down at my legs, and you were beside him. There was blood. Like he'd bitten me."

His face twitched. A quick unstitching as the muscles in his jaw worked to hold it in, but she saw it. The briefest flash of rage, and then his face slipped back into a mask of calm amusement.

"You're right. That is a weird dream. Makes sense though. Given that someone spiked the punch last night. Rum isn't quite the same as a couple glasses of champagne. Honestly, I'm surprised you aren't worse off. Happens about every other year. Apparently, Pastor Jordan had a time last night with Caitlin puking her guts out. Poor thing. Best thing is rest and lots of water. I'll bring you a glass."

She stiffened as he pressed a kiss to her forehead and wrinkled his nose. "And a hot shower. You smell like three-day-old roadkill."

She watched him go, her skin still crawling.

There'd been plenty of nights she'd had too much—her head pounding as she swore up and down she'd never drink that much again. But whatever was in the punch ... she didn't think it was something as simple as rum. She'd woken with the taste of it still in her mouth. Sweet enough to cover any other taste. Sweet enough to make her believe her father's lie. There'd been something in the punch, but it hadn't been alcohol.

And he wanted her to believe it had all been a dream because the truth was so much larger than any nightmare her mind could conjure.

Had Grant bitten her? Was that what she'd seen when she fought through whatever they used to drug her? Some sort of fucked-up vampire role-play? She touched the bandage on her thigh, tried to peel it away, but it tugged at her raw skin, and she hissed in a breath. She didn't want to shower, didn't want to move, but it would make taking the bandage off easier. She needed to see. Needed to know if the horror of her memory was true or nothing more than a nightmare.

She undressed carefully, her joints and muscles a series of knots and aches she knew wouldn't come undone with anything as simple as hot water. She wanted to slip out of her skin. To wash herself clean and forget. Grant. Her father. The blood and teeth. The press of fingers against her inert body.

The water could not be hot enough. Hard enough. It could scorch her through, pull her muscle from bone, and she would not be able to forget.

She let the water wash over her, her fingers at the edge of the bandage as she thought of what she would find beneath it.

But when she peeled the bandage away, there were no bite marks. If she didn't know any better, she would have assumed she cut herself shaving, but the wound on her leg was more than a simple cut. She winced as she poked the skin around it. Circling the cut was the beginning of a bruise. The perfect shape of a mouth.

She shook her head, the pain getting worse by the minute. She did not want to know this. Did not want to face that her father and his church cronies drugged the girls at the Purity Ball and led them into the woods to do what? Drink their blood as if it were some sort of sickening Communion?

She turned and retched, her nausea and disgust so much the same as her stomach cramped again and again.

Her mother had not wanted her to participate in the Ball. Had feared it without ever knowing why. All those Sundays ago, she told Vera about her fear. Her memory of that night. The scars. The heaviness of her body. That her father had told her she fainted. And the sound. The same sound Camilla heard as well. The sound of someone eating.

Her mother.

She cut the water, quickly toweled off, and threw on jeans and a t-shirt that was not her father's. She could push through the headache. Could push through the pain from the cut. She needed to get to the tree.

The phone was still under her bathroom sink, and she sent up a silent thank-you as she typed out a message to Brianna and Noah.

> Going to the tree NOW. If you don't hear from me in two hours, something went wrong.

She slipped the phone in her back pocket, let the bathroom door ease closed, and stepped into her bedroom. Her father had left a sweating glass of water on her nightstand. Frowning, she put it to her lips as a test and let the water fill her mouth.

She immediately spit it back into the glass. A strange grit clung to her teeth, so she went back into the bathroom and spit into the sink. Rinsed her mouth with the tap until she could no longer feel it. She lifted the glass to her nose and sniffed. There was no discernible smell, but she could make out the clouded granules resting at the bottom of the glass.

"Should have stirred better. Or brought me more punch," she said, and spit again.

She had to get to the tree. But doing so meant getting out of her room and downstairs without her dad noticing. If the water was supposed to ... do whatever it was supposed to do, he would assume she was passed out in her bedroom, not sneaking out of the house to go find the Dark Sisters.

No sound leaked through her door, so she pulled it open bit by bit until she could see into the hallway. All quiet. She took one step out, letting the door close behind her, and then paused. Going downstairs meant passing directly by her father's office, which is where he likely was. If she made any noise, he would hear.

She imagined herself light and transparent as air even as her heartbeat weighed heavy in her chest. Pictured herself as a ghost drifting through the quiet house. At the stairs, she paused again, her hand brushing over the guardrail.

She had taken the first step down when she heard voices, and she froze.

"She shouldn't have woken up. They cry sometimes, but they aren't supposed to wake up. Two full glasses. That's the dose. Not three miniature ones."

Another voice murmured something that sounded like an apology, but it was too low, too quiet, to make out.

"She's upstairs. Hopefully asleep. She already thinks it was a dream, but I figured why not hedge our bets, so I gave her another dose. Make it all seem like a dream."

Again, she tasted the grit in her teeth. The water that should have left her sleeping emptied down the sink instead of down her throat.

She took her foot off the stair and backed into the hallway, her muscles wanting to cramp from the strain of moving so slowly. Unless her father and whoever he was talking to decided to leave, she had no way of getting out without being seen. She pulled the phone from her pocket and checked the clock. Fifteen minutes gone.

She was contemplating the drop from her window, whether the distance was great enough to break a bone or whether she could run before her father caught her on the cameras, when from behind her came the distinctive click of a door opening.

She whipped her head toward the sound, her heart surging. Her mother's bedroom door was opening, the nurse in the doorway, her face turned away as she mumbled something about Pastor Burson.

The nurse had not yet seen her, but it was only a matter of seconds before she turned and saw Camilla standing there. Camilla who was supposed to be drugged, likely courtesy of the nurse's stash.

Her bedroom was too far away, and she couldn't go downstairs without the possibility of her father seeing her. Only one door was close enough, and she slipped silently inside just before the nurse turned around.

She held her breath as the nurse's footsteps passed her and then went down the stairs. Only once she could no longer hear them, did she turn and fill her lungs as she took in the room she'd never been allowed inside.

Her father's office.

A desk, much like the one in his office at the church, dominated the center of the room. But where she'd expected a chaotic scatter of notes and files and frames with family photos, there was blank, gleaming wood. The only items on its surface were her father's glasses and a single Bible.

Everything was neat and orderly. Nothing about where he spent all his time crafting his sermons spoke anything at all of the work it took. Her gaze drifted across the room to a massive bookcase that housed a surprising collection of secular reading choices—Jonathan Swift, Samuel Johnson, among a scattering of other dead British men.

And standing to its left, in pride of place, an empty acrylic case she knew was supposed to hold her father's first edition King James Bible. It had been passed from pastor to pastor since Hawthorne Springs built its first church. Her mother had told her on the day her father received it, he'd cried more than on their wedding day.

For years, the Bible rested inside the family safe, concealed with a number of other valuables in her parents' bedroom, but her father never wanted it out of his sight. It was a reminder of their heritage. Of his duty. And so, he'd had the case specially made by some munitions company. The tech engineered to protect against damage by any and all acts of man or God and designed to filter out the damage from UV light, so her father no longer had to keep the Bible in the dark. He showed it to Camilla only once, on the day he transferred it to the case, but she'd been seven years old and far more interested in her horse, Pricci, than in heirloom Bibles.

Her gaze fell again on the desk and the Bible resting on it that should be inside its case, and she realized she'd seen it more than once. Again, her heart surged as she thought back to the night before, when she'd seen the Bible in her father's hand as he knelt beside Grant.

In defiance, she stepped toward the desk and pulled the Bible to her, its heft a surprise. She expected it to crumble against her ungloved touch, old as it was, but the leather was smooth against her palm as she flipped it open.

The pages lay flat beneath her fingers as she took in the scrawled ink that covered the board and endpaper. A series of names she didn't recognize all connected with spider-thin lines until what formed was something like a web. She traced the names downward and then across to the other page until she saw her mother's name and then her own.

So not a web. A tree. The roots of her maternal family going back to the first two: Anne Bolton and Florence Dudley.

Her brows knit as she stared down at the names in confusion. This was her father's Bible, passed down from the preacher before him. She'd never been told it was an heirloom from her mother's side. If it was, wouldn't her father have included it in the diatribe he gave her about it all those years ago? And if it wasn't, why was the tree there? It was possible her father had done it, wanting to leave his own mark, but the entries looked to be in different handwriting, the ink from earlier entries markedly faded compared to her own. And wouldn't he have transcribed his own line rather than his wife's?

She followed the names back to the beginning, noticing for the first time the inscription at the top. Beside it, a deep, rust-colored stain blotted the page, and she traced her fingers over it as she read.

And from their blood will we prosper.

A shiver ran through her, and she pulled her hand away from the stain. Blood.

"Camilla?"

The voice ran through her like a shock, and she slammed the Bible closed. Grant stood in the doorway. He was still wearing his suit from the night before, his tie loosened and the top button undone.

"What are you doing here?" she asked, hating the tremor in her voice.

"I wanted to check in on you, but your dad said you were sleeping it off. Someone spiked the punch, I heard. Your dad asked if I would come up and grab his glasses." He pointed to the bifocals resting on the desk. "You feeling okay?"

She stared back at him, taking in the gentle, worried expression plastered on his face. She wondered if it was difficult for him to wear that mask at all times, or if he'd worn it so long it felt like honesty.

"Must have been jet fuel because I didn't think I had that many glasses. Not enough to have blacked out," she said, choosing her words carefully. She needed him to think she believed their lie, that every word was more mild flirtation and nothing more.

"I can't help but feel the tiniest bit responsible. I didn't even think to try the punch myself. I've never liked sweet drinks like that, you know?" He ran a hand over the scruff on his chin and offered a shrug she knew was meant to look sheepish. A dog caught with his nose in the treats.

His gaze shifted to the desk where the Bible still rested beneath her hand and then quickly to the empty case. Her heart accelerated.

He put his hands in his pockets and rocked back on his heels. "Apple doesn't fall far from the tree, I see."

She swallowed against the lump of fear building in her throat. "What?"

"You prepping for next week's sermon?" He pointed at the Bible and took another step into the room.

She wanted to back up but held herself still. Couldn't let him see she was afraid. That she suspected, whatever all this was, he was only playing his part.

"I didn't think he let anyone near that Bible, but I suppose it's fine. What with you being blood and all."

Blood. She froze. The bloodstain in the Bible. The blood on his and her father's chins. There was some connection there, but she couldn't see it. There were too many pieces missing. Her mind cycled through it all, and she felt her mask falling. It was too much. Too many things she still couldn't slot together.

"Grant," she began. And he smiled. The smile he gave her that first night. The one that told her she was the only important thing in the room.

"It's okay. It'll all be okay." He pulled his hands from his pockets, his cell phone at his ear as he advanced on her. "She's upstairs. In the office."

Her mind went clear. Once, she and Noah argued over who would be the first to die in an apocalypse. She insisted it would be her, that she would malfunction in the face of any sort of violent end, but Noah hadn't agreed.

"You're tough. Tougher than you think," he said.

She hefted the Bible upward and threw it at Grant's face with every ounce of strength she had. Maybe all those hours of Pilates had paid off after all. It landed with a meaty crunch, and he dropped his phone as he threw his hands over his nose.

"What the hell?" he shouted.

"I hope it's broken, you absolute *fuck*," she said as she lowered her shoulder and then ran at him. The force of her body caught him off-balance, and he staggered backward as she pushed past him.

Her only hope was to make it down the stairs and out the door before whoever was on the other end of that phone call made their way to the office. She hit the stairs at full speed, gripping the banister as she flew down. Her blood moved through her with a singular intent. A chorus that sang of escape.

Nothing moved downstairs. No shouting or flurry of movement came from the kitchen as she imagined her father would come barreling out to cut her off. She could have collapsed in relief, but she didn't allow herself to slow, her feet hitting the marble hard enough to sting through her shoes as she ran for the door.

Grant was on the stairs, his hand covering his nose, which was still spewing blood, and she pushed herself to move faster as she threw open the door and blinked into the sunlight.

"Where's the fire, girlie?" Trent Glover stood before her, blocking the stairs. Behind him were two Range Rovers, the windows too dark to see who might be inside. "You should be resting after last night. Your daddy will be so disappointed."

"Don't you fucking touch me," she said, retreating into the doorway. Any second now, Grant was going to reach her, and she was trapped between them. If she could make it to the kitchen, she could use the door there, but she still didn't know where her father was, and if Grant was moving quickly enough, he could easily cut her off.

He clucked his tongue as the Range Rover doors opened, four of the church leaders stepping out. "Language. Let your tongue in all ways praise Him. I don't think that sort of talk is very becoming of a godly young woman. Don't you think so, too?"

Panic slid down her center, her arms and legs going numb, as he advanced on her. There was only one reason for the Range Rovers.

They were going to take her and lock her away on Retreat, and Brianna and her mother were going to die. She would never see them again.

"This doesn't have to be hard, Camilla. Let's make it easy on everyone, okay?"

She snorted. "Easy? Sure."

The men stepped closer, their hands upheld in a gesture that was meant to placate her. They meant no harm. This was for her own good. Didn't she know?

A shuffling came from somewhere over her right shoulder, but she didn't let herself turn. Better to keep her eyes on Pastor Trent and the other leaders who had not stopped their slow progression toward her. She didn't think she could outrun all of them.

"You need to go with them, hon."

Her father's voice slammed into her like a weight. She felt herself drift up and out of her body, felt her head turn to look back at her father, who stood on the stairs with Grant, a bloodied handkerchief pressed against his nose. She followed that trail of blood down his chin and shirt, glad to know she'd done it.

"Daddy," she began, but Pastor Trent was on her, his hand gripping her wrist as he pulled her into his chest, his other arm wrapping around her so she was pinned against him. Immediately, she began to thrash, her legs kicking as she screamed for a god that had turned his face from her.

He dragged her backward, and she let herself go still, the full weight of her body gone slack. A small bit of advice from something she'd seen on the internet about what to do during an attempted abduction. He stumbled against her dead weight, his grip loosening so she was able to free one arm. She drove it directly backward into his balls.

He dropped her fully then, his hands cradling that hideous thing he likely valued more than anything else in his pathetic little world. She pushed off him, angling her body toward the tree line that would let her disappear and take her to the Dark Sisters.

But she'd forgotten about the other church leaders and the rumors of what they carried in case of a difficult woman. She'd heard the whispers when the women returned to services, how they had to be broken under 50,000 volts of electricity. All in the name of God.

She heard the sickening crack of the Taser, and the world tilted, her teeth clacking together with enough force to break her back molar as she convulsed and then dropped to the ground.

Between them, the men lifted her easily and bound her hands and feet with zip ties before stuffing her into the back of the Range Rover. Her head lolled as she watched her father emerge from the dark of the house, his hand against Trent's back as he spoke.

"Comfy back there?" One of the men turned to face her from the driver's seat and grinned. She tried to spit at him, but her muscles were still twisted into an uncontrollable rictus, and saliva dribbled down her chin.

"Should have put a muzzle on her," the other man said as he climbed into the passenger seat.

"Is Pastor Burson coming?"

"Said he'll be by later. Has some loose ends to tie up first." He flipped his visor down and checked his teeth.

The edges of Camilla's vision went blurry, and the last thing she heard before she slipped away was the sound of the engine turning over and her father telling them to drive carefully. After all, they had precious cargo.

"I'D REALLY HOPED not to see you back so soon."

Camilla's mouth tasted of vomit and blood, and every inch of skin felt bruised as she reluctantly opened her eyes. She looked up at Barbara, who leaned over her and wiped at her face with a damp washcloth. They'd put her back in the same room. She wondered if they'd kept it for her since the day she was born. All those years waiting for her to come and take her rightful place as the bad-girl preacher's daughter.

"But I missed you so much," she croaked.

"I see your sense of sarcasm is still intact." Barbara sighed and dipped the washcloth into the basin at her feet. "I trust you remember how things work around here?"

"I can't stay."

"I don't think you have a choice." She nodded at the zip ties still circling Camilla's wrists and ankles. The mattress beneath her wasn't the plush bed she had last time, but the thin cushion of a hospital bed, complete with rollers. Her heart sank as she looked at the metal side rails. It was better for moving her without allowing her to walk. Whatever their intentions were for her, it didn't involve anything voluntary.

Barbara passed the cloth over her face again, her lips pursed as she examined her work. "Good enough for now. I'll get your meds ordered, and then in the morning, after you've taken your second dose, we'll see if you're calm enough for a shower." She retrieved the basin, stood, and made her way to the door.

Camilla watched her go, wondering how long Barbara had worked for her father. If she'd once been a scared young woman forced on Retreat or if she'd always swallowed all the bullshit she'd been fed with a smile on her face. If she ever woke in the middle of the night in a panic without knowing why.

"Do you remember your Purity Ball, Barbara?"

Barbra looked back at Camilla. "Of course, I do." She smiled. "It was perfect. One of the best nights of my life."

"You ever have nightmares about it?"

"Why would I have nightmares about that?" She turned and resumed her walk to the door, but Camilla noted how she avoided answering the question.

"Have any scars? Maybe on your thigh? Maybe can't remember how you got them?"

She paused, mid-stride, and Camilla knew she'd hit a nerve. She wondered how many women in Hawthorne Springs had sister scars on their thighs.

"If you need anything, we'll be watching," she said, and pointed at the ceiling where the crown molding concealed the camera's eye. Camilla had felt it was there during her previous stay, but at least now she had confirmation.

The lock fell into place behind Barbara, her footsteps silent in the plush carpet. Camilla twisted her wrists and ankles, but the zip ties didn't budge. What if she had to pee? Would Barbara come in with a bed pan? Or would she have to piss herself and then sit in it until someone finally came to clean her up?

Tears sprang to her eyes. She'd tried so hard. She'd thought being good and doing everything her father expected would give her the time to figure everything out, but not even her best efforts were enough. It was the role she'd been raised for, and she couldn't even do that right.

She should have been less afraid, should have gone to the tree sooner rather than falling in line with her father's distractions. The trip to Paris, and clothes, and dinner parties, and champagne, and Grant Pemberton. Now, she would suffer for it.

Again, she flexed her hands against the ties, the plastic cutting into her flesh, and she screamed. She didn't care if the camera heard, or if she was being a disturbance. She screamed again, and the rawness of it soothed her somehow. Fuck every single person who helped her father run his bullshit bloodsucking empire. She would see them all in hell.

The door beeped, the lock clicking open, and Camilla bared her teeth, ready to scream again at Barbara, who'd come to muzzle her or inject her with something to keep her silent.

But the person coming toward her wasn't Barbara. She was younger—Camilla's age—a sweep of dark hair pulled back in a braid. She carried a glass of water and a paper ramekin. The medication Barbara had promised.

She set the water on the bedside table, the ramekin still in her hand as she advanced on Camilla and unsheathed a pair of heavy-handled scissors from her front pocket. She leaned in to Camilla's ear and whispered, "Keep screaming. And keep still until I tell you to move. You understand?"

Camilla shrieked, dug her heels into the mattress, and tried to push herself away from those wicked blades. She should have known. It would be easier if she were dead. A problem solved. The sympathy and support for her father would be at an all-time high if he were to lose his wife and daughter. His wife had been so ill. It only made sense that his daughter would have caught the same illness. They would order closed caskets out of respect for Pastor Burson. No one wanted to see such beauty laid to waste. A clean, easy, *simple* solution.

"Good. That's good." The woman bent over her, the scissors making a wicked snick as they opened, and grasped the zip tie at her wrists.

Camilla bucked, but the woman knelt on the bed, leaned her body weight against Camilla, and pinned her down.

The metal was cold against her wrist as the scissors slid against the delicate skin there. Camilla closed her eyes. She'd pictured something bloodier, but opening her wrists was easier. Less splatter to clean up later. She choked in a breath, and wondered if her fear would release along with her blood. There would be some solace in that.

There was a slight pressure, and then a snap as the zip tie released. Camilla's eyes opened in surprise as the woman slung a leg over to straddle her, the paper ramekin in one hand, the scissors in the other.

"Don't move. Keep your hands exactly like they were." The woman's voice was still barely a whisper. She shifted slightly, her body arched so she could reach Camilla's ankles. "Scream again. Try to throw me off."

Bewildered, Camilla did as she asked, her screams filling the room as she felt that cold slide of metal again, the pressure around her ankles releasing as the woman cut the ties.

"Move your head. Back and forth. Like you're fighting me off." She leaned her arm against Camilla's chest, her thighs clenching to keep Camilla still. "It has to look convincing." She jerked her head toward the ceiling and resumed her work.

The camera. They were putting on a show. And her body, the way she blocked Camilla's with her own . . . She was keeping the camera from seeing her cut the zip ties.

With renewed enthusiasm, Camilla thrashed against the mattress as they fought, her screams turning to animalistic growls as the woman tried again and again to bring the paper ramekin to her lips.

Finally, she sat back on her heels and pulled a cell phone from her pocket.

"She's resisting. I'm going to take her down to medical. No, that's not necessary. I got it."

She put the phone back in her pocket and pushed herself off the bed. She bent, her lips close to Camilla's ear again. "Keep your hands and feet exactly like they are. I'm going to wrap you, but they need to be in place."

She withdrew a thin, white sheet and began the process of tucking it under the mattress on all sides, Camilla restrained beneath. She went behind the bed, disengaged the wheel locks, and began to push.

"Let's go," she said, unlocked the door, and then holding it open with one hand, pulled the bed and Camilla through.

The woman walked at a brisk pace, not as someone in a panic, but the no-nonsense gait of someone with a frustrating job to complete. She had no reason to worry. The hallways were empty, and as they entered the atrium, Camilla could make out the deep intonations of one of the assistant pastors leading the women in prayer. Evening Bible study. Everyone other than certain staff members would be in that room. Everyone would be distracted.

They passed through the atrium into one of the hallways, and then the woman paused, withdrew her key card, and opened a door Camilla must have passed a hundred times during her last stay but never noticed. It was the only unmarked door.

She could not yet fall into it. This slight chance at hope. At release. But as the woman pulled her through the door, Camilla felt the sensation expand, and she dared to envision a future that wasn't the Retreat's walls.

Once the door closed behind them, she quickly stripped the sheet off Camilla. "You're lucky there's no one in here tonight. Otherwise, I would have had to come up with some reason to wheel you through the kitchen. That's where the other staff exit is. This is much easier. No cameras in here. They won't give you any privacy in the rooms, but I guess medical is an invasion too far." She tucked an arm under Camilla's shoulders and guided her up. "Go slow. I don't need you passing out on me."

Camilla rubbed at the indentations left on her wrists. "Why are you helping me?"

"I was the one who got you the note the last time you were here.

Robin Chatsworth? I know Brianna. She called and said she was supposed to hear from you and hadn't and that she thought they might bring you here. Said she would pay me if I could get you out, but it's not about the money. I'll take any chance I can to stick it to these assholes." She grinned and pulled Camilla to her feet. "She's a good friend. I hope you know that."

Tears burned the corners of Camilla's eyes. "The best."

Robin guided her to the back of the room, past a series of other hospital beds and metal tables, and paused when they reached another door, marked EXIT in red. "You'll have to walk. I'd let you take my car, but it'll show up on the front entrance cameras, and I don't have any reason to leave right now. It's about a quarter mile out. Keep right, and you'll see the road. There are woods running alongside. Keep to the woods and off the road. There are cameras and security patrols every hour. They won't see you if you stick to the trees. Once you're out, Brianna said she and Noah will pick you up and take you where you need to go."

Camilla threw her arms around this woman she didn't know but who'd risked so much for her. "Thank you."

Robin squeezed her back. "You're welcome. I'll pretend I'm taking you back to your room. Pile up some blankets and wheel the bed back. It'll give you more time. Now go!" She opened the door and practically shoved Camilla out.

Hunched low, Camilla darted to the right. Her body screamed in pain—in knotted muscle and bruised flesh—but she could not stop. Not when she was finally so close. There was no more room for fear. For waiting. There was too much to lose.

The main road rose up before her in the dark, and she did as Robin said. She kept to the trees, the edge of the road in her eye line as she made her way out.

As she made her way to the Dark Sisters.

She was bleeding when she came out of the woods. Her arms dotted with a series of tiny cuts—the greenbriers her father used as an excuse finally finding her as she stumbled through the dark. She fell at one point over an exposed root. The wound on her thigh reopened, and she could feel the blood seeping past the bandage.

But she was out. That was all that mattered. And there was Noah's truck, pulled almost parallel with the trees and turned off. Anyone driving that stretch of road would have passed by without seeing it.

At the sight of the truck, she laughed and began to run.

The passenger door opened. Brianna dropped to the ground, her feet slipping as she sprinted toward Camilla and tackled her with enough force to almost send both of them to the ground.

"You're okay. You're okay," she said.

Camilla let out a sob of relief as she hugged Brianna. Her beautiful, brave, intelligent, compassionate best friend. She would die for this woman. Again and again.

She pulled backward, swiped her thumb over the tears on Brianna's cheeks, and then stopped as her gaze fell on Brianna's mouth. Joy rendered her immobile as she took in the unblemished skin.

"You're better," she whispered.

Brianna nodded and let out a laugh. "I'm better. I don't know how or why, but I am." She clasped Camilla's hand. "Is your mom . . . ?"

"No. No, she isn't." Her heart squeezed painfully. She looked beyond Brianna at Noah, who stood patiently beside the driver's side door, allowing them their moment without his intrusion. They had come for her and offered their help. They would go with her for this final stretch. She could not be too late.

She looked back at Brianna. "Let's go find the Dark Sisters."

Noah parked in the field, and they walked the last stretch to the tree in silence. There were no words that could give voice to her trepidation. Her need.

When it finally came into view, Camilla reached for Brianna's hand, the clean warmth of it a reminder of why she'd come.

"Do you want us to go all the way with you? To the tree?" Brianna asked.

"It's okay. You're here. That's enough." She dropped Brianna's hand and turned to face the tree.

The black walnut stretched over her, no longer a threat but an invitation. The Sisters were frightening. She could not deny the wild panic in her heart. But she'd spent her whole life being afraid. Told to fear things she couldn't see even as she was told to revere other things she couldn't see. So much blind faith demanded of her at every turn. Fear and worship so inextricably bound that she could substitute one for the other.

She held that thought as she stood beneath the tree. As she studied it. The whorls and broken lines that held something ancient at its heart. She wondered how she'd ever been afraid of those faces in the bark. They had never been faces at all. Only nature in its glory taking whatever form it willed. There was beauty even in what she'd seen as obscene. She knew that now and placed a hand against the bark.

"I'm here. I'm scared, but I'm here. I don't know what you are or what you want, but my mom is sick, and if it's because of you... please. How do I fix it?"

A rustling sounded in the branches above her. The sound of a veil parting.

She drew in a breath, and she looked up and into the faces of the Dark Sisters.

They reached for her, but it was not with the intended violence she once imagined. Their hands were gentle. This was an offering. If only she would put aside her fear and allow them to touch her.

Her head tipped backward, and she lifted her hand. Yes. She would allow it. Camilla knew something of being a conduit. A vessel for someone else to fill. God. Her father. She could do it for the Sisters, too.

When they touched her and the vision came, it was gentle. She'd always thought those Biblical holy men were ripped away when their God granted them second sight. But this was nothing like that. It was a sudden awareness that the world around her had dropped away. Like a submersion into warm water. Like opening your eyes and seeing for the first time.

She saw their names written in her father's Bible. Anne Bolton. Florence Dudley. The first two women of Hawthorne Springs. Not sisters at all, but mother and daughter. Anne with her knowledge and belief in nature's magic. Florence with her strident devotion to her own god.

She saw Anne leading two other women to the tree, sap flowing over their fingers, their palms scarlet as they pledged themselves to the tree's magic so their daughters might always know the prosperity they had found. Florence doing the same, but with a sickness in her heart. A desire for her mother's punishment. How her blood had sunk beneath the earth in the same manner as the others. How nature saw her curse in equal measure and granted it in the ways it understood.

She saw as the women fell sick. The sores on their mouths, and blood, and teeth as they coughed up portions of themselves. She saw the bodies impaled on the branches of the tree, Florence's curse made complete.

She saw as Anne tried to explain to Florence that the magic had given back all she'd asked for. It knew no difference. So many of the women carried betrayal in their hearts. They betrayed their friends. Their loved ones. Themselves. The curse manifested with the same intensity as their abundance.

But if they could accept all parts of themselves, the illness would ease. A virus lulled back into sleep.

Some women were able to accept that darkness and found themselves improved. But others were not.

Camilla wept then, her hand still splayed over the bark. She thought of Tania Fullerton, in love with a man who was not her husband. Of Brianna, who betrayed her out of anger. Of her mother, who would not admit the truth of what she'd seen and allowed her daughter to be punished for it.

And then the last vision came.

A man beneath the tree, his mouth pressed against Florence as he drank her blood. Her husband. The first minister of Hawthorne Springs. That same man, along with other men, taking blood from other girls, as they lay drugged and passive in the dirt. Grant and her father and the other church leaders bent over the girls as their distracted, ignorant fathers imagined their daughters safe under the watch of those holy men, never knowing how their blood would stain the leaders' teeth. Never knowing what they stole.

The blood. He wrote those first names in his Bible. The same Bible in her father's study. The same Bible that had her and her mother's name written in it.

And from their blood will we prosper.

Their wealth. Their abundance. They believed it came from the women's blood.

And they took it for themselves. The Purity Ball a thin disguise for their vampiric ritual. Of course, they would not share it, would not consider that such magic might also benefit anyone loved by the women of Hawthorne Springs. No. They would take it for their own.

And then she saw the man standing beneath Anne as he forced Florence onto the branch. Anne and Florence, their hair tangled together as Anne called upon the light and dark beneath the world that one of their blood might see them. Might see them and open themselves so they might punish those who had stolen what rightfully belonged to them. What rightfully belonged to their daughters and all who were blood sworn to the tree.

She could feel it then. The power. How it burned through her blood. Through the earth. Through the bones of Anne and Florence.

How they called out for their daughters. For their sisters. For the bond that had always flowed through them—the chain damaged again and again only to reknit itself. The way a bone will heal when broken.

Anne and Florence could not speak, but she understood their question.

Will you let us in?

"Yes," Camilla whispered. She worked a hand beneath the waistband of her jeans. There were so many places on her that bled, but it felt right to use the blood from her thigh. The blood Grant and her father had taken from her.

"I let you in. Anne Bolton. Florence Dudley. I let you in." She smeared the blood on her palm against the tree. "Let all those whose blood has been taken against their will come here to this place. Let all those who stole it come here to this place. I think it's about time for a reckoning."

She had never wanted to be a witch, had always been told such things were evil.

But she was one now.

CAMILLA TOLD BRIANNA and Noah about the illness. About the blood. Noah's face blanched when she told him about Grant and her father. The cut on her thigh and how they'd drunk of her.

"Bastards," he spat.

"If you want to leave, I understand," Camilla said.

Noah shook his head, his jaw set in a hard line. "No. I want to be here. I want to see it."

"Me, too," Brianna said.

In that moment, Camilla could not have loved them more.

Together, they waited. For the women of Hawthorne Springs. For those who called themselves the leaders of The Path. Who called themselves representatives of God. This walk to the tree would be a pilgrimage of sorts. A letting out and gathering in again.

The forest was silent. The birds paused in their song to observe the procession of women as it went. The trees were still, the wind unmoving. The moon rinsed all it touched in a pale glow. Each of the women marked by its light. Had there been crowns, they would have worn them like goddesses reborn in a world that had long forgotten them and the magic they carried.

It did not take long for the women of Hawthorne Springs to begin arriving. They left their children and innocent husbands, sleeping and calm in their beds. Camilla and the Dark Sisters had called them, and their blood, however diluted, responded to that ancient connection.

The church leaders came. Youth Pastor Trent and Pastor Wade and their colleagues with bulging eyes and twitching limbs that fought against this command they could not help but obey. Camilla had not given them the option. They had never granted it to her. To the women whose blood they stole. She had seen no reason to be gracious now.

Grant Pemberton openly wept as he stepped into the clearing, his eyes locking on her as he passed. "Camilla? What the hell is this?"

She did not answer but watched as he joined the rest at the tree.

In the distance, someone screamed. The voice was deep. Distinctly male.

Camilla smiled. His scream was a gift.

She hoped the men heard it and knew what was coming.

The women locked away on Retreat took longer to arrive, and Camilla spied Robin among them, her face triumphant as she took her place.

Vera came, pausing to hug Camilla before she too drifted toward the tree.

But there were still two missing. Camilla would not begin until they were there. She kept her eyes locked on the tree line. She was not worried. She knew they would come.

Ada came slowly, her body curled into itself, the disease having left so little of her, but her eyes were bright as she came to the tree and took Camilla's hand.

Behind her was Camilla's father. Pastor Burson. The shepherd brought to his lambs. The slaughter in reverse.

Now, they could begin.

She told it all. The story of the Dark Sisters. The story of Anne Bolton and her daughter, Florence. Of the tree's magic. Of their blessing and their curse and how they might heal themselves.

And she told them of the bloodletting. The blood the church leaders and her father had stolen from them.

She finished and looked at their faces. Took in their shock and rage and sadness. "This is no trial, make no mistake, but if you do not want to see what's about to happen here, you're free to leave now. Some of you will lose a brother. A husband. But you deserved to know what had been taken from you, and who took it."

She waited, but the women remained at the tree, unmoving.

Camilla gripped her mother's hand, her voice dropping so only she could hear. "It'll be him, too."

Her mother's voice was clear. Strong. "I know."

A part of her would mourn. She knew that. She had loved her father. She spent years of her girlhood thinking he was her sun, but she wondered if he had ever actually loved her, or if she had only ever been a usable vessel. A sack of blood to drain.

When Camilla raised her arms and tipped her head to the sky, it was a final revelation. The Dark Sisters—Anne and Florence, mother and daughter—stepping once more into flesh as the magic took root. Their promise finally fulfilled.

"Sisters, let us reclaim what belongs to us," Camilla said, and the women opened their mouths. Yes. They were ready. And she was an instrument. The scale and the flaming sword. A blessing and a curse written in blood.

The tree expanded, a pair of lungs remembering what it was to breathe, the branches unfurling their growth so it draped over her.

Camilla marveled at the sensation against her skin. How soft. How silken. Not at all like leaves.

What fell over her was not leaves but hair. Braids like rope. The branches thick with them.

Camilla remembered the hair her mother coughed up. It felt like a prophecy.

Gideon had joined mother and daughter on a single branch, their hair tangled together as they died. It was only right the men suffer the same fate.

When the braids wrapped around the men's throats, the women sighed.

Camilla stepped forward, the women lifting their voices as she watched the men gag, their lips forming a dying prayer. A pleading she would not hear. Whatever agony lay in their voices she heard only as music. The horror of those delicate tendrils creeping toward their mouths she saw as a beautiful justice.

She went among the men, searching until she found him. Her father. How he choked and gibbered, his fingers bleeding as the nails tore away from his skin without loosening the hair about his neck. Grant beside him, his tongue swollen so it poked from between his lips. She waited for sorrow. For regret. But where her tender heart had once slept, there was now only a stalwart flame burning.

She took Grant's tongue between her fingers and yanked until she felt it tear away. Smiled as the blood trickled down his chin and jaw as she drank in his strangled scream. Once, she'd dreamed about drawing her tongue over his skin. Tasting the salt there. She drew her mouth over him now, bit into his tongue and chewed, the blood like honey. The taste was beyond anything the ignorant girl she'd once been could have dreamed.

She drew what remained of Grant's tongue over her father's face. Wiped his tears with the bloodied stump. "Did you cut me yourself, Daddy? Or did you have your little pet Grant do it? Never could get your hands dirty." She lifted her own hands so he might see. Showed him the blood. How it could all be hers. Be *theirs*.

"Camilla—please," he choked, but the hair tightened around his neck. She had no further use for his words.

All those years. Daddy's precious little girl. He'd pretended to protect her with his commandments, and she'd believed it. No matter. This would be the final bloodletting.

Camilla cupped his chin, let her fingers stroke his cheek. "Bye, Daddy. You should pray. Ask Him to take your pain. See if He listens. Because this will *hurt*."

She stepped backward as the hair snaked up the men's throats, reached past their teeth to the roots of their tongues. The wet sound of torn flesh like music as the women writhed beneath those hanging forms, their mouths open to receive the blood raining over them. Their hands slick with it. Their lips and teeth stained as they drank in the power it held, as they licked their skin clean. Screamed together as one voice as they felt it settle back into their bodies.

Anne and Florence ensured their deaths were slow. That when they hung the men who'd stolen their blood, when they pierced their chests with those same branches stained with the blood of their daughters, they did it with an agonizing deliberateness. Their vengeance required it. Camilla could understand that.

Even without their tongues, the moment the branches broke their skin, the men screamed.

THE SKY HAD begun to lighten when the clearing finally quieted. The bodies hanging from the trees were bloodless and still as the women embraced one another.

Camilla watched as the women drifted away. Some of them would mourn. She knew. It was expected after a loss, no matter how justified. But there was so much before them. So much to learn. To build upon. She placed her hand on the tree and looked up into the leaves, but Anne and Florence were gone.

"Camilla." Her mother stood arm in arm with Vera as they turned away from the tree. She was still frail, her mouth still marked by the sores of the illness, but she stood taller, and her skin had regained its color. "Let's go home."

Camilla blinked away grateful tears and nodded. "Y'all go ahead."

Vera and Ada walked on. She had no reason to fear. Her mother would get better. It would take time, but she would get better. Their power was their own, and no one could take it from them. And now they understood. There would be no more denial of the darker parts of themselves. No more guilt or shame that led to betrayal. They were the sum of all their parts, and there was a beauty in such knowledge.

She knew Anne and Florence would never fully leave her. They were stitched into her. A thread that would not be easily broken. The same stitch that connected them all. Friends. Sisters. Mothers. Blood and sap and earth.

Brianna and Noah came to stand beside her.

"There'll be police," Noah said.

"Yeah. But this sort of stuff happens in Hawthorne Springs, doesn't it? People get sick. Commit suicide on that tree. It's happened before. And we can always pay someone to say exactly that," Camilla said.

She hugged them both to her. Brianna and Noah, who had seen all parts of her and accepted it without question. Her chosen family.

"Thank you," she said.

They hugged her back, and together, they walked away from the tree. Camilla would go home. She would take care of her mother. Maybe she would look for Sharon Hutchins, the woman her grandmother had loved. After that, she wasn't sure. The world was so big. So filled with possibility.

Camilla kept her gaze trained ahead until they reached the edge of the clearing, when she allowed herself to turn back. To look at the tree that had her past and future traced in its bark.

Anne and Florence did not look back at her. They had gone. But the wind still carried their voices and the voices of the women who came before. Her ancestors. A reminder to embrace the truth of who she was in all parts. Not to deny even the darkness she'd hidden out of shame. It was all part of her. It was all beautiful.

She could contain it all.

All the light and all the dark.

ACKNOWLEDGMENTS

To the entire team at St. Martin's Press who worked tirelessly to ensure this book hit all the right notes, I cannot possibly convey the immensity of my gratitude. Alexandra Sehulster, you are beyond brilliant, and I know this book is all the better for your notes and your enthusiasm. Thank you to Ashley Quintana for making certain I was checking all the boxes and meeting deadlines and being so kind about it. And to Julie Gutin, who painstakingly went through every line of text and caught the errors my tired eyes did not, I appreciate your diligence and patience.

To Stefanie Lieberman, Molly Steinblatt, and Adam Hobbins at Janklow & Nesbit for their endless guidance and advice: This book would never have existed had you not steered me toward it as you so expertly did. You continue to amaze me, and I never in my wildest dreams could have envisioned finding such intelligent advocates. I am forever grateful I am able to work with you all.

To the librarians and booksellers and podcasters and reviewers whose work helps get my books into the hands of interested readers, I bow to you. You are an essential part of why I am able to do this thing I so love doing.

Samira Bregeth, Amy Foti, Jen Sellman: Y'all are the steadfast rock that keeps me afloat. I never imagined when I started teaching as a nervous twenty-three-year-old that I would find friendships that would carry me through all these years. Annie Bolton, Ariana Jordan, and Sam Rickard: What an honor and a privilege to have each of you in my life. You have witnessed every step I've made and tirelessly shown up and cheered me on. I will spend the rest of my life working to repay you. You have seen all the light and all the dark of me and have held my hand through every moment. I love you all more than words can say.

To my writer friends who witnessed every high and low and provided a sympathetic ear and endless, selfless advice, inspiration, and tough love when it was needed: Rachel Harrison, you absolute goddess you, you saw this book in its very first iterations and somehow managed to keep being my friend and provide the kindest blurb when it was finished. I don't know what I would do without you. Thank you for the numerous coffee chats and mutual love for trashy documentaries. To Michael Wehunt for being the first writing colleague I ever had and continuing to offer support during this long, winding journey. I'm so thrilled we somehow landed in the same place! Thank you also to Hannah Morissey, Clay McLeod Chapman, Nat Cassidy, Sarah Penner, S.P. Miskowski, and Johanna Van Veen for their early reads and for saying such lovely things about this book.

To my two J's: Thank you for letting me do this. For letting me disappear into a room for hours at a time only to emerge grumpy and hungry and bleary-eyed. You both are my everything, and I go to sleep each night thinking how lucky, HOW LUCKY!

Finally, if you are still here, thank YOU, lovely reader. You could have spent your time doing so many necessary things, and you spent it here with me. I hope you see all parts of yourself as worthy of examination, tenderness, and love.

ABOUT THE AUTHOR

Kristi DeMeester (she/her) is the author of *Dark Sisters*, *Such a Pretty Smile*, which was selected as a Georgia Author of the Year Awards finalist, and *Beneath*. Her short fiction has appeared in publications such as *The Dark*, *Black Static*, and multiple volumes of *The Best Horror of the Year* and *Year's Best Weird Fiction*, and in her short fiction collection, *Everything That's Underneath*. She lives, writes, and makes horror-themed candles in Atlanta, Georgia. Find her online at kristidemeester.com.